RUIN

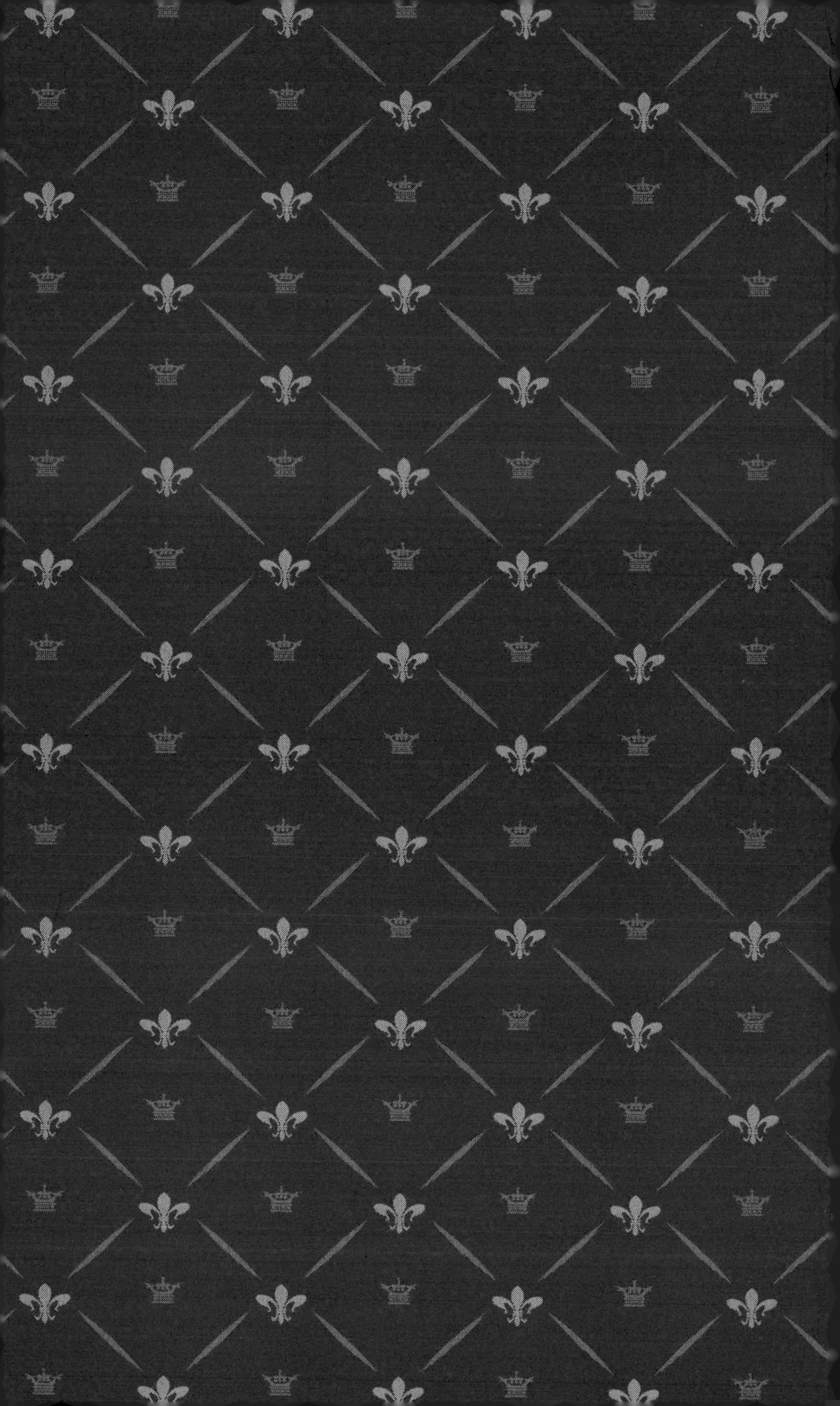

RUIN

FOOLISH KINGDOMS
DARK SEASONS WORLD

2

NATALIA JASTER

Books by Natalia Jaster

FOOLISH KINGDOMS SERIES
Trick (Book 1)
Ruin (Book 2)
Burn (Book 3)
Dare (Book 4)
Lie (Book 5)
Dream (Book 6)

VICIOUS FAERIES SERIES
Kiss the Fae (Book 1)
Hunt the Fae (Book 2)
Curse the Fae (Book 3)
Defy the Fae (Book 4)

SELFISH MYTHS SERIES
Touch (Book 1)
Torn (Book 2)
Tempt (Book 3)
Transcend (Book 4)

Cover design by AC Graphics
Chapter headings & scene breaks by Noverantale
Poet and Briar character art by Mageonduty
Typesetting by Roman Jaster
Body text set in Filosofia by Zuzana Licko

Content and trigger warnings can be found at nataliajaster.com/ruin

For the defiant, the fearless, and the passionate

Touch the princess and suffer her jester's wrath.

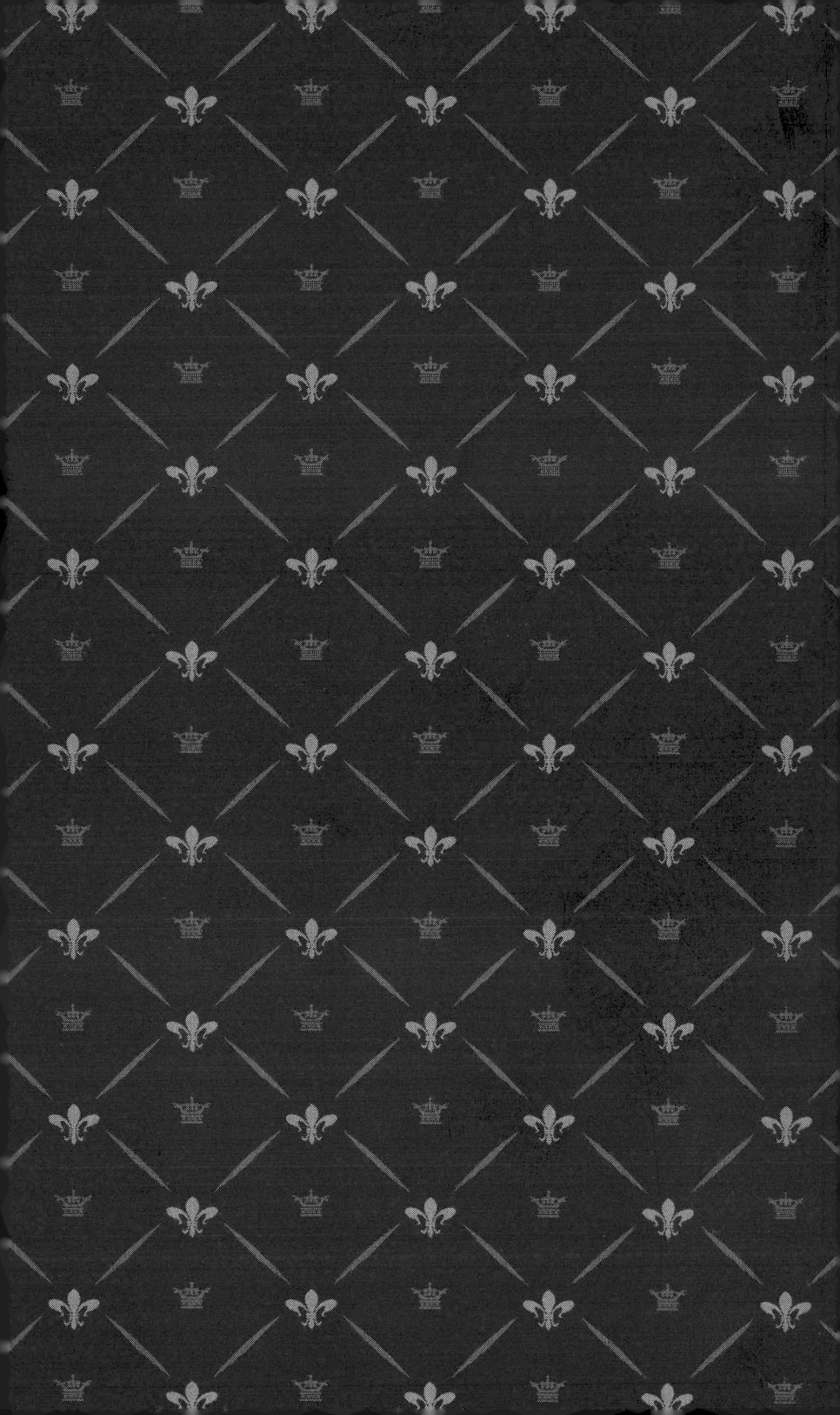

I

Briar

To love my kingdom had been easy. But to love my enemy had been deadly. Yet I would do it again, a thousand times over. I still heard his voice speaking to me for the first time. Wicked. Conceited. Alluring. He had been a temptation, the walking embodiment of sin, as potent as a drug.

I remembered the words he'd said, the rhythm of each sentence, and how they strung around me like cords. The invisible tethers could have either constricted or secured me. Though back then, I hadn't been able to tell which option was the greater threat.

Now I knew better.

I knew *him* better.

The memories embedded themselves inside me. They'd become as elemental as the blood swirling through my veins.

Wherever I went, those memories followed. They accompanied me from one kingdom to another, from a foreign court of debauchery to a familiar one of modesty. The only difference was I'd been a guest in the former nation, whereas I reigned over the latter.

I had always been a good princess. I'd prided myself on it.

Born to rule. Bred to sacrifice.

If you had grievances, I would hear them. If you had wishes, I would fulfill them.

Betray my kingdom, and I would exact punishment. Hurt those who mattered to me, and I would show no mercy.

My whole life, I had belonged to my nation, honored my court. For them, I'd often favored prudence over affection. Always, I did what was expected.

But one crucial time, I hadn't.

One time in another court, I met my match. Soon after, he became my equal. And then, he became everything.

Across The Dark Seasons, the people called me many things.

Highness. Heiress.

Righteous. Willful.

But only one person ever called me a thorn.

For others, I wore a crown. For him, I wore a scarlet band.

If the time ever came to choose between those symbols, I knew which one I'd reach for.

How had it all begun? The answer was simple and not simple at all.

It had started with something more powerful than a crown.

It had started with a ribbon.

2

Briar

The breeze woke me first, the tendril of air brushing my cheek like a finger. I blinked, my eyelashes fanning as the residue of sleep wore off. Visions of a woodland bower and black blossoms faded from my mind.

I had been dreaming of every moment that occurred after I'd first set foot in Spring. Those, as well as every day that had passed since leaving. But now my eyes opened to a montage of treetops painted in ginger and marigold hues.

Mere hours ago, it was afternoon. The world had been covered in the sights and sounds of another Season. But at present, dusk leaked through the carriage, drowsy light spilled across my face, and the landscape had transformed.

At some point, we'd crossed the border. New scenery prevailed, heralding a different environment from the one we left behind. The signs overwhelmed my senses. From the rich gradient of colors, to the statuesque tree trunks rising above the wilderness, to the crackle of leaves beneath the vehicle's churning wheels.

Amid all that, the masculine scents of amber and vetiver.

My lips turned upward. Nothing could stir me to full consciousness as he did. Not even the natural elements of my home, which thrived outside this carriage.

My head rested on a plush pillow encased in velvet. The pillow itself rested upon a set of cobbled muscles—a male torso that rose and fell with steady breaths.

A strong arm encircled the front of my waist, one hand cupping my hip. The other arm banded around my shoulders, holding me close.

I couldn't remember a time when I'd woken up feeling this safe. Nor this happy.

With a contented sigh, I twisted to gaze at the sleeping face looming above. His temple slouched against the upright seat cushions, and his countenance angled toward the window, granting me a view of his chiseled profile. The carriage lanterns glowed. They illuminated a thatch of mussed hair, sealed eyelids fringed in long lashes, and a jawline that could hone a blade.

Puffs of air wafted from a pair of slightly parted lips and rustled the dark layers draped across his visage. He'd always been intimidatingly beautiful. But when he slept, the result was devastating.

Desire, gluttony, and elation overwhelmed the spaces between my ribs. This man shouldn't be real. Yet he was.

And you're mine.

The jester was all mine.

One of my limbs had hooked itself over his lap, while the other tangled with his legs and stretched across the carriage floor. Our bodies sprawled sideways along the upholstered bench. Presently, my cheek nestled into the pillow wedged between us. We had talked, bantered, and flirted ourselves to sleep, but I couldn't recall the cushion being there prior. He must have settled it beneath me after my eyes fell shut.

Beyond the window, a distant figure caught my attention as it stalked through the wild. A proud crown of antlers rose above the creature's head. And from another forest corner, a fox trotted into the brush, the animal's fur as red as my hair.

Every emotion swirling in my stomach coalesced into a single entity: excitement.

Once more, I peeked at my slumbering lover. The clasps of his shirt were undone, splitting the garment down the middle to expose the athletic plate of his upper body. His pectorals broadened with each inhalation. I'd memorized every inch of flesh under the expensive fabric, every muscle carved into him.

I should wait. I should let him rest.

My index finger lifted and snuck into the vent of his shirt. Like a rebel, my touch scaled his chest, ascending to the collarbones and across the ledge of his jaw, and then—

His fingers shot out and caught my hand midway. He held my wrist aloft, revealing it as if evidence of a naughty crime.

My gaze collided with a pair of keen eyes lined in kohl. Irises as vivid as clovers gleamed at me. Brilliant, canny, and very much awake.

"What have we here?" the jester murmured. "A wicked princess, fondling without permission?"

"A princess doesn't need permission to indulge," I whispered. "Not if she's touching what belongs to her."

"Indeed? 'Tis hardly a small thing to own a jester, especially one as attractive as myself. Features like mine don't come cheaply, and I'm not merely talking about my face. Precisely how did this princess earn that right, hmm?" The solid arm encircling my waist lowered, his palm curving to my backside and hefting me into him. "Care to remind me?"

I coiled up his body, aligning my breasts with his gaping shirt. My mouth grazed his—full, hot, and perfectly shaped. "For that, you'd need more rest. Perhaps I should command you to preserve your energy, should you truly wish to please me. As a ruler, I have standards."

"Bossing me around already, Sweet Thorn? But I do love a woman who takes charge."

"Then you won't be disappointed."

His lips swept across mine, snatching my breath. "I'm at your service, Highness."

That devilish voice. Husky with sleep, it possessed a grittier edge, akin to frayed silk. The sound drizzled through me like caramel. My entire being responded, from my nipples, to my fingertips, to my toes.

Finally, his name coasted from my lips. "Poet."

At last, he grinned. That snaggletooth flashed, one of my favorite parts of him. Like a perpetual reflex, the jester's smile probed the rift between my legs.

Anticipation fluttered in my navel as his fingernails dug into my buttocks. With my thighs spread over him, I felt his cock harden. His head tilted my way, that sensuous mouth pushing into mine.

The carriage jolted. Its frame dropped, shuddering as the wheels careened over a depression in the road. The impact knocked cushions to the floor, while two empty chalices and a fruit tureen rattled from atop a recessed shelf.

Our noses bumped. Our mouths struck together.

Surprised laughter sprang from my tongue. Poet grunted a brief "Fuck" before a throaty chuckle rumbled from his lungs. He sat up, taking me with him so that my legs extended sideways over his lap.

After securing me, Poet tucked a lock of hair behind my ear. "Would you say that's a sign from the almighty Seasons to restrain myself? If so, too bad. Because there's no way in hell I plan on listening."

I pretended to give it due consideration. "I believe we can make an exception."

"Are you sure about that? I don't know if I should be pleased or offended that I haven't worn you out."

We had been traveling for a fortnight. But although every muscle in my body ached from sitting in this cabin, the journey hadn't been without its secret charms. Nor its pleasures, especially while cloistered from prying eyes.

Heat crept up my throat. One couldn't tell purely from looking, but we'd made a mess of this interior on a nightly basis. As such, the long trip wasn't the only reason for my soreness. My jester had stamina to outlast an army.

I raised my chin. "As a Royal, I'm not so easily depleted."

"Aye, that's true. In which case, darling Briar, I shall have to double my efforts." Poet cradled one side of my face. "Now, then ..."

Yet before he could clamp his mouth onto mine, the jester's craving gave way to confusion. He reeled back, his eyebrows crinkling in sudden awareness. "Where are we?"

Because I'd sidetracked him, Poet hadn't registered the details outside the vehicle. And to my astonishment, I had forgotten our location as well, once this man's hypnotic eyes had opened.

But the fragrance hit me now. The blend of tartness and sweetness was so ripe, I tasted it on my tongue.

Apples. That, and fertile soil.

My lips wreathed into a smile, that heady thrill from earlier rekindling. Poet riveted his gaze on my features, translated them, and rushed forward. His free hand gripped the tasseled window curtains.

This time, I switched our positions. I wiggled from Poet's embrace, scrambled behind him, and wrapped my arms around his abdomen. Determined to savor his reaction, my attention hopped between the view and his profile.

Beyond the road, sunset poured across the woods. Mist knitted through massive beech trunks, their leafy canopies blooming with spiced colors. Moss germinated from the ground, and exposed roots snarled over the knolls.

Whiskered, prickly, and ring-tailed fauna darted between hedges, the animals' forms moving too quickly to identify their species. But one thing remained true among all these creatures. Some were docile, others carnivorous if you crossed paths with them while unarmed.

Also, one had to beware of touching certain dried undergrowth in these parts. To say nothing of wandering into the wrong patches of fog or underestimating the harvest fields.

The mellow, cloudy wild. The untamed dangers and beauties of this place.

Autumn.

Poet stared in a daze, as if he'd never beheld a forest before. His eyes scrolled across every mesh of branches and shrubbery. He craned his neck to see more, to catch everything before it swooped past. Most of all, the jester's gaze was captivated by the awnings of color draping from the trees.

Resting my chin on his shoulder, I murmured, "We're home."

3

Briar

Poet's attention fell from the canopy. Hearing my answer, his features flattened in thought. Pensiveness strung across his countenance, when a moment ago he'd been enraptured.

I knew that look. Chagrin pricked my throat as I lifted my chin off his shoulder. "Oh Poet, I'm sorry." I inched back. "That was insensitive of me."

My arms pulled from around his stomach, but the jester's fingers tightened, stopping the motion. Immediately, he swerved toward me. "Don't," he insisted, sliding one hand into my hair. "Don't ever apologize for being happy."

"I wasn't thinking. It was hasty to presume you'd feel at home within seconds. You only just left Spring, and you must feel out of place."

"Sweeting, I'm Poet. I'm never out of place."

Even my chuckle sounded apologetic. "I hope that stays true."

"Trust me, I wasn't lamenting. I leave that drivel to the thespians, whilst I'm partial to being a wicked man of verse. It makes life easier." His fingers burrowed deeper into my tresses, his nails grazing

17

my scalp. *"You're my home."*

Tingles skimmed my flesh. Though, I couldn't distinguish whether his touch or his words had done it. Oftentimes, it was both.

I scooted nearer and set my palms atop his own. Like this, the scarlet ribbons around our wrists brushed. In that moment, I knew owning a crown would never feel as treasured as it did to wear this strip of fabric.

It did not matter in which court we found ourselves. I was his home. And he was mine. No matter the Season, that had been our vow from the moment we chose each other.

I heard the pleading in my voice, the wistfulness and apprehension. "I'm just excited."

Poet scanned my face. "As you should be."

"And I'm—"

"Scared?"

I nodded. We'd been over this during the journey, had plotted intricately and thoroughly every facet of our arrival. The customs and mannerisms of this land. How to conduct ourselves in public. How to address each other in front of the masses. What to say, expose, and conceal.

Most of it, Poet and I had perfected while in Spring. We'd prepared as much as we could.

But as the miles shrunk between us and the castle, nervousness consumed me. I wanted this to work. I wanted *us* to work. I wanted him to admire my kingdom, for him to be accepted here. Also, I wanted us to be safe. Yet having one of my wishes granted, much less all three, would be a trial.

I'd made Poet a promise. That did not mean we wouldn't have a struggle ahead.

Whereas threats lurked shallowly under the sinful glitz of Spring, dangers could root themselves deeply beneath the calm of Autumn. All my life, this had been a peaceful nation. But every Season possessed its dark side, whether dormant or not, and my land simply hadn't been tested yet.

Poet brought his forehead to mine. "Nothing will happen to you. I'll shred this world in half first. That is—" he grinned, "—if you haven't already beaten me to it."

I scolded affectionately, "Now you're just being a flatterer."

"I'm being possessive. And realistic. I've seen you in action, Princess. You could bring the enemy to his knees with a mere glance. Trust me, I should know."

"My scowl and your tongue?"

"Precisely. 'Tis an unbeatable combination." Poet glimpsed beyond the window, where leaves rained from the beeches like flecks of gold. "As to the reason for my frown a moment ago—" he glanced back at me, "—take a closer look."

I surveyed the shadows across his countenance. "Nicu."

Poet's mouth slanted. "That's more like it."

"You're disappointed you didn't get to see his reaction to all of this."

He made no reply, because he scarcely needed to. Although Nicu had ridden with us occasionally, Poet's son preferred my mother's vehicle because it had a skylight, and he'd grown fond of the horses driving it.

Also, he and Mother had become a duo. The boy had wooed her quickly, which was a trait he inherited from his father.

During one of our stops, Poet and I discovered my mother snoozing with Nicu in their carriage. Mother's arms had been wrapped protectively around his scanty frame. The sight had brought a private grin to my lips.

But because Nicu was presently ensconced in the queen's carriage, Poet missed his son's response to Autumn. That first glimpse as it alighted the child's face. I'd missed it too.

I strapped my arms around Poet's neck. "But you won't miss it for long."

On cue, our vehicle rocked to a halt. The procession followed suit, a dozen sets of wheels stalling on the road. Bracken crunched beneath the weight of every transport, the knights shouted instructions, and horses nickered.

Impressed, Poet pretended to scrutinize me. "How did you do that?"

The gloating must be evident on my face. "I have my methods."

"Oh, no you don't," he teased, snatching my waist as I grabbed the door lever and attempted to vacate the carriage. I laughed as he yanked me back against him. "Answer the question before I trap you here."

"Can't a princess be cryptic?"

"Not this princess," he threatened. "Tell me."

"Commanding a Royal?" I imitated a glare. "That is grounds for punishment."

"You forget." Poet nipped my lower lip and murmured, "I've commanded many things of you, to which you've obeyed quite enthusiastically."

Don't move.

Behave yourself.

Take it deeply.

Now come for me again.

That's right, Your Highness.

Heat swarmed beneath my dress. My thighs clenched, the slit between my legs pumping with aggravated warmth.

Seasons, help me. With the cavalry dismounting and stalking the perimeter, and the window draperies cast aside to expose us, this did not qualify as a moment to feel aroused. But then, this man routinely brought out those impulses, especially at the most inappropriate times.

I longed to fix my mouth with Poet's, to savor his sculpted body against mine. Indeed, if this jester uttered one more feral thing under his breath, I would be forced to thrust the curtains closed and lock the door. As it was, the reckless temptation wrapped itself like a silk rope around my hips.

Despite having this carriage to ourselves, the luxury of privacy would be compromised once we reached the palace. There, the days would be occupied. And every pair of eyes would scrutinize us.

The activity outside increased. The hollers magnified.

Repressing a groan, I marshaled my thoughts, lest they should turn more explicit.

It had been effortless to predict our traveling party was about to stop. Apart from holding court with Mother, installing myself in the library wing, or harvesting in the fields, I'd never been a princess to sit idle in the castle rather than scout the geography of my nation. Any proper ruler would do the same.

In any case, I identified our location quickly. The globe-like silhouettes dangling from a cluster of shorter trees nearby confirmed this.

"I know this wilderness," I confided to Poet. "I know it the same way you know the wildflower forest."

His lips tipped sideways. "Then what are you waiting for? Introduce it to me."

Gladly. I squared my shoulders just as footsteps approached the transport. An instant later, the door swung open. The motion jostled the exterior lanterns, and a figure appeared, his bronze coat of mail glittering like scales.

The troop had finished inspecting the vicinity. Thus, the soldier's presence could have been timed. Earlier, I'd been too caught up in teasing Poet that I neglected protocol, almost fleeing the carriage without an escort.

Had I been in Spring so long that I'd forgotten such a simple thing? While this frivolous action would be excused in Poet's court, any departure from custom would raise havoc in mine. On that score, I already walked a tightrope.

An elaborate braided bun crowned the knight's skull, with two more plaits weaving up his scalp. A hammer rested in his sheath, and a dagger scar wove across his throat like a crude seam. The man's frown dug into his face as he offered me a callused hand and bowed deeply, "Your Highness."

By nature, he possessed exaggerated manners. Deportment. Courtesy. Nonetheless, that frown deepened in my presence.

I gathered my cinnamon brown skirt in one grip, draped my free fingers in the knight's palm, and descended the carriage steps. My boot heels settled onto the road, hard-packed dirt sinking beneath me.

Nostalgia coursed through my veins, as if I'd been gone for a year instead of two months. It seemed a lifetime had passed. While I no longer felt like the same woman, the Season had not altered.

The aroma of damp soil filled the wild. Amid the caravan, horses clomped in place, their plaited tails swishing. Vine markings climbed up their limbs, looking as though someone had stenciled the equines' coats. But in reality, those markings developed naturally as foals, the color matching the persimmon orange of their irises.

Passing soldiers carried reels of canvas, stacks of fire logs, and spare weaponry including axes, archery, halberds, hammers, sickles, saw blades, and swords. The warriors' fleeting gazes strayed toward me, their features skewed.

Inwardly, I winced. Outwardly, I did nothing of the sort.

A princess does not repent her choices.

A princess must earn her subjects' trust.

I stood by the former and sought the latter. Not long ago, these men and women had respected me, even if they hadn't adored me like Mother. Yet now they doubted my sense of honor and dedication to this kingdom.

I had expected as much. But it still hurt.

Releasing the knight's hand, I kept my shoulders level. "Thank you, Merit."

His movements faltered. Etiquette aside, royals didn't express gratitude.

Stumped, the knight held the door ajar for Poet, who exited the vehicle with casual grace. In the interim, the jester had redone the clasps of his shirt and shrugged into a long coat, the velvet as black as ink and trimmed in copper thread.

Merit inclined his head but kept his attention fixed on Poet, which had nothing to do with attraction and everything to do with the opposite. The soldier muttered around a mouthful of skepticism, the inclination clogging his vocal cords like gravel. "Sir."

Poet had grown used to this. Only this time, instead of merely nodding back and giving the knight his space, the jester paused as his boots hit the ground. He regarded the man with a raised brow. "Sir, is it? You know in Spring, they used to call me the Court Jester. A select few even referred to Yours Truly as 'Master Jester.'"

My eyes bloated. My back tensed.

Everyone within hearing range froze. Mumbles and conversations ceased, men and women-at-arms either gawking or grimacing. Two such expressions that were rarely seen in Autumn.

It fell so quiet, the only noise remotely audible was a woodpecker hammering its beak into a trunk and a leaf breaking under Poet's heel.

"Court Jester" was an accepted salutation in every Season. "Master Jester" was not.

Particularly in this court, the moniker had a deeper meaning. It was not applied lightly.

I read the cavalry's mind. Revered by the Spring Crown or not, loved by their Autumn princess and endorsed by their queen or not, how dare this interloper entitle himself.

This, only moments after crossing the border. Of all the insolence!

Yes, I'd been the recipient of this jester's brash tongue before. I knew the feeling well, back from when I first laid eyes on him.

Merit cast a staggered glance my way, expecting me to intervene.

"I'm over here, sweeting," Poet said, forcing the soldier to glance at him once more.

My gaze jumped to Poet. That's when I caught the furtive twitch of his lips.

Relief whooshed through me. Oh, this conniving bastard.

"Master Jester," he pretended to muse. "Indeed, I remember several people tossing that endearment my way." Then he leaned in and whispered to the knight, "Please don't ever use it. I'm begging you."

The man blinked. Understanding crept across his features, and the barest hint of mirth dabbed into the crook of his mouth. Half the troop followed his lead, chuckling under their breaths. Promptly, they resumed their work.

The soldier bowed and joined his brethren. As he passed, the man attempted to preserve his frown. Yet his mouth still twitched, the pulped scar across his throat stretching.

Poet watched the knight leave, then his gaze cut to mine. "What?" he asked innocently. "Something on your mind, Highness?"

I folded my hands in front of me. "You planned that."

"Which part?"

"You know very well which part."

I'd told him the term *master* held a different weight in my kingdom, though I mentioned this only in the broadest sense. Traditionally, it referred to someone who excelled at their craft. But for the rest, I hadn't gone into details yet.

However, my jester had been cunning just now. He'd charmed the knights into thinking he believed himself unworthy of the distinction. Whereas in truth, the label didn't sound charismatic enough for his taste.

"'Tis the rule of a jester," Poet responded. "Never cut down with bluntness, nor kill them with kindness." He strode toward me, bent his head, and mumbled, "But mock, ridicule, or entice with humor. If not sex appeal."

My eyes ticked sideways, making sure no one heard us. "It won't be so easy at court."

"That's why I'm practicing."

And there was no better place to start. We had talked about this, how befriending this troop would be a wise first step. Obligation to a Royal was one thing. But the true loyalty of knights was not gained effortlessly, which made it more valuable when earned, because the fealty of soldiers was eternal.

Discreetly, Poet sketched a finger along my scarlet bracelet. "By the way? I plan everything, Your Highness."

Damn him. Outside the carriage, we shouldn't be standing so close. I linked my eyes with his and opened my mouth to respond.

"Papa!" a young voice called, the tenor ringing like a silver bell. "Briar Patch!"

We turned as Nicu bounded our way. At four years old, Poet's son was as small as a thimble, his limbs and frame runty for his age. By contrast, those large, wide-set eyes gleamed like emeralds, and his ethereal face beamed with energy.

Poet's demeanor transformed, his expression teeming with an unconditional light. At last, he got his wish. Nicu's explosive reaction to the environment rendered all else obsolete.

He raced our way and slammed into Poet's side. The child's speed compensated for his size, the impact causing the most agile man I knew to stumble in place.

Poet grunted playfully. "What is this? A fae in our midst?"

Gasping for breath, Nicu slung one arm around his father's legs. With his free hand, the boy pointed nowhere in particular, his arm swaying from one end of the setting to the other, unable to tell the difference. "The trees! The leaves! They're made of treasure!"

"Colorful, are they not?" I asked, smiling and kneeling before him. "Like rubies and gold coins."

Nicu's head bobbed. "I saw a deer. It looked right at me."

Behind him, a curvy figure entered the scene. The woman's voice flowed as majestically as the gilded cloak billowing down her voluptuous form. "That's because the deer of this land know a fae when they see one."

Mother joined our huddle. Although she stood as tall and proud as a ship, her expression seemed winded like a sail, the result of spending time with a sprightly child. Yet her gaze took in Nicu like the sun, warmly and without boundaries.

But when her attention strayed beyond us, Mother's visage narrowed into an imperial frown. Aptly, I could guess why. Nicu stirred up a unanimous reaction from our entourage. In my periphery, a few men and women regarded the boy like a poison apple—a cursed thing no one wanted to touch, much less go near.

Poet's eyes flickered to the soldiers, and his profile darkened.

Only at times like these did his resolve wane, the will to defend his son a lethal reflex. His lips flattened, about to lash anyone who didn't turn away by the time Poet counted to three.

Yet wielding that tongue—or worse, his daggers—while angry would only impair the jester's influence. Covertly, I snatched his wrist beneath our mantles. The instant I did, his mouth slackened, disarming like a weapon.

Meanwhile, it took supreme effort to constrain my own glower, to keep it from whittling into a thorn. That wouldn't achieve what Poet and I wanted. Thus, I twisted my head over my shoulder and mirrored Mother's expression—confident, stately, commanding.

Loyalty began with respect.

Respect took patience.

The troop sprang back into action. Armor clinked, and cloaks flapped as the legion trekked into the wild, where they began erecting tents.

Blessedly, Nicu hadn't noticed. The knights' novelty had worn off within a week of travel. We no longer worried about stopping him from leaping on the men and women, his enthusiasm for their attention unbridled. In any case, Nicu was too busy gaping at the towering canopy to sense conflict.

Mother's gaze sought mine, then Poet's. I translated her cautionary stare. This was nothing compared to the reception we would receive tomorrow. Not merely from the court but the whole of Autumn's citizenry.

The combs ornamenting Mother's hair twinkled. She nodded to us, then regarded the jester's son, her attitude softening. "There's a deer herd nearby. Would you like to see it?"

Nicu didn't need to be asked twice. He sprinted toward Mother, who took his hand and guided him into the thicket beyond the road.

At Nicu's whistle, a furry body flew from Mother's carriage and galloped their way. Tumble shot through the fallen leaves, scattering them in his wake. The ferret scurried up Nicu's side and draped himself over the boy's shoulders as they left.

Without Mother having to speak, a trio of armed guards took up the rear. Nonetheless, Poet instinctively moved forward.

"It's safe," I assured him.

The jester wavered. "It'll be dark soon."

"All the same. In thickets such as this one, the beech leaves are impervious to nightfall. They shine through it the way candles would. And wait until you see how radiant the fruit gets. Our lore calls this realm The Shadow Orchard."

Poet rounded on me and raised one eyebrow. "Are we boasting, Highness?"

"I'm informing."

"Pity. A jester responds more to bragging, especially if it's done by a princess trying to impress him."

"I have never tried to impress you," I declared.

"You've never had to," he flirted.

It required a great deal of discipline to curb my grin. "Bragging," I echoed. "So you're saying you respond more to snobbery."

He puffed. "Rubbish. I respond to vanity, which is such an underrated, underappreciated trait. There's a difference."

In that case, I feigned a pretentious swagger. "So if I gloat about these leaves glowing more vividly at night than in Spring, that will relax you?"

Poet chuckled. "Fine. I might be a tad overprotective."

The jester had every reason to be. Also, I'd been the beneficiary of his protective reflexes more than once. "I'm well-acquainted with that."

"Nay." The jester's irises deepened to an obsessive shade of green. "You have no idea."

Our gazes welded together like electric currents. A thousand fuses detonated through my veins. No, keeping away from each other while in a castle packed with nobles would not be easy.

It never had been. Moreover, this court was nowhere near as flighty as Spring. At best, we'd be restricted to the eventide hours while ensconced in our chambers. Even then, our appetites made me question if midnight rendezvous would quench those yearnings—or simply intensify them.

Dear Seasons. What sparked between us had always been forbidden. Except now, this would be a new type.

Two hours later, pits blazed like miniature bonfires through the camp. Tucked into an orchard glade, the fires illuminated this wild in flaming hues, and several expansive tents brimmed with light from within. Against the murk, the interiors pulsated like orange globes.

I counted four dwellings. One for the First Knight, who led this troop. Three for the queen, her daughter, and their "guests." The soldiers slept outdoors, which I did not care for but understood for safety's sake. They could not monitor the orchard while confined, nor react fast enough should the unlikely need arise.

Nevertheless, I trusted this area. As did everyone else. Or rather, everyone except a certain jester who'd insisted on stalking the boundaries twice before being satisfied.

For most of the sojourn, we had either driven through the night or stayed at rural inns. Only a few times had it been necessary to make camp. This would be our final stop before reaching the palace.

Steaming iron pots hung over the flames, the aroma of vegetable stew wafting through the air. Carrots. Potatoes. Squash. And plump, freshly baked bread made from Autumn grain sat on wooden platters.

Most of all, ripe apples perfumed the atmosphere. The orbs dripped like ornaments from the branches, the pomes' skin glossy and so radiant they glowed in the dark, just like the gold and orange leaves of the taller trees.

I dined with Mother in her pavilion. In a neighboring pallet, Nicu curled around a pillow and snored, with Tumble coiled beside his head. The boy had a tent reserved with Poet, but he'd had passed out here after finishing his dinner. Mother had ordered a bed for him until the jester came for his son.

As for Poet, he'd decided to make the communal rounds. Having broken the ice earlier, we thought it a fine idea to take advantage.

I would love to join them. But that would make the knights uncomfortable.

Ironically, Poet's presence was more acceptable. This, despite him being the object of controversy, the source of my reputed corruption, the father of a born soul, and a native of Spring. His position gave him power, but ultimately, he wasn't a Royal. So by comparison, he got away with more.

Throughout the meal, I shifted in my seat. My eyes flitted to the tent flaps.

"You think I don't know what you're doing?" Mother's voice roped around me, tugging my gaze back to hers. Over the rim of her chalice, she pelted me with a perceptive gaze.

I picked up my spoon. "What am I doing?"

Mother set down her drink. "Take care, my dearest."

Yes. This wasn't the first time we'd had this conversation. And she was right.

With a nod, I ate my stew even slower. Although Mother and I had discussed with Poet the social and political complications ahead, I scooped a helping of squash while deliberating further. "We should recap any last minute—"

"No," Mother interrupted.

I stamped my spoon into the bowl. "No, what?"

"We've gone over every detail more times than a scribe and prepared ourselves more thoroughly than a militia. And before you ask, yes. I read your updated pro-con list this morning."

"Once or twice?"

Mother dropped backward into her chair. "Your mind needs rest, Briar."

"Now you're Briar-ing me. A Royal's mind never has time to rest," I persisted. "This is the last night we'll have. Foresight is essential to success."

"Respite is essential to foresight."

My eyebrows flattened into planks. "Poet has been influencing you, I see."

She chuckled. "The rhyme was accidental. Actually, I was quoting your father."

"Oh." I stared at her. "He used to say that?"

"He was fond of manifestos. Like you."

The discovery seized my heart. "I miss him."

Tenderness gripped Mother's face. She leaned forward, extended her arm, and threaded our fingers together. "That feeling is mutual. And that's why I'm grateful every day for you."

I squeezed her fingers back. As I did, my scarlet bracelet grazed her wrist.

Mother contemplated the band, now familiar with the story about Poet's ribbons. "I already gave my blessing. Not that you require it, since I'm certain you would choose his smirk over my approval. It's the same way I felt about your father.

"But there's more. I've kept quiet until now because ... well, I don't say anything unless it's honest. And for that, I needed time." Her gaze met mine. "I like him. He's good for you."

Her words opened a latch in my chest. Yet words failed me.

"Notwithstanding he's got a scheming tongue and devilish habits," Mother sighed. "But he would sunder this world for the ones who matter." She glimpsed Nicu sleeping, then returned to me. "He's changed you, as I believe you've changed him. You have quite an extraordinary bond. Any mother would desire that for her daughter."

I swallowed. "What about you?"

What about everything Mother had on her shoulders? What about the consequences of being a monarch who supported that same daughter?

According to reports, The Dark Seasons spurned me alone for my actions. The continent hadn't condemned Autumn's queen for upholding my choices because they were too busy dwelling on me. I was the one who'd fallen out of favor. But that didn't mean Mother found it tolerable to see and hear of it happening, much less to be the buffer.

She translated my question, and her gaze became distant. Rarely did she react viscerally or immediately.

"A monarch often contends with impossible decisions," she said. "Double-edged swords are an eternal burden for us. I take the gamble because I have faith in you, and because I agree with your beliefs. When rulers make choices, we must ask ourselves not merely what we stand for. We must also ask ourselves what we're willing to die for. You and Poet have your own answers, and I have mine." Her eyes slid back to me, and her mouth curved. "Protect one another. That is all I ask."

I curled our fingers into a ball. Whatever happened, that was one pledge I would never break.

I exited Mother's tent, where four sentinels stood post. The same number of guards were stationed at my own lodging, but impatience and eagerness fueled my steps in the opposite direction. I had no urge to retire. Not with the eventide so crisp and the orchard trimmed in fog.

And not without seeing him.

Nightfall had brought a mild temperature with it. In a month or so, it would be colder.

Tucking my wool coat close, I promenaded through the encampment. My skirt swished over fallen leaves that glinted through the darkness. Soldiers huddled around the burning timbers and tipped back flagons of ale. Some told stories of ancient Autumn and its legendary treehouse colony, while others guffawed and ribbed one another.

But when I passed, each group lowered their voices and genuflected. I reciprocated with smiles, which gave them pause regardless of how often I'd attempted pleasantries while traveling. Over the years since Father died, I had rarely grinned at anyone.

In the interim, I kept my gaze neutral and scoured the camp. All the while, my stomach did somersaults.

Where have you gone?

Apples dangled from the trees like spheres. The orbs threw little shafts of red light across the forest. They provided the same luminescence as candlelight, only in a more provocative color.

I halted under a branch and craned my neck to admire the fruit. My fingers reached out to skim one of the pomes, its skin a brilliant shade of garnet. The pigmented flush was even, the fragrance abundant.

This meant it was ripe. Perhaps too perfect.

One couldn't be overly careful, so I twisted the apple to get a better look at its dainty leaf bowing from the stem. The leaf appeared green, but the trick involved tilting it correctly, to see its true shade. I angled the fruit until a healthy brown color materialized in the leaf, reminiscent of a second layer beneath the surface.

The minor detail relaxed my fingers. This apple was safe.

The weight of someone's attention cut short my admiration of the fruit. Tingles danced up my spine. Slowly, I swiveled my head in the source's direction.

My gaze stumbled across those eyes first. Two shrewd irises pierced through the murk from across the camp, the green as verdant as clovers. He stood amid the knights, speaking to them in hushed tones.

Like a blitz of lightning, Poet's attention skewered the distance and struck my breastbone. With his face banked in the firelight, the jester watched me. And that's when his fiendish lips crooked.

He'd noticed my presence long before I noticed his. For certain, he had trailed my every step.

The realization melted low in my navel.

Technically, this wasn't the first time Poet had feasted with the troop. He'd done so on that initial eventide when we set out from Spring. That was the night he told them the first half of our story, the one he'd been storing in his mind since we met.

Purposefully, Poet had delayed sharing the second half with them. Let it saturate their minds, he had plotted to me. Let them mull over the events, he'd said. Because the longer our forbidden story percolated in the soldiers' thoughts, the more impactful the ending would be, the more it might prompt them to reconsider us.

With all that ale flowing freely, the knights' demeanor became informal. Based on their rapt attention, Poet had been revealing the second half of our backstory with them.

When we left the Spring Court, the jester had narrated our history to me in the carriage. I'd listened with a lump in my throat. So much had happened, and he'd remembered every second of it in lucid detail.

We are a tale for campfires. That is all. That is everything.

Silently, I stared back. With a single look, I communicated every feverish and fierce emotion swarming me. And like a Royal, I inclined my head.

Poet's mouth curved even further. And like an obliging Court Jester, he nodded, the picture of cordiality. The exchange pumped me with adrenaline and a frenzy of need, all of it broiling under the surface.

One additional craving lingered on my lips. I plucked the apple from its bough, then peeked at him once more. My teeth sunk into the orb, a riot of flavor bursting across my palate. Sweet juice wetted my tongue as I let the unspoken command cross my features.

Find me.

Because what the princess requested, she received.

Poet's pupils flashed. Even from this vantage point, I saw it happen. The green irises shrank behind those black wells.

I chewed and swallowed. Then I swung away from him with a raised chin. My skirt and coat sliced through the leaves as I fled deeper into the orchard.

Soon after, a pair of sly footfalls stalked behind me.

4

Briar

The overlapping voices and crackling logs faded. Soon enough, only the chorus of nightfall remained. An owl hooted. Something wild howled in the distance.

Mist cloaked around me, so that I disappeared into the miasma. Yet gold and orange beech leaves emanated dim light, like phosphorescent umbrellas, and apples glimmered from the smaller orchard trees.

I strolled through while coyly savoring my treat. I drove my incisors into the apple, its flesh packed with fluid that spilled down my throat. A moan curled from my lips. I'd forgotten how wonderful they tasted.

The environment reinforced my confidence and steadied my gait. Returning to my roots felt empowering, and knowing he was close invigorated me.

The calm strike of footsteps prickled my ears. The figure moved like a vapor, smoothly and stealthily.

I gulped down another chunk of fruit. A bead of juice trickled from the crook of my mouth. My tongue darted out and licked.

I made sure to angle my head so he would see it. Sure enough, his movements staggered, and I could have sworn a muttered curse drifted from behind.

My lips turned up. I veered in and out of the fog, around the orchard trunks, and through the bushes. Like this, I gave him a tour. I introduced him to my world, and he followed me into the depths without hesitation.

For a long time, we didn't speak. Only the landscape made noise, leaves shivering from above and crunching under us. Whenever they fell from the branches and died, they lost their hues, their light dulling. Yet I found them as beautiful as the ones still clinging to the boughs.

The specter kept coming. He would never stop.

I took the longest route possible, leading him astray. This path would shield us from intrusive eyes.

The farther I went, the tighter my bodice gripped me. My breasts inflated into the corset, and my nipples toughened into pebbles. The nearer he came, the harder my pulse beat, matching the sudden throb in my clitoris.

Consuming the apple to its core, I tossed the remains over my shoulder. I imagined it landing with a thud at his feet. The faintest chuckle rumbled from a few feet away, the sound wreaking havoc through my private folds.

Under my drawers, slickness damped the crease of my pussy. Instead of making it cumbersome to walk, I enjoyed the sensation. It made me feel sexy.

He made me feel sexy.

"You know," I confided, "not every apple in this orchard is safe to consume."

Moments passed before an impish tenor responded. "Is that so?"

I ran my fingers across a trunk and then weaved around its girth. The fog split like a curtain, bidding me entrance. "The stem's leaf will tell you. If it's brown, you're fine. But if it's green ..." I shook my head and lowered my tone, "you will regret eating it."

"And which part of me will suffer?" my stalker asked.

"Your greatest skill," I answered, as if imparting a ghoulish folktale. "The apple will devour it."

"Ah. Like a curse."

"Worse." I stepped around another trunk and pressed my back against it. "Like poison."

His shadow materialized across the undergrowth. It paused on the tree's opposite side, and his husky tone slid around the bend like smoke. "Go on."

"Autumn values mastery as much as honesty, but a poison apple deprives you of the former. It strips you of the skill you value most. A doctor is no longer able to heal people, a mother turns into an abuser, or a glassblower forgets how to work his oven and sticks his hand inside. If not their identities, the deficiencies cost people their loves, their limbs, or their very lives."

"And here, I thought this was a tranquil land."

"It is," I said. "Until it isn't. Didn't you once stop me from touching a Spring rose because a prick from its thorn incited sexual gluttony?"

"Mmm. That was the angel on my left shoulder. The devil to my right is still debating whether I should have intervened at all."

"You are without shame." Yet I bit back a grin. "Nature is benevolent, as much as it's cruel. One moment, it's peaceful. Next, it's gruesome. Like any Season, you must know how to live with the elements and their magic."

Poet purred, "I look forward to your instruction then."

I rotated my head sideways and whispered to his shadow. "You told them."

"Aye," he replied. "After hearing the first half, they were invested in our evocative campfire story. Tragically, I left out the explicit parts. No thanks to your incessant demands, but I wouldn't dream of sullying the warriors' delicate sensibilities with smut."

"Did they listen?"

"What do you think I am? A novice?"

"Did you speak discreetly, or did you theatricalize?"

"Now you're just pretending you've never met me, much less fucked me to within an inch of my life."

"Poet—"

"I might have dabbled in both. A delectable bit of you, a tad more of me. By the end, they were engrossed, if not unsettled. They knew I wasn't bullshitting."

"Of course, they knew," I vouched. "Autumn's first inclination is toward sincerity. It's our foundation, so that makes us more acute to falsehoods. Unless pride gets in the way, we detect it like a shift in temperature."

The jester fell silent. I sensed him thinking the same thing. If that was true, it was fortunate he was a maestro of artifice. It was just as fortunate I was the Season's future sovereign, bred to recognize the nuances of its citizens' behaviors. At court, those skills would foster a delicate balance between honesty and omission.

Thank Seasons, we hadn't been thrust into the upheaval right after crossing the border. We'd been given this blessed reprieve. Just us.

"I'm happy we have this time." I reached backward, my fingers skimming the trunk's coarse veins. "I'm happy your first glimpse of Autumn is like this." My voice cracked. "Simple. Alone."

In a forest instead of a castle. In private instead of among a thousand courtiers.

As though the jester had been expecting it, his own digits met mine halfway. Our fingers lingered, swaying over one another.

I closed my eyes. Unbidden, the memory of how the knights looked at Nicu resurfaced. That, and the boy's trauma in Spring, from which he still suffered occasional nightmares.

Beyond that, I thought of all the innocent prisoners languishing in cages across The Dark Seasons. That part of my kingdom, Poet hadn't yet seen. But he knew enough from Spring. He'd witnessed his share of horrors and been forced to restrain himself, to pace his fury for the sake of long-term change.

I studied a fallen apple rotting on the ground. "How did you do it in Spring?" I wondered aloud, my whisper slipping into the fog.

"How did you see so much yet hold yourself back?"

His fingers stalled on my wrist, then resumed stroking my flesh. "I did it for him."

For Nicu. He'd endured for the sake of his son. "I know that much," I imparted softly. "But how did you survive the pain? How did you tame it?"

I heard the grim smile in his tone. "I didn't."

The answer launched tears into my eyes. Because he couldn't staunch the pain like a cloth to a bloody wound, Poet had let it run its course. While entertaining, targeting courtiers, having sex with nobles, and rising to power in Spring, the anguish never waned.

"Instead of letting it kill me, I let it fuel me," Poet confessed. "You'll do the same, Briar."

"How? We made plans, but the closer I get to home, the less certain I feel." I shook my head. "I want to be more than a princess of a Season."

"Really now," he teased. "Such a greedy heiress."

"I want to be a princess of the people," I stressed. "All the people. How can I rule a nation that would condone treating anyone the way our continent has? How long will I last before I snap?"

"Enough, Sweet Thorn. Don't go there. You're stronger than that. You held yourself aloft when your father died. You did so when you found my son in a dungeon, broke him from the cell, and faced the persecution of every Royal in existence. You're a fucking brushfire."

I clenched his fingers. "How will we manage?"

The jester's answer came simply. "Together."

He pulled my hand nearer, elevating it until his breath coasted over my flesh. He overturned my palm and brushed the sensitive skin with his mouth.

I sighed. This man never failed to soothe and rouse me in one fell swoop.

His digits etched mine, slowly and intently until my joints unraveled. In place of worry, hot embers scorched my skin. His touch opened me under the dress, the lust wetting my drawers.

The jester sucked in a breath, as though he knew. "Alas, Princess. Present concerns aside, it appears you've wandered far from your tent unescorted. 'Tis a dangerous thing in the dead of night."

Adrenaline and longing drained my lungs. "And why is that? Am I still your target?"

In an instant, he pivoted around the tree. I gasped as Poet's face lunged into view, and his solid body bracketed me. Our coats opened, his shirt brushed my bodice, and a rough noise scraped from his lungs as he felt the peaks of my nipples.

Illumination from the apple trees melded with the black of eventide. Amid that, we watched each other.

Poet drizzled one knuckle down the side of my face. "You're always my target. Mine to serve. Mine to protect." His words poured over me like steam. "Mine to fuck."

Molten heat leaked from the cleft between my thighs. My lips quavered, so close to his debauched ones. "And as your monarch, what am I expected to do?"

"Don't you know by now, Highness? Command me. Dominate me." Poet burrowed in, his torso flush against my breasts, his thighs spreading mine. "Fuck me back."

A desperate sound unspooled from my lungs. "You're evil."

A nefarious laugh pushed from his chest. "But isn't that why you led me here, Princess? For your jester to obey your every whim? To fill your lovely cunt with his cock? Would you like him to make you come until your legs give out, whilst on the fringes of your home?"

Seasons. Yes.

I wanted that. I wanted him to take me while still on the edge of this world, where nothing existed but this rural woodland. I wanted what we'd had in Spring, on Lark's Night when he fucked my virginity away. I wanted us to claim this spot, for this wild setting to mark our beginning in Autumn.

Our exhales rushed together. His mouth seethed over mine, and those hooded eyes glittered with a vibrancy that rivaled the leaves. He plastered me to the trunk, one knee digging into the vent of my legs, pressing through the dress until he reached my clit.

A brittle moan broke from me. Poet growled, feeling my pussy react against his leg, the evidence threatening to soak through my skirt.

He braced one elbow beside my head and cupped my jaw with the other. "How I love to pleasure you. How I love flinging myself into the pyre with you."

My eyelashes fanned. I wound my arms around his lower back and dug my fingers in. "Are you mine, Poet?"

"Eternally." He dipped his head and rasped against my throat, the contact igniting my sensitive flesh. "As much as you belong to me."

"Then take what's yours," I ordered, pleaded, whispered. "Satisfy your princess."

With a groan, Poet lifted his head and rushed his mouth against mine. "At your service."

His lips swept in, seized my own, and opened them wide.

Like a blade slicing through paper, shouts ripped through the forest. Poet tore his lips from me, his body clicking in place. His eyes cinched as if detecting something more—something worse—and he vaulted around. Plastering me to the trunk and shielding my body, he crossed his arms and wrenched a set of daggers from under his coat.

A second later, a heavy mass rolled across the undergrowth and landed at our feet. Another second later, bile surged up my throat. Resting in a pool of crimson, the severed head stared at us through a pair of lifeless eyes.

5

Briar

The knight gawked, his pupils vacant and mouth frozen in a shocked grimace. Red as thick as molasses splattered the braided bun in his hair. Another deluge leaked in rivulets from the decapitated stem of his neck.

The jester hissed. He rammed me deeper into the tree and flipped the blades deftly between his fingers. I sensed his eyes dicing across the wild.

Bellows from the camp sheared through the woods. My gasps matched the rampant pump of Poet's chest.

His muscles locked. His height and broad shoulders dwarfed my own.

"Stay where you are," he murmured with calm ferocity. "Don't move."

Terror iced my veins. Nonetheless, I shoved myself against him. Like hell would I allow Poet to cover me while leaving himself vulnerable.

Except I might as well be pushing up against a rock wall. I jerked sideways instead, popped from behind him, and jumped in front of

Poet.

Growling, the jester reacted with the speed of a panther. He seized my waist and whisked me back to my original position.

I grunted on impact. "No, Poet."

"Aye, sweeting," he snarled. "I'm afraid I must insist."

"I won't let you—"

"Truly?" he galled with feigned humor. "I'd expect nothing less than courage from you, but this is no time to fight over who gets to protect whom. This is one battle of wills you won't win."

I opened my mouth. From several paces away, what sounded to be a thick branch snapped like a femur.

My lips welled shut. My vocal cords frayed.

My ears attuned themselves to the landscape, the sounds as familiar as my drumming heartbeat. If a twig cracked or a leaf fell, I would hear it.

Poet had kinetics on his side. A paragon of movement, the jester heard every audible shift in the vicinity.

Blood flowed through the dead leaves, staining the hem of my skirt and the tips of Poet's boots. I peeked around his shoulder to where the head rested.

Those cold eyes, glossy as marbles. That distorted mouth, slanted like a broken bridge.

Recognition churned in my gut. My lungs unleashed a guttural sound. I swerved my head into Poet's spine and clenched my eyes shut. After heaving through several breaths, I pried my lids back open.

Once not long ago, I had cowered in a stairway leading to a hellish jail where Spring kept born souls. While growing up, I used to avert my gaze during Autumn's executions. I had been afraid, but I refused to succumb again. If I could not do this now, I would have no chance later.

I wedged my palms against Poet with renewed vigor. "Let me see."

"Briar," he gritted out. "I do believe we've been over this."

"He was my kin. I need to see!"

"And I need you alive."

Rationally, he was more than right. This wasn't a moment to let sympathy override safety. And while I would defend Poet with my bare hands, he stood a better chance for numerous reasons.

We waited, listened. Footfalls pounded across the bracken, and steel rang as weapons sliced free from their harnesses.

My mind jolted in awareness. I knew those sounds.

Poet swerved, his daggers flying.

"No!" I leaped from the tree. "Stop!"

But those serpentine reflexes outpaced the warning. With a hiss, he whirled from me, thrust up his arms, and crossed the blades overhead. They collided with a pair of broadswords, the collision slicing through the night.

Both figures paused. The male soldier bracing his weapons against Poet noticed me and veered backward. "Your Highness," he panted.

Ashy hair framed the man's angular face, and his eyes glinted as blue as a twilit sky. He stood at Poet's height, and his set of broadswords flashed in the darkness, the weapons as vast as a wingspan. "Forgive me," he said, contrition ticking across his features.

Poet, on the other hand, did not disarm. His eyes slitted as he maneuvered in front of me.

"Poet," I insisted. "It's all right. He's the First Knight."

"Not good enough," Poet remarked, keeping his attention pinned to the soldier. "Call me paranoid. It happens whenever a man's head drops at my princess's feet."

Dozens of bodies flooded the area. The knights skidded to a halt around us, their weapons drawn. Sweat laminated their faces, their expressions ranging from dumbstruck, to enraged, to grief-stricken as they registered the head lulling under the tree. It eclipsed whatever surprise they would have felt discovering me out here with the jester.

The instant they arrived, Poet spun the daggers and disarmed. Realizing the First Knight wasn't a threat, my jester transcended from one impulse to the next, a wholly new fear disrupting his features. His head snapped to mine, and his orbs darkened to a murderous shade.

I understood, because it was the same dread leaching the heat from my veins.

Nicu.

Poet launched into a run. I grasped my skirt and barreled after him. Visions of the last time Poet's son had been in peril—when Spring took him from us—assaulted me.

No, I thought. No, please. No, no, no, no, no!

Ignoring the soldiers' yells, we smashed through the forest, catapulted past the orchard, and bolted into the camp.

Blazes thrashed from the pits. Abandoned crockery surrounded each campsite.

Firelight brimmed from the queen's tent. The assigned sentinels kept vigil at the entrance, with their halberds braced and their eyes stalking the perimeter. Despite this, Poet and I blasted through the entrance flaps, then halted. Mother rose from Nicu's bedside and whipped a finger to her lips, silencing us. With a careful tilt of her head, she indicated the sleeping form bundled under the coverlet beside Tumble, the unconscious ferret curled in the child's arms.

He was okay. He was safe.

No one had touched him.

Poet's face crumbled. He bowed his head, clamped onto his thighs, and unleashed a gust of air. Straightening, he approached quietly, knelt at Nicu's bedside, and drank him in.

Relief choked me as I stared from Nicu to Mother. Her face remained composed, yet her lips had paled, and her upright finger shook against them.

Closing the distance, she cupped my face. "Come," she muttered, then strode outside.

Poet knifed his fingers through his hair, then rose and swung his head my way. Quick as lightning, he charged toward me and grasped my face, his eyes consuming me with desperate urgency. I clutched his jaw, mirroring the act.

Kiss me, my mouth begged.

Make it go away, my eyes implored.

Our lips hovered, panted, brushed. But we couldn't. Not like this.

44

We would not kiss out of dread. We would only kiss out of strength. Poet growled, then dragged himself from me. With one more hectic look at his son, he snatched my hand in a viselike grip and led me into the woods.

Half the troop had returned, having raced after us. Presently, they patrolled the camp and picked through the expanse, searching for evidence. Yet not a single plate or bedroll had been tampered with.

I stalled in contemplation. "Nothing's disturbed."

Poet inspected the soldiers. "And none of them have wounds."

Which meant whoever dismembered the knight hadn't intended to make a scene.

As Poet and I left the camp, the troop brought up the rear. We returned to the orchard, where the rest of the knights had sunk to their knees beside their brother-in-arms. Mother idled, with her hands folded and chin lowered.

The acidic stench of death was so concentrated, it singed my nostrils. Poet's fingers tightened around mine as he guided me forward. The squad parted for us, and when the sight came into view, my hand shot to my mouth.

They had located the body. It rested under the knight's head, with a pile of golden leaves arranged around him.

My intestines roiled. Anguish stung my eyes.

Withdrawing from Poet, I stepped forward. One of the knights muttered, "Your Highness, I wouldn't—"

"Leave her be," Poet ordered.

My leaden feet carried me to the fallen man, where I descended beside his kneeling brethren. I scanned every facet, from the braided bun to the scar across his neck. Whatever monster did this to him had traced the scar's outline, slicing through as if finishing the job.

I remembered him opening the door for me a few hours ago. I remembered Poet coaxing a laugh from this mannerly soldier. I remembered his name was Merit.

I gulped a mouthful of guilt, a lungful of agony. The knights had closed their comrade's eyes. Though it was technically Mother's duty,

45

I extended my shaky hands, plucked a leaf from the pile framing him, and set it on his forehead, in the custom of Autumn.

But it didn't feel like enough. Nothing would ever be enough to atone for this. The man deserved more from me.

With my eyes stinging, I gripped the hem of my dress and gave a rough jerk. The fabric split, breaking along the seam. However, it snagged, refusing to budge further until a blade appeared in my vision.

Poet held out one of his daggers. Grateful, I accepted it.

It took another series of rips before the first swatch tore free. Everyone watched, their jaws loosening as I plaited several lengths of wool and laid it carefully over the man's wound, where the neck and head should meet. I did this as though it might bind him back together, at least in the afterlife.

Stunned silence clogged the area. I filled it with a benediction. "May Autumn keep you warm, Merit."

An ancient saying, a declaration of unconditional respect when a person passed on. I couldn't say what startled the group more, my gesture or my words. Customarily, neither were ever granted by a Royal. Not to someone with a lower rank.

But I didn't care.

For the remainder of our journey, we would preserve his body and then transport him to the castle's crypt. Until then, I gained my feet. I swayed, and Poet caught me, his hands anchoring my hips.

Mother said, "There was an intruder."

"Who?" Poet and I asked.

The First Knight replied in a gruff tone. "We don't know. They vanished. I can attest that we were all together, but Merit had been alone. He'd taken his leave, to wash up by one of the streams. He hadn't been gone more than a few minutes."

"That's why the camp was undisturbed," I concluded to Poet. "It wasn't an ambush."

He shook his head. "It was singular."

"But why this knight?" Mother questioned. "What offense did

he commit?"

"None." A muscle ticked in Poet's jaw, and he tugged me closer. "He wasn't the mark."

"No, he wasn't." My words cracked like a shell. "He was the warning."

The men and women stirred. Repulsion marred their expressions as the First Knight replied, "They left a message."

Arrested, we watched as he lowered himself to the ground and gently lifted Merit's chainmail to expose his bare chest. At which point, vomit sloshed in my stomach. It took everything in me not to keel over.

A bloody rendering of shards was carved into the man's flesh. Like a hideous sketch, it resembled a broken relic, with its pieces scattered and raining down his torso. It made me think of something delicate, akin to chips of glass.

Murmurs and curses resounded through the orchard. Proper Autumn had long been a nation of sense and serenity—of charity, humility, and benevolence. Therefore, none of us had beheld these imprints in our lifetimes.

"What the fuck," Poet hissed.

I stared in a daze. "It's more than a message."

"Aye," the jester agreed. "That, it is."

There could only be one reason for this to occur. There was only one cause for such a crime in a nation that had seen peace for over a century. So soon after my transgressions in Spring, after I'd chosen to bind myself to Poet and his son, which had essentially publicized my sympathy for born souls, as well as implied my support for equality. Yes, there could only be one reason this would happen now.

Poet knew, as well as I did, what this insignia meant. My jester was fluent in the art of marking people.

The man's body had been a canvas. But the symbol cleaved into his corpse hadn't been meant for him. Rather, it had been a warning meant for someone else.

Like a scarlet ribbon, this symbol was a target.

6

Poet

Her finger rested on her chin whilst she slept. The sharp little digit perched on the sharp little ledge of her face, because even in dreams her mind remained restless—deep in thought, endlessly contemplating. Wicked hell, but she constantly found ways to hammer nails through my fucking chest.

Briar's body lay curled beside me, with her cheek burrowing into the pillow. Her plush mouth splayed partially open, small puffs lurching into the air. At the foot of the pallet, her bare feet threaded with mine.

Dawn leaked into her tent. Drowsy rosy light embossed the grass, the traveling trunks, and the snuffed candles. Along the canvas walls, a mural of tree silhouettes filtered in like shadow puppets.

Faint morning rays draped across Briar's limbs, making a slow crawl to her hips and the pert breasts inflating from her bodice. I had shed the coat and gown from her body last night. She'd barely kept her eyes aloft whilst I stripped her, then she passed out the moment I tucked her against me.

Now she coiled into a shell, clad in nothing but a corset embroidered in wheat stalks and muslin pants that cinched at the ankles. 'Twas the fashion of Autumn for undergarments to be longer, to ward off the chill as well as preserve modesty down to the final layer.

Perish the thought. As if that ever deterred me from peeling every stitch of fabric from her curves. To the contrary, it merely stalled the unveiling, making the thrill last longer. For that, I could hardly complain.

The corners of my lips crooked, then my mouth flattened just as quickly. The ramps of Briar's eyebrows dipped in unconscious deliberation. Ever the bookish Royal. Ever the tenacious princess. Slumber failed to sedate this woman, scarcely stopping her mind from churning.

She needed a calm night, a full one without interruption. My thorn should be dreaming about the illuminated manuscripts she would add to her collection. This princess should be dreaming of all the fuckery I planned on doing to her.

She shouldn't be dreaming of death. She shouldn't be depleting herself.

If she didn't take care of this gorgeous body, I would do it for her. Tonight, I would strip, stroke, and satisfy Briar to the point of no return. No matter what obstacles lay in our wake, I would fucking make it happen.

My finger stole out to sketch her cheekbone, then spasmed to a halt. A streak of red materialized on my digit. Blood crusted a lock of Briar's hair, the crimson a grislier shade than the burnished red falling around her face. This must have happened when she bent over Merit last night.

I'd washed remnants of the dead knight from her features once she fell unconscious. Yet evidently, I missed a spot. My knuckles bent, and my nostrils flared.

It's more than a message.

Aye. That grotesque symbol bleeding from the knight's flesh had been a warning to an intended target. And that target currently slept beside me.

To sympathize with born souls, and then to pledge herself to the father of one, marked Briar as an untrustworthy and disloyal princess. Neither she, nor Avalea, had officially declared their intentions for emancipation, but the people weren't naive.

Still, the majority of Autumn admired the queen, so attacking her would be considered a more drastic risk. Whereas Briar's status had deteriorated, making her the weaker link in the public's estimation. Thus, Avalea wasn't the issue. Her daughter was.

At the very least, everyone suspected that Briar's personal choices would affect her political ones. From that, changes would arise. If not now, then over the years to come.

But whoever the fuck lopped off Merit's head yesterday had reached their limit, for they wouldn't touch my princess. Oh, quite the opposite. My blades would touch them long before they had the chance, and I wouldn't be as quick about finishing them off, as they'd been with the soldier. I would draw out the pain until their shrieks breached the treetops.

Sunrise melted through the tent and warmed Briar's profile. My fist opened, and I forced my knuckles to relax. Reaching behind me, I searched for the discarded shirt I'd removed hours ago. It slumped on the floor beside the pallet.

Plucking the garment from the ground, I used the sleeve to wipe Briar's hair, gently cleaning the blood from her locks. Thankfully, the fabric was dark enough to conceal the evidence. She wouldn't notice.

As I finished and tossed the shirt aside, a slender noise floated like a wisp from Briar's lungs. She shifted her hips, then pouted her lips. My eyes sank into her as those lashes fanned open, and her languid gaze drifted to mine. Instantly, her brows smoothed out, and her lips wreathed into grin.

The look struck where it counted, puncturing me between the ribs.

Briar hummed as though she'd slept for half a day. If it had been up to me, she would have. Yet the resilient woman managed to subsist with far less.

She moved to speak, but I placed an index finger against her mouth. *Hush.* Then I cast that finger to the bundle nestled between us.

Briar followed the trajectory, to where Nicu's runty body nuzzled into the pillows. His blanket rose and fell, in tandem to his respirations. The coverlet obscured everything but a tuft of shaggy dark hair and the tip of a ferret tail.

My thorn smiled wider. I leveled my head off the pillow, rested my jaw in one palm, and savored the view.

After last night, there was no way I'd leave her alone. To that end, there had been no reasoning with either of us about having my son and his furry familiar bunk here. No number of guards would satisfy my princess, nor me.

My heart rate tripled as Briar reached across the pallet, took my hand, and molded our digits into a fist. Desire and longing consumed her expression. I threw the same look at her.

If we were alone, I would already be inside this princess. I'd make her come for hours on end, until last night fled her mind.

Yet this feeling, right here, was equally profound. Everything that mattered rested on this pallet. So help me Seasons, no one would get near them.

They're mine.

A deadly noise scrolled up my throat, but I contained it. Nonetheless, Briar registered whatever expression altered my features, and her eyes stumbled down my naked chest to the baldric harnessed at my waist. I wore only loose pants and the dagger's sheath.

She sobered. Her gaze clung back to mine, searching for an answer I couldn't give. Instead, I offered what was in my power.

I mouthed, *I'm here.*

Her steely irises softened, and her lips moved. *So am I.*

Always. She had no idea how far I would go to prove that.

The princess's muscles relaxed, and for a long time we stared, trading silent thoughts. All the whilst, our fingers danced together. At length, the sun dragged itself through the forest, enhancing the landscape's outline.

Determination set Briar's chin. No time to waste, life was precarious, and it would only get harsher by nightfall.

But not yet. She pointed across the tent in invitation, then scooted backward, her movements delicate.

I mimicked the action. We left Nicu and Tumble sleeping as Briar circled the pallet and grabbed my hand.

"I want to show you something," she whispered with a conspiratorial eagerness that dabbed a sly grin into the corner of my mouth.

She rushed me across the tent, past the tall candle tapers. A coat of arms—bronze leaves, gilded stalks, a pair of intersecting axes, and a red fox—embellished the entrance flaps. Their seam divided the artwork down the middle, where a cleft of light pierced through.

Several paces away, the armored outlines of soldiers patrolled the vicinity. With a tug on the tassels, Briar released the flaps, which spread like drapes.

Instinctively, I slung my arm around her midriff and clutched the hilt of my blade with my other hand. Nevertheless, an exhale pushed from my lungs. The cusp of dawn brought a new world into stark relief, in severe contrast to the one we'd left behind.

Before us, a panorama of orchard trees sprouted across the woods, each trunk belted in mist. Apples hung from the boughs, their skin glistening with condensation.

I had been mesmerized with Autumn from the onset, but this exceeded my initial impression. The spiced colors were thicker, heavier than in Spring, and when you paid attention, the hues contained more variety than my fucking wardrobe. The environment wasn't as perfumed, but everything else was denser. The moss shades seemed older too.

Rather than petals, the scents of earth, woodsmoke, and pomes filled the air. Crisp, hearty, and sturdy. I saw, heard, and inhaled Briar in every crevice.

"I know you had your first glimpse yesterday," she said. "But not like this."

"Marvelous," I uttered. "Now I understand."

Why she loved it here. Why she'd missed it.

Briar leaned her spine into my chest. My head tilted to her profile, near her proud chin and freckled nose. Flush with renewed energy, she beamed at the view. Her hair hung down like a flaming river, the locks unkempt.

This woman didn't have a penchant for makeup or jewels. Just as well, for I preferred her like this—unadorned, natural, radiant.

My teeth ached. I wanted to bite that chin, swipe my tongue across that mouth, tear open that bodice, and make her even more flushed.

I surveyed the corset, the elevated peaks of her lovely tits, and the gauzy pants billowing around her limbs. A slit would be hiding between her legs, a tight rift through which my fingers could fit and pump.

Seasons all-fucking-mighty. Only the presence of my sleeping son and the desperation to keep them both safe prevented my cock from thickening.

The flaps led to a short marquee exit, which lent us some privacy. The patrolling knights wouldn't notice us unless they stumbled past. All the same, the thought of anyone glimpsing a centimeter of Briar's body produced a vicious tick in my jaw.

I moved closer to the princess, tugging her nearer, harder. "Quite gutsy, my thorn," I murmured into the crown of her head. "What do you mean, exposing yourself like this?"

"Jealous?" she teased.

"Obsessed," I corrected her. "You shall be the end of me, just as you've been the beginning of me."

"I don't care what they see."

She meant it. At least, this morning she did.

Be that as it may, I doubted the exposure of Briar's corset, dainty trousers, and bare flesh—much less my unclad torso and low-slung pants—would disrupt the knights at this point. Too much fucked-up chaos had occurred since we made camp.

Beyond that, ever since Briar knelt at Merit's side and set the plaited swatch of her dress over his wound, the men and women had been regarding her with a rekindled light.

Briar swallowed. "For this moment, I would risk more outrage."

I groaned. "Those are tempting words, Highness. You're lucky we aren't secluded someplace where I'd be free to corrupt you."

"I cannot promise how often we'll be alone after this. Nights, yes. But daylight is another matter. That's why I don't care who sees us now. This morning is ours."

"Spoken like a ruler," I muttered into her ear. "Then again, denial is part of the fun. Waiting all day will only make fucking you tirelessly all the more intense later. I'll pry you so deeply, you'll feel every inch of my pent-up cock."

Briar shivered, gooseflesh rippling across her arms. "I hope so."

I released the dagger hilt and banded my free arm around her clavicles. "Do better than hope, sweeting. Believe it."

"I wish that were the only thing I could think about. I knew we would face threats, but not so soon. And not to this end." She clamped onto my forearm. "I'd thought perhaps Merit had consumed the wrong apple, which could have impaired his ability to fight back. But the skill he valued most in himself was mentorship, not combat. Most importantly, I did not smell tartness wafting from him. All the same, he was a proficient warrior, which meant the attacker was too.

"As for the markings carved into Merit's chest, they're not recognizable symbols apart from the glass-shard-like appearance, and I cannot make sense of them. I've never witnessed such a maiming in Autumn." Her voice shook. "For this to happen the moment I return …"

Indeed. Whatever those markings represented, it had to do with us.

What exactly did this shadow enemy want? Moreover, to what end?

I twisted Briar to face me. Cupping her jaw, I tacked my forehead to hers, and my thumbs raced across her skin. "Know this, and trust this. The setting might change, but not us."

She faltered, a weary grin struggling to break through. "You sound idealistic."

"Hardly," I hissed against her mouth. "I sound right."

Briar's mouth trembled, and a needy sound unraveled like a vine from inside her. My lungs compressed. The same feverish urge crackled across my tongue.

How I wanted to snack on that willful lower lip. How I wanted to sink my teeth in and taste her. How I wanted to make this woman forget, to kiss the fear from her, to fill her with a stronger emotion until it was all she knew. How I wanted to make her toes curl, her spine tingle, and her pussy throb for more.

The latter was impossible with Nicu in this tent.

The rest? That was fair game.

The princess's eyes sealed to mine, pleading, wanting—asking. And fuck it all, but a harsh noise rumbled from my throat. I swooped down, our mouths shoved forward—

And a windblown noise chopped through the fucking woods. The insufferable racket splintered us apart, the disturbance honking from a horn-shaped instrument that one of the knights blew into, to signal the hour.

A frustrated growl launched from my chest. "Bloody hell," I gritted to the canopy. "I'm going to kill someone."

Briar's laugh resounded under her breath, equal parts amusement and anguish. "We're late."

My gaze dropped to hers, and I must have looked feral, because pink sliced up her cheeks. As the sensible one in this rogue relationship, she inched further back, which failed to mask the unfulfilled desire smoldering in her pupils. Though on the bright side, anarchy and sensuality looked rather fetching on her.

I cemented my feet to the ground, in case they got ideas. The only other alternative would be to throw Briar over my shoulder, carry her to the nearest hidden recess, and fuck her up against the first tree I saw.

I'd sworn not to touch this woman, not to unleash with her, much less fondle or kiss her whilst inundated by death threats. However much I relished the thought, I had standards about Briar's first orgasm in Autumn. Nonetheless, the heiress possessed a habit of break-

55

ing my rules and spurring me to do the same.

How many times had we been interrupted since passing the border? How long had it been since I pleasured her? Mayhap a full day since my tongue probed hers, since the rhythm of my cock had made her shout.

Not that it mattered. My appetite for this Royal was a perpetual, incurable condition.

Another word for it was addiction.

Briar retreated another step, because one of us had to be the stronger and smarter player. Though it didn't help that her nipples poked through the corset, the material not nearly thick enough to shield her arousal.

My mouth watered. Blessedly, my cock behaved and stayed down.

Briar's head jerked between the entrance and Nicu, who stirred and mumbled, which meant he was about to wake up in three seconds, and Tumble would follow suit.

The princess and I stared at each other, then broke into quiet chuckles. I hadn't made her whimper, but at least this moment made her laugh.

Once the mirth receded, her features reinforced themselves. She nodded, and I met her gesture with a wicked inclination of my head.

The magnetism reminded us of a crucial fact. We didn't need to touch. Not in order to connect, nor to collide, nor to conquer. Whatever distance they tried to put between us, whatever enemies came our way, not a fucking soul would succeed.

That private vow resurfaced several hours later, about to be tested when the procession of carriages trundled out of the woods, and Autumn's castle rose into view.

7

Poet

The flags materialized first. The morning fog had yet to evaporate, mist still clinging to the air. As the carriage wheels ground along the road, the castle's bronze pennants speared into the haze.

With my arm strapped around Briar's waist, I used my free knuckles to hold aside the window curtain.

The towers came next. Fronted by vast harvest fields that soared twenty feet high and a lower town with orderly pitched roofs, the castle's brown masonry stood proud. One of the highest structures housed the same type of horn the knight had blown at dawn, which must be the equivalent of Spring's tower bell. At our approach, the apparatus emitted a funneled baritone noise that spread across the vista.

Compared to the circular architecture of Spring's palace—which boasted more curves than a courtesan—Autumn's monoliths were blocky with flat roofs. Shutters bordered every brattice and window, and wooden boxes overflowing with cattails jutted from the sills. And whereas Spring's turrets were corded in wild ivy and ornamented with stained glass, this palace was streamlined, with more attention to craftsmanship than embellishment.

Rustic yet refined. Handsome in its simplicity.

Like someone I knew quite well.

Speaking of which, the object of my everlasting obsession studied me in my periphery. I felt the brush of that Royal gaze and slanted my head in her direction.

Briar curled against me, her irises liquid mercury. "Well?"

I raised an eyebrow. "You're making it rather hard to compliment the view when I have a much more fetching spectacle in front of me."

"You're prolonging my anticipation."

"'Tis a jester's job. But if it pleases you, now I know what a library would look like if it were a castle."

Briar's complexion warmed. And really, my description couldn't be truer. If a book repository were a fortress, it would resemble this one—a castle built for reading instead of revelry.

I fitted a lock of Briar's hair behind her ear. "This world suits my thorn. It seems everywhere I go, I'll be reminded of you."

She nuzzled against me. "I'm counting on that."

Contentment outweighed the trepidation in her voice. After hours plagued by the unknown, speculating with me about the identity of last night's attacker, and quizzing me for the third time on the fundamental customs and prominent court players of this nation, the crinkles in her chin smoothed out. At last, there was that look I wanted to draw from her—relief and joy, however compromised they might be now.

For my part, I would be lying if I said certain mercenary inclinations had abated. Neither Briar, nor her mother could guarantee our enemies didn't reside in the castle. No matter the Season, every court possessed its share of conspirators, all hidden behind veneers of loyalty, simpering compliments, and ceaseless ass-kissing. Public scrutiny and riots weren't the only risks. Things got trickier if court members disagreed with a Royal's actions.

Across The Dark Seasons, a sovereign was beloved until they weren't.

We had anticipated civic discontent and intended to meet with

Autumn's Royal Council to discuss potential unrest and threats against the monarchy. We just hadn't expected an attack within hours of setting foot in this realm. But as a man fluent in duplicity, I should have remembered this crucial rule: strike your prey when they're unprepared.

A jester never made the same mistake twice. The enemy wouldn't get past me a second time.

But although hunting down the murderer and shaving the skin from their body appealed to me, Briar took priority. If I could extend her pleasure for this arrival, I would do it.

I opened my mouth to tease her, to keep that grin in place, when a critter squeaked from the opposite side of the carriage. Tumble sprang off Nicu's lap. For most of the trip, my son's energy had toggled between explosive and exhausted. Awake, he turned into a hurricane of noise and movement, thoroughly wiping himself out within hours.

Now his eyelashes flapped in wonder. Two rings of green sparkled as he lurched upright, and his attention hurtled to the window. "Oh!"

While watching my son, I whispered to Briar, "Three, two, one—"

Nicu lunged across the bench. But instead of mashing his face against the glass, my son threw open the sash and popped his head through the curtains. Briar barely had time to jolt upright, much less emit a sound of dismay.

Half of Nicu's body was already flopping out of the casement before my arm slung around his scrawny waist and hauled him inside. "Ah, ah, ah," I snarled like a goblin and hoisted him against me.

To prevent Nicu from grunting in protest, I dug my fingers into his stomach and tickled him. He squirmed like a fish. The octave of his giggles flew out of the vehicle, where anyone within a mile radius could hear the silvery tenor. My son possessed an otherworldly voice, as musical as a flute.

My actions distracted him enough that he momentarily forgot the setting. Briar's alarm dissolved into humor as she watched me regale my son into hysterics. She joined in the laughter, and I *rawrrrred* at them both, until our chuckles overwhelmed the carriage.

Riled up by the cacophony, Tumble galloped across the floor, his long body darting around our boots.

Horse hooves clomped beside the window, and a muffled voice uttered, "Er, Your Highness. Is something amiss?"

Briar fought to swallow her mirth, her skin as ruddy as Nicu's. "No, thank you," she called out. "All is well." On that last note, she clapped a palm over her lips to stifle another round of guffaws whilst the confounded soldier rode ahead.

Tears streamed down Nicu's cheeks. Worn out, his boyish cackles faded as he slumped calmly on my lap. He gawked at the view without leaping into action, a tactic I'd used infinite times to prevent my son from hurling himself into danger's path.

Another centimeter, and he would have plummeted headfirst from the vehicle, having not registered the distance to the ground, nor the carriage's girth. However, telling him why it wasn't safe to suspend himself out the window of a moving carriage, let alone scrambling or falling from one, wouldn't register to him.

But Seasons, he was getting faster and slipperier every day. In the future, his speed would rival my own, if not surpass it.

As the procession rocked toward the edifice, statuesque field stalks bobbed on either side. Tumble hopped onto Nicu's thighs. My son leaned forward, absently running his fingers through the ferret's fur while engrossed in the scenery.

I pointed to the foliage and murmured, "You see that, my love?"

"Mmm-hmm," he answered. "They're giant plumes that brush the sky."

He shimmied to the edge of my limbs and reached out. "Can I, Papa?"

"Slowly," I instructed. "Stay close to me."

He listened, his hand hovering from the window, attempting to feel the vegetation as it swam by. My eyes ticked to Briar, who gazed at us, her eyes molten gray.

We traded a look that sank to the marrow of my bones. Aye, my son had a fierce magic of his own, capable of wiping away the darkest of worries.

For part of the route, the harvest fields crowded us in. Their stems drummed against the carriage walls, creating a percussion rhythm.

Briar shifted to the bench across from us and laced her fingers with Nicu's. "Like this," she said, then extended their arms until the stalks grazed their fingertips. "It's wheat. You know what flour is, right? Well, this is what we use to make it. And some of the fields grow corn too."

At the sensation, Nicu gasped. Another snicker bubbled from him whilst his digits danced across the stems.

Fuck, how my jaw ached from the vision. I joined my hand with theirs, and together, we felt the rows rush by.

The road broadened, the fields split wider before disappearing behind us, and the paved dirt lane transformed into bricks the color of mulch. The lower town materialized, with shops, restaurants, taverns, forges, market stalls, and houses of timber and plaster clustered together. Instead of rolling through, we veered into a private lane bordered by high walls and snaking parallel to the city, then emerged in a vast pasture inhabited by colossal maples, the trunks reaching impossible heights, nearly as tall as the castle itself. Finally, we swayed through a barbican suspended over a moat and under the gatehouse's raised portcullis.

Courtyards rimmed the castle, shaded by more soaring maples. Under the largest tree, a throng of figures gathered. I counted around a hundred, a fraction of the greeting Briar received in Spring, where citizens had cheered the Royals' arrival, flung petals at their feet, and whistled.

So Autumn's reputed modesty was true. Alas, no such spectacle here. Instead, they folded their hands in front of them and waited.

Naturally, I would have pouted about the lack of fanfare, if I didn't have other things to worry about.

My eyes scanned the unfamiliar faces. A brunette with eyes the shade of mulberries. An elderly man with a shaved head. An androgynous male, handsome with dark skin and whorls tattooed up his fingers like gloves. I scoured the company, picking apart their expressions for signs of concealed bitterness, veiled deception, or at least a modicum of genuine levity. But wicked hell. I detected nothing but decorum and a millennium's worth of breeding.

Censure and intolerance, indeed. Oh, there was that. Unanimous criticism of Briar weighed down their mouths and pursed their lips, to say little of how they'd receive my son. From their manners alone, the resemblance to Briar—Pre-Poet—was uncanny.

But fury? Enough rancor to commit treason?

Either this lot was too dignified to let it show or too inexperienced to know how to be openly pissed off. Or they were just that good at shielding their emotions, as Briar had once been. They could be sophisticated performers. It would take a jester to know, once I'd been here long enough to peel back the genteel layers.

But one thing was for certain. They didn't adore Briar.

Not like they reputedly adored her mother.

Nicu made an enthusiastic noise and feasted his eyes on the succession of faces, from men and women dressed in layers of suede, leather, and wool, to servants outfitted in brown and black livery. He squirmed like a frenetic bunny, eager to hop from the vehicle and jump on the first person in his path.

Although we'd agreed I would distract Nicu during our arrival, Briar's pupils flashed with some type of inspired thought. My thorn took charge and intercepted before I could, bending over until her face leveled with Nicu's.

She spoke in a hushed tone. "Have I ever confessed, I'm a nervous princess?"

My son gawked at her. "But you're so brave. You slay leenixes and dungeon guards."

She waved that off. "Yes, but I'm not always brave. Sometimes I need a friend to hold my hand, otherwise I get anxious and lonely."

Promptly, Nicu snatched her fingers. "I'll stay with you, Briar Patch."

"Would you? I'd be so grateful."

He bobbed his head, thrilled by the task. Mission accomplished, for he regarded the crowd with less zeal than before. One of the many talents my son possessed was empathy. He wasn't the type to leave a friend behind.

Case in point, Nicu and Tumble were practically adhered to each other. The ferret scaled Nicu's arm and wound his limber body around the boy's shoulders like a shawl. At that moment, my son couldn't have looked more like a woodland fae if he tried. More than that, Nicu had a way with the fauna, bonding with them to a striking degree.

Fallen leaves flew into the air as the queue of carriages rolled into the courtyard and ground to a halt. Stallions flanked us. Knights swung off their mounts and spread out, harnessing their weapons and taking their positions in various corners.

The carriage door creaked open, and steps unfurled from the floor.

Briar glanced my way and mouthed, *Jester*.

I gave her a sly wink. *Ruler*.

She anchored her chin, the picture of a Royal who never took her decisions lightly. A woman who didn't back down once she made up her mind. And how exquisite. If this was what I could expect daily, it would be increasingly difficult to keep my greedy paws off her.

More to the point, it would be fucking impossible. This had already been a challenge during the trip, and I had constantly failed to behave.

Briar cupped Nicu's face once, straightened her spine, and slipped from the vehicle. Her fingers lingered behind for a second longer, enough for those digits to stroke my thigh and cause mayhem in several regions of my body.

It served me well. My flesh crackled, a magnetic buzz streaking through me.

Time to do what I did best. Time to perform for the masses.

I'd chosen a deep green coat and black leather vest patterned with gold leaf at the collar. Elegant. Confident. More understated than I usually opted for, but my flamboyant side would need to pace itself.

That hadn't stopped me from tracing kohl under my lower lids, nor painting a small diamond under my left eye. Come now. I wasn't about to deny the finer embellishments in life.

I smoothed out my coat, corralled Nicu and Tumble, then ducked through the exit.

The knight holding open the carriage door regarded me with a nod, meeting my eyes and inclining his head.

Well, well. This genuflection was new.

And interesting. Until now, this squad had only grunted in my general direction when necessary. Apart from the campfire tale I'd spun for them during the journey, the soldiers regularly avoided eye contact with me. Bonding with them in the orchard had been due to the mass quantities of ale they'd guzzled. Plus, the story of Briar and me had lured them, as stories did.

My boots struck the pavement. When they did, the air shifted.

The crowd stirred, the assembly of bodies twitching like birds. More than one pair of eyes widened, and I discerned a few intakes of breath from male and female spectators alike.

My mouth twisted. Call me a shallow being, but no one could deny it. Sex appeal had a knack for disarming.

Briar stood poised. Her head raised high as she waited to present us.

Quickly, I scanned the party. Based on Briar's description, the attire set them apart. Dignitaries and advisors in robes stood at the forefront, the only figures who hadn't reacted to me beyond narrowed, measured gazes. Nobles and courtiers gathered behind them, and upper servants hovered on the outer fringes. The knights of Autumn fenced everyone in, their numbers increasing as more warriors joined the congregation.

Harmless creatures? Fatal impostors?

We would see. Likely many were debating the same of me as we sized each other up.

Splendid. This jester had his work cut out for him.

And yet, we had only begun to cause a fuss. With a slight flourish and without delay, I swept toward the carriage and offered Nicu my hand. The instant his little fingers landed in my palm, a chain reaction surged through me.

Outwardly, I moved with easy grace, like a careless feline. Inside, a lion's roar tore up my throat, and protectiveness cemented my muscles into a shield.

Instead of skipping down the steps, which tended to confuse him, Nicu opened his arms for me. I caught my son around the waist and bundled him against my chest.

The instant we turned, the brushfire ignited.

8

Poet

Half of them gasped, spurts of noise popping from their mouths like explosives. Jaws unhinged. Lashes flapped. One advisor had the nerve to grumble, the planks of his eyebrows diving deeply.

Our audience saw what I had feared for years, what I'd spent my life keeping secret. Nicu's expansive eyes. His fae-like appearance. His tiny nose and broad mouth. That, plus the ferret lounging across his shoulders.

They saw a stripling who defied what they viewed as normal. They saw a boy who would otherwise be declared property.

As in Spring, these people saw what they called an alleged "simpleton." Only the monarchy's endorsement prevented the guards from clamping Nicu in irons.

Privately, my molars ground together. Publicly, I rubbed my son's back and absorbed the scene through an unruffled mask. My expression dared anyone in the vicinity to open their fucking mouths. For if this crowd didn't play nicely, my tongue would do something about it.

Briar's head tilted in the herd's direction. Her features tapered, skewering the onlookers with an imposing frown.

Although she wanted to recruit these people to our side, that might take decades. In the meantime, the princess emanated natural, keen-edged authority, balanced with the right amount of integrity.

But for fuck's sake. You would think they'd never seen anyone like Nicu. And mayhap some of them hadn't. As for the rest, they'd only beheld born souls withering behind cage bars and inside dungeon cells.

Unfazed, Nicu beamed at the party. "Are they here for us?" he whispered.

"Aye," I lied in his ear. "But remember what you promised Briar Patch?"

He nodded and squirmed to break free. After a moment's hesitation, I caught the princess's eye to prepare her.

Her commanding frown thawed, and she extended her hand to Nicu, encouraging him. Cautiously, I lowered my son to the ground, where he sprinted to Briar and snatched her fingers.

Nonplussed, the spectators watched as he tucked himself to the princess's side and peeked at the courtiers as if they were made of sugar—like an overwhelming treat. Only Nicu's vow to Briar curbed his impulse to fling himself into the crowd and hug every stiff figure in attendance. And finally, the courtiers reined in their astonishment, so he registered none of the commotion.

The door to the second carriage swayed open. In unison, everyone lowered their heads as Queen Avalea glided from the vehicle, the train of her cloak swishing behind her. Her face mirrored her daughter's—regal, impenetrable, and unapologetic.

Her eyes latched onto Briar. After spending the last four years raising my son, I knew that look. To say the queen had been worried about her daughter since last night would be an understatement. Riding in separate vehicles hadn't alleviated the terror, because nothing ever did for a parent.

Avalea tore her gaze from Briar and nodded my way, broadcasting a swift declaration of approval. After that, she joined her daughter beneath the central maple tree. This time, the flock held themselves back from swooning. As one, they sank to the floor, submitting themselves to the ruling pair.

My lips slanted. By extension, this moment forced them to prostrate themselves before my son. I doubted that fact escaped a single person.

The clever women had intended this, a risky but necessary move we'd plotted in advance. It obligated this crowd to accept Nicu and reaffirm their allegiance, an avowal that would have dire consequences should anyone break it.

Briar stooped before Nicu, who craned his head skyward at the towers. "Would you like to see inside?" she invited.

The woman might as well have asked if Nicu wanted to explore the inside of a rainbow. He beamed, speechless for once.

I'd never stalked through a castle with my son in plain sight. After years of protecting him, of keeping him to myself, my reflexes tensed. I braced myself, ready to spring at anyone who came near him.

Then I forced my joints to relax as Avalea and Briar strode across a patterned runner. At which point, I relished the sight of my son waddling between them.

I brought up the rear, sauntering through the kneeling party. They pinned their attention to the bricks, yet I caught more than one neck flush scarlet. Not to mention, several pairs of eyes scowled at my passing limbs.

The attendees rose and scattered, a chunk of the court retreating to separate wings and quads, their voices breaking into murmurs before the doors had shut behind us. The rest followed in our wake, the entourage including advisors and knights.

The next thirty minutes flew by in a whirlwind. We paraded from the main foyer with its beveled ceiling, then through a network of halls, each one divided by mezzanines.

Spring flaunted its splendor—marble, mirrors, columns, and curved edges. Its layout sprawled high and wide, the acoustics echoing every mischievous laugh and moaning orgasm.

By contrast, Autumn prided itself on refinement, from the rich wainscoted walls and polished wood floors to the lantern sconces, square rooms with bulky furnishings, and compact passages outfitted with oil paintings encased in brass frames. The condensed halls gave the place an intimate feel, made for introspective whispers instead of gales of mirth.

Toasted colors filled the corridors—russet, auburn, and sage. The passages smelled of unusual fragrances, sweet but hearty. Among them, I recognized cardamom and woodsmoke.

Every vase held dried foliage, from maroon sunflowers to rye stalks, not a single vessel containing a mixed variety. I filed each species in my head. Sooner rather than later, I'd need to acquaint myself with the flora and fauna's magic, from their mysticism to their mayhem.

On that note, my eyes scanned the walls. Camouflaged outlines marked the secret passages, each hidden outlet cleverly placed.

Briar slowed until we walked abreast of each other, with Nicu between us. Avalea glided ahead. Her advisors fussed on either side and cast me periodic glances.

My thorn leaned in and prompted, "Wait for it."

"Oh for Season's sake," Avalea said, exasperated and on cue. "Speak your mind. The jester won't bite."

"On the contrary," I remarked behind them. "I'll nibble."

Briar folded in her lips, withholding a scandalized laugh. Whilst glancing ahead, she smacked my arm reproachfully with the backs of her knuckles.

"What?" I taunted. "Spoiling my fun already?"

"I am your sovereign, after all," she reminded me.

The court hadn't yet heard about the attack. That would come shortly, once everyone had rested. In the meantime, the queen's coterie launched into a series of updates, from financial affairs, to civil disturbances, to social disputes about a guild called the Masters.

Briar and I paid attention as often as we could with my son in tow. Nicu's head flapped left and right. Uncharacteristically, he stuck to me and Briar like plaster and kept mostly quiet, too flabbergasted to do otherwise. As for Tumble, the creature blinked at our surroundings, his body bobbing to the rhythm of my son's footsteps.

Eventually, Nicu regained his confidence and asked Briar, "What's that?" and "What's that?" and "What's that?"

The knights kept surveillance of every alcove and stairway. The warrior from yesterday—the First Knight—caught Nicu peeking at him. Although man's stoic expression didn't change, he dipped his head. "Young Master."

Nicu returned the favor by giving the warrior a toothy grin. "You have metal feathers."

"These?" The knight indicated the plates of his armor, then grunted, "Yes. They do look like wing plumes, don't they?"

Impressive. Few people interpreted Nicu's wayward, lyrical speech accurately. The man looked about twenty-ish, his features honed and demeanor serious. He didn't strike me as the coddling type, yet those dark blue eyes glinted with impartiality and ... respect.

As Nicu chatted and the soldier listened, I tipped an inquiring brow at Briar. She shrugged, pleasantly surprised.

I took advantage of the interim and assessed Her Majesty's aides. Stepping nearer to my thorn, I murmured, "Should I cause trouble with them?"

"Only if you tell a joke," she replied with a straight face.

I gave her a cautionary look. "Insulting my jests, are you? There are consequences for that."

After a beat, her lips twitched. "I know."

Ah. Fucking temptress of a princess. She was in a bold mood, but dangling that line like a morsel would get this woman punished the second I cornered her alone.

"That's daring of you, Highness," I warned.

"Everything a Royal does is daring," she assured me.

"You're right. I shouldn't worry about them." A clandestine smirk filled my voice. "They should worry about you."

Briar's expression remained neutral, but those eyes flared with determination. "We'll know more tonight during the welcome feast."

"I do enjoy a meal served with a side of intrigue."

"Then I expect you to slay, Jester."

"And I expect you to enable me, Princess."

"Who are they?" Nicu asked, eyeing the figures trotting beside Avalea.

I cupped my hand. "Gargoyles who were rejected by their fated mates."

My son nodded. "That's why their faces are made of stone, even though someone chopped off their horns."

The First Knight frowned, apparently unfamiliar with the concept of a joke.

Briar swatted my wrist and mouthed, *Don't tell him that.*

The advisors mentioned something called Reaper's Fest, which centered around a bonfire ball. My ears perked. It sounded like my kind of affair.

Residents stopped to bow and gawk. As the Spring Court's infamous jester and the monarchy's prized gem, I was no stranger to this attention. But Nicu wasn't. The sensory overload made his pupils gleam, and every time his feet shuffled from our huddle, I intercepted with a riddle for him to solve, or Briar reminded my son of his pledge to stay beside her. Either that, or the First Knight noticed, stepped smoothly in Nicu's path, and shared tidbits of Autumn lore, including a story about mystical acorns, which thrilled my son to no end.

After trekking through more wings, more halls, more stairways, and more mezzanines, we arrived in the Royal wing. The advisors departed looking winded from the velocity at which they'd spoken, each of them patting their brows with handkerchiefs, whereas Briar's Mother hadn't broken a sweat.

One foyer comprised two doors studded with black pegs. Briar gave Nicu an anticipatory look. "Come," she urged.

She swung open the partition and led the way. The second we entered, Nicu gasped, "Ohh."

And my fucking ribs constricted.

The nursery's size was modest by a Royal's standards, which I suspected was intentional. Beyond the antechamber, we stepped into a room with a canopied bed, a row of windows with high latches—safely out of my son's reach—that offered a view of the Royal stables, where equines and stags grazed. On the walls, moldings framed panels of wallpaper that depicted forest settings, remarkably similar to Spring's wildflower forest. A cupboard held puppets, animal costumes, and makeshift potions. A rocking horse stood in a beam of sunlight, and a bookcase lined one corner, where leather-bound fables and fairytales packed the shelves.

I noted a nightstand, a miniature armoire, and Nicu's lone trunk already placed at the bed's footboard. A locked grate fronted the fireplace, which bloomed with flames. The barrier wasn't necessary, since my son had grown up near a hearth, and he'd learned a long time ago that fire hurt. Still, the precaution loosened a kink in my neck.

The soldiers closed the door, giving us solitude. In addition to the room's reduced size, it contained a scarcity of knickknacks and only the most essential furnishings. The lack of clutter would make it easy for anyone to remember to place every object back in its original spot. Yet it was humbly luxurious, every stick of furniture exuding quality.

The moderate collection of toys and books was the perfect amount. Not too many to disorientate Nicu, nor too few to bore him. It gave my son a place of his own, a space to indulge to his heart's content.

It was effortless for Nicu to navigate. It took all his needs into account.

It was the sort of room I'd always wanted for him.

Tumble scurried from Nicu's shoulders, scaled down his form, and sped around the interior like a windup figurine. The ferret sniffed and nipped each item until locating his bed, which had been brought in with the rest of Nicu's things. The critter inhaled the familiar scent, visibly stumped that it had ended up here.

My son turned a full circle, his mouth ajar. His brows crinkled with a mixture of awe and bafflement.

The queen folded her hands in front of her—Briar had inherited that pose—and grinned as he took in the space. Meanwhile, her daughter glanced between me and Nicu, uncertainty consuming her features.

I wanted to say something, to assure her this was perfect. Yet every possible compliment, witticism, encouragement, and general syllable dried in my throat. My tongue flopped around in my mouth, a useless thing for once in my life.

"I'm, umm ..." Nicu twisted my way, then scanned the queen and princess's expressions. "What is ... I don't know ..."

"This is for you." Briar stepped forward. "A special place just for you. Do you like it?"

He blinked. "For me?"

His head veered in my direction, searching for guidance. I broke from my stupor and let my boots carry me across the room, where I hunkered in front of him. "These chambers are a gift, love."

A thrill lifted his chest, but weariness buckled across his face. I knew what he was thinking, and I was about to answer when Briar squatted next to us.

"Look up," she prompted.

We did. And that's when the reality of this place did me in. I'd been planning to rectify this one detail with Briar, but she beat me to it.

A lantern hung from the ceiling. Strung from the fixture, three distinct cords looped in different directions. One led toward the antechamber, another to what I presumed was the bathroom, and the other curved here. Each strand was the same color it had been in the cottage where Nicu was raised.

An orange ribbon swung to the bed, where his stuffed gnome sat against a mountain of pillows. His childhood blanket topped the mattress, spread above a matching orange coverlet.

Nicu's teeth flashed with glee. "Happy orange."

His favorite color.

Despite this new environment, the gnome situated as it had been on his old bed reassured Nicu. In his mind, it confirmed this was his room. As did the colors and ceiling ribbons.

Except one thing was missing. I saw it on Nicu's face seconds before he asked, "Jinny's not here?"

Briar's expression faltered. The question splintered me in half. It wasn't the first time he'd asked about Jinny, and it wouldn't be the last. If his things turned up here, where was the woman he grew up with?

Nicu had bawled whilst saying goodbye to Old Jinny, unable to comprehend where we were going, what leaving meant, and why Jinny wouldn't be there. It had taken a few rounds of explaining for him to grasp it all, and still he still craned his head to search for her.

I tapped my finger against the scarlet ribbon wrapped around his wrist. "She's here. Remember?"

Nicu's features relaxed. I used to tell him the same thing whenever I left him with Jinny—that if he touched the bracelet, he would feel me close.

My son would ask again tomorrow and the day after, until it sank in. We'd take it moment by moment. But for now, Nicu nodded and gripped the bracelet with his free hand.

I slid my head toward Briar. Her grinning profile ripped me to pieces. Though, the princess didn't notice, for she was too busy relishing Nicu's glee as he raced across the room and hopped onto the bed.

I gazed at her, unable to utter a fucking word. She did this. How had she managed to coordinate this, when we'd been on the road until three seconds ago?

In my periphery, I caught the queen observing us. Discreetly, she turned away, perched at Nicu's bedside, and offered to show him around.

Eventually, Briar's eyes crept toward mine. A timid but endearing shade of pink puddled in her cheeks. "Forgive me, I …," she trailed off, averted her gaze, and licked her lips. "I might have drafted a sketch of this room and dispatched one of the knights ahead of us. He arrived early, to have the arrangements made." She spoke to the floor, rather unlike her. "I did my utmost to remember everything about his room at Jinny's, and I kept everything you told me in mind. I was rather meticulous in the sketch, actually. But I wanted to make sure he felt at home." At last, Briar peeked at me under her lashes. "Is this okay?"

She was asking far too late. And she knew it.

Not that it mattered. If this woman had ever left me speechless before, nothing compared to her sneaky actions now. And that included when she'd risked her life to help me commit treason by rescuing Nicu.

"Poet?" she whispered. "Is this okay?"

My jaw moved, and my mouth followed. The words came out low and gritty. "I'll tell you later."

Those cheeks darkened further. Her pupils skipped across my face, searching for a more definitive answer. Usually, she saw through my veneer. But right then, I did well to mask everything surging through me.

Had she overstepped? Had she angered her jester by not consulting with him?

Oh, I enjoyed making her guess. She would get my feedback later, but until then, I made sure she felt the intensity of it. My eyelids hooded, and I imagined my irises deepening to an unfathomable shade.

Briar's throat bobbed.

Another throat cleared.

The princess lurched to her feet. Tipsy from her reaction, I followed at a lazier pace.

Avalea must have finished her tour with Nicu. Presently, my son flattened himself on the floor beside Tumble and stroked the creature's fur. "It's okay," he coaxed. "I'm here."

The queen sequestered herself near the windows, where we joined her. After another glance at Nicu, she clipped, "Roundtable tonight."

Briar wavered. "Shouldn't we postpone until morning?"

"Absolutely not. What happened last night must be dealt with as soon as possible, before the feast."

I shook my head and echoed Briar's concern. "Do that, and we won't have time to rule out suspected players."

Avalea paused. "Go on."

"Assassins would expect us to deliberate immediately," Briar spoke in a hushed tone. "We can't summon a forum until we know whom to trust. It will affect what we say and omit."

"In order to ferret out—pun intended—potential enemies at court, we need to exhibit patience," I reasoned. "A juggling act of restraint and resilience. Let them see us drink and revel, which will inspire them to do the same. Eventually, a tongue will slip, or a pair of eyes will stray."

It always happened. But typically, assassins needed time to fuck up.

Avalea processed the logic, though not without reluctance. She was a mother, after all. Some unknown cocksucker had indirectly targeted her daughter with a cryptic warning in the form of a severed head and bloody corpse markings.

I had just as much of a thirst to slit their throat. Except I had to know which throat, and I couldn't afford to be wrong. None of us could.

That was why we'd decided before leaving the orchard not to make the details public. To that end, Avalea had gotten the knights to swear against any disclosures. Merit's death would be announced tomorrow; however, the particulars would not be part of that broadcast. Soldiers fell whilst in service, especially during voyages, which would make it easy to downplay. No one would learn where the attack happened, what had been carved into the knight's flesh, or if there'd been a reason beyond random bandits.

Any slip could reveal how much—or how little—we knew. The less our enemies thought we suspected, the better.

The queen's chest deflated. "Very well," she agreed. "Tomorrow, we deliberate. Tonight, we … juggle."

My mouth curled. "If I may be so bold—"

"Is there any other way with you?" Briar wondered.

"Leave the verbal juggling to me, Majesty."

"You're rather confident for a newcomer," Avalea commented.

"Correction," her daughter stated wryly. "He is versatile."

"Wordplay works the same everywhere," I advocated. "'Tis only the content, pacing, and inflection that changes."

"In other words, everything," Briar summarized.

"Is that all?" Avalea mocked. "I assume I'm supposed to find your riddles reassuring?"

"Never fear. Jesters train not merely with props, but with their tongues." I kicked my head toward Briar. "Besides, I've had practice against a powerful Autumn opponent."

Reluctant approval flitted across the queen's face. "In that case, I'll retire." The woman bobbed a finger at us—"Behave yourselves," she commanded—before promising Nicu she'd return to say good-night in a few hours. Then she pivoted and sashayed through the door with armed guards at her heels.

Briefly, I considered Nicu. "That leaves one more quandary."

Fretful, Briar followed my gaze. "The soldiers will look out for him."

We'd been over this. Having my son twenty-four hours a day in an unknown castle, in a foreign nation, required me to trust Briar's judgment. That was the easy part. Among the knights who'd accompanied us, the princess and I agreed to delegate a pack of them to Nicu's protection, to patrol his chambers nonstop, whether or not Briar and I were around to watch him.

But after last night, our standards had changed. I felt a mercenary urge to reject those plans entirely and staple myself to Nicu's bedside.

Briar's palm landed on my forearm. "We have no choice. Our allies are few and far between. Neither of us can be with him every moment of the day. And do not give me one of your clever juggler analogies. You know I'm right."

My mouth tipped into a humorless smirk. "And however sexy you look when you're right, this is one time when I wish you weren't."

Footsteps approached. A masculine voice cleared. "If I may—"

Briar and I pivoted toward the soldier idling between the antechamber and Nicu's bedroom. When the queen exited, the door had been left ajar. Moreover, the princess's frown and my glower didn't help matters.

"This is a private conference," Briar stated.

The First Knight lowered his head and weathered our skepticism. "Your pardon, Highness. I did not mean to intrude, but your presence is requested for a briefing in an hour. I've been instructed to keep you abreast."

Like her mother, Briar kept her own retinue of councilors. "Poet and I will be there," she replied.

But the soldier ventured another step. "I can guard the boy."

Despite his unflappable kindness to Nicu earlier, Briar and I stiffened. Registering this, the man's eyes clicked toward Nicu. For an awkward few seconds, the warrior struggled with his next words, as if they'd never left his mouth before. "I had a younger brother ... like him."

My eyebrows slammed together. The princess blinked. Was he admitting ...

The knight pressed forth, a muscle leaping in his jaw. "He died when he was six."

My features slackened. Fuck. He was.

"Oh," Briar stuttered. "I-I'm so sorry."

"I was but a lad, only three years his senior." The knight regarded me. "Yet I remember him."

We fell quiet. Clearly, Briar hadn't known this about the soldier, nor did her mother. This was likely intentional on the man's part. Whilst he hadn't outright confessed to treason, the fact hovered in the air.

If Briar and her mother hadn't known about the child, he couldn't have been claimed as property. What happened to that boy and how he died, the knight wouldn't volunteer. This man had already revealed plenty, and though questions stacked in my head—What condition did the boy have? Was it the same as Nicu's?—I was the last person who would press him for more.

I gave the knight a once-over but failed to detect an ounce of treachery. Surliness aside, he radiated sincerity. Moreover, his behavior with Nicu made sense.

No one would confess this information to a Royal if they didn't trust their ruler's mercy. As with everyone, the knight had heard about our crimes in Spring, and that must have influenced him. Like me, he served the monarchy despite the intolerance toward someone who mattered to him.

This soldier was no killer in disguise. He was a sympathizer.

Briar and I surveyed him, then traded silent glances.

"There are crucial things you should know," I told the man. "About his care."

"The child has difficulty with orientation," the soldier cited. "Spaces and distances, chiefly. He identifies objects by where they're placed as much as what they are, so every item must be kept where he initially found it. Nothing must ever be moved." His mouth tipped sideways, out of vigilance rather than amusement. "And he's rather enthusiastically friendly to strangers, which can be a problem."

Well, fuck. Had I thought it possible for someone other than Briar and Jinny to read my son this smoothly? There was an intuitive aura about this man. And beyond that, his actions revealed something more.

He cared enough to pay attention.

If Nicu was like his brother, the knight must have quietly noticed him, absorbing what others disregarded because my son was either invisible to them, or he repelled them.

Briar's profile alighted. "I do believe the jester is silent because you've impressed him."

"The princess knows me well." I pointed at the man. "Consider yourself lucky. Impressing me is difficult, and many have tried."

The knight wavered. "I can perceive people and their needs. Or so I've been told."

And the intrigues kept coming. That type of skill sounded visceral for someone who didn't seem capable of cracking a smile. Then again, I hadn't been in the mood to banter when I introduced Briar to Nicu. My thoughts had been buried in a darker place.

"Exceptional or not, we're grateful," Briar said. "Though I would simply conclude you're more empathetic than many, and that makes you more observant."

"She's the practical one," I said. "I'm the poet who liked your mysterious explanation better. We can discuss Nicu's care later, before the feast."

The knight nodded. "I'd be honored for the instruction, Master Jester."

Ugh. I refrained from gagging but wiggled my fingers in dismissal. "None of that. It's Poet." But when the man's pupils dilated as if I'd instructed him to say the word *pussy*, I amended. "Or *Sir*, if you insist."

Satisfied, the knight bowed. He backed away and headed for the door.

I opened my mouth to call out, but Briar's voice got to him first. "Wait a moment."

The knight paused at the threshold. "Highness? Sir?"

Briar wanted to introduce us, but my mouth jumped ahead. "Your name?"

Those twilit eyes flew to Nicu, who had relocated to the toy cupboard with Tumble. The man studied my son, then redirected his attention to us. "My name is Aire."

My mouth tilted. "Nicu," I called out. "Come here."

My son dashed across the room and skidded in his tracks to goggle at the armored figure. "You're the raptor with the metal wings." Before the man could respond, Nicu pounced, launching himself forward and strapping his body around the man's limbs. "Can I fly like you?"

The man grunted on impact, surprise puffing from his mouth. "Knighthood takes practice, Young Master." He untangled himself from my son and knelt. "But with training, we might make a warrior of you yet."

Nicu nodded. "Are we friends?"

"If that's all right with you."

"This is Aire," Briar announced.

"Aire." My son examined him. "Like the air we breathe. That's why your eyes mimic the night sky and the wind swoops under your feet."

That meant he liked the blue of Aire's irises—which matched the firmament—and thought the man walked agilely, with as much fearlessness as a bird of prey cutting through a cloud.

Seeming to understand, the soldier wavered, then ruffled Nicu's hair and rose. When he left the room, my son darted to the rocking horse, which Tumble had proceeded to chew on.

Silence descended. Briar and I swerved our heads toward one another.

"Soooo," I drew out. "That was unexpected."

"But welcome," she agreed. "Who would have imagined? Yet I believe Aire's trustworthy. First Knight aside, there's always been something about him—something gruff but fiercely loyal."

"I had the same feeling. He gives me grumpy-but-good vibes. Not my favorite combination, but I'll overlook the lack of sin and mischief, considering the rest. And trust me, my morally gray trickster instincts were primed to scrutinize."

Briar folded her hands behind her back. "Aren't they always?"

Our exchange from earlier rekindled. Now that we might have found a solution for Nicu, my mood darkened, spurring me toward other nefarious intentions.

Like a good little princess, Briar registered the change. Instantly, her attention tacked on to Nicu. Without him as the buffer, my thorn wrestled her features into place. Unfortunately for her—and fortunately for me—the attempt failed to dilute that attractive flush.

As much as my tongue enjoyed plying her with a variety of sensations, sometimes words ruined the effect. In the past, the absence of them also caused an uproar among a select few of my targets.

On purpose, I stayed quiet.

"Would you like to see your suite?" she rambled. "It's right across the foyer, and there's a passage connecting your bathroom to Nicu's. That will make it quicker to reach him. Also, my suite neighbors yours, just in case. So I can get to him as well."

"My room can wait," I intoned, my voice rough and downright predatory.

Briar gave a start. She surveyed me with a dubious expression. "No rush? Not even to appraise your wardrobe?"

"I'm much more interested in what I'd find in your wardrobe."

Her breathing hitched. "It's not as opulent as yours."

"Then we'll have to do something about that, won't we?" I stalked nearer. "First, I would have to see your closet and find out what I'm dealing with."

"Are you denying that you've contemplated the size of your sanctuary? That you haven't obsessed once about its size?"

I braced my palm on my chest. "What makes you think—"

"Only the mere fact that it required an entire carriage to haul your belongings with us."

My eyes slitted. "You're about to cross another line, Princess."

With her confidence restored, Briar raised an imperial brow. "A dozen massive crates."

"Half a dozen." Then I recounted in my head and shrugged. "Three-quarters of a dozen. I'll have you know, that's minimal for a jester, and it included accessories." I flashed her a wolfish smirk. "Then again, I do love when you call me out with those pursed lips."

"Flattery will not excuse excess."

I plucked a tassel from her cloak and rubbed it between my thumb and forefinger. "That depends on which manner I'm excessive. There are so many options."

I would have reminded this woman how many illuminated manuscripts accompanied us from Spring. However, she was as defensive of her prized collection as I was about my impeccable attire. Besides, Briar's lips quivered fetchingly under my touch, and whilst I enjoyed my share of tension kinks, presently I'd rather see her flustered than vexed.

Here we were. New land. New court. Enemies lurked unseen and unknown. We had meetings to attend, maneuvers to plot, and schemes to orchestrate.

But for all the dangerous games ahead, another one came to mind. Ill-timed but all-consuming.

I cocked my head. "Hmm. For a sovereign newly returned to her seat of power, you're looking rather overheated," I remarked, deadpan. "Any such reason, Your Highness?"

Briar adjusted the intricate pin spearing through her fishtail braid. She lifted her chin, laced her fingers together, and pretended to ignore my taunts. "It's been a long day. I must be tired."

"Then you should rest," I indulged, taking her hand and brushing my lips against her knuckles. "Restore your energy."

Her wrist trembled. "Yes. For tonight."

Tonight. The feast.

Aye, that's what she'd meant. But I hadn't.

For I would see her long before then.

9

Briar

I took a deep Autumn-scented breath. The rich, brisk aromas of this land filled my senses. Wheat and corn. Apples and cloves. The essences rushed to my head until it spun.

At last, I was home.

Standing at the balcony, déjà vu overcame me. Not long ago, I had done this same thing, except I'd been ensconced in a different Season, unaware of what was about to happen, who I would meet, and how he would change my life.

Now both worlds converged. He was here, in this castle.

An hour had passed since I last saw him. Any moment, he might walk through the door.

My lungs released the familiar Autumn fragrances. I sighed them out, my exhalation shaky. I had hoped the fresh air would settle my nerves, yet the anxiety flapped inside me like a moth.

My dressing robe swished across the rug as I stepped back into my suite, where a fire crackled inside the mammoth fireplace, its mantel crafted of intricate rosewood. The apartment included inlaid chambers connected across two-floors— antechamber, bedroom, sitting room, athenaeum, study loft, bathroom, and wardrobe. A winding staircase led to the study, which overlooked the lower level.

In the sitting room, I halted beside the blaze and proceeded to gnaw on a fingernail. I felt my brows dipping. A knitted quilt slouched over a chair, the folds misaligned and the fabric wrinkled. I strode to the seat and straightened the blanket, then refolded it again, then rearranged it in several variations before satisfied.

Also, the books heaped on a table fronting the hearth were piled too high, the tomes in danger of tumbling like bricks. I tidied them, breaking the volumes into groups and stacking them in alphabetical order.

Whipping around with my fists on my hips, I noticed candle wax had leaked onto the brass tapers lining the mantel. I scratched the bases clean and tossed the wax debris into the flames.

Moreover, the gallery wall in the antechamber was a mess. Oil paintings hung lopsided, leaning an extra half inch to one side. I marched to the wall and adjusted the frames, then retreated backward to survey the result.

Come to think of it, the paintings had been fine the first time. I should have left them alone because now they looked even more off-kilter.

And the pillows on my bed needed fluffing. And the balcony curtains bunched too closely together across the hanging rod. And were those my fingerprints on the window sashes? Oh gods, they were!

Hysteria fired across my chest. Which other parts of the room should I rectify?

Indecision gripped my ankles, stapling them to the floor. At last, I broke free and hastened to the athenaeum where a succession of built-in bookshelves embedded into the walls. My hands rushed across the spines, nudging them into place and straightening novels that had tipped against one another.

I needed more bookends. Heavy ones.

When I progressed to the anthologies, aggravation got the worst of me. The weighty titles sloped, fussy to reposition. "Damnation,"

I muttered. "Move."

"Careful, Your Highness. That's a dangerous request."

I spun on my heels. A gasp leaped from my soul and scraped across the room, so that I sounded like a shocked raccoon. In the process, a thick book dropped from my fingers and struck the ground, followed by three other volumes that plummeted around my feet. One by one, they hit the floor in a sequence of thuds.

A tall silhouette filled the archway dividing my bedroom from the athenaeum. He leaned against the frame, his posture gloriously lazy. That wicked mouth slanted as he watched me through irises gleaming with mischief.

Perfectly disheveled hair. Elegantly slouchy.

The jester wore a netted shirt with an indecently low neckline that offered glimpses of his torso, the tightly woven fabric stretching over grooved muscles and exhibiting more abs than a human should rightly possess. The shirt slipped into the waistband of his leather trousers, the sides paneled in the same netting, and his favorite boots clung to his calves.

He looked far too unrealistic for his own good. I would bet he'd taken two minutes to make himself look presentable, where it would have required a mere mortal two hours. It wasn't fair. And yet, my breath caught.

Poet's lips flexed deeper, as if he was cognizant of my thoughts. "Telling a jester to move will only make him come closer. As I've warned you before, be careful what you ask of our kind."

That gleam prompted me to cross my arms and fix him with a scowl. "I trust you're aware that nature has spoiled your vanity rotten."

"Makes sense," he drawled. "It enabled me to create a child, as well as inspire those lovely lines of scarlet rushing across your cheeks."

An influx of heat snuck up my throat, but I saw no point in denying it. "Are you finished congratulating yourself?"

"When would I ever be finished doing that?" Poet jerked his chin to the fallen titles. "Such a violent display. Any more fussing, and you're going to traumatize those poor books."

"I didn't hear you come in," I said, the statement so obvious I could have cringed.

"Ah," he hummed. "So it wasn't me you were ordering to move? Otherwise, say the word, and I'll very much oblige. Though I can't promise it will end innocently."

The firelight sketched his chiseled features in ochre. I retreated a step, confounded by this restless energy fizzing through my limbs. One would assume I'd never been alone with this man, never felt the pulse of his cock driving in and out of me.

Poet advanced, his sculpted form materializing fully into the room's glow. Like a panther, he sauntered my way. "Aren't you going to show me around? 'Tisn't polite, leaving a guest to wander on their own. Where are your manners, Princess?"

I forced my legs to stay put. "They're in the same place you left your modesty."

A fiendish grin draped across his face. "That's more like the sharp thorn I know and crave."

"I will do even better. When entering a Royal's suite, proper decorum and outright subservience necessitate you letting the guards announce you first."

"In other words, how did I make it past them? Do you really need to ask?"

No, I did not. The jester moved like a shadow when he needed to. Nonetheless, I was curious.

The show-off lasted three seconds. "I'm Poet," he bragged. "Also, I may have overworked my silver tongue." He pinched his thumb and forefinger together. "Just a tad."

"In other words, you manipulated the guards."

"I may have convinced them the princess's lover is an exception to the rules, and you wanted privacy with me. Was I wrong?"

How often this man disarmed and emboldened me. How often this devil swept me from one impulse to the next, one emotion to the other.

Whereas my voice had been trembling a second ago, now I fought to keep a neutral face. "You're not wrong—aside from the part where I'd already instructed them to admit you without alerting me."

Poet stalled halfway across the athenaeum. "Well, well. And here, I thought you were going to let me boast about my skills."

"I'm certain you'll give yourself plenty more chances tonight."

As if I'd handed him an invitation, the jester's pupils glimmered with intent. Yes, I had left myself open for that one.

"You know," he continued, "I expected this to be more complicated. Pity, since I'd grown rather used to the idea of skulking through the halls and claiming you behind everyone's back."

"Lots of things will get more complicated," I reminded him. "But not this."

Poet had once predicted he would have to sneak into my chamber on a nightly basis. Although every court in The Dark Seasons knew about us, Autumn preferred discretion. But as I'd assured him on the way from Spring, waltzing in here wouldn't make a great difference at this point. Yes, finding time together would be increasingly difficult, chiefly when the sun was up, when we had to conduct ourselves in public. By contrast, intimate evening visits weren't the problem.

Then again, Poet should not have strolled in with a gaping shirt. This kingdom gossiped as much as the next, and that visual would get around the wings, from courtiers to servants.

I should scold Poet. I should reproach him.

I should move my blasted feet.

"Not this," Poet echoed in thought. "I beg to differ. It might have been effortless to enter your refuge, but it will be a challenge keeping you quiet. I know how loud you get."

Lava coursed down my spine and pooled between my legs. "When you say things like that, I can barely think."

"Nay, sweeting. I believe you get lots of thoughts whenever I open my mouth. Though you have no idea how much I appreciate the feedback."

"Is Nicu asleep?" I blurted out.

Those orbs flashed like green scythes. "Am I making you nervous, Highness?"

"Certainly not. Of course you aren't making me ... No. Why on earth would you ask that?"

Instead of calling me out on the lie, he simply stared. Poet and I had met with my advisors earlier, then I'd left to refresh myself and ended up falling into a dead sleep, which lasted longer than I expected. Later, I'd returned to Nicu's room with the jester and helped him tuck in the child. After that, we parted ways to unpack. So basically, I had wasted my breath asking.

This, from a princess who rarely wasted her breath. Poet knew as much.

The lush rug sank under my stockinged feet. I shuffled in place, wrung my hands. Was the jester making me nervous?

No. Yes.

Never. Always.

Poet's gaze flitted from my restless toes to my fidgety hands. Some sort of awareness glossed in his eyes, and his purr softened. "It's because I've never seen any of this."

By Seasons. He was right.

The deduction brought every frenzied emotion to the forefront—doubt, fear, arousal, pride, and more doubt—until the root of my angst became clear. I'd been obsessing over the appearance of my suite for one reason.

I'd never had a man in here before. I never had *him* in here before.

That same conclusion reflected on Poet's face. Sometimes this jester understood me better than I did myself, though I could not say whether the knowledge angered, mystified, or soothed me. Perhaps all three.

I gestured around the space and heard my voice wobble, teetering between tenderness, shyness, and anxiousness. "These are my rooms," I said. "This is where I grew up."

Poet's attention swung from one chamber to the next. He swiveled toward the bedroom, where the bed stood on a dais and an intricate wood awning projected over the headboard, its drapes puddling on either side. As the jester's head slanted about, I followed his progress and examined the area with fresh eyes.

Medallion patterned rugs stretched across the floor. Plush armchairs, a settee, and a table fronted the fireplace. Brass candle stems, oil paintings, and ceramic pots filled with dried blooms accented the empty spaces.

Relics of my childhood filled in the crevices, along with memories of my father. My favorite quilt since I was thirteen. The music box on my nightstand, which Father had gifted me, which played a lutist's tune.

In the athenaeum, the inlaid bookshelves rose high, crammed with volumes. The central shelf displayed my treasured illuminated manuscripts, the oldest of which sat open like a museum artifact. Protruding sconces bled muted light onto the texts, and oversized upholstered seats graced the area.

The items I owned ranged from the priceless to the practical, but Autumn did not wear its extravagance on its sleeve. We valued understated luxuries, like a cashmere sweater with no embellishments other than fine stitching and quality fabric.

My only indulgences were books and expensive writing instruments.

In the study loft overlooking the athenaeum, Poet would find more shelves, along with my antique writing desk, an assortment of quills, and a smaller fireplace. But the jester didn't venture up there. Instead, he strolled past me, his scent gripping my lungs on the way.

I turned, watching him mosey down the shelves at an unhurried pace. It gave me time to process the sight of him among objects from my past, mementoes I had accumulated over time. Pieces cultivated from experiences and relationships.

I want to see every truth about you—everything raw and real.

The memory of his words, spoken to me in Spring's castle, unraveled the knots inside me. It didn't matter if every keepsake wasn't as blatantly lavish as the possessions of a Spring monarch. Costly or not, this was my haven, and I meant for Poet to see it.

The paintings could hang crooked. The books could topple over. His judgment did not matter. And it very much did.

I wanted him to value the raw and real. I wanted him to see each fragment of who I was, and for that to be enough.

Poet ran his fingers along a set of book spines. Then his hand stalled, halting in place as he tapped one digit against a particular title. "You're missing an installment here."

"It's a rare collection," I replied, moving to stand beside him. "I've been trying to find the last book in the series, but it's been a struggle." I tucked a lock of hair behind my ears. "It was the first thing I'd ever read, an epic saga about a ruler and how she fell to ruin, but then rose to power. The final book is an extended epilogue of sorts, but there's only one copy in existence. I have been searching for years."

Poet studied the set. His index finger rapped the spine in thought, then he twisted my way like a serpent—smoothly and swiftly. He drizzled his knuckles down the side of my face, scorching a path along my skin. "I fancy what you've done with the place. Did you honestly think I wouldn't?"

My eyes stung. I tried to compress my shaky lips, but they buckled into a sheepish laugh. "I feel silly for overreacting."

"The strong-willed princess, feel silly? Rubbish. I suppose we'll have to fix that, hmm? In what other ways can I make you overreact?"

His silken words caused a profusion in the cleft of my thighs. My pussy tightened, and the tight nub at its center throbbed. The outbreak of sensations overwhelmed me. We'd only just arrived, had only stepped into this fortress mere hours ago.

Him, the controversial jester. Me, the tarnished princess.

I'd been banished from one court and discredited in another. My homeland did not trust me. Hundreds of courtiers and soldiers lurked outside this room, their eyes open and ears perked.

Meanwhile, the confidential parts of my life existed in this suite, tucked within these walls. Now the jester had seen all those things. And though he made this space feel even safer, perspiration surfaced on my palms.

Frantic, I scrambled backward like a petrified rabbit. "A tour," I piped. "You wanted a tour." I lifted my index finger and feigned confidence. "I can do a tour."

My limbs sprang into action. I moved too quickly to gauge his reaction, hastening into the bedroom and clumsily waving him over. Fleeing to the balcony, I resumed my original position from before he'd entered the suite.

Outside, distant corn and wheat fields rustled like waves under a dome of stars. Across the castle grounds, mist laminated every chunk of masonry, patch of grass, and exposed root. In the courtyards, maple leaves glowed through the murk.

This being the Royal wing, the immediate vicinity was exclusive to Mother and me. And with the feast beginning soon, everyone was indoors anyway, preparing for the event. No one would see us from here.

At the platform's rim, cattail boxes jutted from the foundation, the stems shaking like limbs. I rushed to the ledge and gripped the stones. Seconds later, boots stalked toward me. The jester's gait was calm, lithe, and graceful, which meant trouble. He approached like a vapor—encompassing and hard to escape.

Goosebumps raced up the flesh of my nape. My stomach flipped inside out. The slot of my pussy clenched, liquid coating the seam.

Like a specter, his shadow fell across mine. The whipcord body of a dancer blended with my silhouette. Masculine heat radiated from inches behind.

I threw my arm toward the vista and pointed. "To the south, we have the lower town. Millers, builders, and brewers run their businesses from there. We also have a bookbinder's emporium, a mapmaker's stall, and a renowned carpenter's shop.

"Beyond that grow the harvest lands—corn and wheat—which we've named The Wandering Fields. We call it that because people who don't know how to navigate them can get lost there forever. It's even vaster than it looks, an optical illusion that protects the castle from intruders and serves as a form of execution to criminals. Some of the condemned are dropped in there, unable to find their way out and never to be heard from again."

I sensed this giving Poet pause. "That's lethal for such a saintly Season."

"Every court has its limits. And nature is never exclusively good or bad. In ancient times, giants were keepers of the fields, since they were the only ones tall enough to see over the stalks and lead wanderers through. When their culture died out, it was up to the people to learn the routes for themselves. Some have—harvesters and farmers mostly. Others haven't."

"Correct me if I'm wrong, but there's a perfectly functional road leading between the fields. Invaders could simply use that."

"And be spotted by the watch? I thought you excelled in the best ways to travel undetected."

"That's why I'm suggesting the least evident route. There are plenty of healthy shadows to play with along that road, if you know where to look and how fast to catch them. Also, wouldn't raiders know to beware of the fields?"

"Only if they're of Autumn," I clarified and continued pointing. "Then the orchards and beech forest—that's where we came from," I added unnecessarily. "But if you keep going and veer east, you'll enter fox territory, where the creatures are guarded by mavens." I backpedaled to explain. "Fox mavens are a solitary group, mainly comprised of women, who are essentially fauna keepers. And to the west of The Fox Dell lies The Forbidden Burrow. And farther afield, you'll reach The Pumpkin Wood, where The Royal retreat stands secluded."

Poet's netted shirt billowed against my robe, electrifying each vertebra.

I flapped my arm and prattled, "After that, there's The Lost Treehouses. It's an abandoned colony, but—"

Poet's muscled arms extended past me, fencing in my body. His hands rested on either side of my own, his knuckles relaxed compared to how my digits clamped onto the ledge. As the jester's statuesque form leaned over me, his breath coasted across the back of my ear.

Dark amusement coiled from his lips, that voice of his thick and sultry. "Go on," he persuaded against my delicate lobe. "Tell me more. I'm at your disposal."

The graze of his incisors incited mayhem. I pressed my thighs together, desperate to quell the pulse in my clitoris. My lips parted to say more, but Poet's mouth pressed kisses along my profile. His full lips seared across my jaw, the contact threatening to unbuckle my knees.

I rolled my head forward, attempting to maneuver out of range. But he only swept aside my unbound locks and whispered, "Too much, Highness?" Then he switched ears. "Or not enough?"

"Both," I admitted.

"I should hope so."

With that in mind, he etched the opposite side of my neck in a slow, lazy drag.

Flurries scattered across the right side of my body. The ripple effect descended between my legs, where fluid seeped through the gap in my drawers. It felt empty there, hollow yet so very deep.

I grasped the banister, unsure if I was trying to stop myself or use the facade for leverage. My backside arched into Poet's trousers, and a harsh noise splintered from his lungs. At the same time, his cock rose into the wedge of space between our hips, the stem of his erection firm and thick. Through the leather, I felt every inch, from the broad pommel to the base.

My thoughts fogged. The upheaval caused by his proximity captivated me, my body churning, squirming against him. I swayed my waist, skidding my bottom over that cock, the ridge solid and twitching for me.

With a groan, Poet warned, "You shall pay for that."

"I should hope so," I muttered in a daze, tossing his words back at him.

A lusty chuckle brimmed from his throat. "Spectacular woman."

"I'm not so sure about that. I don't know why I scurried away from you, even while I wanted to fling myself at you."

"Mayhap it was part of my devious plan. Makes the chase more rewarding in the end. 'Tis often the response I incite in people."

"Not me. Or rather, not always. I'm no frightened mouse."

"Nay, my thorn. Sometimes you've wanted to punch me."

"Only when you deserved it."

"You *are* spectacular," he insisted. "And you know it. Allow me to propose a theory. You weren't scurrying away from me; you were luring me like a tigress."

My lips peeled into a grin. "I knew there was a reason I wanted you on my advisory team."

"Haven't changed your mind then? In that case, I'll have plenty of suggestions in the near future, as will my cock."

I quivered like a string pulled too tightly. I couldn't decide whether to nuzzle against him or grind my hips harder into that long mast distending from his waist.

The scarlet ribbon strung around his wrist tickled my flesh, managing to catch my attention. Inebriated from need, I raised my arm impulsively, where a matching bracelet encircled my own wrist. The sight broke through our delirium. Heady, we watched the bands rub delicately in the half-light.

"Do you think anyone noticed us wearing them?" I wondered.

"People only see what they want to see," Poet mumbled. "That's a blessing and curse."

"And do you like what you've seen thus far? In the carriage, you said I was your home, but ... do you *feel* at home?"

The jester clasped my hips and wheeled me toward him, the current buffeting his tousled hair and my errant tresses. "Nicu's here." His head lowered, and his mouth abraded my own, soft and strong. "You're here."

That was all. That was everything.

I savored his answer, letting it fuel me like an elixir. My earlier nervousness had to do with more than his impression of my suite, more than being alone with him for the first time in these chambers, and so I needed to know ... "Are you still cross with me?"

Poet froze, then sketched my cheek with the pads of his fingers. "Meaning, am I still pissed off that you outfitted Nicu's room in advance without asking me?"

"Something like that."

"Something like that," he repeated hotly against my mouth. "You did trigger a clamor inside me, but not in the way you think. I was in a feverish state because in that moment, I loved you more than I ever have. And I wanted to fuck you deeper than I ever have." His voice lowered, audible only between us. "You asked if I was done congratulating myself. Truth be told, I'll never be done when it concerns your pleasure. Not until I've made you come long and loudly."

More fluid leaked into my undergarments. My lips shuddered against his. "These feelings never end with you. They never recede. How is that possible?"

Poet's mouth twisted. "I don't fucking care."

I gulped, the confession slipping as if I'd consumed an overabundance of wine. "Neither do I. Yet too much of a good thing can be dangerous."

"I could never have too much of you. I'm addicted, my thorn."

"But I need to know if it can fade." My fingers snuck into his hair, the layers as rumpled as bedsheets. "I need to know, so that I can stop it from happening. So I won't lose this."

A throaty noise rumbled from Poet's chest. His gaze descended my form, skimming over me candidly, thoroughly.

What he saw made his eyelids hood. And in my daze, I recalled the dressing robe. The gossamer neckline dipped low, a sash bound the garment closed at the waist, and the hem cascaded to my toes. Etched in a lace pattern at the bodice and splitting down my limbs, the robe barely concealed my naked breasts. Underneath, a pair of drawers gripped my hips and shielded the patch of damp hair at my core, and stockings hugged my limbs up to the thighs.

Poet riveted on me like a starving man, the effect spine-tingling. The pink disks of my nipples studded through the material. When his eyes landed there, the peaks toughened further, to the point where they ached.

Just by looking at me, he knew how wet I'd become.

Wet. Wanton. Waiting.

So often I'd felt his cock primed inside me, pumping tirelessly through the flanks of my pussy. Because of him, I was no longer a virgin. Yet in this court, on this balcony, and at this moment, I felt like one.

The tumult since last night. The horror and lingering unknown. Everything compiled, begging for release and respite.

My heart jumped. My blood stirred, as though simmering in a kettle. My body prickled, desperate to reap an hour of joy.

To claim it. To defy the odds against us.

Once upon a time, I would have covered myself. Now I stood before his green gaze and let myself be worshiped. I hid nothing, allowing his feral expression to pour over me like melted honey, letting it fill my senses to the brim.

"They'll never take this away," I told him, my tone growing firm. "Say it."

The pulse in Poet's throat accelerated. "Such honed words. They sound more like a command than a wish."

"Would that please you?"

"There's not a fucking thing you could do that wouldn't please me."

"I'll be sure to quote you in the months to come. I might prove the jester wrong and vex him beyond capacity."

"Oh, sweeting. I never said you wouldn't vex me. I said it's impossible to displease me. Even in fury, I'll enjoy punishing you, feasting on you, and satisfying your whims. Anger me, and it shall only make my cock harder for its ruler. Indulge or enrage me, and it will only change the depth in which I fuck you."

Seasons save me. A tremulous noise slipped from my tongue, because I knew what he was doing, delaying my gratification for the sake of a tease. Poet could draw this out until it crushed me, until I succumbed to pleading. He had done so before.

This man, whom everyone idolized, feared, resented, desired, and coveted. This trickster, the most renowned celebrity in The Dark Seasons. This devil, as sexy as he was deadly.

This jester was mine. And I was his.

The inside fireplace sucked oxygen from the balcony and licked every corner of the platform with burning light. Simultaneous indignation, outrage, and defiance flared through my being. Far too late, I remembered who I was—the princess who sprang a child from a dungeon, outwitted a roundtable of Royals, and hoodwinked the Summer King into signing a vital document; the woman who played a battle of wills against the most formidable and adored man on this continent; and a queen in the making, who'd dared to expose her true self to her nation.

To own her choices publicly and with dignity. To face the naysayers head on.

Invisible enemies could threaten me all they wanted. They wouldn't win this game. I'd played against enough mighty adversaries to know I wasn't an easy target. Nor was my lover.

How dare these silent figures assume they could try. How dare they assume they would prevail.

Let them wage a losing war. As I promised Poet in Spring, and as Mother had reminded me, I knew what I stood for. And because of that, I knew what I would die for.

In the meantime, I would do what I'd pledged. I would persevere. I would thrive. I would riot. I would welcome bliss and soak up my raptures. And I would dance through the fire with this man, regardless of who lit the match.

Those kohl-lined eyes devoured me. The weight of Poet's stare strengthened my resolve and drenched my undergarments. A ferocity of emotions collided, stoking my words like timber. "As your sovereign, I gave you an order."

"Spoken like a force to be reckoned with," he responded, matching my whisper. "Very well." That's when his pretty visage sharpened like the edge of a knife. "They'll never take this away."

"Tell me we'll never let them ruin this."

He sidled nearer, his tone equally rampant. "We'll never let them ruin this."

That precious snaggletooth poked from his mouth like a delicacy. My tongue watered, eager to flick against it.

We could make love. If I asked, Poet would oblige. Even then, he would pry me wide.

But I didn't want it slow and sure. I wanted it primal and passionate.

I closed the distance. My nipples pierced the robe and scraped his torso, the raw tips of my breasts abrading that partially transparent shirt. And with the slightest restraint, I spoke through my teeth. "Now prove it and fuck me."

Poet clapped his palm around the back of my neck and hissed, "Your pleasure is my command, Highness."

At last, he hauled me forward. And his ravenous mouth slammed against mine.

10

Briar

A moan launched from my throat. My body struck his, and my breasts mashed into the cobbled wall of his torso. In a hectic flash, Poet's mouth clamped down and yanked me into a full-bodied kiss. No pause. No pacing. We surged into it, our nostrils flaring from the momentum.

His lips captured mine, slanting and shoving against my own. An impassioned noise grated from his chest, so that I felt the ravenous vibration like a tremor. That wicked mouth pulled me in, tugged on me. It folded over my lips and contracted in a dizzying rhythm that sank to the marrow of my bones.

His powerful jaw worked me into a frenzy, the impact kicking my head back. My limbs dissolved. My heart launched into my throat. Our mouths writhed, rocking together and depleting the oxygen from my lungs.

The jester kept a steel hold on my nape. His free palm lunged to my backside, gripped one oval, and boosted me against him.

His tongue rode across the seam of my lips in a single, shameless stroke. My eyes flew to the back of my head. Willingly, I parted for him. My mouth broke open on a fractured whimper, bidding him entrance.

Poet's hot tongue flexed inside, striking between my lips in a sinuous tempo. With skillful precision, he licked into me. The flat of his tongue swabbed my own, teasing and sketching until blood surged to my pussy.

The slot of my body contracted. My clit swelled beneath the dressing robe, the friction resonating as my pelvis skated over his heavy cock. I curled into him, rubbing my core into the jester's erection, the intimate pellet of flesh at my center abutting his crown, which expanded against me.

A brittle sound cut from Poet's lips. In response, his mouth snatched mine harder, hauling me into a kiss that penetrated my folds like a deep, desperate thrust.

My pussy slickened, so drenched that a bead rolled down my inner thigh. Poet's palm flew from my nape to my skull. His fingers burrowed into my hair and clasped my scalp, while the other hand tightened on my buttocks, the better to fasten me in place.

His mouth tore into mine. He pumped his tongue with the same vigor he'd pumped his cock into me on numerous occasions. The effect split my next moan in half. This jester kissed me with every muscle he possessed, marking me in this new kingdom, possessive and protective.

I returned the kiss with equal dominance, because that was how we'd always collided, from the time we were enemies. I raced my mouth against his, taking his tongue into me, my scalp tingling with each probe.

As he plied into my mouth, need streaked through my walls. I dripped for his touch, his kiss, his body. A determined cry snuck up my throat, because pledges only brought us so far. Poet may say words had as much power as actions. Nonetheless, this thing tethering us was still decadently forbidden.

I tasted our illicit bond in the wine glazing his tongue, which strapped around mine. I felt it in the thrust of his lips, intoxicating and indulgent.

Heat from his pectorals rushed through me, scorching the robe. Poet breached that barrier as if it didn't exist, just as he had with everything that tried to separate us. Any obstacle, he shredded to pieces.

My nipples poked into him, and a shudder tracked across the jester's muscled frame. He hoisted me into the cliff of his chest, the temperature of his body branding me.

His tongue gripped mine and sucked hard. I chanted, moaning for more, my plea husking into his mouth. Poet hummed and drew on me, suctioning until my ankles sparked.

I rose on my tiptoes, taking the kiss, taking it all. We heaved into each other, his lips beating against mine.

Mercilessly, Poet peeled his mouth away, only to trap me in his voracious gaze. I whined but quickly swallowed the protest, stunned by the magnitude of his attention. His features cinched, so taut I couldn't tell if he wanted to fuck me or commit a crime.

I licked my lips. "Why did you stop?"

"Stop, Highness?" he husked—and I gasped as he whipped me around, steering me toward the landscape. Then he jerked my spine into his torso, swiped my hair aside, and murmured, "I've only begun."

On the final word, he sank to the notch of my neck, his lips capturing the soft patch of skin. A startled moan ejected from my throat. My head reeled against him, and I reached overhead and backward, my hands grappling for any part that would anchor me.

Poet rasped. While lapping on my skin, he assisted by securing my fingers to the ramps of his shoulders. He suctioned my flesh into the sweltering cavern of his mouth, his tongue sweeping over my pulse point.

My pussy thrummed. I clamped my teeth into my lower lip, shutting in a plaintive cry.

This only made the jester behave crueler. He continued his assault while reaching in front of me to pluck open the sash of my dressing robe. The fabric vanished from my body and puddled around my feet, divesting me of everything but the drawers and thigh stockings. My breasts lifted into the air, the pink crests ruching. Humming his approval, Poet's thumb traced their circumference, teasing the disks, urging them to toughen further.

My jaw unhinged. My fractured moan leaped into the night.

The eventide mist grew opaque, a miasma that coated the castle walls. Even if passersby were permitted to roam the grounds near the Royal wing, they wouldn't be strolling at this hour. And with an overhang shrouding this platform, nor were we visible to the looming tower windows. Though none of this mattered, not with his hands sizzling over my flesh, his digits playing with my nipples, and his mouth sucking on me.

Eager to torment him, I swatted my hips into Poet's cock. I imagined the effect taking place under those leather pants, the shaft widening, its weight growing dense. Veins would thread around his erection, and liquid would rise from the top slit.

My buttocks undulated, skimming from his sac to the head. Growling, Poet wrenched his mouth from my neck. He cupped my breasts, squeezed them in his palms, and walked us forward two steps. At the balcony's ledge, he unlocked my arms from around him and fastened my hands over the rim, just as I'd been gripping it earlier.

Fixing me in place, he leaned forward and muttered against my temple, "Don't let go." Then his thumb sailed across my upper lip. "No matter what I do to you."

My stomach dropped. My hesitation—that we might be caught by someone walking in, that we could not do this yet, that we should wait until the dust settled—dissipated. In its place, the jester's velveteen words slid over me, the intonation stroking like a sly finger along the crease of my pussy.

I nodded. For good measure, I grabbed the railing harder.

A breeze buffeted my hair. My eyes trained on the vista, where trees lanced the sky in a profusion of colors. Reds, oranges, and golds. Shades that burned through the hazy thicket, sultrier than ever before.

Months ago, I would have called this moment obscene and unworthy of a Royal. Not because it was bad to feel pleasure, but because it lacked discretion. Now a thrill eddied below my navel, coupled with a new kind of vigor.

From mere inches behind, Poet's body emanated heat. The shadow of his outline sliced across the stones, the dark slash of his form lurking over me like an incubus.

Anticipation slithered up my spine, deliciously formidable. My own outline slanted toward the ledge, my hair falling untamed around my shoulders. Like this, I bent my hips and watched his likeness.

Indecision pulled two urges from me. I yearned to watch his silhouette, to witness what he would do. I longed to see our shadows collide and break into motion. But more than that, I wanted what I never had with anyone else.

I craved the unknown.

My gaze swerved away and clung to the panorama. At first, I thought a current was rustling the waistband of my drawers, but the slow tug told me it was him. The jester's knuckles trickled over the material, tracing it patiently.

Despite the faint touch, my lower half thrummed. He etched the filmy garment from left to right, then draped a single digit over one hip, down to where the drawers ended just under my buttocks. The material quavered, the hem adorned with tiny beads.

Several fingers joined the first as Poet's hand trailed the embellishments to my inner thigh. My respirations thickened. An uproar of sensations scattered across my flesh.

To torment me further, he progressed to the opposite leg. I sensed him tracing the material calmly. His digits fondled the trim, tucked so close to my aching walls.

This near to my folds, he must feel the heat originating from there, the temperature pushing through my intimate slit. Liquid filled the crease of my pussy, my arousal spreading through the undergarment. At which point, Poet switched direction. He reached in front of me, where his fingers traveled more succinctly between my thighs.

I parted reflexively for him, and the opening in my drawers trembled when he made contact. His digits circled the entrance, each pass languid. By contrast, heavy breaths chuffed from his lungs and matched my own exhalations.

When Poet reached a spot where I'd drenched the textile, he hummed in satisfaction. "Such a sweet thing," he crooned—then used two scissored fingers to split the seam wider, quick and fast. "So easy to shred."

A whimper coiled off my lips as his fingers breached the fabric and skimmed along my pussy, smearing the wetness. He brushed the hair nestled against my flesh and swirled the arousal over my clit.

My fingernails cleaved into the ledge. My eyes squinted, tempted to squeeze shut.

Just as swiftly, Poet withdrew from under the fabric. His digits climbed my hips and returned to the waistband.

Ever so slowly, the garment slid from my body. The cloth trembled down my thighs, then my calves. My drawers landed atop the dressing robe, both of which I heard Poet kick aside.

I stood poised before him, my naked bottom and dripping folds exposed. Only the stockings remained, the garment clinging like film from my toes to several inches above my knees.

The jester sucked in a breath. At the noise, pride rushed through me. I'd never known it was possible to feel equally regal and sexy.

"Stunning," Poet said. "Magnificent."

"Powerful," I imparted. "Queenly."

His body pressed into mine, the slab of his chest brimming and packed with muscle. His decadent voice drizzled into me, hungry and helpless. "Dominant."

And that's when I knew. The stockings would remain.

Poet straightened, and the rustle of fabric brushed my ears. My eyes flitted to the side. His shadow peeled off his shirt, revealing a bulk of skin and sinew, every inch of his dancer's body carved and smooth.

The jester's hands fell to the buckles of his pants. Again, I tore my gaze away and forced myself to stare at the landscape. Anchored against the balcony, I listened to material rippling down his limbs, the sound like a hiss.

I fantasized about his tight buttocks flexing, the divots caving in as they always did whenever he breached me. I imagined his cock rising from the fabric. I pictured the heavy sac, the column of flesh, and the ruddy head.

Cattails quivered from the wooden ledge boxes. Amber and vetiver imbued my senses.

Poet's palms landed on my hips. "Bend for me, Your Highness. We're going to need plenty of space for me to properly service your cunt."

I licked my lips. "No one has ever spoken to me as you do."

"And if I have my way, no one ever will," he growled.

"I used to hate you for speaking to me so indecently."

"Is that all you felt?"

No. I had felt a thousand feverish, agitated, seductive things. But I didn't say that, because I didn't need to.

Poet ran the tip of one digit down my spine, inciting a flurry across my flesh. "At your request, I'm going to make you feel so many things, you'll lose count."

"I only want to feel *you*," I confessed.

Because I love you, and I need you, and I cannot lose you.

Another weighty breath expelled from his lungs. "You'll always have me." Naked, he sank nearer to me, twisted his head over my shoulder, and pressed a kiss to my cheek. "Now be a good princess and spread yourself wider. Show your jester that fetching pussy."

I tilted forward, enough to bare my entrance. At the same time, I set my feet farther apart, my thighs splitting at a greater distance. The position put me on full display, my private flesh fanning out for him.

Even without seeing Poet's reaction, the "Wicked hell" that tumbled from his lips said enough. That, and the palpable dampness suffusing my walls. My slit was glistening for him.

His fingers shackled my hips. In one quick motion, the jester lugged me into him.

I gasped, my buttocks folding into his pelvis. His length and width were considerable. The mast stretched against my backside, then dipped underneath to the seeping cleft of my body, his bulbous crown poised at my slot.

Poet angled my waist, fitting our hips together. My knees quaked like chinks about to break from a precipice.

His cock nested into the vent of my thighs. The firm tip nudged my walls in a taunting gesture.

"Oh," I grunted. "Poet."

"What's that?" he droned. "I can't hear you, Highness."

Damn him. For all our urgency, the jester possessed a remarkable talent for prolonging the torment.

My nipples puckered at the thought of defying and antagonizing him. I violated his rule not to move. My backside inched closer to the bulge protruding from his hips, my buttocks tapping his cock.

Poet uttered a serrated noise that penetrated my core as much as the stiff peak of his body. "Vicious thorn," he accused.

"Foolish jester," I replied. "Thinking you could give without getting back in return."

"Then by all means," he invited. "Wreck me more."

And then his hips swiped forward. And his cock pitched between my walls.

His length pried through my pussy, its girth spanning the tight sheath. The crest of his cock lodged inside, deep and high. On impact, my body hefted upward, and a hard moan burst from my mouth.

Poet groaned with me. The bulk of his frame hunched, his joints vibrating against my own tremulous limbs.

My inner muscles sealed him inside, clinging wetly to his solid flesh. For a moment, it seemed like we might draw a breath, that we might compose ourselves and take this slowly, steadily, and softly. That's what this arrival deserved, did it not? This night should be a gentle consummation.

But now I knew. As the jester had proven to me often, hard didn't mean harsh, just as delicate didn't mean subdued. Passion could be attained either way.

We didn't wait, didn't pause, and didn't stray. Instead, Poet dug his fingers into my hips, leveled himself, and snapped his waist forward. At the same time, I rammed my buttocks into him.

We met in the middle. My pussy and his cock rushed together, the heat of his erection spreading my folds. The collision extracted another moan from me, another haggard growl from him.

Like this, we hammered into it. I took a second to acclimate before getting a sense of how our bodies tilted. Then I looped my waist away from him, just as he reeled backward, his cock slipping out of my walls. And after a beat, we flung our bodies at each other once more. I squeezed the ledge, braced myself, and used it to push back, my opening swatting over him. Simultaneously, Poet's lower half jutted into me, the pome of his cock striking through and hitting a spot that made me cry out.

Then again. And again.

We rocked against one another. Poet's erection jutted between my pussy in a fervent tempo, the thick heat of him slinging in and out. His hips pivoted in a circular motion, drawing so much wetness from me that I smothered his cock.

We had achieved this position several times since he first introduced it to me, but I'd only ever remained stationary, awed by Poet's movements and growing accustomed to pleasure from this angle. But now, my confidence grew. I rolled with the jester, my arousal smearing him from crown to hilt as he rode my hips.

My folds encased his erection, the damp clench of my body parting for his thrusts. Inside me, I felt his tip pulsate. With each lance of his waist, the head enlarged, so that I envisioned fluid leaking from the slit.

Our waists separated, then drove into one another. My fingernails bit into the stone, my hair tumbled over my shoulders, and my breasts jostled from the cadence.

Poet unleashed a gritty, possessive noise. He undulated his hips, entering and retreating fully, his pace serpentine. Neither slow nor rapid, this man embodied the art of rough lovemaking and sumptuous fucking.

My rear folded under his, each pump of his thick cock shoving me closer to ecstasy. A yelp flew up my throat. However, if I let it out, the whole kingdom would hear. Despite this being a pious nation, the commotion would not be mistaken for something innocent. And while I wanted to transcend the judgment, I still wanted to lead this world.

I still wanted to earn that. Screaming out a sequence of orgasms would not be wise. Though that didn't mean I was about to stop this. I would never stop this.

The forbidden secret of us wetted me anew, as much as the sleek punch of Poet's cock. I compressed my lips, muffling the sounds threatening to cannon from me and splinter across the vista. But it became increasingly difficult as Poet whipped his hips succinctly into me, his cock snapping to and from my body. He was simply too skilled, his body too agile for me to resist for much longer.

Yet I wanted it longer. So much longer, deeper, harder, faster.

My head fell forward. I gave into the temptation and beat my backside into Poet's lunging cock, my pussy chasing the apex of sensation.

The jester felt my walls flutter as much as I did. "Aye, my princess," he encouraged in a dulcet tone. "Help yourself to me."

Seasons have mercy, but I did. My arms and thighs burned from exertion, and yet I could not contain myself. I pursued this feeling, sought to end and delay it. With each pelt of my hips into Poet's groin, more brittle cries gathered on my tongue.

On one particular lurch, the jester hissed. His erection rose higher, stoking a point inside my pussy that sent an electric current up my spine. At last, a renegade cry broke from me, sharp but thankfully faint. I had sounded as if I'd cut myself.

Perhaps I had, because nothing could feel this potent, this blissful. Pleasure indeed hurt; it sliced you open, made you bleed, drained your breath, and crushed your heart. But the outcome, and its reward, were worth it.

Small sobs cracked from my mouth. I simply couldn't help it, and why should I deny it?

Poet nudged my thighs, steering them farther apart. "Wider, sweeting. So much wider."

Understanding the command, I lifted one foot and elevated it on the balcony's lower molding. This parted my folds even more and changed the slant. Poet hunkered over me, covered my hands with his, and clenched our fingers together. The scarlet ribbons strapped around our wrists pulled snug and abraded one another.

Like this, he charged into me. His waist sloped higher, and higher, and higher.

Tucked into him, my joints gave out. I held on and let him take over, let my jester service his princess, let him claim me.

And claim me, he did. Poet's waist bucked, accelerating the pace. His cock sprinted through my pussy, the crown striking a spot that eradicated my willpower. Tiny jolts rippled across my walls. I sobbed against my closed mouth, so the clamor was discernible only between us.

Poet didn't force it from me. He knew why I struggled to keep everything in, even while my pussy began to spasm in short bursts of release. Not quite there, yet not far from oblivion.

This was merely a prelude. Until then, the sensations climbed, teetering on the brink.

Poet held back as well, grunting under his breath. Those illicit hips whisked against my core, his erection flexing into me. His forehead landed atop my nape, and his breaths siphoned with my own, the exhalations in tune with every sling of his hips.

He worked into me, fucked deftly into me. I took it all, absorbing him like a virtue and a vice.

Like a weakness and a strength. Like everything raw and real that existed in this one fleeting, dangerous, extraordinary life.

I would have my crown, and I would have him, and I would defend both. I would savor them, protect them.

No other option would do.

Poet lifted his head, his chin hovering over my shoulder. We faced the vista and slammed into each other, our moans rushing into the atmosphere. Mist glazed the castle walls, condensation spread over my flesh, and wetness gushed from my pussy.

The desire to unleash clashed with the desire to suppress. Despite my intention to moan privately, the rapture seizing me from head to toe challenged those limits. And although Poet aimed to follow my lead, to heed our surroundings, and to fuck me discreetly, his shuddering form taxed the limits even more.

In fact, he nearly breached them several times, with several pistons of his hips. The pommel of his cock nocked inside me, the tempo instinctive. His waist chased after the wild noises I made. He hunted them with the senses of a prowler, on a mission to extract every octave I possessed, on the brink of ripping my voice apart. This man had always done this to me, and it was impossible to stop now.

Or rather, I made it impossible for him. Somehow, I alone did this.

My insides thrummed with each jolt of pleasure from the jester's cock. He'd told me not to move. He cautioned me against this. Which was why I did the opposite.

Indulgently, my fingers found their way between my thighs. Poet's breath caught, the noise sounding suffocated. Yet he didn't stop me any more than he halted his cock.

No, he kept going. As did I.

With him suspended behind me, the jester had a clear view of my ministrations. I dipped my hand into the vent, through the curls thatched over my intimate lips, and flattened my thumb over my swollen clit.

We sighed. My moan was a wisp of noise. His was guttural, tortured as if pushed through a grater.

Experimentally, my fingers played with the kernel at my center. I encircled the protruding flesh, eternally stunned by the sensations washing through my damp folds. Every nerve-ending seemed to reside there, then scatter to other precipices in my body—my scalp, my knees, the tips of my digits, and the soles of my feet. I rolled the peg, the stimulation aggravating and addictive.

Matching the rhythm of Poet's cock, I teased my pussy. The pads of my fingers cinched the bud, rubbing it continuously. I patted the flesh, simultaneously alleviating and creating friction. Inches away, under my split legs, Poet's erection pounded in and out of my cleft.

Eagerness motivated my hand closer to where he impaled me. When my knuckles abutted his length, I cupped myself. While he flung his cock between my folds, I worked the soaked seam in tandem to his movements.

Poet rasped, "Wicked fucking hell, Briar."

And I could not tell which drew arousal from me—my hand or his words. Either way, I flooded my fingers and his cock. My mouth trembled, the cries hardening into steel, ready to burst like a pipe.

I felt his eyes ducking to where my digits and his broad length met. Both entities joined at my delicate opening, my wetness glossing his flesh.

I liked knowing this. I liked marking him this way.

Just as I liked being claimed.

A hard kiss and a sweet fuck.

Recalling the words he'd spoken long ago, I attempted to block another moan.

A tear wrested through the atmosphere. The stockings clinging to my limbs must have torn, because air brushed the exposed skin of my front thigh. Although the finespun undergarments were the only things I wore, we had ruined them. For all the jester's vanity about clothing, he cared less with his erection buried inside my pussy. And I liked that too.

He fucked me sweetly with his cock. So only one thing was left.

"Kiss me," I implored. "Kiss me hard."

At the request, my jester seethed. "Soon, sweeting."

"Your princess gave you an order."

The world jolted as he released the balcony ledge, hooked his arms around my middle, and hoisted me upright. I released my core and gasped as my back struck his chest, the pectorals and abdomen lacquered in sweat.

His mouth chafed against the trench behind my ear. "And your jester told you not to move."

With both of us standing, he kicked my legs apart, and his cock launched upward. I yelped. There was nothing for it, the angle of his erection stunning the oxygen from my lungs.

We had never made love this way before. My mouth fell open on a long, silent string of moans as Poet gripped my breasts and kneaded them until the nipples puckered into his palms. Anchored like this, he threw his backside into it, his cock vaulting into my pussy.

Expertly, he thrashed his waist. The broad tip pivoted into me, the stiff ridge of his body slipping and sliding through my walls.

Astonished sobs slid off my tongue. He shot into me, opened me so thoroughly, so firmly. Every strong thump of his cock caused my being to disintegrate and my folds to spread farther.

The back of my scalp landed against his shoulder. Helpless, I clasped his nape and writhed in front of him, my pointed breasts bouncing.

The sensations mounted and gathered speed. The jester groaned and increased momentum, his buttocks sprinting, his cock lashing into me, so that all I could do was hold on for dear life. Pleasure accumulated as our groins rushed together. My clit throbbed like a pulse, and the flanks of my pussy fluttered, the result pouring onto his crown.

So close. So very close that I shook from it. So close and so badly that I might weep or shriek.

Poet registered the change in my body and sought to destroy our resolve. With abandon, he powered into me, putting his entire frame into it. He hauled his cock between my folds, picking me apart, striking that spot over and over.

My body seized. It locked, held, froze.

And I broke. Heat and pleasure collided in the juncture of my thighs, and my pussy convulsed, shockwaves coursing through my blood. The orgasm slammed into me with such force that I flayed against Poet, who held me tightly.

An avalanche of moans shattered from my tongue. I came so loudly the jester twisted my face up to his and slammed his mouth onto mine. He spread my lips open and swallowed the cries splintering from my lungs, the torrent endless and falling into the well of his throat.

At last, he kissed me hard. All the while, he kept whisking his cock into me.

Clamped together, my sobs flowed into him, the noises brittle and sharp. I quaked, my naked body flush with his. My pussy contorted, the folds gripping his cock and wetting it fully.

As my body continued to spasm, Poet's hips struck mine with quick, shallow jabs, his cock streaking into me until his muscles condensed.

Then he broke with me. Unleashing a long growl between my lips, Poet combusted, his form shuddering. His cock twitched inside my pussy, his tip releasing into my cleft and spilling warm liquid.

Our bodies pulsated into one. We kissed, our mouths sealing deeply while he came, so that I felt the reverberations down my throat.

At some point, our hips ebbed to a halt. Once the moans subsided, Poet detached his mouth from mine, and we collapsed against the balcony. Air sawed through my lungs, and Poet slumped over my body, careful not to mash me into the railing.

His chest pounded, its pace as rapid as my own. Spent, he absently plucked the top of my stocking and released it. The material snapped against my flesh, and he mumbled, "How many pairs of these do you have?"

An exhausted laugh burst from my mouth. The jester lifted his head, drew his hard cock from my crease, and wheeled me around.

Those husky green eyes glittered with lust and mischief. "Come here."

Except I didn't have time to *come here*. Poet registered that as well, because the instant his hands flanked my midriff, intending to jerk me into him, a knock rapped against the antechamber door.

Without warning, the partition swung open.

II

Poet

Shit. I whisked Briar sideways, cutting off her squeak as I spun her from the balcony and reeled us out of view. The princess's sweaty back bumped into a stone foundation. I pressed her there, against the wall separating the platform from her suite.

Inwardly, I flattered myself for being a connoisseur of multitasking. Outwardly, I performed the crucial movements. My palm shot out, cupping the back of the princess's skull before it knocked into the facade, whilst the other hand blasted to her mouth and clamped over her lips. Her pupils imploded to the size of saucers, shock flashing in the black wells.

We held fast, peering at one another. My torso plastered itself to her breasts, the luscious flesh warm against my pecs and those pert little nipples tapping me like pink rocks. I lacked the capacity to focus on what this position did to my cock. Fortunately for those nether regions, I had pulled out of Briar's beautiful cunt in time, otherwise the last three seconds would have hurt.

Hinges winced, and the door to her suite parted. A pair of footsteps sashayed into the sitting room and paused at the central fireplace.

"Briar?" Avalea called out.

If I thought the princess's eyes couldn't goggle any wider, she proved me wrong. Those orbs dilated to the point where they ate her fucking face. A petrified, mortified shade of red slashed across Briar's complexion. Her eyelashes flapped as if she was questioning—hoping, praying, wishing, deluding herself—whether she'd identified the voice correctly.

The queen fell silent. Flames crackled in the grate, audible from this distance, as detectable as the monarch's knowing silence.

There could only be one reason why she hadn't investigated the rest of her daughter's chambers, much less checked the balcony. And not just because the double doors leading outside were open.

Nay. The queen likely hadn't budged because Briar's clothes were scattered across the fucking platform.

My eyes clicked toward the evidence. The robe lay in plain sight, heaped in an expensive puddle, along with the princess's soaked drawers. I tried to be inconspicuous whilst surveying the clutter, but I should have learned by now that Briar saw, heard, scented, and felt every move I made.

Eyes glazed with the remnants of pleasure and newfangled terror, the princess followed my gaze. When she located the pile, a squawk of humiliation clogged her throat. Thankfully, the woman managed to conceal this frantic response behind her sealed lips.

Our attention surged back to one another. Around the corner, I sensed the weight of Avalea's gaze, which hadn't bothered to scan the rest of the apartment. She'd seen enough, because a tiny draught of air hitched in her throat.

Indeed, she had spotted the scene of the crime, where Briar's discarded garments rested. And like any parent with intuitive skills when it came to their offspring, I felt the Royal drawing the right conclusion, as well as the culprit behind it.

After a pause so thick it could have sliced the castle in half, the queen sighed. "At least you waited until past sunset."

She could have been directing that to her daughter or the man who'd been snapping his cock inside Briar not one minute ago. In any event, Briar's chest caved. Her eyes soared heavenward and fused shut in abject misery.

I couldn't help it. My lips tilted. She just looked so cute and so thoroughly fucked, in more than one respect. Besides, long ago I told this woman that corrupting her was among my greatest achievements. Why would I stop now?

Avalea's tone slanted, torn between reproach and wry amusement. "With Aire assigned as Nicu's watchman—a fine choice, by the way—I expect you at the feast in no less than half an hour. That's all I came to say."

Lucidity cleared the sex-and-shock-induced haze. Now Briar rolled her offended eyes, which only broadened my leer. My thorn hated being reminded of things she already knew.

I could defend the queen's natural impulse to look after her child, no matter how old that child was. However, it was much more fun watching the princess's reactions veer from one extreme to the next. Last but one hundred percent not least, her damp pussy mashing against my erection made it impossible to think diplomatically.

"I assume you need no help getting dressed, so I'm leaving," the queen announced, then cleared her throat. "And do pick up that mess. Someone might get the wrong idea."

Briar's eyebrows slammed together. Humiliation forgotten, exasperation in full force. The second my canines flashed, and my shoulders shook, her pupils sliced my way. If her mouth weren't concealed, I'd have gotten a glimpse of her chin crinkling.

Footsteps sauntered from the room. This time, the door melted into its frame with a faint latch click. Discreetly done.

Briar tore my hand from her mouth and barked, "Not funny."

"On the contrary," I muttered.

I saw myself reflected in her gaze, from the rumbling chest to the smarmy grin. The princess glared at me, and glared, and glared. And then she bunched her mouth, repressing the mirth before finally letting it out. She fell against the wall, framed her cheeks, and released a disgraced laugh.

"Oh my Seasons," she hissed, shaking her head.

"Agreed," I chuckled. "We're off to a splendid start."

The knights guarding the alcove leading to Briar's room would have warned the queen I was here. That aside, I doubted Avalea had anticipated a show. At least, not this early.

My temple landed against Briar's as we glanced at the deserted knickers, sprawled right where I left them after stripping her down to those delectably tight stockings, which still hugged her thighs.

For pity's sake, those thighs. They shook on either side of my own. Trapped like this, I felt the dewy aftermath of Briar's climax. Her arousal coated our skin, evidence that she had come all over both of us.

I should applaud my reflexes for achieving the impossible under duress. Never had I reacted so fast whilst hungover from an orgasm. Doing so after making Briar come wetly around my cock elevated my skill to a whole new level. Taking her against the balcony and making her shout into my mouth had been nothing short of excruciating bliss. I swear, my body had been levitating.

Perspiration lined the bridge across Briar's hairline. Her hands fell from her cheeks, and the more she relaxed, the more our antics brightened her irises from steel to sterling.

She stabbed a fingertip into my abdomen. "You are going to ruin me."

Like a sly devil, I bracketed my arm overhead. "Consider it payback. You did it to me first."

Her complexion ripened. But then she grunted, dropped her forehead between my collarbones, and muffled into my skin, "However will I face her tonight?"

I spoke into the princess's hair. "Fear not. Your mother has seen what I look like. She'll understand."

With a rosy scowl, Briar jerked back and smacked my arm. "You are the vainest man on the continent."

"It's a habit, not to mention a fact of life. Would you like me to stop?"

She sobered, and her words flowed like nectar—tart, thick, and appetizing. "Never," she stressed. "Never stop."

"Excellent," I husked right before my mouth snatched hers.

I yanked this Royal into a kiss, hard and deep, determined to make her feel the flick of my tongue down to the crease in her thighs. With a moan, Briar glued her lips to mine and opened for me like a well-behaved ruler. The seam of her lips spread under the pressure of my tongue, which licked its way inside. I crooned and dragged my hands to her ass. Cementing her against me, I bent my head and flexed into the princess, probing her heat with slow, deft swipes.

Her breasts quivered. In the gap of her legs, slick hair brushed the base of my cock. Her arms scaled my torso, and her waist curved against my frame.

I imagined the freckles sprayed across her flesh. The little beauty mark tucked under her forearm. Cursed me, I could spend hours feasting on every inch of her skin and still leave this balcony a famished man.

She rocked her mouth with my own, and her fingers spanned my jaw. I'd barely begun to properly suck on that sweet tongue, but the innocent contact blasted heat to my sac.

Groaning, I pried my lips away. Fuck, this woman intoxicated me to the point where I practically slurred "Now then. What's this rubbish I hear about dressing yourself?"

Her mother implied Briar wouldn't need help getting ready. Not with me in the room.

Still ... "No maid? No retinue of ladies?"

Briar blinked, winded from the interrupted kiss. "Oh," she breathed, then waved that off. "Our custom is vastly different in Autumn. The Royal family doesn't keep an entourage of ladies. We only require one."

"So that's why I never saw you surrounded by anyone but guards in Spring. Except this one lady you speak of was absent."

"She took ill and couldn't make the trip. As a hospitality, Queen Fatima's ladies were at my disposal, but—"

"I can guess how you felt about that."

Briar's expression fell, and her gaze became remote. I crooked my finger beneath her chin and lifted her face to mine. "It's okay to miss them."

She swallowed. "I didn't think I would, but they became my friends. My lady here—it appears she's fallen in love with the nurse we employed to take care of her. The family doesn't approve, so they've run away together; I received the message once I arrived. In any case, we got on fine, but it wasn't the same as with Cadence, Posy, and Vale. I miss them. I miss Eliot so much. And I ..."

Her words cracked, as brittle as a twig. My thumb stroked her chin whilst certain ideas took root in my head.

Disappointment didn't suit this woman. We would have none of that.

"I gather you'll be without a lady for a while," I said.

She nodded. "I'll find another, but it takes time."

"Hmm." I tapped Briar's speckled nose. "Meanwhile, whoever will dress you?"

Awareness pinched her features together. "Poet," she said, drawing out the name like a warning.

"You've come to the right jester. Half an hour, is it? That won't do for a princess who's destined to stun the room."

"It's not necessary. I am perfectly capable of outfitting myself."

"Naturally," I dismissed, releasing my grip on her ass and stalking backward. "Come with me."

Naked, I turned. Raising my arm, I snapped my fingers and took her hand with my free one. Briar fell quiet as I guided her into the suite, where the blaze flooded the wainscoting in gradients of orange.

Truly, it was an impressive space. Simple but elegant. Studious but comfortable. The browns, greens, and creams fit my thorn, as did the chests, sideboards, inlaid bookcases, and loft that appeared to house a writing desk.

The walls carried her scent—tart apples and crisp parchment. And I was particularly fond of the bed, expansive enough to drape Briar in several angles across the mattress.

Ignoring the temptation, I led her to the wardrobe. On the way, my ego registered the heiress's attention latching on to my bare ass. The taut shape. The divots she loved to admire. The way everything flexed as I walked, in addition to whenever I fucked her. The weight of Briar's gaze teetered between my endowments and the direction they took us.

My mouth crooked. I could slow down and prolong her appraisal. However, nosiness quickened my steps, even more than when I'd explored the size of my own appointed coffers. Whilst I hardly expected to find the same pleasure trinkets I kept among my clothes—all of which I'd brought with me—everyone stashed secrets into their closets. A year's worth of rutting in my court had taught me that.

What enticements would I find in the princess's repository?

Off the bedchamber, we passed through a short corridor, where a pair of doors stood ajar. I hadn't needed Briar to point the way. My sixth sense as a trendsetter detected where to find the magic.

The princess's silence thickened once we crossed into the recesses of her wardrobe, where a chandelier strung in leaves hung in the center. The candles must be molded of Winter wax, which was known to burn for days before melting to the base. It also illuminated warmer yet brighter light than most tapers, all without polluting the air.

Almighty Seasons. The collection halted me.

The rectangular room was deeper than a tunnel and included four alcoves, two on either side. One end contained shelves packed with sweaters, scarves, belts, and hair accessories. Inside the opposite niches, a plethora of dresses, skirts, pants, and blouses hung along the rods. But instead of organizing them by articles of clothing and color, the princess had cataloged her attire by outfit. Each garment and its corresponding pieces were arranged together, including the coats, capes, and shawls. And in some cases, the shoes and boots.

I hadn't surveyed the fabrics yet, and already this might be the first time someone's apparel outdid my own—at least in methodology. Briar's systematic mind bluntly presented itself in full view.

"Well, well." I twisted to admire her under the chandelier. "An heiress *and* a liar. You've been holding out on me."

The princess regarded the wardrobe with less enthusiasm. "I don't have the time to decide what goes with what. This makes it easier."

In Spring, ladies-in-waiting usually took charge of what a Royal wore. I liked that Briar didn't follow that ridiculous and downright offensive rule.

She released my hand. I took advantage and sauntered down the alcoves, my fingers tracing the brocades, velvets, taffetas, and a multitude of other textiles. My digits danced over intricately laced sweaters with ruffled turtlenecks, thick dresses patterned in plaids, tapestry-woven jackets like the one Briar wore in Spring's archive library—when she'd fingered herself to the sound of my voice—flowing gowns with trains, and articles wrought of supple leather and glittering chains.

Nothing so darkly vain as my own style. However, the stitching bespoke of a prized artist. At some point, I'd need an introduction to her tailor.

To say nothing of what lay inside the drawers. Inside, I found treasures that put to shame every smutty, kinky, taboo, erotic, and pornographic novel I'd ever read. The choices lay folded before me like aphrodisiacs. Corsets and bodices embellished with gemstones, fringed little undergarments, smocked knickers—all with cords and slits that begged to be spread apart—and stockings ranging from sheer, to meshed, to quilted.

In a particularly salacious mood, I hooked my pinky through the elastic leg of one of those compact drawers and raised it to the light. From behind, I felt the heat of Briar's flush.

"Should I have asked permission first?" I inquired.

Her gulp flooded the room. "No," she whispered. "I want you to touch them."

My cock jumped. I wouldn't bullshit about this. For I would have peeked even if I hadn't been sure she would allow it. I was in love with her, but that didn't mean I'd lost my penchant for unscrupulous and gluttonous deeds.

My fingers hated to, but I set the flimsy item back in its place, slid the furnishing closed, and resumed my quest through the room. Alongside woodland colors, foiled and jewel-toned options dominated the space.

"I'm impressed. Polished like the rest of this castle, yet much more engrossing." I drew my finger down a fitted navy sleeve that ended in sharp points above the wrist. "None of these reveal much skin, though." I veered my head over my shoulder to where she lingered, still as naked and ravishing as me. "Ever thought of experimenting?"

She crossed her arms over those fabulous tits and arched an eyebrow. "I'm with you, aren't I?"

Ah. I gave her a devious smirk, then crooked my finger to beckon her. "Show me what you have in mind."

Briar complied and headed for a panel of ivory silk adorning one of the mannequin busts propped like museum statues throughout the closet. She reached the garment and wheeled the bust my way. I clocked my head to the side and tapped my jaw, auditing her selection.

Scooped neckline. Elbow sleeves.

Like the front, a glossy panel of material would dip across Briar's back, yet the overall shape ensured the design stayed modest. Below that, the dress narrowed into a nipped waist before fanning out into multiple layers for the skirt. Promptly, I fantasized about ripping the divine thing off Briar, the first chance I got.

"Elegant color," I listed, stalking up to the Royal and circling her. "Discreet cut. Sophisticated but authoritative."

"My thoughts precisely," she concurred.

I stopped in front of the princess, my bare hip nudging hers. Ignoring the temperature swirling in my groin, I dragged my digit over her ribbon bracelet. "And will you be wearing this?"

Briar held my gaze, her voice softening. "Will you?"

"Aye. Only not where they can see it." At her gaping look, my mouth slanted. "Not there, you naughty princess. I mean, under the sleeve."

"I would have assumed you had every intention of exhibiting your scarlet signature."

I pretended to give it some thought. "That would clash with the fuchsia."

A reluctant chuckle tripped from her lips. "Is it worth suggesting you choose a shade that compliments Autumn, at least for tonight?"

"And abandon my flashy Spring roots already?"

"I would never ask that of you. But it would show that you esteem our culture. Consider it a preemptive measure for when you open your mouth."

Grinning like a fiend and hardly about to deny it, I pointed to the carpet and twirled my finger. Understanding, Briar wheeled away from me and faced an upright mirror framed in ornate mahogany carvings. The fixture was mounted at the far end of the wardrobe and extended to the ceiling.

This provided a sumptuous view of her freckled ass, the skin still rosy from where I'd gripped and bent her over. Changing course, I returned to her stash of intimates, plucked out a few choices, and prowled up to that majestic ass.

Armed with the dainty items, I halted inches from her and met that sterling gaze in our reflection. Then I knelt and cupped her ankle until she registered my intentions. Blood consumed her cheeks as she lifted her foot, enabling me to peel the torn stocking from her leg and then repeat the action with the other limb.

After that, I unspooled a fresh pair of stockings up her smooth limbs. "What exactly do you think I'm going to say to this court?"

Her upper thighs pebbled whilst I unraveled the material over them. "I've met your tongue," she declared.

"You've also met my tact," I reminded her. "Fine. How about I wear red instead? To match your hair. We're conspirators, after all."

She peeked at my stack of bracelets. "You're already wearing red."

I drew out the silence for a beat. "That, I am."

After smoothing the stockings in place over her thighs, I held open a pair of sheer drawers. With another bashful flush, Briar stepped into them. She kept still as I slid the knickers over her ass, the thatch of hair shrouding her pussy vanishing behind the material.

Fuck. I stood while fixing the drawers over her waist. Even my feigned nonchalance felt like a kink, like indulging in foreplay, except in reverse. "I'll wear whatever Her Highness wishes. How's that for indulgence?"

I glanced at the princess's likeness and found her visibly binging on the V of my hips.

Caught in the act, her gaze swerved to my face, and her throat contorted. "Go with the fuchsia. I will not have you change for me."

"Because you'd like to make a splash?"

"Because I want you as you are."

Goddammit. How long did we still have? My itch to snatch this woman and shove her against the closest flat surface grew worse.

Nevertheless, I doubted a quickie would satiate me. It never had with her. Our sexcapades were the reason we'd stocked up on bundleberries, arming ourselves with enough Spring contraceptives to enable a warren of rabbits.

I aligned my chest with her spine. "I'd been jesting. Actually, I was thinking of platinum instead—also shamelessly defiant, mainly on account of the design rather than the color, but the metallic is lofty enough to pass most people's inspections. For the rest, it'll help me root out the strictest prudes of the bunch. Thoughts?"

A small grin crept across her face. "Perfect."

"And I think what you meant earlier was, are *we* going to wear the ribbons?"

"It would convey our commitment to each other."

"It would also intimidate our audience."

"Too much, too soon?" she interpreted.

"You know the answer to that," I replied. "Change pisses people off."

Briar nodded to herself. "Particularly when it's expedited."

Aye. Seeing us together tonight would be enough to rile them up. With a flourish, I swept a corset over her breasts. Seasons, I would never understand the need to suffocate women in these infernal torture devices. However, inflating the tops of Briar's tits would make up for it.

"Accessories?" I prompted.

"I was thinking perhaps a diadem," she replied, failing to disguise the tremor in her voice when my fingers grazed her nipples. "Mother will don her crown. However, anything grand for myself would be too imposing for a homecoming of this magnitude. A simple glittering headband shall suffice."

"Describe it," I said.

"There's one in the castle vault, thin and made of crystal leaves. It arcs over my scalp instead of encircling my forehead. Though another option has the same crystals, but larger and clustered with pearls."

My fingers coasted over the corset laces, smoothly crisscrossing the strings through their grommets. "I would choose the former. Sticking to one precious element will let the gown stand out. What else?"

"Fashion advice from a Spring native," she teased. "What shall my subjects think?"

"I prefer the term *Spring icon*." With a long, lazy pull, I looped another cord through the hole, making sure she felt and heard the material gliding into the opening. "Also, I have as much experience in stripping clothes from bodies as I do in dressing them."

A rosy hue blossomed across her shoulders like an enticement. As my fingertip skimmed that blush, Briar trembled in a rather fetching manner. I cemented our gazes and resumed affixing the corset to her bust. The garment gripped her a little tighter, enough to claim this woman but not enough to steal her breath.

"Droplet crystal earrings and a corresponding necklace," she whispered.

Languidly, I threaded another cord through another hole. The corset shrunk, cradling her body. "Scale back on the matchy-matchy, my thorn. Considering the crystal diadem and ribbon bracelet are already part of the equation, opt for just the earrings. 'Tis a cardinal rule. Always wear one less embellishment than you think you need. Like I said, allow the dress to do the work. That's how you'll glamour them."

"When you put it that way, then perhaps my crown is a better option," she contested.

"Nay. Let them know you surpass that." My eyes swallowed her reflection as I tied the base of the corset into a knot. "Show them you can slay, with or without it."

Ambition and confidence lifted her chin. Just as swiftly, her nipples shoved through the fabric, the indentations animating my pulse. "I see why Basil and Fatima pampered you," she flattered.

My mouth tipped sideways. I veered away, detached the ivory gown from its bust, and swept it in front of Briar. "With permission, Your Highness."

She inclined her head, the gesture absurdly provocative. I positioned the gown over her, pulling and tucking it over Briar's waist to give us a preview in the mirror.

Except something vital was missing. Or rather, something desperately needed to go.

Briar gasped as I bent my head, sank my teeth into the sleeve seams, and bit through several threads. The stitching yielded enough for me to unweave the elbow length fabric. Tossing aside the superfluous material yielded a cap style, which I pulled farther down her arms to create an off-shoulder neckline. This bared her cleavage and spine, low enough to compliment the gloriously sharp architecture of her body, but not so low that her subjects would faint or spit out their ale. Moreover, the alteration changed the fall of her gown, accentuating her proud shoulders with more finesse and giving the illusion of added height.

However regal, the dress had been overly chaste and appeasing. But the ivory color had allowed my sly fingers to play with the cut and add understated provocativeness. Rather than sacrificing power, the change enhanced everything important. She would conquer the room without them realizing it.

"Magnetic yet indestructible," I purred. "See for yourself."

Cautiously, Briar twisted to marvel at the gown. What she saw brought a glint to those metallic eyes.

I hovered nearer and scraped my lips over her warm cheeks. "You're blushing. Do you like it?"

"How did you do that?" she wondered.

That meant yes. "I never take anything at face value." My mouth pecked her earlobe. "Can you handle it from here?"

In the chandelier's flickering light, Briar pivoted toward me, her fingers clutching the gown to her body. "I thought you were going to work on the rest of me."

"Oh, I have every intention of working on the rest of you later. But you'll be wearing far less." And because her grip on the dress loosened, as if she might drop it, I ducked my head and fixed her with a candid look. "Did my cock make your pussy feel good?"

Despite the pink staining her cheeks, Briar scowled. "Stop it."

"Are you sure? If not, I'll fuck you again. Why else do you think I need to leave in the next ten seconds, before I explode and haul you up against the wall?"

Briar tossed the gown to the floor. "You're pulling a Poet. You're doing that thing where you use sex-talk to divert from serious matters. And you only do that when you're nervous."

'Twas a strike to the chest. I hadn't known I'd been doing that. Yet she was right.

It was true, I wanted her again, as often and long as possible. But I also flirted and teased and tempted whenever I didn't want to think about all the other shit on our plates. And when unmasked, I was just as unhinged as she.

The quandary wasn't about facing a court I didn't know. For I'd done that once before. Nay, what lanced through me was seeing Briar among those people, seeing how they affected her, and seeing what that did to us. I'd said as much from the beginning, when I tried to break from her in Spring.

To this day, I feared she would crush me.

True, I was overreacting. In general, poets tended to do that, particularly if they were addicted to the source of their inspiration.

But after having a man's head roll at our feet, witnessing this court balk at the sight of my son, and tipping Briar over the balcony until she came brokenly against my mouth, these recent events had me scatterbrained. 'Twas pitiful and beneath a jester such as myself.

I towered over this princess, yet I couldn't have felt smaller. "They don't make me nervous." Gently, I sketched her jawline with the tip of a black fingernail. "You do."

She blinked, and the creases in her forehead vanished. "Do not do that." She grabbed my hand, fisting it with hers. "It's us. A tale for campfires."

That is all. That is everything.

My muscles loosened. "Aye."

Briar nodded and licked her lips, an impromptu thought surging to the forefront. "We'll need our own language in there."

Perform for the masses but keep the script hidden. That, a jester could do in spades. As could a princess.

I gazed at our bunched fingers. "I've often found hand gestures communicate many things."

Briar rubbed her scarlet bracelet between her thumb and forefinger. "Whenever you're talking to someone, and I do this, it means what they're saying is truthful and safe. And if I do this—" the princess tapped her chin, "it means they're lying, so be careful. Because if they're lying, they're also listening, watching, and remembering."

Mmm. I liked where this was going.

"And if I do this—" I improvised by drawing my finger across my lower lip, "it's a warning not to answer the question. And this—" I mimed flicking a piece of lint, "—means humor them."

We plotted a few more hand signals, all of them to be used mutually. If either of us thumped an object onto a surface, it meant we'd hit a nerve. But if either of us smoothed out an invisible wrinkle from our clothing, it meant we had impressed someone.

And because I couldn't resist, I pretended to trace my finger around the rim of a cup. "As for this, it means I still feel the wet clutch of your cunt around me." I banded my arm across Briar's waist and stalked my lips against hers. "And my cock is still hard for you."

She sucked in a breath and smacked my chest. "Don't you dare signal that to me in a room full of people!"

"It would be all your fault," I defended. "As for the rest of them, I have some practice being the newcomer in a court. That didn't stop me from owning everyone in those halls by the year's end. I know when to repress my tongue and when to flick it like a whip."

Briar combed through my mussed hair. "Fact: That is called pacing."

"Correction." I waggled my brows and yanked the woman harder against my naked body. "It's called foreplay."

Which is why I made good on the temptation and fucked her again, this time against the wardrobe mirror.

12

Briar

My heels clacked against the floor. I stepped into the athenaeum just as Poet turned. The instant his eyes landed on me, the book he'd been perusing dropped from his fingers and smacked the ground. His famished gaze slid down the ivory off-shoulder gown clinging to my form, the neckline scooping lower than it had before. Droplet earrings swung from my lobes, and the slender diadem sat atop my head, the gems twinkling. To finish everything off, I'd left my hair undone, the locks flowing freely around my face.

Fire scorched the jester's retinas. His mouth worked, but nothing came out beyond some type of undomesticated sound.

Pleasure eddied through my veins. I felt those orbs absorbing me like starlight—something that burned beautifully, its light reaching across an impossible distance. Also, I felt him mentally stripping the ensemble from my body.

My stomach flipped. Yet his attention was not the only factor. Poet had changed as well, outfitting himself in new leather pants and a black coat that defined the contours of his frame. Large platinum buckles studded the upper garment, the elaborate metallic flashing. I failed to detect a shirt under that coat, which bared his throat and clavicles.

We met in the middle while admiring one another. Poet squinted as if I'd perpetrated a felony, the painted whorls under one eye shifting. He stole my fingers and swept his mouth across my knuckles. "This isn't a fair fucking fight, Princess."

The exposed ribbon around my wrist shivered. A voltaic meteor shower invaded the place where his breath touched my skin. "I disagree," I responded, blatantly sketching his physique. "I believe we're on equal ground."

He straightened. His cunning mouth lifted to one side. "Shall we?"

Ten minutes later, we paused at the threshold. Sentinels flanked the doorway but maintained an inaudible distance from us, as did the knights trailing Poet and me—the ones who journeyed with us from Spring. Beyond the hammered brass entrance, murmurs drifted from inside the hall, along with the clinking of glasses and the background strum of a violin quartet.

As the music reached Poet's ears, he groaned. "Really?"

I elbowed him. "It's a beautiful tune. Quiet, melodic—"

"Boring," he interpreted. "Are we attending a feast or a funeral?"

"That depends on whether you keep your mockery to yourself."

"Pity. The world classifies Autumn as virtuous, yet the last two days have proven otherwise."

I twisted his way fully. "We are not all immoral."

And he turned to face me. "Tame your scowl, Sweet Thorn. I know that because I know *you*, but now you're telling me I'll be castrated fatally if my jester filter doesn't stay in place?" He scoffed like a glorified snob. "As if anyone could handle me besides you."

"I wasn't referring to *you* being in danger," I clarified.

Poet perked up at that. Honestly, he should have seen the response coming. I knew how quickly he could eviscerate a packed room merely by exercising his tongue.

Yet that wouldn't set the example we wanted. The jester was just

lamenting because the music didn't measure up to Spring, the kingdom most renowned for its artistry.

His eyes dipped, raking over my dress. An enigmatic and downright carnal impulse brimmed in those pupils. Swiftly, we rotated
back to the door, our shoulders brushing and sending electric shocks
up my system. Perdition, he'd been inside me more than once in the
past hour. We needed to contain ourselves. Like him, I kept my attention trained on the double doors instead of the suit that molded
to his body.

Poet spoke while staring ahead. "Are you saying you fancy this
tragic mess of a tune more than Eliot's lute playing?"

"Are you implying this discussion is necessary three seconds before making our debut?" I scolded.

"Debut," he echoed. "I like the sound of that."

Brat. Scoundrel. Troublemaker.

"I know what you're thinking," he intoned.

I grunted. "If you wish for me to dwell on your finer attributes,
then stop whining."

"If you want me to behave, then stop teasing my sex drive with
that fucking gown. Every organ in my body is responding, including
the most inconvenient one."

My cheeks baked. I swung toward him again. "Need I remind you,
the off-shoulder part and lower neckline were *your* idea—" But the
smirk he directed my way cut off my lecture. My lips flattened as I
stared at him. "You bastard."

"In so many ways," he acknowledged smugly.

"Libertine," I accused.

"Bibliophile," he teased.

We shared another long look. Heat rose between us like lava about
to spill over. Our fingers linked and squeezed, and we wheeled toward the entrance.

"Be on your guard," I mumbled while fixating on the doors.

"Be at your fiercest," he replied while doing the same.

We had our strategy mapped out. Arrive with our arms looped

together instead of with our hands entwined. Promenade side by side but in a formal manner. Keep our gazes neutral but attentive to everyone who approached. Invite questions but keep answers brief. Save the subtle retorts and veiled warnings for the crucial moments.

And when all else failed, ask about the state of the harvest—Poet might have rolled his eyes at this—which no Autumn resident could resist discussing in detail.

Finally, only use humor as a last resort. This rule was for Poet, though I had my doubts whether he would listen.

As for flirtation tactics, well … just, no. Not in Autumn.

He released my fingers and crooked his elbow like an escort. I hooked my arm through his. Poised and positioned like chess pieces, we crossed the threshold and entered a new kind of battleground. And with each second that ticked by, a sequence of events occurred.

"Her Royal Highness, Princess Briar of Autumn," resounded like a trumpet from the footman's mouth. Hundreds of murmured conversations ceased, the violins slid to a halt from the musicians' dais, and heads banked in our direction. Everyone reeled our way as Poet and I stepped into the scene.

Throughout The Dark Seasons, each court judged in its own way, to its own distinct octave. Sinful Spring chortled and ridiculed openly. Temperamental Summer snarled or shouted, regardless of who was watching. Placid Winter slit its eyes, every gaze cold, cutting, and calculating. And discreet Autumn concealed its reproof behind dignified stares, as smooth as polished wood.

Such expressions greeted us as we paraded into the feast, the train of my gown slicing a path behind me. Attendants genuflected, countless heads wrapped in crespines, headbands, and elaborate nets ducking in subservience. The crowd maintained its composure, but I caught the set mouths and stiff postures as everyone's gaze plunged to the floor.

But once Poet strutted fully into the candlelight, a tornado might as well have blasted through the area. Because not all of them had been present when our procession rolled into the courtyard this morning, the courtiers gawked against their wills. Eyes flared wide. Lips parted. As the crowd straightened, numerous pairs of feet shuffled backward, while others took involuntary steps forward. Nonetheless, all heads craned, the better to see.

Curiosity motivated any citizen. Apparently, beauty and reputation achieved the same feat, only to a greater degree.

My knuckles flexed over Poet's forearm. Whether out of possessiveness or protectiveness, I couldn't say.

It could not be out of envy. I would never covet how Poet's physicality attracted people.

Yet the way most women blushed, and how scores of men adjusted the brooches glittering at their necks, mirrored the reactions he drew in Spring. With that black and platinum outfit, his verdant irises lined in kohl, and paint ornamenting one conniving eye, this man exuded raw sensuality.

Such a novelty was unfamiliar to my people. It was like watching a graceful jaguar prowl into the space—dark, hypnotic, and gorgeous. Not least of all, dangerous.

I knew this phenomenon. I had experienced it once, while alone in a dimly lit hallway.

To this day, I still felt the same upheaval whenever the jester sauntered into a room. If I had assumed my nation would be immune, I'd been wrong. On the contrary, Poet's effect spanned Seasonal borders.

The hairs along my arms raised. He must have noticed the change, because his thumb stroked my flesh.

Yours. Always.

This land. This jester.

I hiked up my chin. *Mine.*

At last, the attendees remembered themselves. Some went so far as to bristle, offended that a mere glimpse had struck them dumb. I empathized with this reaction too.

An advantage or a drawback? That remained to be seen.

Their gazes returned to me. That's when they noticed the dress.

The ivory color rippled down my form, the skirt cascading around me like water. By contrast, my exposed shoulders straightened. Because Poet and I had collaborated on the ensemble, it achieved the balance we'd been aiming for.

Proper. Noble. Fearless.

I'm your princess. And I'm one of you.

I'm your leader. And I serve you.

I'm different. And I'm the same.

Appreciative glances mingled with ambivalent ones. Poet had been right. They regarded my dress the same way they would have a crown, and the pure ivory color balanced the risky neckline, allowing both to coexist.

A moment later, Mother stepped into the hall, her figure outfitted in a swirl of sapphire. Again, the footman lauded, "Her Majesty, the Queen. Avalea of Autumn."

She glided in like a ship—able to shove the ocean out of its way. Stalling beside us, my mother completed this united front. Flanked by my jester and my queen, hope coursed through my veins.

Father used to say the first step in anything was the hardest. Mother gave us a covert wink, then sailed forward.

My grip on Poet's forearm loosened in relief. But his thumb continued its inconspicuous stroke over my flesh.

As we moved into the crowd, my joints unlocked. It would be all right. Whatever passive-aggressive remarks or shrouded insults the court threw our way, we could do this.

Spring's great hall boasted a Royal dais, rows of tables, and a performance floor—a space meant for entertainment and dancing. But Autumn's assembly room had the opposite effect. Built for deep conversation and savoring the meal itself, rich wainscoting lined the walls—a signature feature of this castle—patterned rugs covered the floor, and the mouth of a giant fireplace roared with flames. It was the largest inferno in the palace, apart from the one in the ballroom, plus the bonfires during Reaper's Fest.

Despite the number of guests, the room achieved an intimate quality. It was meant to be shared rather than monopolized. A single

U-shaped banquet table furnished the space, unbroken and uniform. Intentionally, the arrangement blurred the lines of hierarchy.

Vines coiled across the table, the cords embellished with acorns reminiscent of legendary ones that possessed ambiguous magic. High taper candles rose from the mesh of foliage. Plates with deliberately mismatched leaf patterns extended across the surface, and bronze glass chalices waited to be filled with hard cider. Every chair was fully upholstered, made for guests to curl up in while eating.

One would think we had walked into a common area rather than a dining hall. One would also think these court members embodied such comforts. Instead, they regrouped from the initial sight of Poet and me. Their amazement shifted, transforming into looks of consternation, as dry as twigs.

Nonetheless, we'd been given a sign. Their intolerance could change with time, if we learned how to slip through the cracks.

Political decisions would affect that. As would social interactions.

And so it began. In this kingdom, conversations preceded the meal. Courtiers broke into groups, each of them sipping cider while attempting to conceal their impressions of us.

Observing the rules of etiquette, I guided Poet to a huddle of Mother's advisors. Decorum required us to acknowledge them first before anyone else. Several members of the Royal Council cast us sober glances as we approached.

"Cheery bunch," Poet remarked.

I withheld a laugh. "You promised to behave."

"Naturally. So long as they compliment my outfit, no one shall get hurt. And so long as they praise your gown without any of the men foaming at the mouth, no one will lose their limbs."

"Fact: You're horrible."

"Correction." He leaned sideways and murmured, "I'm effective."

His silken voice penetrated my senses not a second before we were upon the group. I struggled to purge the warm color from my face, then cleared my throat.

The cluster acknowledged us with bowed heads. "Your Highness," they chorused.

Two women, the first with a gap in her front teeth and the second with cropped hair the color of clay. One man with inked skin and a series of braided hoops dangling from his left ear.

"Ladies. Gentleman," I greeted. "May I present, Poet. Court Jester of Spring."

"Newly of Autumn," he amended on cue.

Appeased looks crossed their faces, but only fleetingly. Winning them over would be a task, considering the jester's reputation as a valued advisor to Basil and Fatima. No dignitary appreciated their authority being challenged or undermined, but their approval would go a long way with the rest of the court.

"Pleased to make your acquaintance," the first woman stated, only half-lying as her eyes soaked in Poet's countenance.

Transfixed, the other female had forgotten to speak until her peer nudged the female's bicep. Knocked out of the trance, the council member schooled her features and added, "Well met."

"How extraordinary to find ourselves in Spring's midst," the gentleman with the braided hoops said, all the while inspecting Poet's platinum buckles. "I gather it's your first foray into this kingdom, as Basil and Fatima have never brought their trained fools with them during visits."

"Licensed fools," Poet corrected smoothly. "Jesters are picky about accuracy when it comes to their credentials. You understand, I'm sure."

The man's brows rose an inch, recognizing the corner Poet had backed him into. Disregarding someone's status purely to demerit them was a delicate balance. If done wrong, it made the speaker look either uneducated or lazy, neither of which neat and tidy Autumn citizens valued.

"Quite," the advisor muttered. "Rumor tells us you used to be a confidant to the monarchy."

Rumors. Hearsay.

Used to be. Past tense.

Absently, I readjusted one of my droplet earrings, the gesture visible to Poet's eyes.

He's baiting you. Check your ego.

Poet noticed the signal and shrugged to the man. "Nonsense. I was merely their lucky charm."

"That is apparent," the councilor replied with another glimpse at the ornamented coat buckles. "Your people exhibit such eccentric tastes."

Oh, for goodness sake. I predicted Poet's response.

"I couldn't agree more," he replied. "It takes a practiced eye to notice."

Another direct hit. Mild yet ironic.

Distress filtered through the man's visage. My jester had dropped the implication at his feet like a booby trap, preventing the councilor from commenting further.

We excused ourselves. Idling too long in anyone's company wasn't appropriate. It implied partiality, and we did not want to be seen as disingenuous.

Time to separate. If we also appeared too attached, it would be viewed as a weakness. Not to mention, a vulnerability. Whoever had killed Merit, and for whatever ultimate agenda, they had to be in this room observing us.

The second we parted, courtiers traipsed my way in batches. I welcomed their attention and accepted their salutations. We chatted discreetly about Mother's role in the Peace Talks, my "excellent" choice of gown, and recent opposition from certain trade workers about who rightfully earned the title of Master.

All the while, the masses struggled not to glimpse my lover. Despite the ostentatious platinum buckles, the puma black of Poet's attire proved to be as undeniable as his tongue. I didn't need to hear the conversations to know he left each person who approached him flummoxed. The man could spin words like gold, maintaining refined and intelligent conversation while maneuvering the discussions in his favor. He turned criticisms into compliments, reproaches into encouragements, and derision into banter. The man was able to gauge which partners were worth beguiling, which ones required more formal efforts, and which attendees needed to be put in their place without embarrassing them. This method was especially fortunate for the latter, as I'd often witnessed Poet's skill in ridiculing his opponents, which otherwise bordered on ruthless.

Periodically, I peeked over the rim of my chalice. From this vantage point, I watched him render most of the guests tongue-tied once he was finished with them. Suavely, he humbled himself to this crowd while reminding them of the power he'd earned with his former monarchs.

To have the Court Jester's approval was to gain an advantage, particularly with the Crown. You wanted him as an ally, not an adversary.

At regular intervals, we glanced at each other. The moment this happened, the air thickened with humidity. An invisible force sizzled from his end of the room to mine, so that hot coals glowed in my stomach.

The pull drew us back to one another occasionally, the effect resembling a dance. Systematically yet instinctively, we retreated and united. Whenever among the groups, we communicated through hand signals.

I rubbed my scarlet bracelet. *They're telling the truth.*

He tapped his chin. *She's lying. Don't call the woman out, but let her know you're aware of it.*

I drew my finger across my lower lip. *Do not respond to that.*

But when the jester ignored the command and engaged the speaker, my eyes snapped to him. *I said, do not respond to that.*

Yet Poet nonchalantly traced his digit along the lip of his cup, reminding me of what it meant.

I still feel the wet clutch of your cunt around me. And my cock is still hard for you.

The cove between my breasts tingled. I guzzled my drink and dropped it onto the nearest tray, then reached for a vessel of cool, effervescent water.

We detached ourselves again. As we traveled individually through the hall, nobles murmured to one another. Servants idling at the further corners inspected us as well.

Only the soldiers who had traveled with us paid the jester and me little heed. They kept vigil of the hall, their eyes dicing across each face and measuring every movement. Yet once, a female knight registered my attention and inclined her head.

Awareness dawned. Something had shifted in the forest when her comrade died. Instead of obligated, the gesture felt voluntary. To that end, one of the men shadowed Poet, a sickle gleaming at the warrior's hip.

The jester was aware of it, as he remained cognizant of a thousand details. I would bet he'd already inventoried every potential weapon in the vicinity, including the butter knives. Provided we were dealing with sacrificial fanatics, if anyone revealed themselves as an enemy, Poet would send the nearest piece of cutlery flying in their direction before his bodyguard had a chance to register an attack. And that was assuming Poet forgot the dagger harnessed under his coat and resorted to silverware.

Be that as it may, the soldier's inclination to shield Poet eased the crick in my neck.

Unlike with me, attendants flocked to Mother and vied for her attention with genuine enthusiasm. Because she had presented herself as a disciplinary Royal, the world did not blame her. Thus, the court's bias prevented them from scorning their queen, even while she vouched for my choices and endorsed Poet and Nicu.

Amid the feast, I overheard hushed conversations rehashing the story of the jester's seduction and my subsequent rebellion.

"Poor Majesty."

"The shame must be taxing on her."

"But look how she carries herself with aplomb. So loyal to her offspring, despite how the princess has conducted herself."

Thankfully, Mother could do little wrong. On that score, the guests cast her empathetic looks.

Good. Let them continue to love her. I would rather she be re-lieved of the burden than weather it on my behalf.

Besides, my actions had nothing to do with her, and I would never allow anyone to think otherwise. I chose this path. No one else. And if Autumn still supported at least one member of the Royal family, it was to our benefit.

I inserted myself into a clique of female nobles. "What a pleasure," I exclaimed. "It's lovely to see you all again."

The perplexed women blinked and uttered, "Your Highness."

That I approached them with such an amiable demeanor was new behavior—warmer and more welcoming than I used to be. It was the sort of thing Mother excelled in. Although Autumn was a polite society, congeniality won the greatest loyalty.

Though considering how we singled out and treated certain people, this was the grossest of hypocrisies.

No one seemed able to reply, so I adjusted my tone back to normal. "Tell me. Do you think we'll have a good harvest this year?"

Their stupefied faces relaxed, and their pupils brightened with fervor. At which point, the replies overlapped. By the time they bowed and shuffled to their seats, I'd gotten a full report on the state of our fields, including a lecture on why sourdough remained superior to rye.

Many asked about my time in Spring and the outcome of the Peace Talks. Equally as many salivated to ask about Poet. Nine times out of ten, they pretended to be ignorant of the answers, even though most of the particulars had already circulated.

"How long will he be staying with us?"

"Did you travel together?"

"Does he have a title?"

Typical. They weren't asking out of curiosity. They were reminding me of my circumstances, forcing me to repeat them. To acknowledge the repercussions, because although I was their sovereign, I had tarnished Autumn's relationship with Spring. This was their chance to satisfy a grievance without making a scene, to exact compensation from their heiress without issuing a demand.

And while everyone knew I'd traded for Poet and his son, they purposely didn't inquire about Nicu. It would be imprudent to demonstrate an interest in what they ignorantly considered to be a plague of nature.

I accommodated, giving them what they wanted. Poet would be living here indefinitely. Yes, we traveled in the same caravan from Spring.

Then I gave them what they didn't expect. To the last question, I could have told them Poet had been offered a peerage by Basil and Fatima but declined it for reasons that were none of their concern. More importantly, I could have reminded them that "Court Jester" was a title. A coveted and influential one at that.

Instead, annoyance peppered my lips. "He does not have a *noble* title," I emphasized, then shrugged and murmured just before taking a sip from my chalice, "But he has a tongue."

This may not be Spring, but Autumn residents had an imagination. I left them with that, walking away as they clutched their pearls, and the faintest gasps toppled from their mouths.

In the maw of the fireplace, game roasted on a spit, the animal's flesh crackling and juices spitting into the fire. The aroma mingled with the tartness of baked plums and the savory whiff of russet potatoes. More than anything, the amplifying scents announced dinner was about to begin.

Poet caught my eye from the other end of the room. We maneuvered around the throng and met on the outskirts. Each of us faced in the opposite direction, our profiles parallel as we assessed the feast.

Our mingling held three objectives. First, to reintroduce myself and initiate Poet into society. Second, to attain hints—from their personalities to their quirks—about the assassin's identity, should they reside in the castle. For the time being, we'd accomplished both.

Finally, one goal remained. To perform for the masses. For what we had in mind, Poet needed to accumulate tidbits about his audience.

"Are you ready?" I asked.

"Aren't I always?" he assured me.

I pinned my gaze to passersby but leaned nearer to his scent. "How will you know what information to use?"

Shrewdness and cunning filled his voice, so that I pictured that devilish mouth quirking. "I'll know."

Wryly, my eyes slid toward the basketweave patterned floor. "I'm expecting specifics."

"Specifics spoil the fun and ruin the drama."

"In other words, it steals your thunder."

"I do enjoy being the center of attention. That aside, if a jester reveals all his secrets, it dilutes his leverage. Does a chef tell everyone what goes into his best dish?"

Fair enough. "The chef would at least disclose the ingredients to his sovereign."

"That's why the chef isn't a performer." Poet's tenor brushed my skin like ebony satin. "That welcome feast in Spring, when we met? I knew which of your buttons to press, did I not?"

Memories surfaced. Me, walking into a feast that could have been mistaken for a bacchanal. Him, dancing in a funnel of smoke like an apparition. The way my thighs shook under the table while I watched him. The moment he made an example of me in a packed hall, granting every Royal the favor of a lit candle—all except me. We hadn't spoken yet, but the jester had known precisely how to strike. Already, he'd known where to penetrate me.

Poet did press a few buttons. Including an intimate one he hadn't been able to see. That alone had vexed me.

I restrained a huff of amusement. "I still have a grudge about that."

His octave lowered to a devious whisper. "Then punish me later."

Villain. Knave.

I fiddled with an errant wisp of hair tickling my neck, the motion enabling me to duck my head closer to him. "Have enough ribbons ready."

A choked sound tripped from Poet's lungs. I strolled away with a repressed grin, the satisfaction of leaving him there bringing a lightness to my steps.

I migrated to the banquet table. As I reached my seat and set down the chalice, a buxom shadow puddled across the drinking vessel.

Mother appeared beside me. I stared at the assembly room while addressing her. "Do you suppose this kingdom will ever comprehend its double standards?"

The queen chuckled grimly. "I would love to see that day." She touched my shoulder, the contact drawing my gaze to hers. "Count your blessings tonight if that's the only challenge we face, dearest. This storm has been brewing for a long time, since the era before you and Poet. It's only that you two were brave enough to be the spark." She inched nearer. "Now allow that spark to flare."

I rested my palm over hers. "That is inevitable."

We took our seats. As we lowered ourselves, the crowd hushed and followed suit. They listened as Mother raised her chalice and toasted to our homecoming, to our reunion with the court, and the upcoming Reaper's Fest celebrations. And despite my widespread infractions, the knights and nobles clapped in earnest.

"And now," Mother announced, extending her arm toward a dark silhouette that flanked my other side. "I give you our newest addition to the court. Poet, the Court Jester of Spring. Now of Autumn."

The revelers applauded dutifully. I wanted the freedom to present Poet myself, but had I given that speech, it would have been deemed an impertinence. Officially introducing my corrupter would be seen as flaunting my choices. But coming from the queen's mouth, it demonstrated her blessing of the situation and, thus, elevated Poet's reception.

A hive of bees sprang from my navel. Pride tickled my scalp when the jester stepped into view. As always, he'd manifested to my right like smoke.

Towering in front of his chair, Poet's gaze scrolled over the congregation. An erotic dance like the one I'd first witnessed in Spring would be too excessive. However, a gesture from his origins, combined with a greeting of his own, would be appreciated. So instead of enchanting everyone with the kinetics of his body, my lover swayed them with the proficiency of his tongue.

With a bow, he swiped a fresh goblet from the table and held it aloft. Beneath the table, his free fingers slid privately over mine. Those bees swarmed up my knuckles, and I reciprocated, brushing his hand in return.

"Hear this now," Poet began, his voice unspooling like silk through the hall. *"Look this way. From root to bough, this is Autumn's way..."*

The verse poured from his mouth, eloquent and lilting. Poetry originated in Spring, but the stanzas came from an anthology of Autumn lore. From the giants who once kept vigil of our fields, to the lost acorns imbued with magic, he tied each of the myths together. The guests stirred, reluctantly impressed.

That he knew this. That he'd taken pains to learn this.

After conversing with the attendants, Poet took what he'd heard and inserted it into the recital. He blended artistry with knowledge, historical context with social awareness. The result became a magnetic rendition of this Season's roots, combined with the traits of its citizens. Their morals and values. Their concerns and hopes. Seamlessly, the jester blended everything together through fluid rhymes, neither audacious nor mild.

Mesmerized, people leaned forward in their seats. The cunning jester slayed them with unscripted words, using the narrative to draw them into his sphere. Like a magician and a seducer, he juggled his audience between his fingers, holding them spellbound.

Heat percolated through me. I watched his commanding profile sketched in firelight, unable to fathom that this devilish creature belonged to me. That he wanted me as much as I wanted him. Enthralled, I glazed my fingers over his and felt his wrist shiver.

When he finished, I shook myself out of the daze. The spectators did the same, needing a moment to recover.

Then they burst into applause. Some rose to their feet and clapped, the noise drumming through the space and growing in pitch.

My palms smacked together. I felt a smile threaten to break

through my face.

The jester's mouth crooked as he raised his chalice. Turning my way, he inclined his head to Mother and me. Straightening, the fiend afforded me a wink.

But when he glanced once more at the courtiers, the chalice froze in his grip. His fingers tightened on the drink, his knuckles flexing and several veins inflating from his hand. He choked the vessel with such force, I worried it might crack.

One figure applauded louder than the rest. Like a phantom, the attendant stepped from the hall's entrance, as if he had entered during the commotion. Or perhaps, he'd been there long enough to listen to Poet's triumph.

My shocked hands ceased clapping. My fingers dropped into my lap.

Standing less than twenty feet from us, the King of Summer slammed his palms together like paddles. "Bravo," he boomed, then tapered his venomous gaze at me. "It appears my timing is perfect."

13

Poet

What. The. Fuck.

Like a boogeyman risen from the ashes of hell, Rhys stood near the threshold, a corona of firelight burning around him. As he stepped deeper into the room, illumination from the volcanic hearth slashed across his neck.

Appropriately, this brought to mind my greatest fantasy of seeing the cocksucker beheaded *and* simultaneously roasted to cinders. The bonus of his cremation would be for good measure, if only to make sure he stayed dead. One couldn't take chances, because who knew how many extra lives he had.

Alas. This wasn't the reality. Nay, the King of Summer's ghost hadn't just paid us a visit. As much as I'd like to verify it, my soul would have sensed the moment this king drew his last breath. I would have felt it like a perverse sixth sense.

Instead, the bane of everyone's existence hijacked this moment with a snide grin ticking the corner of his lips. Or rather, I suspected that's what his mouth was doing beneath the flaccid mustache drooping from his face.

Here I'd been, at the start of my inaugural performance in Autumn. History in the making. The genesis of a fresh beginning, a path to forging a relationship with Briar's people.

I'd had them. Regardless of those who scorned what I stood for, they hadn't been able to object once my tongue began to flick words into the air like flavored confetti. They'd swallowed what I gave, letting it melt into their systems, and liked the taste of it.

I'd fucking had them. For three minutes of applause, they had been mine.

Aye. This Royal must have bargained his soul to a warlock, in exchange for his own form of clairvoyance. He'd known when to interrupt me, shortly before the bonus epilogue could lurch from my mouth and work its glamour.

His presence leached the revelry from the room and shocked everyone into stillness. Their clapping hands seized. Murmurs chopped through the hall.

To my left, Briar's eyes flashed in recognition, then hardened into steel plates. The man had caught her so off guard, she failed to mask its effect. The princess scowled, her freckles shifting like a broken constellation.

Queen Avalea went still, her fingers choking the arms of her chair. Her stumped expression testified that she hadn't expected him.

Summer knights loitered behind Rhys like statues. Their burnished capes were embellished with some kind of reptilian skin, likely the flesh of an endangered species. Either that, or a venomous leviathan native to one of Summer's countless islands.

The soldiers' features bunched as tightly as fists, and their fingers locked around the hilts of their curved swords. These men and women acted as though they hadn't seen a good orgy in a decade, much less sampled a fine wine. From that deprivation alone, magma would pour from the tops of their skulls at any moment. Perhaps living near a thrashing ocean and getting sand up your asshole on a frequent basis did that to people. Or the nip in the autumnal air pushed them so far out of their comfort zone, they didn't know how else to respond, apart from festering.

In any case, this crew didn't need a fight. They needed mass quantities of booze and copious amounts of groping.

From the opposite recesses, Autumn soldiers maneuvered closer, also clamping onto their weaponry. Summer's behavior made sense. Although peace had reigned on this continent for a century, millennia of evolution had wired Summer's blood with enough short fuses to detonate a city.

As for benign Autumn, I would call the knights' offensive stance out of character, if they weren't citizens of a likewise prudent culture. And if they hadn't recently witnessed one of their comrades lose his head and get his torso disfigured.

The guests shuffled, unsure whether to rejoice over this surprise or flee before the troops launched at each other. The tension between the warriors grew so thick, I could slice a wedge of it and heap the thing onto my plate like the world's shittiest appetizer. Not least of all, reports about what happened between this ruler, Briar, and me lingered fresh in their minds.

The King of Summer let his eyes scroll over the congregation as they bowed, curtsied, and did everything short of throwing maple leaves at his feet. I didn't have to be a native to conclude the alcohol and overstimulation had gotten to everyone. The Court Jester of Spring. The King of Summer. Neither of whom they'd ever seen individually, much less in the same room.

When those toxic orbs landed on Briar and me, the princess's fingers snatched my hand behind the table. It wasn't every day a fire-breathing nightmare interrupted the honeymoon. Henceforth, the temperature drained from her digits as they latched onto mine.

I clasped her hand back, to keep her warm, to keep her upright. And to keep myself from whipping out a dagger and hurling it at the king's chest, aiming in vain for something resembling a conscience.

If Nicu were here, the sight of this man would resurrect my son's trauma. The mere thought of Rhys getting near Briar or Nicu motivated my free hand to move. I reached toward the inner pocket of my coat, where the first blade rested.

If this man came back for my son …

If Rhys came within a thousand feet of Nicu …

But nay, he was safe. Aire and his men had the suite barricaded from unknown visitors.

And I knew a thing about targeting people. The king may hold a grudge bigger than my ego, but my son wouldn't be worth the effort to him anymore, much less the bloodshed. Not when this shark could trade for any born soul he wanted, and with any Season.

Whatever reason the shithead was here, Nicu wasn't the target anymore.

Rhys peered at me and Briar as though he could see through the tablecloth to where our hands linked. The instant his attention cemented to the princess, that mouth lifted into a sneer under the nest of pubic hair germinating from his face.

The sight infected me like a virus. My retinas exploded. I saw so much red, 'twas a wonder a tsunami of blood didn't flood the area.

I maneuvered in front of Briar, cutting off his view of her. To which he assessed the motion with relish before turning away.

Avalea recovered quickly. The muscles of her countenance twitched into place as she pasted on a congenial expression.

"Your Majesty," Rhys greeted the queen as she detached herself from the chair and flounced to meet him across the room.

"Majesty," she repeated, each of them genuflecting.

They murmured in hushed tones. Then Rhys nodded in gratitude and strode from the hall with his minions in tow.

Conversations hatched across the court. On either side, members of the Royal Council grumbled theories.

The queen swung toward the assembly and fixed them with a gracious smile. "Please," she invited, swinging her arm to the place settings. "Eat. Drink. We shall return shortly."

On that note, she pinned me and Briar with a swift look before gliding from the room. We followed her. Stalking around the table, we pursued Briar's mother through the double doors. Yet instead of heading to the Royal wing, the queen bustled toward an unknown alcove with a legion of soldiers behind us.

Like fuck would that suffice. I shook my head and jetted in the opposite direction, to the tower stairwell.

A hand shot out and clamped around my wrist. I whipped toward Briar and fumed, "Let. Go. Sweeting."

"No," she clipped. "Not unless I come with you."

My tongue faltered. Her words quickened my pulse, filling the gaps with warmth. Had I honestly expected her to react any other way?

We rushed up three flights of stairs and strode into the Royal wing, where Aire and two of his men stood post outside Nicu's door. The First Knight saw us coming and met us halfway down the corridor. He lifted his hand to stay our panic. "We've been informed. He's safe and will remain so."

Briar sighed in relief. My chest deflated, and I carded my fingers through my hair. "Thank you."

"His Majesty brought a troop with him," Briar prompted. "If you hear commotion. Or any disturbance—"

"I'll know before Summer has a chance to breach this wing," Aire finished.

"Your hearing is that good?" I asked.

I'd meant it as a bland joke, but the man's eyes dimmed like a storm-riddled sky. "I won't need to hear them."

Whatever that meant, I believed him.

Briar and I checked on Nicu anyway, peeking inside the chamber where he nuzzled into the sheets with Tumble. After that, we returned to the alcove where the queen had been heading. The more ground I covered, the harder my boots smashed against the surface. Although my gut had rationalized the king wasn't after my son, I'd needed to make certain. But several other possibilities remained, one of which had to do with the way Rhys leered at the princess.

Like a target.

I snatched Briar's hand and strode in front of her. She made no reply but pressed closely to my side.

The alcove led to another wing, which housed only one structure. We entered a vast repository where a network of built-ins lined the wainscoting, with floor to ceiling books wedged on the shelves. Briar's face relaxed marginally, and the rest became clear.

This was the library.

Among the stacks and reading cubicles, a few passages led to solitary doors. "We conduct our roundtables and host meetings in the library wing," Briar explained.

Knights flanked one such chamber at the end of a short hall. A waiting soldier pried open the partition, and we passed into a compact room where a modest fireplace flailed with heat, books crammed the walls, and wing chairs bordered a coffee table. The door closed, insulating us inside.

Avalea swerved from the window where she'd been pacing and fixed us with a perturbed stare. That she didn't ask what took us so long pumped up my admiration for this queen. She knew where we'd gone.

"Is he all right?" she asked.

"Yes," Briar answered.

The princess did so because I couldn't speak yet. I stalked to the fireplace, needing to grab something, anything that would stop me from reaching for my blades.

At the mantel, I seized the rim and leaned into the pyre with my head bowed. A muscle rapped in my temple. The ledge of my jaw fastened. If I unshackled my fingers from the sill, I would likely go on a Summer killing spree.

Silence infested the library's chamber. We stood in our respective corners, processing the situation.

With a growl, I broke from the mantel and rotated on my heels. At the same time, Briar and Avalea joined me by the flames. The princess's fingers bunched into a knot, whilst her mother wrung her own hands.

"He was still in Spring when we left," Briar said, her head jumping from me to Avalea.

The queen nodded. "Rhys is here to deliver the born souls that Briar and he negotiated for during the Talks. He must have sent Summer a missive to corral twenty dungeon inhabitants and have them brought here."

"Doubtful," I countered. "In the time it's taken us to travel, a message would have needed just as long to reach Summer. Even more for that asshole's council to select twenty born souls and have them parceled to Autumn. There's no way Rhys could have accomplished that so quickly."

Briar's shoulders fell. "Not unless one journeys by ocean."

Shit. I'd either forgotten or blocked out that fact. Unlike the rest of the Seasons, Summer traveled exclusively by water. Its seafarers wove sails from materials native to their coves, which accelerated the ships. Moreover, the hulls were constructed with the bones of deceased swordfish, which enabled the vessels to shift sizes and quest through a variety of waterways, no matter how narrow or vast. Those advantages, plus the fierce waves rolling from one shore to the next, made any trip infinitely quicker than by land. Thusly, Summer could swallow distances and surpass a falcon's speed if necessary.

"Very well," Briar conceded. "Yet there's no reason for the King of Summer to depart from Spring only to come here directly, merely to be present for the transfer of prisoners."

Avalea swallowed. "No. There isn't."

My gaze incinerated holes into the rug. I spoke through my teeth. "He's not just here for the trade."

They fell quiet, their silence agreeing with me. But more than that, never in the history of The Dark Seasons has a monarch strutted into a kingdom without notifying his hosts in advance. Not unless that monarch intended to wage a war.

The king's unprecedented and spontaneous arrival spared us about three seconds of plotting—what to say, what not to say, when to be direct, when to be cagey—before the Queen ordered the sentinels to bid Rhys entry.

At which point, I did what I'd always done in Spring. Summoning every ounce of restraint left, I leaned one shoulder against the mantel, arranging myself like a knickknack and the very picture of lavish boredom. To the outside observer, I gave the impression of a dandified fool rather than a lethal deceiver—one who would sooner hack off the king's flaccid cock with a flick of my blade than play host.

Aye, I was flattering myself. I needed something positive to motivate me.

Briar perched on the edge of a wing chair and folded her hands in her lap. Her eyes ticked over to me, then clocked toward the door as Rhys paraded inside like a glorified insect.

Adding insult to injury, his saffron linen cloak slithered behind him, its lengthy hem chafing the rug because some incompetent genius had neglected to study the basics of design. And though I valued excess, the monstrosity of a garment involved an overabundance of sashes, plus a severe lack of insulation.

Ugh. If the man couldn't hire a decent tailor, much less a logical valet to select weather-appropriate textiles, then what sort of advisors attended the king's forums?

Fewer things depressed me as when someone made the wrong fashion choice. For fuck's sake, I hadn't thought I could hate this imbecile more. Life was full of surprises.

The doors shut behind the knights, both military forces stationing themselves outside. Flames from the grate snapped and spewed embers. Outdoors, a gust kicked against the windowpanes.

I'd heard about Summer's castle, which sprawled horizontally instead of vertically across jagged ocean cliffs, the vista as sharp as coral reefs. People said the fortress stretched so far along the horizon, it blended in with the range. With a monarch like this one, I supposed the citizens needed all that room to scream.

In any event, it was hardly a shocker when the king appraised the chamber and commented, "Such a quaint palace. The residents must run into each other often." His attention swung between Briar and me. "Though I've heard forced proximity has its merits in the end."

"Your Majesty," Avalea said, her features taut like a snare as she gained his side. "We weren't informed of your impending arrival. Is Giselle in attendance with you?"

"My queen is on her way to Summer. She longs for the sea, and this is hardly a social call."

"Nevertheless, how unfortunate we hadn't known to anticipate a visit so soon after the Peace Talks. Otherwise, we would have set a place for you at our table."

"Yes. Apologies and so forth for interrupting before you had a chance to fill your plates. The sun sets so quickly here, I neglected to remember that you dine at an early hour. Terribly inconsiderate of me to forget our cultural differences."

Firelight burnished the inflammatory red of Briar's hair and highlighted the crystal leaves in her diadem. With artificial politeness, the princess suggested, "Perhaps a missive went undelivered, Sire?"

"No, it didn't," he dismissed. "I came unannounced."

"Very renegade of you," I drawled, the dispassionate words leaking off my tongue like acid. My eyes raked over his attire, which couldn't possibly serve him in this climate. "Didn't you hear? Autumn has a dress code."

The king strode to the chair opposite Briar, swept off the ridiculous cloak, and tossed it like a rag onto the cushions. Without glancing my way, he spoke to Briar's mother. "Someone tell the jester that subordinates wait to be addressed by a king."

"Point me to one, and I'll take your advice."

You fucker.

Authority threatened. Masculinity challenged.

Trying to feign nonchalance, was he? He picked the wrong juggler to test. I hadn't pushed his buttons so much as pounded my fists onto them, all without ruining my manicure.

Predictably, the shithead wheeled on me. The bushy planks of his eyebrows slammed together as he groused, "I see your tongue is still attached to your mouth. Most unfortunate. I'd hoped the queen would come to her senses and order it hacked off before you'd reached the castle. Or at the very least, your cock. That, too, has done enough damage to Autumn."

So original. Nevertheless, my left knuckles bent, curling toward the blade stashed in my coat. Carefully, I flexed my digits until they relaxed.

If he thought the princess or her lover would take that bait, Rhys was a greater dumbfuck than I'd assumed. Briar merely stared at him, her features as placid as a lake. And just as difficult to see through.

The queen was another matter. Rhys glanced at Avalea, whose nostrils flared. Like an afterthought, he dropped himself onto the wing chair, made himself at home, and grunted, "No offense meant."

"Every offense taken," she objected, moving to stand between him and her child. "You had my daughter arrested, attempted to execute her lover, and sought to claim his son as property."

"None of which is out of my jurisdiction," the king reminded her, then leaned around Avalea's voluptuous form and regarded me. "Nor did I claim your spawn as property."

I spoke around the barbed wire entwined in my throat, my words managing to come out blasé. "Oh, I'm sorry. That must have been my other son—Licu."

"I didn't have a chance to claim the simpleton, because you stole him from me."

"You mean the part where your ass got tricked into surrendering him? That wasn't stealing, that was intelligence." I knocked my head toward Briar. "And *that* was all her."

"None of your grievances hold water," Summer griped. "I acted within my rights as a monarch—a ruler ordained by the almighty Seasons."

"Would you like us to leave you and your phallus alone, so you can finish stroking it?" I proposed with a dramatic sigh.

If he had horns, they would have sprouted. "You miserable, illegitimate fuck—"

"Don't you dare," Avalea interrupted, her voice as thin as a layer of ice. "You have entered my house without notice, undermined my rank, offended the Court Jester, and refused to acknowledge my daughter."

"On the contrary," the king snarled. "I have every intention of addressing the princess and her whore in great detail."

"Don't keep us in suspense," I prompted.

Already, purple suffused the man's face. I saw the budding implosion. Excellent, since the angrier Rhys grew, the sloppier his bullshit became. And without knowing which game he was playing, we needed him clumsy.

Placating Rhys, verbally licking his balls, and kissing his ass would yield nothing. He wasn't here to be nice. Until we got wind of his agenda, the best course of action was to cherry-pick at his evident weak spots.

Except Briar darted her eyes to me and rubbed her scarlet bracelet rather hectically. Which meant not only was the king telling the truth, but my thorn had an amendment to this warning. The harsh grind of her fingers against the ribbon made it clear.

Quit while you're ahead.

Like her, I recognized the fine line I treaded between mockery and malice. The queen had fallen victim to the same impulse, and although I had every confidence the princess could pick up our slack, it was best to tamp down the fury. Similar to Rhys, the more pissed off I felt, the less tactful I became.

The king drummed his fingers on the chair arm. "I would speak with your offspring and her fool alone."

"You would also presume those wishes will be granted without having been earned," Avalea stated.

"If I'm not mistaken, we made a bargain in Spring. You got to keep the simpleton bastard of this demonic heathen, all in exchange for twenty of Summer's mad. Clever and successful, considering how badly my court wants to purge itself of such useless burdens. As I already informed Your Majesty, I'm here to deliver what I promised."

"Is that all?" I asked. "Rather pedestrian of a monarch to make his own deliveries."

"I wasn't done."

"And my question was rhetorical."

Mostly. That he wasn't done had been obvious from the moment he darkened our doorstep. Like fuck was he here just to parcel off his prisoners.

"As this was a negotiation between your heiress and myself, and as the jester was an unfortunate side effect of that negotiation, I require a private audience," Rhys dictated.

Avalea opened her mouth, but Briar's voice swept through the room. "It's all right," she said. "We will speak with him."

Her mother hesitated, then nodded in acquiescence. "I'll wait in the alcove. And the guards will remain outside these doors."

"As will mine," Rhys replied.

I stared at the king and spoke as though caressing a razor blade. "No need," I told Avalea.

"So we agree on something," the man grumbled. "I won't be long, and I suspect a bloodbath would take more time than this discussion will."

That wasn't what I'd meant, but okay. Even if he did pose a threat to Briar, my blade would find its way into his ball sac before he could quack for help or Autumn could barrel in and defend their princess. After that, I'd go for the king's jugular. Or perhaps I'd lop off the whole volatile noggin, slowly and with the dullest knife in my collection.

Although enough heads had rolled in the last two days to give me a lifetime of nightmares, this one I would enjoy. And I wasn't above treason. For I'd proven that once before.

Avalea stormed from the chamber. The blaze swallowed most of the oxygen in the room.

The king's temper subsided, the capillaries in his veins no longer in danger of bursting. The purple drained from his complexion, replaced by the hint of a pompous grin.

As if he owned this fortress, Rhys gained his feet and toured the room, which seemed more fitting considering how often he'd shuffled in his chair during the Peace Talks. Summer citizens were known to be a restless bunch. Truly, I hadn't expected him to last as long as he had in the wing chair. But now, he weaseled along the chamber's perimeter while studying me.

He might as well be slinking across a chess board. Briar and I watched every move he made, dissected every motion. Keeping our faces neutral, we waited for our opponent to position himself like a rook.

"I applaud your performance tonight," he lied. "Quite engrossing, watching you prostitute yourself to the masses, all for the sake of … what?" He spread his hands. "Acceptance? Notoriety? The same popularity you exploited in Spring? The freedom to fuck Autumn's princess without consequences?" He came full circle, stopped at the back of the wing chair, and gripped its frame. "Or perhaps it's something more. I can't help but wonder."

"If you keep talking long enough, you might figure things out for yourself," I replied. "I hear that's what sovereigns do."

Rhys tightened his hold on the chair. Signet rings bridged across his knuckles, likely squeezing the circulation from his fingers.

The princess vacated her perch. "Why are you here?"

His attention leaped toward her. "I've heard you're rather hands-on for an heiress, working the fields alongside your subjects. Maybe you've inspired me to do my share of actual labor. Maybe I decided to personally escort the maddened fools I promised you because I've had a change of heart about the distinction between leadership and servitude."

"That would require knowing where the heart is located, Sire," Briar stated calmly, as though she'd made an innocent comment about the weather.

Rhys slitted his eyes. "What does that mean?"

I grinned politely. "It means fuck you."

"Poet," Briar warned.

The king sheared his gaze my way. "In Summer, I've had men decapitated for less."

"And in Summer, the ocean drowns people for no reason," I reminded him. "It appears you don't set the bar very high."

"Poet."

160

But I ignored Briar. "You might want to work on your confidence threshold, if it merely takes a jester's tongue and a princess's frown to insult you."

"Are you disputing the might of a king?" Rhys demanded.

"Not at all," I demurred. "I'm denying the presence of one."

"Poet," Briar clipped under her breath. "Enough."

My head snapped in her direction. As our gazes collided, my pupils expanded. For some reason, needles jabbed up my spine.

Oh, Briar saw through his horseshit. She knew Rhys wasn't inspired by a single thing she did. But didn't she grasp the veiled condescension he was throwing at her? Commenting on Briar's willingness to labor with her subjects had been a snub. Rhys was implying she didn't know the difference between being a farmer and being ruler. He was trivializing Briar, calling her incompetent.

Talk down to my thorn, and my daggers will come out. Besides, we agreed that if I could rile up the king, I should. So why the fuck was she stopping me again? My temper was in check now.

I felt the king's eyes skipping between us. "Lovers' quarrel?" he gloated.

The question snipped our trance in half. Briar's features twitched in awareness, and I wagered mine did the same. Fuck, he'd gotten to us without trying.

The moment reinforced itself. We exchanged another brief look, swearing not to let that happen again.

"Enemies who become mates," the king mused. "Enticing premise, I'm sure. But what happens when those mates can't agree on how to be allies? Who's right, and who's wrong?" His voice trickled through the room like oil, hazardous to slip on. "Who wins the argument?"

"It's not about winning the argument," Briar said. "It's about understanding the argument."

"That could be why there are two of us and one of you," I added.

"For how long?" Rhys contemplated.

In my periphery, Briar dragged her fingernail across her lower lip, as if she had an itch.

Don't answer that.

When neither of us replied, the prick shoved himself from the chair's rim. "You know," he continued, "after your crimes and subsequent deception during our bargain, I kept telling myself those were isolated incidents. I convinced myself you two were irrelevant—beneath my retribution. If someone matters little to you, why waste time on them? Why make the effort?"

While pretending to mull that over, he strolled toward Briar. I twisted from the mantel and tracked his progress, my fingers clenching the dagger under my coat.

Rhys halted in front of the princess. "You got your little varmint of a half-wit. I got a chunk of the mad off my hands. And I got to see you ridiculed on Lark's Night."

Then he stepped around her. And my fingers released the dagger.

Rhys joined me at the fire and balanced an elbow on the mantel, essentially mirroring my posture.

Though come now, I did it better. And I looked better doing it.

"Even your insolent recital in my tent, plus that dramatic lip-lock between you two, I could forgive," he told me. "I was enraged at first, but the public tends to forget such stunts when in the throes of a sunset carnival. Especially if that public consists of Spring residents drunk on narcotic petals, circus revelry, and unbridled smut. So they stumbled from one entertainment to the next, which diminished your attempt to humiliate me. Of course, that made me feel better."

His facade changed, eagerness curdling his features. He leaned forward and spoke in a hushed tone, like an ocean current hissing against sand. "And here's where it got interesting."

I quirked a brow. "Careful who you're talking to. My kind are master storytellers, which makes us the toughest of critics, should anyone dare to spin a tale for us."

"Using the term *master* so casually in this nation is rather brazen," Rhys answered. "Even for your status."

Briar had mentioned the title having a greater meaning here, chiefly when applied to someone with skills. That's why Merit and the troop had gotten flustered when I made that joke back in the forest. However, I had the feeling there was more to it, and the princess hadn't gotten to that bit of Autumn trivia yet. Still, none of us had time for a detour.

Briar's shadow bled across the floor as she approached. But she only made it halfway, a strange expression warping her freckles. She paused in an oval of firelight that magnified her silhouette, the blaze giving off an optical illusion, as if the princess's likeness bore cracks. As if her outline were so brittle, it might shatter if she moved another inch.

She flattened a hand over her stomach, like she knew what the king was about to say. The motion was so acute, I felt her premonition like a puncture wound. What's more, her ribbon bracelet reminded me of all the people I'd ever targeted, as though I should have seen this coming, as if I should detect when someone was targeting me in kind.

Oh, I had known. I just hadn't been aware to what end.

What the fuck did the king have on us?

Rhys's mustache lifted in triumph. "I think this sequence of events will engage you, seeing as you and your princess are the main characters."

"I should hope so," I played along, my voice fatally calm. "Despite the awful costumes they made us wear, Briar and I were the sexiest people at the carnival, not to mention the most interesting."

"Are you sure?" the king asked whilst the flames dashed across his face. "Or were the key players those born fools you set free from their cages while no one was looking?"

14

Poet

A nasty taste spilled across my lips, bitter to the point of rotten. The putridness was so extreme, it paralyzed my tongue. Beside me, Briar's outline radiated dread. I felt her reaction like a magnetic thing, which raised the hairs across my forearms. I couldn't say when, but at some point, the princess had foreseen this outcome. And now, it made belated sense.

The king knew. He knew what Briar and I did before we left the carnival, before we fled and dissolved into the forest, to the secret bower where the atmosphere inspired provocative impulses in its visitors. There, I had fucked the princess until she came three times in an hour.

But prior to that exquisite episode, we'd done something equally mutinous. After rushing from Rhys's tent, we skulked to a remote area where born souls were kept in pens. The sunset carnival had set up those enclosures so that revelers could torment the prisoners for kicks.

Unable to digest another fucking moment of it, Briar and I had set them free. A treasonous act, and the second one in a row for us, having just rescued my son from a dungeon several days before. We were pardoned for that, thanks to Briar's deception against the Royals, which negotiated me and Nicu from Summer's hands.

But that we'd dared to flout the rules once more, on the night of the carnival? Well, that had been as necessary as it had been felonious. Moreover, it was a long, healthy middle finger to Spring.

We'd taken the risk, because how could we not? Besides, the revelers had been tipsy on wine, stoned on petals, and intoxicated by their own self-worth. They'd been too eager to dance and horny as fuck to bother with the prisoners. It had been the perfect opportunity to set the captives loose without anyone knowing or pointing the finger.

Loud music. Even louder moaning.

No witnesses. No proof.

The revelers and Royals had discovered too late the prisoners' absences. And since the captives were never found, everyone chalked it up to a simple escape. Never mind that Spring believed many born souls to be useless and unintelligent. Instead, they assumed the prisoners were so wild by nature, they must have found a makeshift tool or a heavy rock to break open the padlocks.

As Briar and I had expected, sinful Spring assumed we wouldn't do something so rash as to break another law. From their points of view, the disreputable princess and jester were too smart to be that flagrantly stupid.

Oh, but that was the brilliant part. For I had taught my sweet thorn how to play the fool—thusly, to deceive. That was the trick of it.

Never would we have left human beings to deteriorate. So we did the inevitable. And we'd gotten away with it.

Or so we'd thought.

Rhys grinned, elated with himself. His face creased with such vindictive glee, he resembled a caricature of himself—a distorted, exaggerated vision. Apparently, Summer natives exhibited their pleasure just as swiftly and erratically as they expressed fury. The miserable fucker relished our reactions to the point of obscene.

His jubilant voice contaminated the room. "Don't you remember? A Royal is always served by an entourage. Though sometimes that retinue isn't publicly revealed."

Briar found her voice quicker than I did. From her static position at the room's center, her response thrust into the space. "Spies."

"Something like that," Rhys acknowledged. "I find it remarkable that Summer is the only monarchy who keeps certain members of its court camouflaged. We have our councilors and troops, however it's wise to keep some loyal confidants obscured. I would say this very moment is a prime example of that."

"You had someone follow us," she translated.

"I had a few someones follow you," he corrected. "You never know when one witness will end up with a sword in their gullet. Always best to have spare minions on hand and alternative stratagems in place. I would advise you to take notes, Highness. For future reference when it's your time to reign. Providing you get there, of course."

My tongue sizzled. "Do *not* threaten her unless you'd like a weapon lodged in your mouth."

Rhys's nostrils flared. "Touch me, and you'll be disemboweled before an audience by sunrise."

"Touch her, and it'll be worth killing you."

"Enough," Briar demanded. "You've both had ample time to pound your chests. What do you want?"

The king spoke to her whilst staring at me. "Ultimately, I'm here to blackmail, not to execute. However much I'd enjoy the latter, the former is more appealing, as the suffering will last longer. What do I have in mind, you ask? I shall gladly oblige.

"Liberating fool slaves not once but twice in succession. A child is one thing, but a group of adults?" He tsked. "That you didn't learn your lesson the first time led me to thinking what else you might be capable of, and what you might be hoping to accomplish together. Outside the bedroom that is, or wherever else you swap bodily fluids.

"From the scene you caused during the roundtable at the Peace Talks, to the moment you freed those prisoners, I started to wonder. If a jester and a princess will go so far to set abominations loose, how many more will they try to save?" He cranked his head toward Briar. "Or more critically, what will you stand for in the future? What kind of leader will you be to this nation? What will you lobby for?" Then his gaze slid back to me. "And when will you start?"

Okay, but the prick wasn't asking himself any questions other people across the continent weren't asking too. I would hardly call this train of thought novel, despite the visible kudos he gave himself.

A deceiver knew when to stay quiet—to make that one eventual strike count.

Now that the shock had worn off, I took the opportunity to recline deeper against the mantel, as if I'd found a technicality in his speech but wouldn't show that card yet.

I sensed Briar picking up on this. In my periphery, the princess squared her shoulders. Moreover, she folded her features into the picture of unapologetic composure, regardless of the mayhem charging through her.

Our shifts in demeanor spurred Rhys's mustache to flap quicker and with less finesse. "A simpleton boy, a bastard whore, a soft spot for born fools, a proclivity for rebellion, and a list of offenses long enough to make a professional fugitive jealous," he itemized. "You've accomplished quite a bit in a short time. A former 'good little princess' who fell from grace and now makes decisions based on her cunt as well as her sympathizing heart. That is a recipe for ruin, not merely for yourself but an entire kingdom."

"How I rule this court and this land is none of your business," Briar censured.

"Except it is," Rhys hissed. "As the one who reigns over Summer, it is very much my business who my nation has dealings with and what my allies sanction. Especially when it comes to universal law, in *addition* to natural law, and most certainly if it has anything to do with born fools. Your revolting behavior has branded you as untrustworthy, unreliable, and unstable, which will not serve the future of this continent. If you two shits were thinking of campaigning for the emancipation of those abominations, you are a threat to The Dark

Seasons." His glower hurtled my way. "As the king of an allied court, it is my duty to prevent that."

I flicked open a tinderbox resting on the mantel. Plucking a length of tinder—a small, dead twig longer than the king's cock—I tapped the stem's tip against the surface. From the corner of her eye, Briar saw the message.

You've hit a nerve. Go deeper.

Her gaze swung to our opponent. "Telling everyone what I did won't ruin me any more than I already am," she parried.

"Trust me, I've learned the inconvenient way that pointing the finger at you doesn't work that easily," Rhys bitched. "Not to the degree that would satisfy me."

At last, mockery sat on my tongue. "Satisfy you. I thought we were talking about the so-called protection of this continent, when really, I should just go fetch you a yardstick."

The king's cataclysmic fist hammered into the wall above the mantel. His knuckles rattled the facade so loudly the knights strode closer to the door, each fighter bracing for entry.

No matter. I held his scowl without blinking.

"The preservation of The Dark Seasons is my calling," he vented, then festered at Briar. "As it should be yours, Princess."

"Our definitions of equality, protection, and preservation are somewhat different," I drawled.

"You've made that clear. And like you two, I've had to get more creative with my methods." He flexed his hand and forced it to settle on the mantel. "So no, announcing what you've done won't get me what I want." Then that fucking gleam resurfaced, this time with a malicious light. "But setting more fools free on Autumn lands will."

Confounded, my eyes clicked over to Briar. She met my gaze, her own confusion evident.

"You might say I got the idea from you after learning about your sneaky escapade on Lark's Night, before you two raced from the scene," Rhys continued. "By the way, where did you go after that?"

Scarlet pooled in Briar's cheeks. Thankfully, the king had so little practice in the art of seduction that he failed to register this. More likely, he interpreted her reaction as anger.

I gave Briar a covert shake of my head. *He's bluffing. He doesn't know.*

The cocksucker wasn't bullshitting about having spies on our tail when we set those prisoners free. But he was clueless about where Briar and I went afterward, and how I'd buried myself inside her lovely pussy within that same hour. I heard the telltale flatness of his question; if he had known we'd been fucking for the rest of that night, his voice would have possessed a different tone.

Rhys's minions hadn't had time to be voyeurs. Whoever they were, they'd been too preoccupied acting as informants and reporting to him. The King of Summer wasn't a patient man.

But how the fuck would setting born souls free benefit him and destroy Briar?

"Your logic is wanting, Sire," Briar said.

Rhys vacated the mantel and took up position beside an ancestral portrait. "You got twenty of the mad from me." Then his eyes glinted like algae. "But I got to choose them."

Another chess piece slid into place. The magnitude of what he'd said roiled in my gut. Did he mean to …

Yet I saw the answer crawling like a scorpion across his face. Aye, he fucking did.

"I know the contents of my prisons," he summarized. "I know every moronic and crazed animal who rots there. I know what each one is capable of, and I know which cell every inhabitant occupies. It's hardly difficult to send that information to my council. Or did you think I would choose randomly?"

"I wasn't even aware you could choose intelligently," I replied.

The man glowered. "I thought jesters read people better than that."

"Only if our blood is the same temperature."

"Then I suppose I'll have to take that as an advantage. End your crusade, or my conspirators will set the mad loose on the public."

Loose. As if they were beasts hellbent on mutilating the first innocent bystanders they came across. Even though he'd curated the prisoners, Rhys tended to make assumptions. To that end, only this ignoramus would presume every maddened soul was a violent individual who'd attack unprovoked.

Some might. Most wouldn't.

I recovered from the sucker punch. "Alas. If no one's educated you on the nature of violence—ironic, considering your lineage—someone should have told you it's not that simple, biased, or insular."

Rhys's spiteful chuckle scraped through the chamber. "And if no one has educated you on the nature of, well, nature—ironic, considering *your* roots—someone should have warned you it can be just that simple."

Realization dawned. Perplexed, Briar swatted her head between us.

I spoke to her through a mouthful of fury. "A deception."

A sham. A facade.

The princess's eyes widened in horror. The king would orchestrate a heist of the prisoners and turn it into some macabre form of theater. The captives would be freed, but they wouldn't be the ones to commit murder. Behind the scenes, this massacre would be up to the ones who'd liberated them.

Rhys's spies would find victims to kill. And after mauling them, those spies would make it look like the mad had done it.

My disgust ran rampant. Although Rhys saw all born souls as plagues, this travesty abused the captives as pawns.

One, the tactic would reinforce what the public believed about born souls. Two, Rhys's assassins and their victims wouldn't be the only ones to worry about.

Nay. The public would be.

Here, his plot exceeded my expectations. If anyone at court saw a maddened soul trotting about the castle unshackled, that courtier might run.

Or they might intervene. Indeed, they might do it aggressively.

They might presume the captive was fragile, unable to resist. And whilst some born souls would indeed have less fight in them, less ability to defend themselves, others would have more.

If court residents exercised their so-called duty—worse, if they felt outrage—they might not accost a born soul gently. That could get ugly fast, and that ugliness could spread if more players got involved in a brawl. Crimson would flow through the castle halls and court-yards, to say nothing of what would occur if the captives reached the lower town or outlying villages. Altruistic as this land prided itself on being, it had never been tested this way. On that score, farmers and tradesfolk knew how to wield pitchforks and blades.

Human beings were harmless until faced with a threat, wheth-er that threat reflected reality or not. Like I'd told Briar, people saw what they wanted to see.

Who knew how it would end for either party.

But it would never end well for Briar. Because she'd negotiated for those twenty souls, the public would blame her for the carnage.

She struggled to collect herself. "Your conspirators have no au-thority to infiltrate our dungeons. They wouldn't make it past the guards."

Technically, true. Yet her point scuttled through my mind like a bad omen. As a man who'd spent a year passing in and out of shad-ows, leaving the castle undetected whilst venturing to see Jinny and Nicu, I predicted where this was headed. Hence, I anticipated Rhys's response like a slow-motion blow to the face.

"They won't make it past the guards," he echoed victoriously. "Oh, child. They already have."

Loathing rushed up my throat. "You fucking parasite."

Briar gawked in revulsion. "It was you."

The camp attack. The knight's severed head. The blood soaking the tips of our boots. The markings carved into Merit's chest—crimson illustrations resembling something like shards of glass—left behind by the attackers.

His spies had done that. They'd gotten past a camp full of trained soldiers without being seen or heard, merely to prove they could. They'd beheaded their victim, then left a token of their affection, emblems of their leader.

Their leader, who wore a crown on his head and an unrepentant look on his fucking face.

In Summer, I've had men decapitated for less.

Briar's features cinched like a noose. "Maiming one of our knights while unprovoked is an act of war," she seethed.

"Yes, it is," the king acknowledged. "Except I'm not waging war on Autumn. I'm waging it on you."

"You would harm innocent people!"

"You have much to learn, Highness!" he belittled, his octave reaching its boiling point. "They're called casualties of war. Get used to the term if you insist on being a nuisance and an enemy, rather than a compliant sovereign. If you weren't so invested in the liberty of abominations, none of this would be happening. Blame yourself, not me. I'm doing what a king must to protect his world!"

"You would endanger these prisoners and the people in my court. All for the sake of keeping born souls manacled."

"For the sake of this continent," Rhys growled, his spittle flying. "For the sake of having a worthy ruler succeed your mother. Not an impressionable slut who opens her legs and yields her power to the first man who—"

My blade flew across the room. Its tip diced through the king's sleeve and pinned him like a flea to the nearest wall. In seconds, I followed the dagger's path, cannoned in his direction, and blasted him into the facade, my arm bracketing against his windpipe. The wall shuddered, rupturing like a fault line, and the neighboring painting crashed to the floor.

The man gargled, the veins in his throat popping. His neck bobbed against the tip of my second blade, which I angled at his thrumming pulse. If he so much as squeaked to his troop, my weapon would pierce his larynx.

Briar broke across the room and grappled for my shoulder. "Poet," she implored. "Stop!"

"Now, now," I cautioned him, then flipped the blade and positioned it at the head of his cock. "You've insulted the princess. Apologize, or you'll be leaving here with one less trait to compensate for."

The king spluttered like a juvenile. "Get your paws away from my dick, you savage alpha lapdog."

"This isn't a dick," I raged, sliding the tip to his balls. "It's a prop."

"Poet." Briar snatched my bicep and whispered harshly, "Don't. Please."

The knights of both courts crammed behind the door, steel ringing and bracing. They sensed something, but because we'd been hissing, they couldn't be sure. That would change the moment I turned this motherfucker into a eunuch.

Inevitably, Briar's features hardened. "I issued you a command, jester."

Wicked fuck. My fingers flexed over the dagger's hilt.

True, I would peel the flesh from his bones and tear any court in half for this woman. Not that she needed me defending her. And she did look glorious when she took charge.

But that wasn't the only reason Rhys's life—and his disposable pecker—hung in the balance with me.

I thought of Nicu. I thought of that murdered soldier. I thought of everyone who would be caught in the crossfire, if the king made good on his threat.

I knew a bluff when I heard it. This wasn't one such occasion.

A trickle of blood dribbled from Rhys's neck where I'd pricked him. In his own Season, he could have me drawn and quartered for this. To say nothing of the penalty for threatening certain low-hanging fruit.

Briar's voice gentled, and her digits loosened on my arm. "Poet. Not like this."

A muscle in my jaw throbbed. Reluctantly, I whipped the daggers from Rhys's cock and sleeve, then juggled them into their sheaths while sauntering backward.

The king sagged, then jerked his clothing in place and barked with the furious dedication of a zealot. "A wise choice, whore. I'll show mercy for now, if only to watch your downfall before you're both set on the chopping block."

He wiped the blood from his throat and stood between us, puffing himself to his fullest height. I had a good six inches on him, but that didn't matter. His head practically inflated, knowing he'd gotten to me.

"Stand down or pay the price when your subjects fall and this kingdom blames you for bargaining maddened murderers into their land," he told Briar. "In only one of these cases shall your heads ultimately remain attached to your necks."

She lifted her chin. "My mother would never—"

"Indeed, she wouldn't." He beamed as if he possessed the power to shit gold bricks. "But the public would."

Briar fell silent. Her elevated chin wrinkled.

The king drilled into that weak spot. "If my conspirators set the mad loose to flee your dungeons and harm Autumn's citizenry, your subjects will never trust a thing you do or say again," he emphasized. "You might have a chance of redeeming yourself after Spring, but you won't after this." Rhys diced a finger between me and the princess. "And if I hear so much as a whisper about you campaigning in the years to come, I'll make good on this promise."

Meaning, his cult would tell him. Meaning, they would stay here to keep track of us.

"*For inheritance of the Seasons,*" the king quoted from an old continental aphorism. "Every worthy Royal, noble, and commoner is blessed with a sound, rational mind. That is the will of nature. And when the will of nature speaks, we listen. The decision is yours, Highness. Born fools or your people."

Correction. Her people or her people. There was no difference.

If the public condemned Briar for her choices, it wouldn't stop there. As a bonus, Autumn might take its venom out on the ones who mattered to us.

Nicu. Avalea.

Once the news reached farther, that discourtesy might extend beyond the borders to Spring.

Jinny. Eliot. Cadence. Posy. Vale.

Either way, checkmate. This kept us on a leash and left no future for my son. Not if we lost the power to inspire change.

"You're asking me to make an impossible choice," Briar uttered.

Rhys shrugged. "I'm a king."

Tragically true. And kings never asked.

The Royal piece of shit opened his arms. "Fuck each other hard. Live happily ever after. Be a joyous little 'found family.' Count your blessings. Reign free." His arms fell to his sides. "Just don't overdo it and end up crossing me in the process."

My head didn't know what to do with this man. However, my tongue did.

As the king strode to the door, I murmured, "Your Summer minions can't stay invisible in Autumn forever. They may know how to disguise themselves, but so do we."

Briar and I would find them. We would root them out like weeds.

The king paused with his hand suffocating the door knob. He cast us a sidelong glance, firelight seeping into the crevices of his face. "Who said they were of Summer?"

15

Briar

The moment King Rhys left, my knees gave out. The room shifted, tilting askew. I stumbled backward onto the wing chair and clutched the seat cushion, fighting to regain my equilibrium.

From the hall, the knights' muffled voices clogged my ears like water. In response, Mother instructed something to her soldiers, all of them crowding outside the ... Which room were we occupying? I could not recall.

Suddenly, a dark figure materialized. Poet stooped at my feet, his body hunching between my legs. He tipped his head to look at me, that gorgeous face trenched in worry, and he murmured things I couldn't hear.

But how I wished I could. How I longed to soak up his voice, to have it fill me with relief, to wash away this past hour like a bad dream.

When I failed to respond, Poet's fingers gripped my hips, as though I might topple sideways if he didn't prevent it. Perhaps that was true. Around me, the chamber spun, blurring every object.

The blazing fire. The window overlooking a murky landscape. The jester's green eyes flaring with concern and a lingering tinge of vitriol.

Images of Merit's severed head flashed through my mind. That, and visuals of the people who'd recoiled from Nicu upon our arrival. The boy smiling as he explored his bedroom. The hazy view from my balcony while Poet made love to me hard and fast. The jester's verse luring his Autumn audience at the welcome feast.

Rhys's victorious grin. Poet's knife angled at the man's throat, ready to slash His Majesty's head from his neck.

My desire to stop the jester. And my desire not to.

So easy. It could have been so easy.

16

Briar

The shock wore off at some point. It happened after Mother blasted through the room like a raging goddess, after she and Poet exchanged words while I sat immobile, after the jester and my queen spoke to me in steadfast tones meant to fortify my resolve. At last, Poet's touch brought me out of the hypnosis.

I blinked at the brutal lines of my lover's face and heard him mutter, "He did this to you. So help me, I'll kill him for it."

He laid that offer before me like another of his temptations. By some force, I summoned the will to shake my head, silently discouraging him.

Next, I listened to snippets of what Mother said. Her gentle words echoed what already flitted through my consciousness, inherent after a lifetime of training.

A princess does not shrink under pressure.

A princess must not lapse before her people.

I longed to nestle with Nicu under a blanket. I yearned to be stripped and fucked softly by Poet, to have him hold me in the darkness, where nothing could penetrate us. I wanted to curl up with

Mother on a sofa while sipping cups of hot cider.

I latched onto Poet's face. *I cannot do this.*

His features tightened, and his irises blazed. *You can, my thorn.*

Mother fixed her own gaze on me. *And you must.*

For one moment, I wanted to be a normal woman, living a normal life. But then the urge faded. I had a duty, and I had a nation to defend, and this was no time to wilt.

This wasn't just about me. I hadn't been the only one threatened, a fact I would not allow.

Poet offered his hand, palm up. My fingers landed there, feeling him clutch me.

With conviction, I broke from the paralysis and returned to the feast with my family. I pasted on a serene expression, as if nothing amiss had occurred, as if my insides weren't tangling into knots.

Mother reassured the baffled court that Summer had merely been passing through and stopped here on a matter of quick business. Regardless of the scandal between Autumn's princess, Spring's former jester, and Summer's monarchy, the king harbored no animosity toward the citizens of this kingdom. Naturally, he would have rejoiced in staying, but after such a long term at the Peace Talks, Rhys needed to return to his own court as soon as possible.

This exemplified Rhys as a man of dignity. Their princess had offended him in Spring, yet he'd come here bearing no ill will, nor an ounce of animosity. It reassured everyone that the rift between our nations wasn't expanding.

In short, Mother had lied. She'd done so to protect her subjects. Though I cannot say if the crowd believed her.

The meal progressed, more subdued than usual. It lacked the ripple of delicate conversation and intellectual debates that normally accompanied the scent of roasted game. Our guests dined and drank in weary contemplation, the impact of Poet's enthralling performance overshadowed.

The whole time, Poet ate with one hand. His free fingers clasped mine under the table, his thumb caressing my ribbon.

I took the necessary bites, succulent meat flaking to ash on my palate. The food lacked taste, so that I swallowed flavorless chunks and rinsed them down with bland liquid that sloshed in my chalice.

Violins strummed. In the custom of Autumn, speeches were made by the highest members of Mother's council. They welcomed us home, though the recitals came out stunted and awkward.

At midnight, Poet led me up numerous flights of stairs and tucked me into bed. After that, my chamber dissolved into blackness. Though at one point, I stirred against a solid chest and a pair of arms encasing me. The tempo of someone's pulse rapped in my ears, and a voice poured into my head like liquid velvet.

Sometime after that, I woke up lucid. I bunched the quilt in my fingers and gawked at the overhead awning. My throat bobbed as two opposing emotions crept across my flesh, one of those sensations chilling me to the bone.

I came from a purportedly benevolent kingdom. I had never been tempted to aggression before.

Not until the jester. Not until his son.

In Spring, I had slapped Cadence. I'd threatened a dungeon guard and hurled a rock that cracked against another sentinel's skull.

But even then, I had never wanted someone dead. I'd never felt such violence toward another.

My love had wrought the best of me. Yet that same passion unearthed other impulses too. Darker ones.

I had wanted Poet to end the king, the way that tyrannical monster ended one of my knights. I'd wanted to watch it happen.

Nonetheless, I pulled myself from the sinful impulse. Otherwise, I would be no better than Summer's monarchy. In which case, what else would I be capable of doing for the ones I loved?

The second emotion chafed my flesh. I tore out of bed, realizing halfway to the fireplace that a nightgown hugged my frame. Poet must have undressed me before I fell unconscious.

My jester had also slept here last night, because the sculpted imprint of his form had made a dent in the mattress. I swerved about, only to discover the suite empty. A precious timepiece constructed by Winter's inventors ticked on the mantel.

My eyes bloated. Ten o'clock?

A gritty premonition lurched into my mind. Everyone would have broken their fasts by now. The court would be about their business. And Poet, Mother, and I would be …

No. *No.*

My knuckles bent into fists. I snatched my robe from the settee and thrust my arms into the sleeves, then marched from the suite. Ten minutes later, I pounded through the library, located the right passage, shoved open a pair of fifteen-foot-tall doors, and stormed into the council room.

"You started without me!" I protested.

A trio of heads snapped in my direction. Poet, Mother, and the First Knight.

I halted partway between the entrance and a rectangular table, the furnishing surrounded by wood-paneled, book-lined walls. Anthologies, lexicons, scrolls, compendiums, atlases, encyclopedias, historical accounts, and political decrees filled the shelves. My unshod heels pressed into the floor; the surface was inlaid with a bronze leaf that spread its tips across the ground.

The jester stood on one end of the table, and he twisted my way the second I entered. He wore a charcoal coat etched with studs and a corresponding pair of dark gray leather pants that disappeared into knee-high boots. An eclectic mix of worry, relief, and admiration slanted across his face as he took in the spectacle of me.

My open robe and visible nightgown. My shabby, cascading red hair. My bare toes.

The fists hanging at my sides.

"Morning, Highness," he said. "Your scowl is a sight for sore eyes."

Flirting would get him nowhere. "And I'm apparently late to the proceedings," I accused.

Aire's head darted between us. He sought out Mother, who had risen from her chair at the table's head. "Briar—"

"You started without me," I repeated, drawing out the words for emphasis.

Despite this fact, no one else occupied the room. At this hour, the Royal Council would have normally attended our roundtable. I'd anticipated as much, which instantly seemed foolish. Rhys had blackmailed us, revealing his knowledge that Poet and I had committed not one, but two crimes in Spring. Moreover, he'd forecasted our intentions for born souls.

Naturally, the council shouldn't know about this. Nor had we originally planned to inform them about our ambitions yet. Not with our reputations walking a tightrope, the court already on edge, and our situation fraught with risk. We'd intended to ease into that relationship over years.

My rationale caught up with me. Transparency and loyalty aside, we couldn't broadcast any information about Rhys. Not until we ascertained the identities of his informants and knew whom to confide in, assuming anyone outside this room would champion us.

I had raged through the castle in my nightclothes and with my hair snarled into a nest. The scene I'd caused in broad daylight had been witnessed by servants and courtiers alike, the news of which would spread to the council.

In an instant, I knew how my conduct would appear to the court and what assumptions they would make. Truly, I could flog myself. With the doors sealed to the point of soundproof, not even a sorcerer could eavesdrop on this conversation. With that assurance—and on the pretense of normalcy—this inner circle had chosen to meet conspicuously. But because they'd opted out of my presence, the court would get wind of that fact, along with my reaction to it.

Neither boded well for my reputation.

Mother's actions, I comprehended. Whether or not I participated, Autumn's queen needed to proceed.

Aire's participation, I also understood. He had pledged to keep Nicu safe, confessed his own secret to us, possessed an unflappable demeanor that surpassed any other soldier, and had proven himself trustworthy thus far. We needed all the allies we could get.

Poet was a different matter. Always, I wanted and needed him by my side, but that wasn't the issue. While looking at him, another emotion cut to the forefront, wounding me terribly. I hardly required a mirror to see the anger littering my face; however, Poet saw more. The hurt must linger under the surface, because his features shifted.

He approached my side, his expression unsurprised yet apologetic. "You were exhausted, love."

"I'm fine," I stressed, inching back from him.

If this man brushed a single part of my body, I'd relent. And I couldn't do that in front of Mother and Aire. Our effect on each other was a privilege, but it was also private.

My eyes slitted. *We should have talked in confidence about what to do. We should have confided in each other before involving anyone else.*

Mother wasn't just anyone. She was my family, her support was paramount, and I would never exclude her.

All the same, the bond between Poet and me came first. We'd sworn that much to each other, and we had agreed to consult one another before making decisions and taking actions. Yet here he was, helping Mother oversee this meeting in my absence while I appeared feeble and incompetent to anyone outside this room.

Poet absorbed every unspoken accusation. "You were *exhausted*."

"I heard you the first time," I defended. "And I'm not weak."

"No one is saying you are."

"You should have waited for me."

"Frankly, sweeting, I'm not in the habit of waiting to protect someone."

"And I'm not in the habit of letting others fight my battles for me."

Something I'd said marred Poet's features. A hundred replies sliced across his face before a lone muscle rammed into his jaw. That's when I saw it. Beneath those kohl-lined orbs, lavender puddled under his lower lashes. The crescents signaled he hadn't slept much, if at all.

I thought of his unyielding embrace while I slept. And just like that, my shoulders fell. He would never undermine my position. He would protect and preserve it with everything he had. Yet the jester would also take care of me, first and foremost.

Which did I want more from him? Which did I need?

Behind us, Mother's chest deflated. A slew of emotions filled her voice, namely contrition and pride. "You are your father's daughter."

Aire trained his eyes on the facing wall, where a carved map of The Dark Seasons spanned the facade. While averting his gaze, the First Knight gestured to my lack of attire and cleared his throat. "You're, um …"

Poet maneuvered in front of me. "He means your lovely tits are showing."

No, they were not. The outlines perhaps, but I wore two layers of underclothing. My nipples were hardly in danger of making an appearance.

Yes, he was attempting to lighten the mood. No, I wasn't up for it.

But yes, I'd been wrong to lash out. My mouth opened to apologize, but the jester moved aside, inclined his head, and swung his arm toward the table with elegant mockery.

I forced myself not to reexamine the tousled mess I'd presented to every resident promenading through the palace. Swiftly, I knotted the sash of my robe. Then I stepped around him.

Poet followed and pulled out a chair for me. I sat while muttering a curt, "Thank you."

He leaned down, and his timbre slipped into my ear. "At your service."

Sarcasm or flattery? Banter or annoyance?

Both perhaps. I sensed my conduct creeping under his skin, just as his behavior did mine. He would call me stubborn, unrelenting.

So be it. I bristled either way.

The meeting commenced, with Mother and Aire recapping the details from the past hour. I sat upright as though I wore a dress instead of a nightgown, had boots on my feet instead of flashing bare toes, and kept my hair braided instead of tattered. The whole time, I avoided Poet's penetrating stare as he lounged across from me like a lazy devil.

Yet the more we turned over the events of last night, the more Poet's mood darkened. His fingers flexed around his chalice. His jaw locked, chiseled enough to file stone. Whatever attempt at humor he'd offered me vanished, those livid eyes deepening to a verdant green.

We had foreseen an uphill battle with this kingdom. But we hadn't predicted Rhys taking up arms from the sidelines and forcing us to reexamine where we stood, including how to combat our enemies—visible and invisible—from this new position.

If our foes had an ultimate leader, now we knew who it was. Rhys posed a greater threat than anyone at court. But it was also clear that some residents of this palace were working for him.

Who said they were of Summer?

The question seared my chest, as it had last night. After Merit's death, we'd been aware there could be resident traitors in our midst. But to get outright confirmation—and to know they chose Rhys over their own rulers— peeled something from me, leaving my flesh raw to the touch.

Mother massaged her temples. "The spies are most certainly at court."

Poet tapped the table, sunlight bouncing off his glossy black fingernails. "The spies are everywhere. Some of them witnessed the princess and me going rogue on Lark's Night, but there was no mistaking the size of Rhys's head whilst he told us about his cult following." The jester motioned to himself. "It takes arrogance to know arrogance."

His hand dropped to the chair arm, where it slung over the side. "Not only was that cocksucker bragging, telling us how important it is to keep part of one's retinue hidden, but it's not as if Summer citizens joined our caravan. All the soldiers traveling with us were recognizable to you three, were they not? That means Rhys's spies are scattered between Spring and Autumn.

"And if his flatulence—not to mention the length of his mustache—is any indication, Rhys likely goes the extra mile, especially to compensate for the lack of girth in other parts of his anatomy. Therefore, it's plausible he's got additional snoops in his own court, as well as in Winter.

"Treason against one's sovereign is an inconvenient risk, so how he managed to win over these moles with his charming personality is a mystery. Three possibilities, then. Either Rhys possesses paranormal glamour, or he's roofied people to his side, or he's an excellent scammer with an impressive ability to mind-fuck vulnerable candidates."

"Or he's a king," Aire remarked. "That tends to intimidate people."

Poet wiggled his fingers. "Pff. His pedigree is as questionable as his wardrobe."

"Convincing courtiers to switch allegiances—betraying one Royal in favor of another—would take more than intimidation," Mother warranted.

"It would take a bribe," I asserted. "Currency is a substantial motivator. Or like Poet said, an effective speech. That, plus an investment in similar interests such as prejudice. As an additional measure, Rhys must have conveyed what happened in Spring to his Autumn informers and likely skewed our actions to make them sound villainous. If someone is a convincing speaker, propaganda and manipulation can go a long way."

"In any case, we sniff them out," Poet finished, then glanced my way. "It doesn't matter what the fuck Rhys wants from us."

In other words, we wouldn't give in so easily. Blackmailed or not. Threatened or not. Rhys couldn't expect us to surrender our campaign for emancipation without a fight. We had risked our lives for Nicu. Did the king really think we wouldn't do it again, or for the rest of the people who deserved to live freely?

I nodded. "If he has us under surveillance, we must be vigilant."

Mother regarded Aire. "Our military force should be monitored."

Aire folded his hands over the table. "With all due respect, my brethren are not under Rhys's influence. We've sworn an oath."

"So do monarchs, but that doesn't stop them from breaking those oaths if they're anything like Rhys," Poet contested. "Vows are fanciful, fickle things. Oftentimes, the biased will concoct excuses and escape clauses. To say nothing of those who simply break their pledges in favor of political and personal gain."

"Even so, I know them to be on Autumn's side," the knight testified.

"What makes you certain?" I probed.

He stared back at me. "Because I've already surveyed them."

Mother studied him. Poet and I swapped a look, recalling Aire's cryptic remark about sensing a person's true nature. We trusted the soldiers who journeyed with us; they had a unanimous alibi for the night Merit was killed. But the legion who'd been stationed here could not be disregarded.

That said, Aire had always possessed a remarkable ability to assess the men and women under his command. Not once in the years I'd known him had this soldier been wrong.

The jester and I nodded to Mother, vouching for Aire's declaration. After a moment's deliberation, she yielded. "I'll accept that for the time being."

"We need to focus on sifting through the rest of the court," I said. "Researching Summer's history with Autumn might assist us in identifying potential spies. Perhaps there's a hint in our timeline—former alliances, debts owed, or unusual reports that connect court members to Summer."

"You could simply hide the prisoners His Majesty brought from Summer," Aire reasoned. "They could be relocated to The Lost Treehouses. I'm no superstitious advocate for lore or myths, but few people dare to enter that place. It's suitably isolated and easy to monitor."

Poet shook his head, dark layers slumping across his brows. "When you've trained yourself to move undetected, you've also trained yourself to see in the dark. If Rhys's minions were able to infiltrate our camp, that makes them perceptive. They'll know if we attempt to relocate any born souls. Nay, we need to deceive, not play defensive." His eyes slid to mine and glittered. "We need to trick them."

"In what capacity?" I deadpanned.

His sexy mouth twisted, the sight infuriating me anew. "By giving them a show. We're known as a defiant couple, which means they'll expect us to deliberate or delay our decision. Best to make them believe we didn't bother, that we've folded quickly, and that we're complying with Summer. All the whilst, we'll set out to yank off their masks."

This made sense. A jester and princess knew how to perform.

Mother argued, "That will make you look frail and susceptible to them. It will nullify your chances of presenting a strong front."

"Rhys might take further advantage of that," Aire added. "He could require more conditions from you."

"Quite the contrary," Poet argued. "If we play this carefully, the opposite will happen."

"Rhys feels emotions to the extreme," I interpreted. "It's as easy to gratify him as it is to enrage him. He won't push his luck because he'll be too busy congratulating himself on the victory. Perhaps his spies will do the same, which means our deception could ensnare them."

"The more blatantly we attempt to ass-kiss the Autumn court, the more our enemies will assume we've seen the error of our ways," Poet concluded. "Since appealing to this nation was our goal from the beginning, the farce will come naturally. The more we succeed, the more Rhys's cult will believe we're no longer a threat, and their disguises will slip."

"That's a rather delicate balance," Mother observed.

"So is penning the perfect sentence," I said.

"And juggling seven sets of balls," Poet remarked.

The double entendre caused my lips to fold inward. I would not let this devil off the hook that quickly. No matter how effortlessly he could make me laugh, nor how intensely he looked at me, nor how deeply that neckline slumped to expose his collarbones.

So we would feign compliance while hunting this court for traitors. To outsmart this mysterious cult, we would become tricksters ourselves. Spies to root out the spies.

A creaky noise from someplace in the room severed the trance between Poet and me. Mother was watching us. Aire had pinned his gaze to the map, pretending to examine the Seasons' geography.

The discussion resumed. As an extra precaution, we listed ways to solicit public approval. Poet suggested including Reaper's Fest in the plan, after we explained the annual tradition to him. One night every year, our kingdom honored the ancient holiday by abandoning our prudent ways. We donned masquerade costumes, illuminated pumpkins with candles, and lit pyres in the forests, villages, and castle courtyards. The evening served as a departure from propriety, when everyone was free to explore their inhibitions—lawfully and within reason, of course.

The main event consisted of a bonfire ball. Although I'd been banished from Spring, and the Peace Talks had just concluded, we would invite Basil and Fatima to the revels. Despite how we'd insulted them, the sinful and impulsive monarchy possessed its own double standards. On that note, they enjoyed surprises as much as the fae of folklore.

According to Poet, welcoming Spring to our sacred holiday would flatter them. Plus, it would show we aimed to keep good relations with the Season.

Whereas in secret, we would continue planning for the future. For equality. For the freedom of born souls. We had snuck around one court before, and we could do it again

Two hours later, the meeting adjourned. I visited Nicu and Tumble, spent as much time with them as possible, then buried myself in the library. This hadn't changed about me. As cultural creatures of habit, it gave the residents a modicum of relief to hear of my retreat into the stacks.

By nightfall, I sat in my chambers, in front of the fire with a pile of books scattered on the rug around me. A blanket swathed my hips, and the flames toasted my skin. Yet my eyes ached, and frustration compelled me to shut the manuscript I'd been rifling through.

Behind me, the door cracked open. My heart leaped as I swung toward Poet. He leaned against the partition, the weight of his body closing it.

The latch clicked. I stared flatly at him while my insides hummed, a restless buzz stirring from within.

His untucked shirt hung around his waist, and the sleeves were rolled up his forearms. Beneath those clothes, he would be smooth and solid. And just as mesmerizing.

I evaded his gaze and scowled at the fire.

"Evening, my thorn." I felt him moving across the room with that customary feline grace. "I thought I would find you in this spot."

"Because you know me so well?" I said to the blaze.

Poet didn't take the bait. I peeked as he hunkered to the floor and lounged beside me, one knee propped up and his wrist hanging over the edge. "As well as you know me," he answered, then cocked his head. "Does that scare you?"

Never. Always.

Time and again, it proved impossible to hide from this man. What magic did he have, to expose me to this degree?

A set of brass bookends hovered under my nose. I glanced at the objects in Poet's hand. "Peace offering," he said. "It's not the missing book you've been looking for, but I do have excellent taste in scholastic decor."

I recalled how he'd watched me fussing with my shelves, trying to arrange the titles without them tipping over. The bookends would keep the volumes in place.

My resolve slipped a notch. With quiet gratitude, I accept the items and set them on my lap. The wind howled outside, and firelight pooled across the floor.

Poet murmured to my profile, "We can't do this apart, Briar."

My voice croaked. "Then you should have woken me."

"Or you should have trusted me."

I snapped my gaze to him. "I do."

But for some reason, his features constricted. "Is that right?" he inquired suavely. "In the library wing with Rhys, did you trust me when you ordered my tongue to retract?"

Indignation seared across my lips. "You were letting fury get in the way of your tact."

"Such a tricky balance, isn't it?" the jester intoned. "Just like when you were letting your pride get in the way of your logic."

I swerved fully his way, the bookends sliding off my thighs. "I didn't need rest. I needed to be there."

"You were," he bit back, his tone brimming as quickly as mine.

"Only because I woke myself up," I vented, my glower inches from his. "What would have happened if I'd snoozed through the whole thing?"

Poet's eyes narrowed. "Then you would have been refreshed, which would have done fabulous things to your cheeks. Especially to that strong-willed mouth—"

"Stop doing that!"

"Doing what?"

I slapped my palm on the ground. "After what happened at Peace Talks, haven't you compromised my role in meetings enough?"

"Ah," he hissed silkily. "So I've triggered you, is that it? Perhaps you should remember how you reacted the last time we locked horns in a conference, which didn't work in our favor."

"It was my right and my responsibility to be there today," I berated. "This is my kingdom, and this is my problem. Rhys dropped that ultimatum at *my* feet!"

Something altered in Poet's expression, darkening the planes of his face. We stared at each other while the flames threw heat our way. His eyes dropped like rocks to my mouth, which escalated my pulse and caused his pupils to swell.

I felt the intensity of his stare between my thighs. Anger and something equally molten collided inside me.

His next words diced like blades. "Don't you mean *our* feet?"

Remorse struck me between the ribs. He had flashed that same look in the library's council room, when I'd declared no one should fight my battles for me.

I had said my battles.

Mine. Not ours.

My lips parted to reply, to make amends. But Poet pushed off the carpet, whipped away, and stalked to the exit. Without looking back, he tore open the door and slammed it closed behind him.

17

Poet

Headstrong, relentless woman!

I strode from Briar's apartment and tracked past the guards hovering on either side of my suite. "Out," I growled, ramming my palm against the door.

As the partitions blew open, the sentinels didn't need to be told twice. My savage expression and livid command propelled them from the recess. Discretion was the standard in Autumn, to the point where raising your fucking voice was considered a misdemeanor. That much had been clear upon entering the feast last night.

In short, watching me throw a hissy fit violated their canon of behavior. And keeping vigil of a jester from the continent's most debauched Season wasn't the preferred assignment anyway. If I needed to fester in private, the guards would oblige with gratitude. Wisely, they scattered like mice and took up residence at the alcove's entry.

I prowled into my suite and threw the door shut behind me, the wood panels crashing into their frames. Verily, I paced the width of the room, my boots slicing back and forth across the rug.

Aye, this was Briar's kingdom. But nay, this wasn't just her problem.

On Lark's Night, right after I'd made her come for a third time in the wildflower forest, hadn't I argued with Briar about the problems we'd face if we stayed together? I predicted she would be consumed by her position, and I would be consumed by the loss of her, to the point where we'd grow apart.

Yet we swore not to let that happen. Her fights would be my fights. My demons would be hers.

We'll rule and love like warriors.

Briar's promise from that night lanced me in half. When it came to taking risks for her, I'd never been immune. Breaking my own rules, tearing down the walls, and verbally or physically impaling anyone who meant the princess harm had become a permanent reflex.

I'd believed her word and welcomed the gamble with open arms. Yet already, a chink appeared in the scaffolding. She'd laid claim to this shitshow with Rhys, declaring it her responsibility instead of a feud that belonged to us both.

Visions assaulted my head. Those steely eyes reflecting the flames. That determined mouth spewing righteousness at me. The proud resentment radiating off her like a humid gust—the wet heat of it.

A sweltering flux coursed through my veins. I halted in front of an upright mirror and wrapped my fist around its pillared frame. As usual regarding the princess, it took a while for my blood to cool, to reduce from boiling to simmering.

Only then did I scan the area with calm eyes. Naturally, I'd done a thorough appraisal of these quarters once Nicu was settled. My suite had been furnished in the same manner as the rest of this castle, like a well-crafted study or library.

Except I'd noticed some departures from the norm. The ornateness and height of the gold mirror above the fireplace, although paintings typically graced the mantels here. The bookshelf filled with verse and erotica. The deep green accents, like in my previous chambers.

Silk pillows that nonetheless complimented the thermal bedding. Stained glass embedded into an ornamental window, the hues throwing a kaleidoscope of colors across the walls.

The sheer size of my wardrobe. The number of cupboards, drawers, compartments, and racks carved into the cedar recesses. The vanity table housing my pigments and face paints, the alcove of upright mirrors that showed a person from all angles, and the small dresser drawers, each one suitable for hoarding pleasure trinkets.

Extra bedding was stored in a cabinet, the collection dyed in various shades of orange. This, in case Nicu crawled into bed with me.

Elements of Spring. Things I prioritized.

Pieces of me that she'd replicated. Just as she did for my son.

These intoxicating sights had followed me into her room last night, had fueled my blood whilst I fucked her on the balcony. Now the same visions produced a rift in my chest, a shredded sensation.

Although the bathroom in my suite connected to Nicu's chambers, entering from an unfamiliar passage would confuse him. Getting my son accustomed to the basics required time. Never mind the complications of living in a castle.

Until he got used to things, I took the longer way around. Exiting my suite, I strode down the corridor and found Aire leaning against the wall and exercising one of his swords with the casual prowess of a veteran warrior. The knight's wrists and arms rotated the weapon as if it was attached to his body. He moved lightly, effortlessly, and unpredictably, mimicking the wind itself. The sword synchronized with him, swooping like the fringed wing of a raptor.

To the inexperienced, it gave the impression of mindless swordplay. The way Aire spun that weapon made it seem easier than it was.

Hmm. I'd enjoy matching up against someone of my standards. I sensed a practice session in the near future, preferably with a large audience. And splendid timing, for I needed an excuse to wield a sharp object.

Worse, I hadn't trained in over a week. My muscles and reflexes currently despised me.

Aire noticed me coming, speared the weapon into the sheath at his hip, and straightened. "Master Jester."

I scoffed. "None of that. We talked about this, did we not? It's annoying and not nearly provocative enough."

After a moment's indecision, he nodded. "Sir ... er, Poet."

"That's more like it."

The man relaxed against the wall and regarded me with a wry lift of his brows. "I think you scared them."

To clarify, his eyes ticked over my shoulder to the alcove entrance, where the guards now stood after fleeing from my suite. Aye, hissing at them hadn't been the cleverest idea and not my finest hour. Definitely not if I wanted to lure this court.

I'd make up for my snafu with the guards later. In the meantime, I slanted my mouth. "'Tis an unfortunate side effect of crankiness." My attention darted nonchalantly to Aire's sword, then back to him. "I'd be more vigilant with a child like mine in your midst. Swing your steel this near to where Nicu could leap outside at any moment, and you'll be in for a harsher surprise."

And my knife will find its way into your esophagus, whether or not I like you.

Aire frowned, his face pinching like a dart. "It's not the sword that truly ails you."

How in the wicked hell?

Never mind. This gruff bastard registered too much for his own good.

I cocked my head, impressed but a little unnerved whether I'd lost the knack for duplicity. "Am I that transparent?"

The knight stared back. "No."

Again with the cryptic shit. If I could entrust him with Nicu, but he couldn't spill to me or Briar about whatever unique ability he possessed, it had to be something vital.

That aside, Aire patrolled this area with the same dedication of a warrior invested in combat. When in truth, any other knight would consider this assignment a downgrade—to watch over a child everybody viewed as unnatural.

If this went through the knight's consciousness, I detected no sign of it. Surly but honest came to mind. This man didn't smooch anyone's ass, and he didn't justify himself. My approval of him doubled.

I nudged my head toward Nicu's door. "I'll take it from here."

Aire stepped around me, but my next words stalled him. "Thank you again. I know this isn't what you're used to."

That was putting it mildly. Nonetheless, the knight grunted. "There's no need, Sir. It's an honor. I am fond of Nicu, and he's a member of the Royal family."

My brows slammed together. "Who told you that?"

His expression didn't change, but a staunch light banked in his irises. "She did."

Nicu hurtled himself into my arms as I squatted just inside his antechamber. "Papa!" he squealed, as if days rather than hours had passed since we last saw each other.

"What have we here?" I fake-gasped, squeezing him against me. "A fae enchanter?"

My son giggled and tangled his fingers around my nape. "Briar Patch was here. She read storybooks with me and brushed Tumble's fur, but then she left to wear a crown. But she told me she's coming back."

Of course, she did. That promise, my thorn would never rescind, no matter what stewed between us.

I spent the following hour juggling acorns for my son's delight; wrestling with Tumble, who squeaked and bounded across my chest; playing a shadow puppet game with Nicu, using our fingers to form animal shapes against the walls—in which my sneaky fox hunted his graceful doe; and listening to his enthusiastic chatter as he invented folktales about the stars, the celestials being his latest preoccupation.

But at one point, Nicu's attention diverged from the constellations. Tumble hopped off my son's lap as he dashed across the room, grabbed a tiny wheat stalk from his nightstand, and twirled the stem in his fingers. The young reed must have been strategically placed there, in order for him to identify and remember what it was. A token meant to remain close to him whilst he slept, like the scarlet ribbon hugging his wrist.

I hunkered beside him. "Where did you get that?"

"Briar Patch gave it to me," he answered, tracing his finger over the kernels. "She wants to show me the wheat fields."

"Does she now?" I drew out.

He nodded and altered his voice to sound like the princess, the better to quote her. *"The stalks will tower over us like the giant field keepers of old. And if we look closely, we'll see their shapes in the stems, kernels, and leaves."*

I wanted them to spend time together. I wanted Nicu outdoors, like he was free to do at Jinny's cottage.

This whole time, he'd been glancing regularly out the window, his longing evident, the sight gnawing at my gut. Incidentally, it had been safer for him to roam through Spring's forest whilst hiding from the Crown than it would be under the protection of Autumn's monarchy.

But hadn't Briar said The Wandering Fields could trap a person if they didn't know the way? Hadn't she claimed its vastness protected the castle from intruders but also served as a form of execution?

My son lacked the ability to orient himself. In a fit of enthusiasm, he could scamper through the rows and stray, if Briar and I weren't careful. He'd be unable to find a successful route, unable to comprehend how he ended up meandering in the first place. Likely, Nicu wouldn't even guess he was lost until long after he attempted to leave.

With Rhys's spies lurking who the fuck knew where, touring any landmark could expose my son. He'd be an open target. Although the princess and I had become the king's primary agenda, I couldn't take risks.

Briar would rationalize as much. Yet she'd made this promise to my son. And being someone who remembered things verbatim, Nicu would enshrine this promise. He would hold her to it.

So I couldn't be present for a roundtable without her, yet it was fine to make plans involving my son without talking to me. Oh, I'd be having words with the princess about that.

"I've got a hush," Nicu whispered.

"Is that so?" I inquired. "A secret, hmm? Do tell."

"She said I'll be protected in the fields, so long as I stay close to you and her. She said I'll never be alone if you're both near."

Fuck. Something inside me caved in. Of all the things that woman had ever said, this proved the most accurate. The princess would guard him with her life.

"And what must you do to guard yourself?" I quizzed.

We'd gone over this many times, so Nicu repeated, "Be brave but smart, and know the difference."

My lips tilted. "That's my fearless, gorgeous successor."

"Huzzah! I'm gorgeous!"

"And why is that?"

"Because I'm Papa's fae."

I wheeled my fingers for more. "And?"

"Because I'm Nicu." My son thought about that, then he nodded and tangled his arms around my neck. "I like being me."

My forehead planted against his. "I like that too, my darling."

18

Poet

The hours bled into days. The days merged into a tug-of-war. The longer time passed, the more intense our discord became. Unspoken words clogged the air. And other, less inviting comments ransacked whatever space we occupied.

"I disagree," Briar stated, her tone cordial.

I lounged in my seat, toyed with my chalice, and responded with non-committal sarcasm. "Which part?" I crooned. "The part where I said Spring would react more favorably to an invitation if it were delivered less formally? Or the part where I reminded you that I know Basil and Fatima well enough to be right about this?"

The princess returned my stare, her gray eyes flinty. Along the table, the council members' heads swatted between us like paddleballs. Half of them concealed frowns of disapproval—because how dare we smolder this hotly during a formal conference—and the other half blustered because we'd left them out of the debate.

Frankly, they hadn't been able to keep up with us. The pace of our argument had left every occupant in the dust.

We'd been discussing our plans to welcome Spring for Reaper's Fest. Although we hadn't informed this committee about Rhys's vendetta, the annual bonfire ball was a safe topic. Moreover, it gave the advisors a solid reason to approve of my participation. If I was going to attend these conferences from now on, best to start with something I had clout and supremacy over. That would set a precedent and thaw their apprehension.

The Royals of Autumn might know the Royals of Spring to a political degree. But the Court Jester knew Basil and Fatima to an intimate one. Plus, not only had I held sway over the monarchy, but I'd dominated their revels. I knew my Season's penchant for entertainment, and I knew what forms those galas took. If Autumn intended to regale Spring in the matter to which it was accustomed, my advice was paramount.

This much, Briar and I had rationalized. However, the meeting had plummeted from there.

"We don't want to appear desperate," Briar argued, an olive satin gown cinching her form and cupping her breasts.

My eyes snapped from the swells to her face, which stained a fetching pink color. The shift in her complexion could be the result of exasperation or more enthralling possibilities. "Desperate? I think it's a bit late for that," I drawled. "Besides, where's the folly in a little desperation? It has a magnificent impact on one's complexion."

Like an itch I couldn't stop scratching, Briar's combative flush deepened. The hue intensified to red, as pigmented at her hair, which she'd trussed up in a primly netted headdress ornamented in beads. She choked the quill in her grip, the tip dribbling ink without her realizing it. "Sending a parchment of epic verse depicting Reaper's Fest is not the Autumn way. They'll see right through it."

"Even better," I replied. "They like excess, and they'll enjoy making us grovel."

"It's dramatic."

"It's Spring."

Those fucking netted beads would scatter from her hair if my hands got to them. That quill would pour more ink and stain our clothes if I propped her ass atop the surface.

By Seasons. I shifted in my seat.

Back to the subject at hand, dammit. Briar was lucky I hadn't suggested employing a courier to do a striptease as part of the invitation. Not that any Season—including Spring—went that far to get each other's attention. But it would have been amusing to see the council's reaction. I'd have tested that limit if a certain Royal wasn't mentally flogging me from scalp to sac.

Our voices remained level, yet every word lashed across the room as Briar and I sat opposite each other. What's more, I knew that particular shade dousing her clavicles as they rose and fell like overworked pumps. Under the skirt, frustration had caused slick heat to nestle in the tight hairs between her thighs.

Almighty hell. My tongue watered as if this were some perverse, antagonistic foreplay.

At the table's head, Avalea's brows crimped. Her eyes ticked between us, not unlike the advisors who squirmed uncomfortably.

"A tidy missive isn't going to impress my former sovereigns," I told Briar. "Nor would it entice a hermit, much less a pair of monarchs who like their parties showered in glitter and booze. Their Majesties will want us to spoil them."

"I suppose you would know about being spoiled," the princess bit back.

Oh, Sweet Thorn. Watch your fucking mouth.

My lips twisted. "That's the perk of earning what you receive."

Briar's nostrils flared. "Are you implying that Royals don't earn their positions?"

"Is that what I said?" I deflected, juggling her words like daggers, like props to play with.

But aye. I'd implied as much. Majority of the titled were born into their power. Everyone else had to work for it a little harder.

Nevertheless, that I believed Briar had earned her crown in spades wasn't a point I should need to make. Yet her expression begged to differ.

Someone coughed. Someone else muttered to the queen, "Your Majesty, I must insist..."

"I propose a traditional invitation," Briar appealed to the table, rivalry frosting her voice. "A simple, dignified solicitation. That would show we haven't changed and we're not a flighty nation."

She couldn't be serious. My princess was too smart for this bullshit.

"It would also show you have no concept or regard for the vagaries of Spring," I said. "And I haven't even gotten to the ironic part."

"There is nothing ironic about my recommendation."

"Oh, my mistake. I thought we were talking about a revel where people donned masquerade costumes, ignite bonfires, and ditched propriety for one night. You're hosting a spree, not a tea party." I raised an eyebrow. "Do you want them to show up or not?"

Briar bristled in her seat. "I'll assume that question is rhetorical."

"You're free to assume many things. I can't promise the outcome will be what you expect."

"Because I'm not as fluent in Seasonal allegiances as you?"

I shall amend. Watch your fucking mouth—or I'll watch it for you.

My elbow crooked, and my forearm bent as I leaned across the table. "Because unlike you, I'd rather utter promises I can keep."

Briar flinched. Avalea swiveled her withering gaze from her daughter to her daughter's lover.

"With all due respect, Your Highness," one of the women interjected. "The proper method of handling Spring might be more suited to someone who wasn't banished from their borders."

Now the stricken princess blanched. For all their discretion, Autumn was remarkably straightforward when it came to the truth. The wounded shimmer in Briar's pupils resurrected a brutal part of me.

I diced my head toward the advisor, my tongue ready to flay her.

Simultaneously, Briar recovered and pelted the female with an imperial expression.

The queen did the same until the councilor begged Briar's pardon, then Avalea drummed her manicured nails on the table. "We'll pick this up tomorrow."

The discussion shifted, briefly tackling a growing disagreement between a small number of trade workers and a guild called the Masters. I vaguely recalled the subject from when we arrived, in addition to Rhys's passing comment in the library wing. But before the roundtable could get into it, the advisors insisted we return to the subject at a future date, when the council had more testimonials to present.

The meeting carried on, the debates consisting of environmental concerns and library maintenance. Not knowing a bloody thing about the difference between barley and flax, much less how to inventory book collections, I reclined and observed.

I'd used this tactic back when Spring first appointed me as its Court Jester, and the method provided several benefits. One, the chance to study the advisors' idiosyncrasies and scrutinize them for hints of subterfuge. Two, the opportunity to grasp the scope of Autumn, for when I finally got to flaunting my tongue in earnest. Three, the bonus of riveting my gaze on Briar whilst undisturbed.

At last, the princess regained her footing. She contributed to the conversation with ingenuity, her knowledge of the land so vast it won nods of appreciation from the committee members. The woman radiated authority yet absorbed everyone's viewpoint like a sponge—like a Royal who cared and saw them as equals.

Pride clashed with irritation as I watched her. In the crawl spaces between these moments, Briar made a concerted effort to forget I was there.

Oh, but we'd perfected this dance in the past. Thereupon, I made it impossible. Whilst she scribbled notes, I fastened my gaze to the princess, making sure my attention melted through her skin.

Only when the fine hairs of her nape rose did I look away, satisfied.

That night, I took her expression to bed. Sweat licked across my chest, and need raked down my skin as I gripped my aching cock. My hips flexed, lunging upward into my hand with rampant speed.

Her face, her voice, her words. They swam through my head like hallucinations, toughening the length of my erection. I tugged on the flesh, pulling in cadence to each retort that had punched from her obstinate mouth.

Those words belonged to me. As did she.

My cock shuddered. With a growl, I spasmed into my palm, her name splintering off my tongue.

A pear orchard occupied the northern end of the castle. At sundown, the fruits glowed with the same phosphorescence as the apples had in The Shadow Orchard. The orbs radiated like lanterns, illuminating the rows in pale green light, enough for me to observe the princess harvesting after dark.

Briar's brisk footfalls clamored in my ears. She had paired a smock bodice dress with a belt, and her hair fell freely but for a single braided lock that dangled like a cord. The woman had discarded her shoes and elected to prance around barefoot, her unshod toes peeking from the hem.

The effortless princess couldn't have looked more bohemian if she tried. As she passed one of the trees and munched on a pear, my arm shot out from behind the trunk. I hooked around the princess's middle, looped her against me, and yanked her into the thicket.

Briar yipped. The basket tucked over her arm struck the grass. Pears avalanched, along with the one her lips had been nibbling.

I spun us around. The princess's back thumped against the tree, where I crowded her in, my arm bracketing overhead. "Not so fast, sweeting."

Recognizing me, her eyes tapered. "What's the meaning of this?"

My attention flitted to the half-eaten pear on the ground, where the shapes of her teeth had burrowed into the flesh. I'd meant to say something different, but a tantalizing alternative came out instead. "Did that hit the spot?" I cooed darkly. "Or should I?"

Briar's pupils inflated, even whilst they sparkled with resentment. My senses ignited, spurred by the signs. A confidential sheen flickered in those orbs, revealing itself like a confession.

She moved to storm past me. I shifted, fluidly blocking her path. "Wait a minute."

Blatantly, I studied her glower and listened to the righteous huff blast from her lips. Yet I saw it on the princess's face. I hadn't been the only one fantasizing behind closed doors.

I dipped my head and rasped, "How was it?"

She knew that I knew, because her body trembled. Just like it must have last night, whilst she'd nestled several fingers between her thighs, teased her sweet damp pussy, and made herself come.

Even so, Briar dissected my smirk like a piece of evidence. "You tell me."

Bravo. Rapt minds thought alike.

Also, this: Whatever visions had consumed her fantasy, and however deeply she'd fucked herself, her flush told me enough. For indeed, it had been very good.

When I made no reply, she reverted to the original question and spoke through her embarrassment. "I said, what's the meaning of—"

"Allow me this," I interrupted, remembering myself. "The next time you make plans with my son, do his father the courtesy of letting him know beforehand."

Understanding dawned across her features. "He wants to see The Wandering Fields, and I want to show them to him."

"However much I love hearing that you're eager to introduce him to this world, it doesn't change the fact that when it comes to Nicu, educate me on your intentions first."

"You cannot keep him cooped up."

"You think I would do that?" I grated, insulted. "Nay, I would have him race through your fields without a care. I would have him turn this whole fucking castle into his playground. But I will also keep him safe. And until I've scouted every inch of the castle's perimeter, you will remember that. Especially when it comes to a place where people can get lost until they die of the elements, providing they don't dehydrate or lose their fucking minds first."

She blanched. "How dare you! I would never take him somewhere perilous. I told you, it's only dangerous if someone doesn't know the way. Well, I *do* know the way."

"I heard what you said," I answered with a silken snarl. "Believe me, I hear everything you say."

"I was planning to restrict our excursion to one row. Just one, which has a dead-end and will be monitored by escorts. There's no place for him to stray, and he'll love it all the same."

"Regardless. He goes nowhere I'm unfamiliar with. Understand?"

"No," she snapped. "No, I do not understand. I would not bring him anywhere that wasn't safe. Why are you suddenly doubting me?"

"Wake up, Princess. I trust your judgment like I trust my own, but this isn't about you. Nicu is my responsibility. I'm his father."

"And I'm his—" But Briar swallowed what she'd been about to say. Her eyes glistened, the sight fracturing a place in my ribs.

I know what she'd been about to fucking say. Moreover, my tongue burned to taste that word in her goddamn mouth. How I wanted to hear it aloud, then to brand it on her with my canines.

I could hitch her legs over my waist. I could pin her against this trunk, tack her wrists above her head, and make her shriek in tempo to my hips.

In turn, she could destroy me.

Then again, too late.

Her pupils expanded on me, like she knew what sort of thoughts rented space in my head. That sharp tongue poked out to trace her lower lip.

Our chests beat together. A force of energy crackled between us like static. My mouth hovered inches from hers, our puffs of air slamming together.

The unspoken word still lingered on the princess's tongue. Condemnation, I wanted to crush her against me and consume it, to draw it from her like a prolonged, overdue moan.

Hiking up her chin, Briar glared. "Don't you mean he's *our* responsibility?"

A jagged breath rushed from my lungs. The retort hit me like a slap in the face, all but calling me a hypocrite. Her voice possessed the same tone I'd used on Briar before striding from her room.

Don't you mean our *feet?*

Briar shouldered past me. And like a bloody fool, I let her go.

The next morning, we stepped into a nightmare.

The dungeon loomed ahead like a tunnel, with exposed roots threading along the crusted walls and chambers cramming both sides of the cavity. Briar and I walked down the conduit in silence. Her mother followed, with several guards trailing us.

Spring kept born souls in dank, filthy, subterranean cells or oubliettes—a horror hidden under layers of marble. Summer shackled its people in caves scattered along humid, mosquito-and-reptile-infested shorelines; though lately, the shithead called Rhys had been considering erecting a tower. As for Winter, it rarely kept the prisoners locked up, since they were routinely used for hunting bait and medical experiments.

For the most part, Autumn kept born souls in cleaner environments than this dungeon. They lived—or rather, languished—in sheds cloistered away on the castle outskirts. But historically, the mad were a different quandary, restricted to this void unless deemed stable.

And although this nation provided its prisoners with the essentials such as latrines and actual mattresses, the place reeked of piss ponds and mildew. Rhys's selection of souls ranted to themselves, picked at their gums, or reclined in their cots and sang about temperamental oceans, their briny inflections akin to cracked seashells.

I hovered near Briar whenever she got too close to the bars. One of the men jumped from a pocket of shadow, and I swerved in front of the princess, though my knife never came out. The inmate was harmless, merely baring his fangs and laughing.

Pity and rage pried my mouth apart. I grinned, playing along and delighting the man. That I couldn't do more for these people crimped my gut.

I heard Briar swallow her grief. I listened as Avalea murmured to the wardens.

The princess and I knelt before separate cubicles. As I passed an apple and a hunk of bread to one of the captives from beneath my coat, I glimpsed Briar's hand, which offered biscuits and a vial of milk to a young woman. Our gazes collided, the heiress's orbs watery and my throat scraped raw.

We fucking hated this.

But the princess and her jester had already been labeled as sympathizers. For anything more, timing was crucial. Ordering humane care needed to come at the right moment, under the right circumstances.

Until then, we dealt with it in slices. We gave what we could whilst Avalea's presence distracted the guards.

We breakfasted with Nicu and Tumble afterward. Then Briar joined the harvest, tucked herself into the library wing, and convened with her mother by early afternoon. At some point, she must have entered my suite when I wasn't there, because I found a classified blueprint of the castle on my mattress.

I exercised my acrobatic muscles on the training yard, soaked up the midday hours with my son, and made use of the blueprint by prowling through the castle through dusk. I did this until I knew the halls, mezzanines, stairways, wings, courtyards, and hidden passages as I'd known the arteries of Spring's palace. Autumn's castle bore a less grandiose size and more structured layout. Therefore, it didn't take long.

This way, I kept to the shadows, the better to overhear conversations whispered about Briar, her sinister jester, and "their simpleton."

Fortunately for these people, my fists and tongue behaved. I couldn't identify Rhys's spies if I managed to snap their necks first.

That same night, I rejoined Briar in Nicu's room, to read him a bedtime story. From there, my thorn and I parted ways.

I didn't slip into her chambers. Nor did she ask me to.

Our little spectacle in the library's council room was nothing compared to the next meeting in Avalea's antechamber. The queen tried and failed to buffer the tension as the princess and I tackled every detail regarding born souls.

From introducing novel approaches for emancipation and humane treatment, to massaging the court's prejudice into a new shape, to which sources we used to accomplish this, we buried ourselves in the topic.

Briar excelled in the research, volunteering to scan texts on Autumn's history—its origins, decrees, ordinances, fundamentals, and any passages that bore technical or ethical loopholes. Since born souls were considered so-called abominations of nature, she planned to study doctrines, journals, textbooks, legends, folktales, and true accounts of the landscape's magic.

Lastly, Briar would balance her findings with medical volumes, especially the ones scribed by Winter's doctors and academics. Whilst that frigid Season valued books for science and scholarship, Autumn valued reading for introspection and reflection. Both could work on our behalf.

I would test the emotional nature of Autumn through creative means. My verse could offer various perspectives, providing it struck a deeper chord with the court. Reciting tales would do the same, since people tended to insert themselves into the characters' experiences.

Bawdy stories worked in Spring. In Autumn, sensitive and angsty ones might have the same impact.

If my narrative tongue failed—miracles did happen—my grin and wit would have remarkable effects. I'd seen that take root already, however much the residents denied it. Call me vain, but the princess wasn't the only overachiever in this castle. If I probed the nobles and advisors with an irresistible crook of my lips or a sultry tone of voice, could anyone hold it against me?

Charm and attraction tended to have potent influences. No matter where a person came from, laughter and longing were universal. So once I found outlets, I would nestle thoughts about born souls into the courtiers' minds, prompting them to consider my words long after.

Introducing Nicu wasn't an option. Using him like that was a deal-breaker. But if they naturally got accustomed to his presence at meals and during outings, the courtiers might unwind enough for their perspectives to change. They might catch glimpses of his sweetness, his winsome spirit, and his brilliant way of viewing the world. They might stop cringing when they looked at him, and they might stop tensing whenever he flung himself in their direction.

Likewise, the novelty of these people would wear off for Nicu. When that happened, he wouldn't leap at them for hugs. Mayhap then, they might relax around him, and they'd have the breathing space to ponder his personality from a different angle.

It could take years. But if my son couldn't woo Autumn, the rest of this continent would be impossible.

Though none of this would be doable before we identified Rhys's informants. Until then, the amount of time Nicu spent in everyone's company had to be limited.

Briar and I talked with her mother about future regulations and integration. We exchanged thoughts about caring for those in need of assistance, how to finance that care, and where it could take place.

We mulled over the dangers, predicted the public's response, and brainstormed solutions.

It wasn't that Briar and I disagreed on any of this. Nay, our connection there proved stronger than ever. We bounced ideas and theories off one another as if we'd been doing it our whole lives. If there was one subject we didn't clash over, it was this one.

The problem was, the princess spoke in a waspish tone. In kind, I replied with a monotone timbre. We might as well be conducting a business trade, if not challenging each other to a verbal joust.

As for how to deal with Rhys and his spies, that's when our voices tightened, our eyes slitted, and our patience thinned. We had to play by the rules whilst beating him at this game. Alas, we bickered in circles about strategies, to the point where I couldn't figure out how this shit had gotten out of hand. With each lap, we fueled the flames.

Despite the tension, we finally found a way around it. Briar and I mingled with the court during feasts. From across the hall, she cast me cursory glances, and I pinned her with lingering stares.

Without speaking, we fell into a routine, necessity eclipsing the animosity. We worked the room cleverly, tactfully, patiently. Gatherings became battlegrounds in which we navigated each courtier as if they were a landmine.

After circulating separately, we reunited to further pursue the masses. I would offer a sly compliment, my own brand of sophisticated wit, whereas Briar took her cues like the ruler she was. She jumped in at the perfect times, adding to my comments with gentility and intelligence. I captivated, and she informed. I teased in a way Autumn slowly responded to, and she rebuilt her steadfast image by sharing everyone's devotion to the harvest and their pride for craftsmanship.

In the midst of that, we analyzed each person, searching for clues—missteps that would identify Rhys's spies. On that score, the second anyone so much as looked at Briar the wrong way, my hackles rose.

A steady stream of growls rustled up my throat, and I pictured the daggers hidden under my coat. I lost count of how many innocent bystanders nearly lost their limbs, how many times I nonchalantly stepped in front of Briar like a barricade, and how often my body felt anything but nonchalant about it.

All the whilst, we continued using the hand signals we'd taught one another. That, and our fingers inevitably succumbed to the lure of physical contact. The forced proximity couldn't be helped, yet the gestures proved natural, intrinsic, fated. Briar would put on a well-mannered ruse and smooth out my sleeve. I would ooze my digits from her nape to her tailbone, inciting shivers down the heiress's back.

At one point, I slipped my arm around Briar's middle, tucked her against my side, and murmured, "Closer, sweeting. We're supposed to look like we're madly in love, remember?"

Her gaze slipped toward me, that expression driving me crazy. Whatever she saw staring back, it must reflect the same thing. Our trance crystalized to the point where it took virtually a full minute for us to peel ourselves away.

From how Briar glowed, one would think my cock had been giving her a healthy dose of orgasms each night. From the way I hovered near the princess with the possessive stance of a bodyguard, one would think she'd been reciprocating that pleasure.

One would think everything was fine. One would think we'd overcome whatever the hell was boiling between us.

One would be very fucking wrong.

Nicu skipped between Briar and me. His elated chatter was addictive as the princess gave him a promised tour of The Wandering Fields. Now that I understood the castle's layout, I could monitor each area as if I possessed twenty pairs of eyes. And knowing Nicu would be able to enjoy himself, to run and play outside, elation filled me to the brim.

My son's profile alighted on every plant stem we passed. Briar's own excitement amplified as she told him stories about the fields' lore and the giants who used to nurture this area centuries ago. She pointed out stalks whose outlines resembled those ancient keepers—if you looked closely enough and from certain angles—and she answered Nicu's rapid-fire questions. No matter how wayward the inquiry, she understood him.

Nicu held our hands as we walked. At one point, the sly little fae detached himself but wove my fingers with Briar's, as if commanding us to stay linked whilst he scampered away. Dashing ahead of us, he cawed gaily, intimidating a hawk sailing through the clouds.

Briar and I stopped, watching my son instead of each other. With a dead-end looming ahead, plus the princess's knowledge of the fields' geography, there was no place for Nicu to wander without us losing sight of him.

So. I may have been overreacting before.

My palm burned against Briar's, a flux of heat scorching my fingers. Her own digits trembled, but she didn't let go.

Fuck. She didn't let me go.

The princess and I swerved at the same time. We stared, the force of it rushing from my pulse to my cock—drastic, abrupt, undeniable.

Then Nicu chirped, "Papa! Briar Patch!"

It broke the spell. Briar blinked and offered my son a flustered smile. Some impulse gave way, and she darted after him. They sprinted through the stalks, the early sunset splashing gold over them.

I stood there, rapt by Nicu's clover irises and Briar's fiery hair. Clad in an embroidered blouse loosely tucked into a skirt, she kicked off her ankle boots and dashed barefooted with him. Her stubborn, perfect mouth parted, and her laughter merged with Nicu's melodic chuckles.

She hunkered beside him and illustrated how to harvest a batch of stalks. A priceless chain glinted along her forehead, the central pendant winking, yet the princess's fingers grew caked with dirt, sweat bridged over her throat, and muck stained her toes. The vision rammed its fist into my chest, the impact upsetting my balance.

She looked as she had back in Jinny's cottage.

Beautiful. Painful.

'Tis the lovely cruel you are.

Briar caught me staring. Pushing a tendril of red from her face, she halted, and her breathless voice stiffened. "What?" she asked defensively.

My gaze must look ferocious. Yet it was for an entirely different reason.

I wanted to eat her alive. I wanted to crush my mouth against every part of her body and stroke my tongue through the folds of her pussy until the climax pooled down my throat. I wanted to punish this thorny princess for every clipped word she'd spoken since the night I strode from her suite.

I wanted to ruin her thoroughly.

19

Poet

Aire's broadswords flew at me like a set of wings. As they sliced through the air, I pivoted from the tips and revolved behind him.

The First Knight swooped around to face me, shock breaking through his concentrated features. I hadn't been in the mood to practice aerial moves. Back handsprings wouldn't tamp down the heat percolating in me lately. However, combat would.

For a start, I'd opted to fight Aire weaponless—my speed against his set of blades. To say the least, the ethical bastard had objected at first, then finally obeyed my request for him not to hold back.

Aire windmilled his swords in rapid succession, the steel blades catching the afternoon light. I swept around his weapons. Sweat darkened the fabric of his sleeveless shirt, which hung unfastened and offered passersby healthy glimpses of his anatomy, all without revealing the whole picture. By contrast, my bare chest glistened openly for viewers.

Courtiers paused in the distance to watch. Numerous pairs of eyes sketched my torso, my physique and skills having always been a heady combination. Many onlookers paid Aire equal attention—mostly females in his case, since the knight preferred women exclusively. From under their lashes, they took stock of the man's rippling abs and biceps.

Over time, our audience grew. The troop who'd traveled with us from Spring ventured onto the lawn, emerging from their dormitories and crowding the surrounding fence. Not long after, they began to cheer, holler, and clap—and not just for their comrade. During a few incidents in which I swerved or flipped out of Aire's path, the men and women beat their fists onto the posts, chanting for me.

Summer would have taken bets.

Winter would have placidly observed.

Spring wouldn't have given a shit who won, so long as the opponents stripped for the occasion.

As for Autumn, it encouraged the battle. But out of sportsmanship, it didn't choose sides.

Ah. I did fancy a spectacle. Indeed, I'd been hankering for one, having been long deprived of a decent *and* consistent bevy of onlookers.

To a chorus of shouts, the knight and I crossed from one end of the training yard to the other. For a brawny male, Aire moved like a gale, swift and seamless, as if the weapons weighed nothing. That made it clear why he outranked every warrior in residence. But whilst he proved himself a worthy opponent, I proved myself a difficult target.

Still, eluding him got old quickly. I grew bored with the monotony and whisked a dagger from my hip sheath. Shearing around the knight, I flicked the blade at one of his swords and knocked the hilt off balance, which distorted his movements.

Aire stopped as gracefully as a raptor landing on its perch. "Impressive," he puffed.

"Genetic," I boasted.

The barest trace of humor slanted the man's mouth. But before the rare mirth could travel to the rest of his face, Aire's expression faltered at something behind me. Suddenly, the clamor faded. Quiet stunted the revelry like a red flag—or like an invitation.

My spine tingled. I knew this sensation like I knew my own pulse, which thumped in a staccato rhythm.

I felt that imperial stare before I turned and locked eyes with her.

Briar stood on the fringes. Her expression was composed, her irises polished like sterling. She'd leashed that flaming hair in what seemed like a complicated weave, with a quill-shaped pin stabbing through the plaits. I wasn't standing behind her to confirm this, but I caught glimpses and discerned the rest.

She wore a pair of fitted hose and high boots. Above the pants, a fetching vest of walnut damask nipped her in all the right places and hung to mid-thigh. Rolled edges along the vest's arm slits complimented her shoulders.

Everything fixed in place. Everything concealed, like a proper Royal.

Oh, but I saw more. Like a superpower, I penetrated deeper, harder beneath the surface.

A tinge of scarlet snuck across her collarbone and plunged into the neckline of her vest. Under the fabric, her nipples pebbled. 'Twas indiscernible to the inexperienced eye, yet I was too familiar with the shapes of those little shells for it to escape me.

I saw the divot between her brows. I saw the bob in her throat. I saw those irises flare as if someone had lit a match to them.

And I saw that stubborn chin crinkle.

Need I remind her, I wore a mask professionally. I understood the trick of it. Thusly, I saw the mutiny occurring behind her veneer.

At the nexus of those pants, a steady throb brimmed inside her cunt. I could practically feel that sweet root thudding, and the knowledge pumped blood to my cock. Blessedly, I was able to control the effect.

Briar's gaze tripped down my body, sketching the muscles of my abdomen. Sweat trickled over my skin, a droplet sliding to my navel and sinking into the trim line of hair that vanished under my waistband. My chest inflated, heavy breaths siphoning through me and causing my attributes to flex.

The princess took great pains to shield her reaction. A few traitorous cracks broke through, yet my thorn refused to give in, working tirelessly to tack her features in place. Just like the well-bred heiress she pretended to be.

Except I'd once cleaved through those walls. Every erect part of me had breached that barrier and exposed the fervid woman underneath.

Saintly but willing to spurn the rules.

Chaste but oh, how loudly she moaned.

Dutiful, but as fierce and tenacious as a temptress.

Everyone bowed in her presence. But I did no such thing.

Instead, I binged on that look and called her bluff. "Princess."

"Court Jester," she said, then folded her hands in front of her, the knuckles so strained they whitened. "Mother would like a word with us before dinner."

Excellent. That gave us an hour to deal with our shit.

More to the point, it gave me an hour to dabble.

Although the queen could have sent a messenger, Briar had chosen to find me herself. She liked taking matters into her own hands.

As did I. "By all means, Highness. Come and join the party."

Her forehead crimped. "Excuse me?"

Naturally. I had overstepped by making a bold request in front of the troop and the distant onlookers. Yet they didn't know half of what I'd already done to this woman. In any event, that wasn't why Briar floundered.

The world needed to get used to our bond. Briar was my princess. But she was also my equal, and if we wanted them to see a matched pair, we had to act like one.

She knew this. She just didn't know what I intended for her on this field.

To trust me or not? Had that changed because of one fight? After all we'd been through?

Nay. Not us.

Not my resilient lady.

Pissed off though she might be, Briar made her choice and stepped through the gate held open by one of the knights.

Pissed off though I might be, heat and rapture spread through my veins.

I glanced at Aire, who hovered with an uncertain expression. My daggers had no place in this tourney, so I nicked my jaw toward the steel staff leaning against the fence. "Would you mind?"

The knight wavered, then harnessed his broadswords, paced to the rod, and tossed it to me. I caught the lance in one hand and proceeded to spin it like a baton. My fingers whipped the object into motion whilst I sauntered backward and sealed my gaze with hers. "I do believe you have time for a little training session."

Briar's eyebrows slammed together. "I beg your pardon?"

My princess never begged. Also, she'd heard me clearly.

Back when we rescued my son from a dungeon, I swore to teach this princess how to wield a weapon. We hadn't had the opportunity during that odyssey from Spring, and life had been a maelstrom ever since. But now, we had no excuse. With Rhys's chickenshit spies running amuck like a bunch of invisible extremists, this moment was severely overdue.

I would fling myself in front of an army to protect Briar. But something might happen to me. In which case, she would have to defend herself, keep herself safe, and keep Nicu out of harm's way. Besides, we desperately needed an outlet to release the pent-up emotions of the past week.

A cocky grin wrung across my mouth as I spun the staff. "You're dressed so appropriately. 'Tis a shame to let a good pair of clingy pants go to waste."

As everyone grew silent, I sensed Briar's awareness of our audience. I had put her on the spot, but so be it. This wasn't new for a Royal, and if she wanted to preserve the troop's admiration, she had to perform for them in a way that blurred the lines of rank. We had to remind them we weren't merely a jester and a princess but also fighters.

Comprehension slid across her face. Ever the logical female, she nodded.

Her acceptance worked on me like a stimulant. Axes, archery, halberds, hammers, sickles, saw blades, or swords wouldn't suit her. Neither would daggers. Briar knew her spirit weapon the moment one of the soldiers offered her a choice from the collection propped near the fence.

She pointed to a belt loaded with short, thin, twiglike projectiles that resembled double-edged thorns or ink quill tips. Like most objects in the soldiers' arsenal, the tiny weapons must be native to Autumn.

My grin broadened as I recalled skipping stones with Briar near Jinny's cottage and how the princess hurled that rock at a guard's skull when we rescued Nicu. She was an expert horsewoman as well as a fearless shot, her aim remarkable for a novice.

An introduction to harsher, harder training that included hand-to-hand combat would commence later, as time went by. For now, the princess had to test her reflexes, amp up her heart rate, and learn how to anchor her muscles, how to maintain balance and speed, and how to exercise all those things concurrently. But to glean what kind of instruction would fit, assessing her strengths and weaknesses was imperative.

Aire retreated to the outskirts with his clan. The crowd murmured and leaned into the fence.

One of the knights handed Briar the belt. She buckled it around her waist without needing instruction, as if … as if she'd done this before.

My staff halted mid-rotation. Throwing stars crafted and gifted by Winter had played a role in some of my earliest juggling acts. If I had to guess, the miniature thorn quills worked the same way.

Mmm. This would be fun. And infuriating.

With my free hand, I demonstrated how to hold and release one. "Like—"

"—this?" Briar inquired, snatching a thorn quill and flicking her arm.

The object whirled across the yard like an asterisk, sliced over my head, and stabbed one of the fence posts. I narrowed my eyes at the object, then swerved toward the princess. So much for assuming I'd need to teach her about stance, aim, and safety first. The proud flash in her pupils told me not to waste my time.

Well, well. She'd been keeping this a secret, had she?

I quirked a brow. "Now let's see if you can strike a moving target."

Her features pinched. "From this range, I think I can hit something important."

Snickers rippled through the troop.

My lips tilted as I wheeled the staff between my fingers. Briar and I circled the perimeter, stalking around one another like a pair of territorial leopards.

She hurled the next thorn quill in my direction, but my staff blocked the attempt, blasting it off course. From the belt, the princess retrieved another weapon. She flung it without pause, the object slipping through my whirling staff.

Briar tried again, this time whilst squatting and aiming for my limbs. I pivoted, twisted the rod behind me, and executed a backhanded block.

Frustration bunched across that regal facade. Her features puckered, and her complexion burned with the sort of indignation that could fry an egg.

Like ammunition, my mouth wreathed into a mischievous grin. And like a fiendish motherfucker, I cupped my palm and flapped my fingers twice, beckoning her.

Come and get it.

That did it. Growling, the princess came at me with a vengeance, sprinting my way and heaving a thorn quill. Over and over, she lobbed them at my weapon and missed—by a fraction, but still.

To my elation, the woman was less an amateur and more a prodigy. She wielded the thorn quills as if they'd been made for her. And for such minuscule projectiles, they had remarkable strength, able to withstand the brunt of my weapon. The thorn quills carved through the air with impeccable direction, reeling straight for the ledge of my staff. They caught me off guard several times, bumping into the rod but failing to disarm me.

Spiraling the weapon from one hand to the other, I circuited behind Briar. As I did, my voice snaked into her ear. "So how did you learn these nifty tricks?"

Briar tore around, reeling so closely that our noses tapped. "Who said I had to learn?" she hissed in my face.

Our gazes were nailed to one another. The crowd vanished, and the voices disintegrated. I inhaled tart apples and felt her outtakes slapping against my own.

Then the moment shattered like glass. The princess's response accomplished what she wanted. Stumped, I stalled my weapon, and Briar seized her chance. Vaulting backward a few steps, she launched a thorn quill vertically. It cannoned heavenward and shot back down, shaving a clean path to my staff and smacking it from my grip.

I staggered, and my ambitious princess went the extra mile. She sideswiped my leg and sent me careening. Except the move lacked flexibility—which was why she landed on top of me. My back hit the grass, and her breasts crashed into my chest. On reflex, Briar braced her palms on either side of my head, her expression split between shock, rage, and victory.

The astounded troop erupted. "Whoa," blasted from their lips, then they roared with triumphant laughter and broke into applause.

With her splayed legs flanking my hips, Briar and I fell into a staring contest that bordered on primitive. Her braid had come undone, just like my fucking pulse. As our lungs chuffed with oxygen, I obsessed about how it would feel to train without weapons.

Only our hands. So much closer. And alone, right where I could press her into whatever surface I wished, where my body could trap hers, where only I heard the sounds she made.

I wanted to snarl at the knights to get the fuck off this field. The command fumed on my tongue but never made it to my lips.

My skin sizzled against hers. Our wild breaths collided, reaching critical mass. Briar's irises smoldered, which matched the heat surging to the roof of my cock.

The crucial question was this: Where did this anger come from?

Part of me couldn't fucking recall anymore. Had we been clashing because of that paltry argument in her suite? Had one trifling fight simply led to another, and another, and another?

Or had we perpetuated this friction for another reason?

I couldn't tell if the tension brewed from animosity or desire. Were we fighting out of fury or foreplay? Were we suffering from it?

Or were we enjoying it?

Neither of us brought up our little training session later, when we joined Nicu in his room. Instead, we spent time entertaining his imagination, making sure he enjoyed his dinner, and slowly getting my son acclimated to the Royal wing. To that end, Briar and I had ordered more ribbons, each one connecting our suites to his, so he would know where to find us.

Later that night, I made a prediction. She would punish me for what happened on the field. Verily, this woman would vanquish her jester for his sins.

In the great hall, a member of the Royal Council blabbered to me about the current dispute over how trade workers earned the rank of Master. Or rather, how they didn't earn it because the distinction was inherited, as with many titles over generations.

The man vented whilst casting routine glances at my coat. I'd gone shirtless underneath, with only a few rows of thin gold chains holding the vestment closed, a panel of skin showing through like a tease.

Webbed streaks of kohl splayed under the lower lashes of one eyelid. I was going for a corrupt-prince-meets-paranormal-shifter look. Considering the man's discomfort, I'd succeeded.

Normally, I wouldn't have pushed my wardrobe this far. Not yet.

However, I hadn't been dressing for him.

The sentinel announced her name. The council member ceased chattering.

Glancing at the entrance, my head did a double take. The princess walked into the great hall, thus confirming my prophecy. She wanted to kill me.

The champagne gown clung to Briar's body, its cut as dangerous as the metallic color—radiant and capable of intoxicating someone with merely a few swallows. Like the effervescent drink itself, she went to my head before I knew what the fuck was happening. And if the heiress had caused this jester to lose his grip on a book that first night, she now lit my skin on fire like an arsonist.

The deepest V neckline in history plunged to the princess's navel. The gown's fitted waist flared into a skirt that shimmered as she moved, matching bands encircled her bare biceps, and a spiked, golden crown rose from her head. Briar's sideswept braid, combined with a lack of other jewelry, softened the otherwise lustrous ensemble. It also made the silver rings of her eyes stand out.

Several males reappraised her figure, practically licking their chops. At which fucking point, jealousy slashed its way through me. My fists curled, and my retinas fired on all cylinders. I must look demonic, because the minute her fan group checked my reaction, the hounds whirled in the opposite direction.

A wise choice. Unbeknownst to them, they'd just spared their balls from an unpleasant end. Another millisecond, and I'd have wiped the floor with their carcasses, the better to illustrate a pertinent rule.

She. Was. Mine.

Briar's attention rummaged through the crowd and landed on me. Those eyes slipped down, down, down, tracing the open panel of my coat, my flesh caged in by nothing more than a few chains. She turned away, her throat pumping.

True enough. It seemed we'd had the same idea.

Throughout the night, I sat across the banquet table and watched Briar munch on a cranberry like a scene from an erotic novel. Her mouth chewed, the movements rattling that neckline. Worse, juice stained her fingers and lips a cruel, breathtaking shade of red.

I glided a single digit up and down the stem of my knife, knowing she felt the motions between her legs. Periodically, I caught her staring my way when she thought I wasn't looking. Except I noticed her eternally and to my damnation. I imagined her thighs pressing together under the table. And when she least expected it, my pupils cut to hers at the precise moment when she gulped a swig of nectar.

For good measure and for her eyes only, I lifted a fork to my lips, the prongs holding a wedge of something soaked in sugar. Capturing the princess with my stare, I sank my teeth into the pastry and took a ferocious bite.

Much later, we did our little dance of mingling with the courtiers. But the second she was alone, I tracked behind the princess and loomed at her back. "Alas, I know you're angry with me. But wait for me tonight." My insolent voice leaked down her nape. "I'm going to peel your clothes off and fuck you."

Before I could see what my words did to her skin, I sauntered away.

20

Briar

I hastened through the double doors and shut them behind me. In the darkened throne room, I plastered my back to the partitions as if to ward off intruders. A profusion of heat sloshed in my stomach, forcing me to flatten my palm over it.

Everything ached. Everything scalded.

My body siphoned oxygen, and my heart rate struggled to calm down. I had rushed here after dinner ... after hearing what he'd said. I fled in vain as though those words wouldn't follow me here, as though I had a prayer of resisting them.

Located in a remote section of the castle, the throne room felt detached from the complex. The broad doors muffled any noise traveling through the corridors, any activity beyond.

I craned my head to the ceiling and shut my eyes. After a few minutes, my outtakes slowed. The empty room enveloped me.

Of all my choices for escape, why had I chosen this one? Slumping, I blinked at the space as if it would provide the answer.

It shouldn't be possible for silence to possess its own sound. But as I stood in the shadowed chamber, a cavernous echo filled the space, like the atmosphere itself was breathing. It gave an illusion that the walls and floor could talk, the architecture emitting a hollow sigh as thin as fog. For such a powerful place, where public decisions were made that would affect a kingdom, the room appeared ancient, secretive, and mysterious.

Father and I used to come here at night too. During those eventides when we explored the castle together, at some point we would end up here. He would tell me stories about the monarchs of old, and I would sit in Mother's chair, my short legs dangling over the seat. I would pretend I already wore a crown, and Father would pretend to be one of my subjects.

A wistful smile slid across my lips. Perhaps if I listened closely enough, I would hear remnants of our conversations, the memories lingering in this chamber like ghosts.

A large flag hung from the rafters, its facade bearing Autumn's coat of arms, with its leaves, gilded stalks, intersecting axes, and fox. I stepped gingerly across the glossy floor and ascended the dais, where two chairs presided. Upholstered in supple brown leather and carved with intricate leaves, the high-backed chairs stood in a slash of moonlight. Motes floated in those beams, glittering like pixie dust. It made this place seem archaic, where wonderful and terrible things happened, where judgment and mercy converged.

Battles had been waged and settled in this room. Defeats and victories had been announced here.

The left chair belonged to Mother. The right one was mine.

Stillness permeated the room, so thick it overwhelmed my senses. I could not explain this phenomenon, even to myself. Just as I could not justify many things that had occurred in the past week.

Rhys's threat. Poet's dagger.

The meeting to which I'd arrived late. The fight with Poet in my suite.

The things we said to each other. The things we hadn't said to each other.

The penetrating way his verdant eyes cut through me. The honed way we bared our teeth during arguments. The provocative way he had looked at me when I took Nicu into The Wandering Fields.

The combat session in the training yard. The sweat licking down his naked chest. The heat of his breath.

But wait for me tonight.

Hours later, the depth of his words still stroked between my folds. *I'm going to peel your clothes off and fuck you.*

Here in this vacant refuge, the texture of his voice caressed the trench between my breasts. My finger traced the arm of my chair—a long, slow glide over the smooth wood. By the time my digit reached the edge, the silence vanished.

Something replaced that subtle hum. Something that caused hyperawareness to prowl up the back of my neck.

The doors behind me rasped on their hinges. The click of a latch resounded through the room—definite, intentional.

My pulse rioted, hammering against my breastbone. The percussion buzzed in my ears, so that I braced myself, listening for footsteps. Yet they didn't come, didn't advance my way.

Instead, a dangerous timbre oozed into the throne room. "Sit down."

My flesh ignited like flint against tinder. The delicate flanks of my pussy clenched, liquid pooling there. Warmth puddled in the crease, and a perilous need overcame me.

The black silk of his voice wrapped around my thighs. All the same, I didn't move.

A princess didn't obey or yield that easily.

This time, it came out like a demand, spoken in a hushed tone. "I said, sit down, Princess."

That intonation struck me like a satin whip, like one of his pleasure toys—sinful, artful, lethal. Also, famished.

If I denied him, the jester might suffer. I heard the signs of it—the hitch in his breath and the desperate calm. A nervous but satisfied thrill raced through me, down to the tips of my toes.

My finger perched on the chair's arm. Purposefully, I drew out the moment. It reminded him that while he had the power to order his princess, she had the power to make him wait. To torment him the way he did her.

Now I had my answer. I came here for solace and freedom. And for him.

I hadn't been running from his intentions. I'd been sprinting toward them.

I knew he would find me. He always did.

And like me, he had a promise to keep.

When next we're alone, I'm going to fuck you on your throne.

When he made that declaration on the way from Spring, I'd shivered with anticipation. After dinner, when he told me to wait for him, my flesh had melted. Both times, I'd wanted to give the jester what he craved.

I yearned for him to take me, right here. My flesh thirsted for it.

Finally, I turned and sank into the chair. The upholstery cushioned my backside, the upright seat encapsulated me, and my heels pressed into the floor. All the same, I felt unstable until his eyes accomplished what the throne could not. Those vivid orbs bolted me to the seat.

Any moment, either one of us could take charge.

His dark silhouette lounged against the door. The distance shrunk as we studied one another across the hall. It did not matter how far away he stood. His attention never failed to reach the vital places inside me.

It could be pitch black in here, and it wouldn't make a difference. I didn't need the light to know he was grinning. I felt his every movement like the blood rushing to my head. I felt his every reaction like a heartbeat, the jolt of it ramming into my chest. The effects overwhelmed me, tantamount to an elemental bond.

Dampness coated the cleft between my thighs. At the sensation, I gripped the chair arms. The moment my fingers clenched the seat, he stepped forward.

Each thud of his boots became a throb in my clitoris, which

matched the brisk rhythm of my pulse. I became acutely aware of the crown glinting atop my head, as much the black ink leaking from under his right eye, the webs ending in steep points. Then just as quickly, those facets vanished.

The crown's weight lifted. The green of his eyes consumed my gaze, so that the paint disappeared from his countenance.

One moment, a princess and a jester. Next, a man and a woman.

Two people in a place they weren't supposed to be together.

Lovers who found themselves there anyway.

It was inevitable. As it always had been.

The jester sauntered forward. His open coat swished around his limbs, and the loose chains that barely enclosed the panels glinted. The garment walked a fine line between Spring and Autumn; it showed enough flesh to reflect his true personality, but the gold links kept it marginally tame.

As he drew nearer, Poet plucked the chains from their clasps. The vestment split apart, baring his chest and the muscles tracking into his waistband.

My breath quickened. I yearned to reach out and cup his profile. Worse, I wanted to fist his collar and yank him to me.

Ascending the dais, Poet's outline blended with mine across the floor. "Well done, Your Highness," he murmured with a bow of his head. "Now that I have you where I want you, tell me how to reward my sovereign."

He might as well have passed a baton to me. The authority in his words transferred to my own, and desire seeped from my tongue. "Kneel for me, Court Jester."

Sit down, Princess.

Kneel for me, Court Jester.

Our shadows broke apart. As he obeyed and sank toward my feet, those eyes remained fastened to mine.

With each inhalation and exhalation, my chest rose and fell. He'd positioned himself between my calves, the genuflection forcing my thighs to spread. The skirt of my champagne dress rustled up my limbs, and his leather pants tickled my skin.

Moonlight swam through his features, lacing them in lightness and darkness. With a tilt of his head, Poet sketched my posture on the seat. His irises gleamed with admiration and mischief. "This chair suits you." And because I clutched the seat arms, he flattened his palms over mine and leaned forward. "Allow me to tell you how this shall go." He draped one finger under my skirt and etched that digit from my ankle, to my knee, to my inner thigh.

The instant his fingernail scraped across the slit in my drawers, my breath caught. My pussy flexed, arousal saturating the undergarments, so that he felt it.

Those black pupils expanded. "First, I'm going to taste this lovely seam." His digit moved through the slot and brushed the hair thatched at my core, then found the kernel of flesh at its center.

My lips parted, a tremulous gust of air falling from them. My hands squeezed the chair for balance.

Poet's finger circled my clit, teasing and inflating the stud. Heat sizzled there, and my pussy throbbed harder, heavier.

The jester hummed. "Then I'm going to lick these exquisite walls." His digit raked up and down my crease, coaxing more wetness from my folds, which he scooped up. Withdrawing his hand, Poet brought the gloss to his mouth and lapped it clean, the edge of his tongue flicking. And I swear, his pupils doubled in size from the taste of me.

An undignified sound curled from my lungs. I squirmed, aware that my need had soaked through to the dress and was in danger of tarnishing the seat.

"After that, I'm going to sink my tongue between the tender flesh of your cunt," he rasped. "Once I'm throat-deep, I'm going to pump long and slow."

Patiently, the jester framed my knees and spread them. Burrowing farther into me, he unsheathed a dagger from his boot. With swift movements, the blade cut through the front threads of my skirt, which split the fabric in half without destroying it.

I gasped. Cool air stroked my bare legs, and the gap exposed the dainty material covering my pussy.

Poet tossed the blade. Then he slid his palms over my hips, gave the drawers a gentle tug, and dragged them down my limbs. He chucked them aside, baring the line of my core to his view. Excitement leaked from me in a steady flux, surely drenching the gown and slopping the chair.

I should be ashamed. I should repent for such an infraction.

The way I sat with my legs sprawled and my pussy glistening in plain sight was sordid, pornographic, disgraceful. Yet my clit swelled. My insides only grew wetter and warmer.

With this man at my feet, I'd never felt more powerful, more wanted, more alive. It would take a war for me to vacate this chair.

With a groan, Poet thumbed the breach in my thighs. "I'm going to ride up this precious slot, all the way to this very ... sweet ... thorn." That same thumb grazed my clit, and he spoke while staring at the crest. "I'm going to wrap my lips around it and suck tentatively."

"Poet," I begged.

"I'm going to be gentle until you want it harder, and I'll give what you want, and my lips won't let go." He rolled the peak of skin gently, urging a splintered moan from me. "Then, you're going to come on my tongue. And I'm going to swallow you whole." His digit ceased its ministrations. "Would you like that?"

"Yes," I whimpered.

Poet. Yes.

That was all. That was everything.

His composure snapped. As though my reply had clipped an invisible cord, the jester yanked me by the hips. I skidded to the chair's rim, my thighs splayed apart, and my gasp tripped across the room.

Wasting no time, Poet's head dove between my thighs. His mouth rushed to the groove of my body, the heat of his lips pushing against the private flesh. At last, he feasted on me.

With my limbs flanking his face, the jester's tongue draped up my slit in one long stroke. A fractured cry lurched from my throat. My spine arched, and my head craned backward, the crown slipping a notch.

Poet hummed. Under the skirt, he clamped onto my naked backside, his palms anchoring my pussy against his mouth. The warm flat of his tongue swabbed my crease. He lapped at my arousal, which drew more slickness to the surface, so that I poured onto him.

Another guttural sound rumbled from his chest. With my buttocks locked in his grip, he skimmed the pleat of my body, the edge of his tongue flicking. With every measured lap, he traced the crook of my pussy, rowing over and under.

I arched into the chair and steepled my knees. Anguished moans spilled from my lips. The wretched sensations accumulated, each one surging to my clit.

The jester looped one of my thighs over his shoulder. This changed the angle of his tongue as it rode along the furrow of my pussy. Pleasure tracked up my vertebrae, prompting me to whine and scoot closer. With my left thigh hitched atop Poet's shoulder, my heel slipped.

I sat there, with a lopsided crown on my head, my skirt slashed up the middle, and one shoe dangling from my toes. I was in disarray, a clamor of stuttered cries and incomprehensible mumbles, a wild mess of a princess.

And I did not care.

Seasons, how I did not care.

Poet's tongue drizzled down my slit and sheared between the walls of my core, spreading the folds apart. As promised, he sank into me, through to the hilt. Then he began to pump, his tongue whisking at a steady pace.

Finally, my hands tore from the seat. I clutched the back of his head, urging his mouth nearer. My thighs flared open, and my pussy drenched his tongue as it speared through me, shooting in and out. He plied me repeatedly, flexing between my folds like it was his cock. Using the same tempo, he knew which places to strike.

Poet groaned, the sound gritty. I sobbed and circled my hips, my core riding his tongue, meeting his strokes in tandem. Dear Seasons, it felt so good. So monstrously, agonizingly, terribly good.

I keened as Poet caught my other leg and hooked it over his opposite shoulder. He braced my rear, and I clung to his scalp. His mouth and my core rammed against one another, desperate to bury him as deeply as possible.

The jester siphoned his tongue, probing a spot that had me chanting. He attacked that narrow place, hitting it relentlessly.

But without warning, he withdrew his tongue and gave me another molten lick before reaching my clit. The distended flesh thrummed, hot and sensitive. On a husky grunt, Poet muttered, "Give me that."

Then he snatched the peg into his mouth and sucked.

My shout blasted through the room. I released his head and bit my fist, hoping to stifle the noises as they amplified. With my free hand, I struggled to keep the crown from toppling off my head.

The cinched pressure of his lips was torturous, to the point where I might weep or scream. While his mouth worked me into a stupor, the apex of his tongue swirled around the ridge of nerves, which scattered through me like a brushfire. He etched the tiny crux, then swatted its crest. Disjointed moans cracked from my lungs, the result excruciating.

My vision blurred. The room rotated on its axis.

His mouth took me, devoured me. All I could do was hold on and try not to dissolve. I oozed onto his tongue, my core so wet it glazed my thighs. The pleasure mounted, on the brink of shattering me, of tearing me in half.

My pussy trembled, an impending orgasm raging through me. Poet must have felt the onslaught, the constriction in my core. With a hiss, he tugged on my clit as if spurring the climax faster.

I abandoned the crown, reeled my fist from my mouth, and grabbed his hair instead. My fingers pulled on the roots, mussing his locks. All the while, he suctioned on me, towing my clitoris between his lips and simultaneously etching the tip.

A profusion of heat flooded my veins. I groped his hair and drove my pussy into his mouth. The satisfied octave of his groans embold ened me, the pleasure blissfully aggravating. My body ground itself against him, and the hectic sounds we made consumed the hall.

Sweat trickled down my back. The center of my body dripped with need.

Poet licked voraciously, then switched to mop the slot of my pussy, and finally returned to the small bud. My moans escalated, the noise solidifying into inconsolable shrieks.

Out of nowhere, one of Poet's hands covered my mouth. He knew I was gaining momentum, about to reach euphoria. We felt it as my folds convulsed.

I could come all over his tongue, like he'd predicted. It would be effortless, decadent, and nearly impossible to resist.

Impossible for someone who wasn't a willful princess. As much as he liked to call me that, this man did not know the half of it. But I would show him.

It could not end yet. I wouldn't allow it.

Not until I'd had my turn.

A plaintive sound escaped me before I summoned the nerve to stop him. With only a modicum of sanity left, I squirmed backward. Poet took the hint, his lips loosening as though he knew I wanted him elsewhere. Yet I gave no warning as I seized the collar of his coat and jerked him from me, forcing his mouth to release my clit.

Poet's brows slammed together in confusion, then his pupils dilated at whatever expression he saw on my face. I launched to my feet and hauled him with me, then spun us around. Without pause, I shoved him onto the chair.

His backside hit the seat. I climbed on his lap, split my thighs around his waist, and grabbed his face. "Give me that," I demanded, then sank my mouth onto his.

The jester's breath stalled as I clamped our lips together and forged us into a kiss. My mouth clung to him, rocking in a furious cadence. I plastered my fingers to his profile, fixing him in place while I thrust my mouth against his.

An instant later, Poet recovered from the shock. With a ferocious growl, he threw himself into the kiss. His mouth spread over me, flexing back and forth, sealing us together. Oxygen heaved from his lungs and gusted into mine, the temperature rushing across my tongue.

We took one another's mouths at a rampant pace. The kiss felt dire, repentant, infuriated, and wounded. I could not say if we were kissing to apologize or to vent our grievances. Every emotion converged, stinging my eyes.

Seasons, I had missed him. Each second. Each minute. No matter how closely to each other we had stood, I'd missed him.

I missed his touch, his scent, his heat.

Poet's digits cleaved through my hair. Plaits unraveled from my side braid, and my locks fell around his face.

He grunted as if in pain. Then I realized why. My teeth had nicked his lower lip, yet I knew what that intake of air meant. He liked it.

I did it again. My incisors raked over his mouth, then speared into the flesh, biting him until his skin pebbled.

On a snarl, Poet snatched my lips again and wrested them wide open. His tongue pitched between my lips and whipped against my own. I moaned, taking him into me, the kiss erupting.

Our tongues whisked together, the intensity exhilarating. The contact should rob me of air, should deplete me entirely. Instead, it refueled me. It gave me the ability to breathe again, after suffocating for days.

We kissed, frantic as if it could end at any moment. We kissed, refusing to let that happen. We kissed, unable to get enough of each other, because the possibility of ever growing apart didn't exist.

Poet.

His tongue caught mine. It lapped urgently, hotly against me.

Lust shot to every nerve ending and coiled between my thighs. Wetness pooled from my folds, my pussy pounding with need.

Poet's cock thickened and rubbed against my clit, the friction eliciting another whimper from me. He'd been hard since kneeling at my feet. I had seen and felt it, but now his erection pulsed even harder. The stem rose high, the pome bloating under his leather pants.

237

Seasons. I veered back, tearing my mouth from his with force.

"Let me tell you how this will continue," I panted in a low tone, then claimed his left arm and affixed it to the chair. "I'm going to use this ribbon." Untying the scarlet bracelet from my wrist, I strung the fabric around his arm, trapping him in place. "And I'm going to use this one." Plucking his own bracelet loose, I wound it over his right wrist, fastening it to the opposite armrest.

Poet's nostrils flared. His eyes burned a ravenous shade of green, but he didn't stop me. I had told him once to have his ribbons ready for my use. Despite what he thought, I always kept my word.

With the jester bound and at my behest, I made myself comfortable. My hips rested in his lap, my thighs splayed around his strong waist, and my pussy abraded the heavy mast of his cock. The gown's skirt draped around us, splitting like a curtain from where he'd sliced through the fabric.

My lust smeared his pants. Poet's eyes hooded, and a faint grin tipped his mouth sideways.

I cast my lips over his and whispered, "And then I'm going to ride you on this throne until you climax like an obedient jester. Do you understand?"

That filthy mouth slanted farther. He pushed his lips harsher against mine and jolted his cock upward, pelting it against my sodden walls. "Then what are you waiting for, hmm?" That husky voice rustled against me, the octave as low as my own. "Fuck me, Briar—"

My lips swooped down to shut him up. I swallowed the words, desperate to taste them, to consume them. Starved, my mouth welded to him and sucked us into another kiss.

My tongue flexed with his. My restless fingers dipped to his pants and tore at the clasps.

With several quick jerks, the closures sprang apart. Poet's broad, long cock projected from the fabric. Flushed and dark at the head, it wedged between us, the sight wetting me anew. A velvety bead leaked through the slit in his crown, but although I wanted to lap that droplet and listen to the jester groan, I wanted that speck inside me much more. I needed all of him inside me, so deeply I would never forget what it felt like.

I hastened, my movements clamorous as I lifted my hips above him. The opening of my core poised over his stiff length—and I sank onto him. Poet made a violent noise, and I cried out as our waists locked. My pussy sealed around his cock, drenching him from the sac to the pommel.

Astride his erection, my body expanded, taking him to the hilt. I shifted closer until our chests pressed, my breasts perking against his pectorals. My nipples pebbled, my clit inflated, and my head swam. Blood surged through my navel and simmered between my folds, the sensations primal—critical.

Poet's cock filled me to the brink. The walls of my pussy flared around him, encasing him in me.

I threw myself into it. My body flew against Poet's, my hips grinding onto his lap. I galloped on the jester's cock, moaning openly, recklessly.

Poet's face contorted. He growled and squeezed his fists, unable to move anything but his waist. His jaw unhinged, haggard breaths launching into the room. I felt every inch of his erection as I gyrated my waist, swatting at him until his scalp thumped against the chair.

Like this, I fucked the jester on my throne.

Each time I landed on him, my flesh went up in flames, and another sob lurched from my throat. I watched, mesmerized as Poet's eyes clenched shut. The vision motivated my hands to the finials lining the top of the chair. I grabbed the fixtures and used the leverage to charge at him, my hips pelting his.

His cock tightened inside me, its height extending. The crown struck a wondrous place that dislodged a shout from me. My skin burned, my knees bent around him, and I keened aloud.

Time suspended and accelerated. And then Poet began to move in tandem. With his wrists shackled, he put all his strength into his waist. He jutted his backside and hoisted his cock deeper into me, the impact catapulting through my being.

Again and again, I moaned as Poet rammed his hips into mine. The brunt of it vaulted me upright. My body caught his, both of us rowing into one another.

Yet it still wasn't close enough. Not nearly.

I looped my knees over the armrests, so that my legs hung on either side of the throne. This boosted my thighs higher. Poet purred his approval and launched into me, his cock pounding through my folds.

My pussy opened wider and soaked his erection. Gravelly sounds skittered from my tongue, each noise prompting Poet to haul his cock into me harder, faster.

Fuck me sweetly. Make love to me hard.

Yes, this. Always this.

I rode him, and he rode me back. I was alive, and he was alive, and nothing else mattered.

We fused ourselves together, rushed at one another, as if it would never be close enough. Let no one breach this again. Never again.

Poet flung his cock into me repeatedly, his waist slinging forward with precision. He knew where to mark me. He knew where to afflict me. I arched into him and split myself around his body, my hips and breasts jostling.

Under the dress, moisture trickled down my skin. Beneath the open coat, a sheen of perspiration covered Poet's throat and torso.

I wanted to shred our clothes. I wanted us naked on this throne.

But that would take too long, and I had no patience to spare, no composure remaining. Only one part of me stayed bare. Only one part of him projected from his clothing. That was enough to make us soar.

My pussy ground onto his cock and leaked all over him. The round head of his erection siphoned in and out of me, the stem sloping at the right angle. Tireless, we met each other thrust for thrust, taking one another higher, higher, higher.

My spine curled backward, my hair hung nearly to the floor, and I shrieked up to the ceiling. All at once, my pussy quivered around Poet's lunging cock. Spasms rolled up my thighs. Pleasure compressed between my folds, prompting the jester to double his efforts, driving up into me as I slammed down onto him.

My cries expanded and tore through the room. Poet hefted himself inside me, circled his hips fiendishly, and growled, "Now, sweeting. Give me that again."

Now happened. And I gave it to him.

The orgasm shattered through me like a tide. My pussy fluttered around his cock, flooding him as I hollered to the rafters. Poet hauled his waist between my thighs and roared as he came, his cock twitching while my folds gripped him.

White hot pleasure spilled from my walls and spread to the tips of my being, the orgasm lasting for so long I felt dizzy. My vision clouded. My lungs emptied. The muscles of my pussy grasped his cock, pulsating and prolonging that release until I fell forward and crashed against him.

Poet slumped at the same time. Together, we collapsed into a heaving fit on the chair.

Spent, I wheezed into his chest. My lungs churned, grappling for oxygen.

Exhausted outtakes drafted from Poet's throat, the sound rough. His abdomen inflated with mine, both of us struggling to inhale one another's scent.

There was a pause. Then the gates blasted open. My gaze flew to his, just as his forehead shoved against my own.

"Forgive me," I implored, my voice cracking. "I'm so sorry."

"Nay," he rasped, his features strung. "'Twas my fault. I'm the one who needs to apologize."

"No, it was me. I was stressed and scared. And so, I overreacted about seeing you at the meeting without me. We'd agreed to confer with each other first, before anyone else, before taking any step, but I know you wouldn't have disregarded that under normal circumstances. What's more, I did the same exact thing to you, all without realizing it. When I said the battle with Rhys was my problem alone, I only meant to protect you."

"When I attended the meeting without you, what makes you think my intention was any different from yours? I told you as much, remember?"

"I know." Shaking my head, I repeated, "I'm sorry, Poet."

"Don't be, Sweet Thorn. Like an idiot, I was too pissed off to see the obvious, much less to be reasonable about other disputes. Your excursion with Nicu, for instance. When we argued about that, I should have reminded you of one eternal fact. I do trust you—with all that I am."

"And I trust you more than anyone."

"Still, 'tis your jester who deserves to be sorry."

"You don't need to—"

"Aye, Briar. I do," he insisted. "At least permit this bastard to grovel a little. It's such a good look on me, especially after angry sex."

I blinked. "Is that what this was?"

"I certainly hope so. We've never indulged in that luxury, and my Briar Bucket List is long."

"We were fools," I panted into him.

"So fucking stupid," he agreed, kissing my mouth before showering more kisses to my jaw, the side of my neck, and my chin. "So. Fucking. Stupid."

He kept plying me until I chuckled. "You're going to distract me again."

"Is that supposed to be a warning?" he wondered, lifting his head. "I blame you for being so addictive." He brushed our noses together. "Don't you know? Don't you know how scorching you are? How stunning? How fucking sexy? You have no idea how many times I wanted to drag you away, crush my mouth to yours, and fuck you until we both lost consciousness. You've got no clue what it did to me, seeing you sprawled on the throne, with your pussy waiting for my mouth, only to have you mount me like an empress afterward. If I wasn't your captive before, I am now."

"Flatterer," I teased, then thumbed his cheekbone. "I love you."

Poet draped his mouth against mine and murmured, "I love you more." Then he nuzzled under my earlobe and planted a kiss there.

"And more." Then my throat. "And more." Then between my collarbones. "And more."

My laughter echoed as Poet's mouth found infinite places to nibble. "And more," he growled.

For a while afterward, we sagged against one another and regained our breaths. I tucked my head under his jaw and drifted my hands up and down his sculpted chest.

Fear sliced through my happiness as I remembered the unknown spies in our midst. However, I relaxed a second later. With the throne room located in a remote section of the castle, no one had heard us, despite how loud we'd been.

And even if a spy followed us here, the most they would have heard were the sounds of sex. As much as my cheeks broiled, we'd given them no ammunition to work with.

In tired whispers, we recapped everything that happened since the fight, each of us clearing the air, explaining why we'd acted as we had. It was one thing to vow we wouldn't let our enemies breach us. It was another to face those enemies, starting with the Summer King.

Still, Poet and I had proven ourselves stronger than this. The strain had gotten to us once. We wouldn't let it happen again.

I snuggled deeper into Poet until he cleared his throat. "Sweeting?"

"Mmm?" I muttered.

"As much as I enjoyed the kink, would you mind untying me now?"

"Seasons!" I shot upward to unravel the scarlet ribbons from his wrists. "Oh gods, I apologize."

"You'd better not. I rather enjoy being restrained by a future monarch," he said as his arms slumped free. "However, I was getting antsy to touch you."

"Well, you know." I draped my finger down the side of his handsome face. "My clothes never came off."

I'm going to peel your clothes off and fuck you.

"Ah," the jester crooned. "But I never said which clothes."

"Conniver," I accused.

"Speaking of which." Poet leaned sideways and snatched my un-

243

dergarments from the floor. He tucked the sodden drawers into his pants pocket and flashed me a wily grin. "I'm keeping these." Then I gasped as he jerked me into him, his cock notching against my pussy and his voice a decadent purr. "And I never said we were finished."

21

Briar

I floated past the guards. One of them muttered something about the queen granting someone entry, which made no sense. It must be related to one of the numerous meetings and court sessions awaiting us. Whatever they'd been referring to, it would be dealt with later.

My jellied legs carried me through the entrance. I drifted into the antechamber, shut the door behind me, and dissolved against the facade. Closing my eyes, I traced my lips and remembered.

His hands spreading my thighs. His mouth between my legs. His cock pumping into me. His groan as I rode him, dominating him on the dais, all with a crown on my head.

The throne chair shaking with our movements. The outright scandal of it.

The jester. The only man who could prompt me to do things I'd never thought myself capable of.

I had thought we'd done everything there was to do with each other. I thought I'd felt every emotion in existence by now.

Yet no. Constantly, he introduced me to other sensations. I could not keep track.

An influx of warmth swirled up my limbs. A sigh coasted from my lips—followed by the sound of a feminine chuckle.

From deeper inside the suite, a woman quipped, "Just look at her. It appears our princess has gone rogue."

A second voice chimed in, the intonation flirty. "What have you been up to, missy?"

Then a third voice joined the procession, this one sultry and sarcastic. "And who have you been doing it with?"

My eyes popped open. My head snapped toward three figures taking up residence in my chambers.

The first woman had rich dark skin, burgundy irises to match her hair, and an overbite.

The second female possessed Mother's curvy form and inked blossoms that trickled across her left collarbone.

The third flaunted evergreen tresses, the physique of a swan, and the deceptive temperament of one.

Vale and Posy lounged on the settee beside the crackling fire. Cadence dared to perch on the edge of my bed, with her fingers wrapped around one of the footboard posts and her nails glinting with inset crystals.

I would have reduced this to a mirage. Except Cadence bore the same antagonistic love-hate smirk I'd never forgotten, because she enjoyed catching me off guard.

I gasped and hurried toward them, all while shaking my head in disbelief. "What …"

Astonishment and an inexplicable lightness quickened my steps. The three ladies hopped to their bare feet and bustled my way. We dashed across the space, then halted in the apartment's center.

They beamed. I gaped.

Then the women erupted into excited squeals and opened their arms. An overwhelmed noise sprang from my lips as they rushed at me, crushing us into a group hug and jostling me in kind. Because Spring natives favored surprises, they chortled at my inability to utter a coherent word.

The perfume of wildflowers and the aroma of a wine bottle we'd once shared while exploring Spring's palace struck my senses. Substantial. Familiar. I recovered from my stupor and hugged them back, my grip tighter than I'd have predicted.

Joy. That's what this feeling was.

At length, the ladies broke away in a flurry of chiffon. Bangles clanked from their wrists, and their hair cascaded like waterfalls. My hold on them must have startled the females, because they cooed, "Awwwww."

At least, two of them did. The third female merely raised her groomed brows, impressed by my emotional reaction.

"You should see your face," Vale boasted, combing through my hair.

"Mission accomplished," Posy added while smoothing out my dress. "We left her speechless."

"She was already speechless from something else," Cadence gloated. "We just upped the ante."

My amazement melted into a stunned chuckle. "I don't understand. How is this possible?"

"Who cares?" piped Posy.

But I very much cared. The last time I saw them, I'd been banished from Spring. And as members of Queen Fatima's extensive retinue of ladies-in-waiting, they were obligated to stay loyal to Her Majesty. Lastly, the queen would never allow them to travel here. Not with our relations in a current state of disarray, and certainly not to abandon their posts.

The only way citizens were allowed to cross borders was if both monarchies granted the request. This trio would have needed special permission, starting with Fatima.

I thought I would not see them again. Not for many years.

"Hey." Posy cupped my face. "It's okay."

"No, it is not," I protested, a rock wedged in my throat. "How did this happen?"

"Already jumping to the logistics," Cadence criticized, albeit with a tinge of amusement. "Some things haven't changed."

"Well, it's only been a few weeks," Vale reasoned. "What is supposed to change?"

Nothing. Everything.

It had taken less than a month for Spring to change me. And so much had happened since I returned to Autumn.

I removed my gold crown and set it atop a side table. The ladies guided me to the fireplace, where flames danced inside the hearth. As moonlight crept through the windows and balcony doors, I perched on one edge of the settee while Cadence lounged on the opposite side.

Instead of opting for the neighboring armchairs, Posy and Vale curled up on the floor by my feet. Vale nestled her back against Posy's plush breasts, while the latter wrapped her arms around the other's midriff. It gladdened me to see them still together.

Lack of decorum aside, one thing I appreciated about Cadence was her candor. "Fatima fired us."

The warmth I'd been feeling drained from my face. "No," I demanded. "She did *what*?"

My expression must be stricken because Posy hastened to explain. "Cadence is embellishing. Her Majesty dismissed us."

"It's the same thing," Cadence contested.

Vale snorted. "Not to my woman, it isn't."

"Fired is too melodramatic," Posy asserted. "Dismissed is a more distinguished term, yet it still makes us sound appropriately mutinous."

"You've been reading too many fantasy epics," Cadence remarked.

"And you haven't been reading enough."

"Since you left, Posy has been in a rebel phase," Vale told me. "You influenced people in Spring more than you know."

Dread locked my shoulders in place. My fingers clasped tightly in my lap. If this was true, were they discharged because of me? Back in Spring, these ladies had admitted publicly to spending amiable time with me, but that wasn't a violation. In fact, that had been expected.

As for my crimes, they hadn't been aware when Poet and I rescued Nicu from the dungeon. But perhaps Queen Fatima had falsely accused them of partiality, having assumed their loyalties had transferred to me. And …

"Eliot!" I stressed. "What's happened to him? Is he safe? Is he hurt? Did they—"

"Calm your titties, Highness," Cadence said, ignoring how my face pinched with umbrage. "He's fine. Your favorite minstrel is doing what we were trying to do, only he's doing it better."

"Fatima didn't kick us out of her clique because of you," Posy assured me. "Don't get us wrong. After a certain Court Jester's betrayal and the way we cheered when you two locked lips in front of King Rhys on Lark's Night, the queen was antsy about who remained loyal to her. She was suspicious, but that wasn't the real issue."

"You might have inspired us," Cadence said.

They told me how. After what Spring did to me and Poet at the carnival—appointing us as the Fest Fools—and after hearing our story, and after hearing more from Eliot, nothing felt the same anymore.

Vale, Posy, and Cadence joined forces with Eliot. The foursome traveled at separate times to the archive library and rifled through the texts I'd read during the Peace Talks. Eliot knew which volumes to seek out, because I had mentioned to him before leaving where I'd gotten my information on born souls. The group figured that was the best place to start educating themselves. They'd hoped to learn more, to see things from a new perspective, and take up where Poet and I left off by slowly and carefully advocating for emancipation.

To that end, Eliot set out to earn notoriety within the court. And in Poet's absence, Spring sought and found compensation in my best friend. In turn, Eliot had been using his position to gain Basil and Fatima's favor, to insert himself into their good graces, all for the sake of following in Poet's footsteps, to further campaign on our behalf.

For research, the group was careful to be inconspicuous. Unfortunately, one of the nosy patrons wasn't fooled. Whereas Eliot had escaped the aristocrat's attention, Fatima's ladies hadn't been so lucky. The noble informed the queen of the trio's actions, which led to inquisitions. Scarred by Poet, the Crown now scrutinized its entourage under a microscope.

Out of self-preservation, the ladies denied any duplicitous intentions. And since the aristocrat couldn't prove I'd read the same books as they had, the queen settled for dismissal instead of jail.

That left Eliot to take up the gauntlet on his own. He paced himself, also intending to speak up for me and Poet over time. To absolve us in the Crown's eyes. To nudge their minds toward forgiveness, to void my banishment.

My eyes prickled. Dear Eliot, who helped us break Nicu from captivity and now risked committing treason for this cause.

For us. For me.

The ladies softened, watching my expression shift from fretful to humbled. If they hadn't met me, none of this would have happened to them. Yet after everything, they'd gambled with their freedom, putting their lives on the line to help.

I spoke around the wad in my throat. "I don't know what to say."

"Good," Cadence relished, rising from the settee and striding across the suite to my wardrobe. "We'd rather have the last word."

Never mind. I huffed a dry laugh. "You may have it," I called out. "Also, is this your way of implying you'd like a tour?"

"Oh, we already gave ourselves one," Posy assured me. "Your suite is lovely. A little moody with the colors, but lovely."

"I never imagined a castle could resemble a library," Vale said, glancing around. "It's rather studious."

Politeness aside, they seemed disappointed. Coming from a culture decorated in marble, stained glass, and glitz, I hardly faulted them.

Posy released Vale and wiggled closer to the settee. "So what are the parties like?"

I hesitated. "They're not."

"Told you so," Cadence hollered from my closet.

Posy pouted while her mate patted her shoulder. "We'll fix that,"

Vale consoled. "I heard something called Reaper's Fest is coming up shortly. Spring is buzzing with the news that you've invited the Crown to a ball."

Accurate. But unfortunately for these three, such occasions were annual exceptions.

Cadence sashayed back into the sitting room with my toffee brown dress. She modeled it against her form, the tapestry sleeves fluttering. "Studious vixen," she interpreted. "It might work. I don't mind trying something new."

That latter statement was also true of Spring natives.

I shrugged. "You may keep it."

Cadence dipped her chin and grinned in satisfaction before returning to the wardrobe, no doubt to search for accessories.

My eyes widened with sarcasm. "You're welcome."

"I know," she called back.

Posy and Vale gave me apologetic looks. I sensed what they wanted to ask, though they must feel unsure about it now, especially with Cadence nosing around in my things.

I smiled, elated. "Yes, you may stay at court."

The pair of lovers beamed. Cadence returned and dropped into an armchair. "Can we please move on to the important question? Where is our down-and-dirty celebrity?"

Vale smacked her calf. "You were supposed to wait."

"I have waited," the female argued. "I never said how long my patience would actually last."

"You swore to pace yourself. Does that discussion ring a bell?"

"It was yesterday. Of course I remember. We've settled the technical stuff, so let's progress to the fun. Besides, I'm not asking anything you two weren't dying to know."

Three heads cast my way. The impact of their gazes caused heat to flood my cheeks. It must be past midnight by now, only half an hour since Poet and I parted ways from the throne room. All at once, visions of what we'd done atop my throne surged to the forefront.

"Poet is ..." I studied the rumpled folds of my gown. "He is, um ..."

A beat of silence passed. The ladies surveyed my appearance with newfound realization. The plunging neckline and knots in my hair, which I had tried and failed to tame. The creases in my gown. The split in my skirt, which reached to my knees, which could be mistaken for a stylistic cut, so long as the onlookers hadn't been bred in a Season where bodice ripping was a common pastime.

"Ohh," Posy gushed. "So that's what you were doing before you got here."

"We were otherwise engaged," I tried to reconcile.

"I'll bet you were," Vale teased. "If that blush and the state of your fabulous dress is any indication, that rogue was *engaging* you in a rather interesting position."

I demanded, "How on earth could you know that?"

"Does that mean we're right?"

"First, it's pointless to rehash our origins, but we can if you need reminding," Cadence said. "Second, we know Poet. Third, you've got that I've-been-fucked-senseless gleam in your eyes."

"Makeup sex," Posy guessed.

"Angry sex," Vale insisted.

"Nope," Cadence interpreted, her attention scrolling up and down my frame. "Angry sex that turned into makeup sex. By the way, the champagne color suits you. Though I wager the dress's slit was a convenience rather than a tailoring accident."

I did not care for my privacy to be so flagrantly evaluated. On the other hand, they weren't wrong.

"Okay then," Posy insisted, pressing her palms together. "Leave nothing out."

"Tell us what we missed," Vale said.

They wanted smut, not a summary of the big picture. However, they had missed far more than they knew. And I trusted them, especially after all they'd gone through to support Poet and me.

Still, I needed to consult with the jester first before telling them everything that had occurred. So rather than dwell on that, another question came to mind. As I'd entered the suite, my guards said the queen granted someone entry. They must have meant my three companions, seeing as they'd been permitted to install themselves in my suite without my knowledge. The guards had been preparing me, but I'd been too engrossed in thoughts of Poet to heed the prompt.

Belatedly, I asked, "How did you get here so quickly? Who brought you? And how did my mother know to expect you?"

"There's a confidential river," Posy supplied. "It runs to and from Spring. Basil and Fatima reserve the passage exclusively for their travels, which cuts the journey by more than half. We hired a ferry-man to pilot his riverboat, which cost a fortune since, technically, we were breaking the law."

"The river deposited us to one of Autumn's outlying towns, where we rented a carriage and paid a driver," Vale added.

"Your mother admitted us when we arrived," Cadence finished. "But she wasn't the one who invited us here."

"Indeed," a masculine timbre said. "That was me."

We swerved toward Poet, who reclined against the archway between the antechamber and sitting room. He'd arranged his hair to its usual organized chaos, messy by intention rather than a result of my fingers yanking on the layers. The jester had also changed into a bronze vest and a granite jacquard shirt, along with granite-dyed pants that sank into his boots.

My heart jumped into my throat. The firelight sketched his lazy features, emphasizing the knavish crook of his lips.

Like a set of firecrackers, the ladies launched to their unshod feet and flounced across the suite, intending to attack him. I rose, watching it happen. Yet even in present company, Poet's smoldering eyes fused with mine.

At the last second, he grinned at the women, ready to soak up the attention. But before they could smother the jester, all three ladies skated to a unanimous halt.

Just then, a scanty figure popped from behind Poet.

"Oh," Posy yipped as Poet's son trotted into view.

With his hair matted and those eyes more vibrant than his father's,

Nicu resembled a sleepy fae. His appearance stopped the women in their tracks. They tarried awkwardly, unable to help themselves.

We hadn't introduced them in Spring. There was never time or a safe opportunity. On top of that, we hadn't wanted to overwhelm Nicu more than he already was, nor get him attached to people he would end up saying goodbye to.

Nicu blinked through his exhaustion. The second he registered the women in their frothy gowns, his pupils bloated with glee. "Nymphs!" he cheered and sprinted toward them.

Fluidly, Poet's arm latched around Nicu's middle. He scooped up his son while the boy squirmed with excitement. "Who are you? Who are you? Who are you?" he asked each female. "Papa, look! Nymphs who were birthed from petals. Are we friends? I wanna say hi!"

"Hush," the jester murmured. "They're shy."

The females gawked, aghast at the word. They were the farthest thing from shy. I would have chuckled if I weren't feeling so overwhelmed.

Poet made introductions. "Nicu, this is Vale, Posy, and Cadence. They're Briar Patch's ladies."

"Are we?" Posy whirled, hopeful. "Truly?"

Poet had made an accurate prediction. I'd suspected they were eager to inquire about their positions in Autumn. It was uncharacteristic in this kingdom to have multiple attendants, but I'd broken so many rules at this juncture, what was one more?

"Of course," I told them with a grin. "If it's acceptable to you."

The women brightened, Cadence included. Except their enthusiasm faded into uncertainty as they resumed looking at Nicu. Rather than judgment, they merely watched him with self-conscious intrigue and a bit of nervousness.

He intimidated them.

I realized they did not wish to frighten Nicu. Nor did they know how to react, what to say or do without offending Poet and me. Acutely, I sensed their fear of making a mistake.

Poet held the child fast until he calmed down. "Ladies, this is my son, Nicu."

The women hesitated. Then each of them curtsied and suddenly proceeded to coo over the boy. Another chorus of "Awwwww's" left their mouths—including Cadence's—as they shuffled nearer and shook his little hand, which delighted Nicu.

"You're nymphs from the land of botanicals," he told them. "You sprouted from foliage and petals, and that's why you're just as pretty."

"I like the sound of that," Vale encouraged.

Posy bent nearer to him. "Seasons, you're kind of adorable."

"I created him," Poet bragged. "What did you expect?"

"Nice to know you're still arrogant," Cadence bantered.

While Poet reunited with the ladies and let his son chatter among them, Nicu worked his magic, glamouring the women with his spirited nature. They understood very little of what he said, but once they got used to it, the wayward speech didn't faze them. Having been raised among artists helped with that, and Poet and I took turns interpreting Nicu's compliments.

Nonetheless, whenever Poet looked at me, my cheeks scorched. Although he'd changed clothes, did he transfer my undergarments to his new pocket? Was he keeping them close?

I fought to regain my composure. "You woke him up?"

"This cunning sprite?" Poet shifted Nicu to his opposite hip, since the child wasn't ready to be released, lest he should jump on the ladies. "He pretended to be asleep the second I entered his chambers. Then as I was leaving, Nicu heard a rather impressive number of feminine squeaks coming from your side of the hallway." Poet regarded his son, their noses bumping in the most fetching way. "Dare I say, you're getting harder to catch every day. Headstrong fae. You must have inherited it from the princess."

The implication caused my breath to hitch. Poet heard it and glanced back at me, his gaze melting me like butter.

The women sniggered. Vale waved her arms. "Hello? Remember us?"

I flushed for the hundredth time and cleared my throat. Poet merely slanted his lips into a wicked grin, a witticism about to spring off his tongue.

But Nicu spoke first, *"For the inheritance of the Seasons."*

Poet had made that quip about "inheriting" my trait, and the word must have triggered Nicu's mind. Thus, his pronouncement should be innocent. Yet it swept like a cyclone through the room, sucking the oxygen from my lungs.

Poet's smile dropped. His features narrowed into a frown.

Confusion and trepidation iced my veins as the jester and I balked at his son. Now that the thrill of the ladies had worn off, Nicu merely toyed with his father's wrist ribbon.

The old continental aphorism declared that people with allegedly "sound minds" were the only individuals worthy of existence. It claimed this rule was the will of nature—of the almighty Seasons. Over history, no one had ever contested the ridiculous assumption.

But the problem wasn't just what Nicu had said. It was *how* he'd said it. The voice he used. Nicu had altered his tenor to sound like the person who'd uttered those words to him.

He hadn't been speaking his mind. He'd been quoting someone verbatim.

Rhys had made that same recitation in the library wing. That night, he'd cited the continent's aphorism. Yet the voice Nicu used belonged to someone else—a person who had parroted the king's words, which could be a coincidence. Or it could be something else.

It could be the voice of a follower under his command.

Baffled, our female guests cast their gazes between us. Unaccustomed to Nicu, they couldn't tell whether the problem stemmed from him alone or another source.

"Is everything okay?" Posy asked.

"Did we do something wrong?" Vale ventured.

Cadence wavered, then muttered to them, "I don't think it's about us."

As I started pacing, their puzzled expressions deepened. Something more than the quote gnawed at my ribs. I tapped the backs of my knuckles into the opposite palm. "The Summer King said the attackers killed Merit just to prove they could get past our soldiers. By extension, that means they can get past any barricade, such as the dungeon."

"Summer King?" Posy trilled. "Attackers?"

"Who's Merit?" Vale asked.

Cadence flattened her hands on their arms to silence them. Meanwhile, Poet's glare tightened like a fist. After Nicu spoke, the jester knew where I was going with this.

I paused mid-stride and glanced at Poet. "Why would the king feel the *need* to prove his spies could get past our defenses?"

"He wouldn't," Poet hissed. "Unless we wouldn't otherwise believe that was possible."

The knights and guards wouldn't doubt a castle resident. They wouldn't question a courtier's presence in the dungeon.

I nodded. "His spies aren't at court."

Stumped, the ladies waited for someone to explain.

Poet swerved his attention toward his son. "Nicu," he muttered slowly. "What you just told us. Where did you hear that? Who said it to you?"

Nicu met his father's gaze. "Is this a game?"

"Aye," the jester gritted out while stroking his son's cheek, "Can you tell us?"

To which the child smiled. "The master in the orchard told me."

Poet's eyes snapped to mine, bewildered rage kindling in his features. Council meetings had only scratched the surface, so although he understood what the role of Master meant in Autumn, he still didn't know the full extent of it.

But I did.

Not only did the spies live outside of court. At some point, one of them must have encountered Nicu in The Shadow Orchard. And if one of them referred to themself as a Master, that meant ...

It struck me like dynamite. I knew who the spies were.

22

Poet

She blasted through the halls. The hem of her dress hissed against the floor, the champagne fabric flashing like a torch. We stalked behind her—me and the ladies. Aire had taken Nicu to his room, for this was something my son should never have to see.

"The Masters are a guild of Autumn's finest crafters," she recapped without stopping, her fingers gripping the shimmering layers of her skirt. "They're an elite group of members who inherited the titles from their ancestors. The Master Arrowsmith, the Master Blacksmith, the Master Builder ..." Briar halted and fixed me with an imperative look over her shoulder. "The Master Goldsmith."

Like with Nicu, it wasn't the moniker that struck me. It was the tone she used while speaking—brittle, as if it might splinter in her mouth.

My fists curled. Whatever made her sound like that needed to be extinguished.

"So they're elite peasants?" Posy inquired.

"No," Briar insisted. "Not peasants. In Autumn, these vocations are prosperous. Most of all, for the Masters. They enjoy wealth and acclaim. Like nobles, they own land and keep servants, and they want for nothing. As far as ranks go, it's the highest office a crafter can earn."

"Doesn't sound like they earned it, though," Cadence argued. "Not if they inherited it."

Briar nodded. "It's an age-old fellowship, a tradition created centuries ago. The titles have always been granted to the members' offspring. And while the skills of each trade have been historically passed through familial generations, a small number of trade workers are now arguing the distinction should be freely earned. It should be rewarded, rather than bequeathed as a birthright. Mother and I believe this as well, and we've made it a future goal, but it's a complicated system to reverse."

Ah. The hints about there being a minor uprising against this tradition made sense now. I could guess what these elite heirs and heiresses thought of that prospect. Being a Master was a privilege I doubted they'd relinquish willingly.

The princess whipped forward and charged toward an adjacent corridor, with us on her heels. She stopped beside a nondescript panel and flattened her hand on one of the moldings, which sank deeply into the wall like a mechanism.

The door peeled back, allowing us to pass into a black hole. Because I'd already memorized the hidden conduits in this castle, I knew where she was taking us.

The last time this little clan had disappeared through a clandestine channel, we'd been tipsy off the thrill, howling into the darkness, and on our way to Spring's labyrinth. There, we danced around a water well and confessed our desires. And like a glutton for Royal punishment, I'd slipped my hand under Briar's skirt to trace the opening of her drawers, teasing out wetness from the cleft of her thighs.

No such elation awaited us tonight. This time, our group fell silent as we descended a winding brick stairway. The steps coiled into an abyss, the walls lined in condensation and flaming lanterns that jutted from hooks.

On her way, Briar snatched one of the beacons. "The Masters are nevertheless revered. All this time, their positions have been treated like tenures," she continued, breath pumping from her lungs. "The reason for this is simple. The guild's founding members established Autumn's infrastructure. They have power and influence because they built everything upon which we stand, everything we need to thrive and defend ourselves. Our towns, the armory, this castle."

"Its secret passages?" I murmured aloud.

Briar gulped. "That and more."

Her voice hitched, frayed at the edges. I heard the wounded betrayal a second before she sucked up the noise and fixed her shoulders in place. Nonetheless, her ability to recover quickly didn't stop me from planning all the ways I would gut the ones who'd made her falter.

The ones who sided with Rhys. The miserable cocksucker couldn't have selected more effective traitors.

Vale, Posy, and Cadence quietly deliberated. Likely, they were processing everything, from the story Briar and I had rattled off in her room, to Merit's death in The Shadow Orchard, to Rhys's blackmail, to the Masters.

Notwithstanding, the princess didn't need to say more. If the Masters were scions of Autumn's founding crafters, these members had been trusted and valued, regardless of how the titles came to them. Such alleged paragons were supposed to represent this nation, as their forefathers had. Like a Court Jester and the Royal Council, the Masters worked closely with the monarchy, helping to establish and preserve this land.

But if that was the case, one vital detail didn't make sense.

"Why wouldn't they be at court?" I asked. "If they're top-notch patriarchs, wouldn't they keep quarters in the castle?"

"The Masters reside in their country estates," Briar answered. "They also run forges and workshops in the lower town. But in any event, they're rarely at court. And because admission to our dungeons is limited to castle residents, the guards would require clearance before allowing the guild into the cells."

"That's why they used Merit as an example," I murmured. "It's why they felt the need to prove obstacles like sentinels wouldn't be a problem."

"I believe so. The Masters have their own domains, apart from court. Even for fellowship meetings that last up to a handful of days, they convene farther afield rather than within castle bounds. They prefer to gather an undisclosed location in the woods, which they call The Forbidden Burrow."

Cadence broke her silence. "Talk about giving off some creepy vibes."

"Why's it called that?" Posy asked.

"Because it's unreachable if you don't know the way," Briar answered. "And because only the Royal family has special access, should Mother and I wish to conference with the guild."

"So basically these crafters want to appear cultish," Vale reckoned.

"Exclusive," I amended.

"Authoritative," Briar replied.

"Authoritative. Exclusive. Cultish," I sang. "Regardless, every faction wants to sound as impressive and elusive as possible. Matter of fact, I can relate. I used to think about officially naming my suite in Spring. In which case, giving their rendezvous spot a formal designation is rather jester of them."

At the stairway landing, Briar paused and tossed me a sidelong glance. "Of course you'd compare them to yourself."

"Everyone gets compared to me," I remarked.

Her mouth twitched, but the humor failed to reach her eyes. It had been worth a shot. Besides—and forgive this professional fool for his conceit—I hadn't been exaggerating.

We strode into a crypt. Alcoves dug into the walls of a square room, with an urn at the center that brimmed with flames. Archaic carvings imprinted the ceiling, depicting stories about foxes, giants, and acorns.

At another time, I would have been intrigued to know more. But at the moment, I was having trouble seeing and thinking in any colors other than red. Briar seemed to have connected the dots, and whatever conclusion she'd drawn tormented her.

I aligned myself with the princess as we ducked into one of the alcoves, where a body lay resting atop a tomb strewn with maple leaves. Behind us, the ladies halted on the threshold and gasped.

Spring buried its dead under the trees in the wildflower forest. But Autumn housed a memorial down here, where newly fallen courtiers, nobles, and warriors lay preserved in foliage. The bodies remained here until it came time to transport them to a cemetery in the woods. This gave the person's soul a chance to settle into death, or so I was told.

The Royal family was an exception. They went to a mausoleum located in the pear orchard on the castle's north end, where I'd cornered Briar during our little spat.

The dank air slid through my vest and shirt. The ladies shuffled forward, their heels clacking as they flanked one side of Merit's form, which rested under a gauzy blanket.

Briar showed no sign of being cold. If anything, her mottled complexion signaled she was no longer hurt but very much pissed off. She stationed herself opposite from the ladies whilst I loomed at the soldier's feet. We watched her peel back the covering.

Bile rushed up my throat. Renewed fury surged through my blood.

Cadence grimaced. Posy turned away for a moment. Vale's mouth compressed.

Briar expelled a desolate breath. She closed her eyes, then forced them open to stare at the knight's ashen face. Someone had sewn his head to his neck, but the crimson line remained, pulped and thick.

His weapon of choice had been a hammer, which he clasped to his chest. But he'd yet to be dressed in his armor—that would happen when he was laid to rest—so the markings that sliced into his torso were visible, littering the mauled skin like a fucking diagram.

Initially, we'd likened the imagery to pieces of glass. But as Briar's eyes retraced the sketches, her eyebrows furrowed. "It is not glass," she said, confirming something. "Whoever did this, they didn't draw glass."

Shards, yes. But what other kind?

I planted my hands on the tomb's surface and leaned forward, my head tilting and my eyes jumping from one mutilation to the next. We hadn't been able to decipher what the markings had meant. But now the smaller details became clearer.

The shapes had texture and dimension. As a jester with a penchant for targeting, I was acutely aware of this truth: No symbol was ever random.

The ladies inched nearer, their horror fading as they examined the soldier's torso. Coming from a land of artistry, their gazes shifted, seeing what Autumn folk would likely miss on the first pass.

"But it's definitely a broken object," Cadence added. "Bits of one, at least."

"Aye," I grated whilst holding Briar's gaze. "The object is made of gold."

Gold shards, then. And if one of the Masters was a goldsmith, their talents would include jewelry making. That amounted to one significant piece I'd seen Briar wear mere hours ago when we'd fucked on her throne.

Briar's face burned with outrage. "It's my crown."

23

Poet

ead. Those cocksuckers were dead the instant I got my hands on them.

This was how it stood. Rhys's spies were the Masters—a guild of Autumn crafters who pretended to be loyal to the Crown, all whilst embroiling themselves in trickery and fuckery. They were also the ones who'd infiltrated our camp, chopped off Merit's head, and somehow managed to trade words with my son.

At least one of them had, since Nicu was able to quote from them. Shortly before Merit lost his head, Nicu heard commotion from outside the tent and crept out of bed to investigate, with the queen none the wiser, for she'd been preoccupied writing a letter. My son snuck to the edge of the pavilion, peeked under the flap, and caught the figure whilst on their way to decapitate a knight.

Nicu and this unexpected visitor had swapped murmurs, then my son scuttled to his pallet and fell back asleep. Despite the commotion that occurred minutes later, thankfully he'd stayed unconscious.

As for the rest, my son had refused to tell us what the person looked like. He said nothing more, other than, "I promised her."

Her. That was something, I supposed. On that note, when Nicu quoted this assassin, he'd imitated a smoky voice and something else. For the life of me, I couldn't reconcile it, couldn't fathom it.

But like hell would I believe it. Because if I hadn't known better, I would have said the voice Nicu emulated had sounded like a child.

That couldn't be. Evidently, my brain had to be losing its tact.

But whoever she was, the bitch could have hurt Nicu. She could have stolen him quietly behind the queen's back. My teeth gnashed so hard, I was lucky the pressure didn't crack my enamel.

Under Rhys's command, these bigots now threatened to break the mad from captivity. The Masters would do damage to innocent bystanders, then frame the prisoners for it. The guild had chosen Summer over Autumn, had chosen to dupe their queen and princess, all for the sake of maintaining The Dark Seasons' xenophobia.

Artisans who were part of the legacy that had erected this kingdom would scarcely champion a princess campaigning for social change. Such "purists" would shit on their own monarchy if they disagreed with certain reformist principles. And because of their pedigree, these members had funds, clout, and civil support.

Cunning, indeed. No one would suspect these emblematic figures of committing treason. But everyone would understand their motives, their determination to maintain the so-called natural order of things, to keep born souls at the bottom of the totem pole.

The Masters also had knowledge. Their ancestors built the secret passages in the castle. They designed every lock, forged every weapon. They would know how to enter and exit a dungeon filled with born souls. In which case, it made sense that Rhys would opt for them.

Recruiting the Masters had been a clean shot. As Briar said, they held extended meetings in the woods. Even if Merit had recognized his attackers when they approached, he wouldn't have suspected the guild was about to lop off his head. He'd have disarmed to greet them.

The princess, the ladies, and I picked through the bloody sketch- es, mentally assembling the gold shards. Indeed, the result matched the shape of Briar's crown, not her mother's.

We'd been right. The markings cleaved into the knight's body had been a message, a target against Briar's future reign. But until tonight, we hadn't known everyone who was behind it.

All this time, we'd been searching in the wrong place. But now that we knew the spies' identities, who they worked for, and where to find them, our plan changed. According to Briar, The Forbidden Burrow was located a few miles from The Pumpkin Wood, which housed a solitary cabin called The Royal Retreat, where the princess and her mother found respite whenever they needed it. The retreat was nestled in a shrouded corner of the wild, as difficult to find as the Masters' hideaway.

Thus, the plot. Briar and I would set out to the retreat and tuck ourselves away, then prepare to infiltrate the fellowship. The Masters would recognize her, since the area was hard to reach without privileged Royal knowledge. That meant disguises were out of the question. We had to go in as we were, on the pretense of discussing current disputes about who should be admitted into the guild. This being a touchy subject, the Masters would understand the need for utmost confidentiality.

It was too soon to convict Rhys of his part in all this. That would sever ties with Summer and instigate potential war, with every other Season siding against us. But once we had irrefutable proof the Masters were working toward anarchistic ends, we would either give them an ultimatum or leave with the evidence we needed to arrest the guild members for treason later. Whether immediately or in the long term, we wouldn't spare them.

Changing their minds about born souls wouldn't happen with these fuckers, much less in one sitting. However steadfast the princess was, and however charming I could be, we weren't *that* good. If they were willing to betray their sovereigns in favor of Summer, despite that leading to their executions, we'd get nowhere fast trying to challenge their perspectives. For these kinds of zealots, it would take generations.

At dusk the next evening, we passed through another secret artery in the castle, which tunneled beneath the citadel, the maple pasture, the lower town, the corn and wheat fields, and into the woodland boundary, via a stairway carved into a tree trunk. Apparently, select trees contained outlets leading to and from the palace, including the hulking maples just outside the barbican.

This chute dumped us far from the stronghold and into the court cemetery at the forest border. High headstones frothing with dried flowers packed the glade in neat rows. Leaf vines dangled along the perimeter like a fence, and mist sprinkled the branches.

Inside the graveyard, Avalea, Aire, and Briar's ladies waited, along with two saddled horses. Those stencil-like markings—common among steeds here—twined around the equines' limbs, intricate braids wove through their tails, and their irises gleamed persimmon orange.

Hmm. I wasn't superstitious, but starting a crusade surrounded by coffins wasn't the most encouraging send-off. But for some reason, Autumn citizens didn't see it that way.

The queen whispered fiercely with her daughter, visible puffs of air sprouting from their mouths.

Cadence pursed her lips at the setting. Posy romanticized the area, her expression nostalgic. Vale rubbed her arms to ward off a chill.

Inevitably, the ladies distracted themselves the only way they could in these circumstances—by appraising the First Knight's muscles. In the past, they had reserved that attention for me. But since I was taken and they'd developed a bond with Briar, the women set their carnivorous sights elsewhere. True to form, Posy elbowed Cadence and tipped her chin toward Aire, who tightened the saddles and patently ignored their stares.

Cadence gave his ass a once-over. Despite her visible approval, she shrugged. "Too crabby and too superior."

I could have placed bets on that response. As much as I liked the soldier, Cadence fancied black sheep with tragic backgrounds and questionable integrity—didn't we all?—not courteous grumps with a strict moral compass. The lady also liked to play and didn't enjoy working too hard for her meals. Considering my hand had once been lodged inside her—long before Briar—I could attest to this.

As for Aire, the soldier only responded to damsels. However deadly he fought, this man favored the predictable to the riotous, women who didn't fuck with his straightforward principles. Honestly and no offense to my new friend, I doubted he knew what a sex toy looked like, much less how to get off with one.

Pity for him. Finding someone who turned you into a hot mess was much more inviting.

Briar wore a black merino wool top stitched in lace trimmings, paired with a corresponding skirt and cloak. She strapped a set of thorn quills beneath the mantle, then stashed a few into compartments embedded within the headband encircling her loose hair. My lips tipped sideways. Aye, my smart heiress was full of surprises. The sight of her affixing miniature weapons to her outfit didn't escape my cock's notice, but I did my best to keep the effect from standing too high.

Seasons almighty. I never said my sex drive reacted at opportune times. I came from Spring, after all. We excelled at inappropriateness.

But whereas I had zero trouble stripping the princess with my eyes whilst simultaneously keeping vigil of our surroundings, my sweet thorn only managed to peek at me twice. After we tore each other apart on her throne, she'd been fluctuating between demur blushes and formal speech. The aftermath of throne sex was manifesting itself in her evasive gestures, not to mention my appetite.

I wanted more of her, on every horizontal and vertical surface in the vicinity. The temptation would only increase when we reached the retreat. Secluded. Alone. We'd have tonight, plus a full day tomorrow, before entering the Masters' burrow.

That, in addition to extra days following the meeting. It gave us leeway, in case anything changed, or if we needed to engage with the guild more than once. Overall, this left a lot of spare hours at my disposal.

Avalea clasped her daughter tightly, then released Briar and gave me a pointed nod. *Take care of her.*

I nodded back. *With every breath.*

Aire guided my steed across the grass. As I swung my leg over the saddle and mounted the animal, I overheard Cadence crooning to Briar. "Sure you don't need company?"

Vale bumped the female's shoulder. "They're going on a life-threatening mission, not a fornication binge."

"So what?" Cadence argued. "It can be both."

Posy snorted. "There's no excuse for us, is there?"

Briar scowled, which only spurred the ladies on. Impulsively, they crowded her and began poking and whispering naughty suggestions of how she and I could spend our private time.

Actually, some of the tips appealed to me. Briar, on the other hand, wasn't amused. She kept batting the women away and snapping under her breath, "Stop. Stop. Stop."

My mouth twitched. Another fetching note about these ladies was they liked to watch, if not live vicariously through the coitus. And although they were never audience members, my former exploits had included entertaining a general spectator or two, who observed whilst I bent my partner over.

Yet however appealing the experience, the thought of someone watching Briar naked—the thought of someone watching her come—made me want to rip out the person's throat.

Greedy jester. Her moans belonged to me.

Avalea planted her fists on her hips. "Briar's mother. Standing right here."

Dutifully, the ladies clamped their mouths shut. Nonetheless, I caught Aire glowering as if the exchange had curdled in his brain like sour milk.

Sobering, Cadence fished an envelope from her cape and handed it to Briar. "Had I known you would be ditching us the minute we got here, I would have given this to you sooner. You're welcome, by the way."

Briar took the missive. When she scanned the envelope's handwriting and the wax seal of a lute, her eyes shimmered. "Eliot," she whispered, then clutched the paper to her chest. "Thank you."

"Well, what can I say?" Cadence responded. "The sappy minstrel grew on us. Also, he made me promise a hundred times to deliver the message personally. And I didn't even read it."

Briar let out a sniffling chuckle and slipped the envelope into her cloak. "Commendable."

Cadence, Posy, and Vale grew serious. "Be careful, you two," Posy uttered before the women snatched Briar into a group hug, which she reciprocated.

"Your Highness," Aire clipped, holding out the horse's bridle.

The princess detached from the huddle and hefted herself onto the mare. As I ushered my horse to hers, Aire advised, "Master Jester—"

"Ah, ah, ah," I interrupted. "You know better. It's even worse now that I know where the term comes from."

"Sir," the man revised. "These crafters have strength, but they won't be agile or fast, and they're unaccustomed to fighters with aerial skills." To Briar, he added, "Nor will they anticipate Your Highness capable of aiding her lover in combat. Use that to your advantage."

"You're doubting our ability to deceive already?" I quipped without humor. "Assuming the Masters will go rogue on us? That would take a serious fuck-up on our parts."

"I've no misgivings about either of your verbal skills," the knight vouched. "But neither shall they."

And no surprise there. The controversial princess and her devious jester had outwitted one Season already. Anyone dealing with us would be on alert, sifting through our words for duplicity.

Moreover, this needed to look as innocent as possible. A military entourage would be expected, but it would show less authenticity that we wanted to speak with the Masters in private—that we trusted them to a naive fault. That was precisely why we'd sent the guild a missive in advance about meeting, rather than us showing up unannounced. Formality reigned in Autumn, whereas spontaneity made the people here antsy and circumspect.

Aire concurred with this, despite how much he'd wanted to play guard. As if reminded of something else, his expression grew pensive. At length, he uttered, "It wasn't a straight blade."

Briar stared at him. My brows rammed together.

"The weapon that decapitated Merit," Aire said. "It wasn't a straight blade. I've been recalling it in my mind's eye for some time. A knife or sword wouldn't have made that sort of cut."

The princess shook her head. "It had to be, though." Then she explained to me, "Apart from hammers, the Masters only wield knives and swords. But anything curved would have only come from their trade tools, which they'd never use for violent purposes. The members would consider it a defilement."

"They haven't exactly been living up to expectations, though," I replied. "But if the murder weapon didn't match the Masters' cache, what then?"

"A sickle?" Briar ventured. "It could not have been a saw blade."

"It wasn't." Aire dropped his voice another notch. "It was an axe."

We filed that information away. The queen clutched her daughter's hand once more, her eyes glittering with trepidation. "Protect each other," she told Briar.

The princess kissed her mother's knuckles. "I love you, Mother."

Avalea swallowed. "You have no idea, my dearest."

My thoughts latched onto Nicu. Briar and I had spent the day with him before leaving, the three of us picnicking in the pear orchard. We'd covered all contingencies to make certain he would be safe in our absence, including appointing more guards to the Royal wing, all under Aire's command.

Briar's ladies had also promised to keep Nicu company. For that, the princess and I had coached them on the fundamentals. We hated separating from my son, but we trusted this group to look after him.

A moment later, we galloped from the cemetery. In silence, Briar and I shot past the trees, their offshoots snarling overhead and periodically snagging on our clothes. Marigold beech leaves trembled from the boughs and glinted through the eventide, and whiffs of damp soil permeated the atmosphere.

Reaching a path camouflaged in the brush, we halted the animals. They grunted, clouds of oxygen ejecting from their snouts. The princess and I contemplated the murky route strewn with bracken and illuminated by gilded oval leaves.

The ride would take a while. My ass was going to be cranky when we got there.

Briar's profile cemented, a thousand emotions crossing her face in succession. She was avoiding my stare. Oh, but that wouldn't do.

I glanced at the thorn quills sheltered in the princess's headband. "I do admire a woman who knows how to accessorize. By the way, are you finally going to tell me where you learned those slick throwing skills? It explains why you beat me at skipping stones, not to mention the dungeon guard whose noggin you nearly split in half."

"You are just envious I won that tossing game at Jinny's cottage."

"I resent that accusation. People are jealous of *me*, not the other way around. Though if it were up to Yours Truly, you'd win every game we played. Need I ask again? Never keep a jester waiting."

Her features thawed, a wistful grin cracking through. "Father taught me in secret. No one knew besides Mother. Even our army had no idea."

That accounted for their shock when she knocked me on my ass at the training yard. "They weren't the only ones who didn't know."

She peeked my way, those sterling eyes flashing with guilt. "I'm sorry. I should have told you, but I suppose … it never came up? More than that, I was so used to keeping the proficiency to myself, to protect it from being discovered, I hadn't thought to share it."

"Why wouldn't you want the world to know you're a savvy badass as well as a sexy bibliophile? It's bewitching."

Briar cast me a wry look. "I am not a bewitcher."

Heat rippled across my flesh. I pointed to my face. "Do you see how I'm looking at you, sweeting?"

Her head darted in the opposite direction. A rosy tint flooded her throat. "You disarm me far too often."

"I could haul you onto my horse and disarm you further. That's a trope in certain smutty novels, you know."

"We should keep going."

"Answer the question, and we will."

She sighed. "Must I tell you what you already know?"

Nay. I could guess why nobody was aware of what she could do. 'Twas the element of surprise that worked in her favor, should the need arise to defend herself.

Aire had implied as much before we left. Despite her prickly facade, no one would expect this Autumn princess capable of wielding a weapon. Not with her pacifist reputation and prim breeding. Case in point, this would work to our advantage if the Masters grew stupid, decided not to believe our farce, and got weapon-happy.

Briar stared at the pommel of her saddle, her suede gloves straining over the reins. "Poet?"

"Aye, my thorn?" I inquired.

Her head lifted, and her eyes clutched mine. "Now you know everything."

I want to see every truth about you—everything raw and real.

My mouth itched for her. "Now I love everything."

I snatched her fingers and brushed my lips across her gloved knuckles, making sure the contact burned down to her skin. When we reached this retreat, I couldn't promise to behave myself.

Briar's hand quivered. "And I have everything."

That, she fucking did.

The princess glanced at the road. "Be careful not to touch any wild cranberries or root vegetables that aren't ripe. You can tell by their dull color or scaly texture. They'll cause an outbreak across your flesh, as well as a perilous fever if you touch your mouth afterward." She turned back to me. "Follow my lead."

I winked at her. "Don't I ever?"

Her lips tilted. Snapping the reins, Briar sent the horse flying. Her cloak whisked around her slight frame, and that flaming hair blazed through the shadows.

I shot after her. For miles, we raced through the wild, pounding from the beech forest and through The Shadow Orchard with its treacherous apples. After a series of breaks and sprints, we passed into a woodland cluttered with blanched, warty aspens capped in yellow leaves on the eastern side. Foxes trotted through the foliage, their faces pinched and their fur as russet as Briar's hair.

I remembered her description from the night we arrived at the castle. We'd stood on the balcony, where she nervously rattled off the geography, aware that I only gave half a shit about the details, because all I'd wanted to do was make her moan.

In any case, she'd called this area The Fox Dell. And to the west, ravens sailed over a morass of brambles in The Forbidden Burrow. No wonder it was hard to reach, for the place was a chaotic web of nettles, prickly shrubs, and thorns.

That jungle was where the Masters hosted their shindigs? They came all the way out here, and on purpose?

And people called *me* dramatic.

We blended into the murk, keeping off the main thoroughfare. Briar guided us through shrouded avenues and unmarked crossways. The aspens and spiny brambles faded behind us, replaced by hickory trees crocheted with moss and pumpkins clustering the landscape. The wild gourds bloated across the underbrush and glowed like lanterns. Some were scattered, and others were gathered in batches, with vines curling from their stems and draping over the ground. Like beacons, the gourds emitted orange light, as if someone had lit candles from inside their wombs.

Seasons. The Pumpkin Wood was a darkly lush sight to behold.

Briar threw an expectant look my way.

I huffed. "Oh, knock it off. You know I'm impressed."

Grinning, she urged her mount through the foliage. The hickory trees and incandescent pumpkins split to reveal a structure tucked into the shrubbery. The cabin rose two stories high, with a steeply pitched roof that must be an attic. Brickwork on the bottom level, combined with half-timbering on the upper portion, gave the home a picturesque appeal. Casement windows contained frosted plates of glass, making it impossible for anyone to see inside.

The exterior was humble, refined without being opulent. Passersby would assume a wealthy merchant or solitary noble lived here.

A small stable loomed beside an herb plot. Beyond that, the spokes of a mill abutted a wide pond. The wheel was stagnant but in excellent working shape.

The location brought to mind the coziness of a certain home in the wildflower forest. My ribs clenched at the thought of Jinny. She would like this place as much as Nicu, especially the luminous pumpkins.

We paused at the clearing's threshold. My eyes scanned the perimeter. Next to me, Briar surveyed the environment, her Autumn senses attuning to details I wouldn't notice.

"It's clear," I murmured.

"Yes," she agreed.

We trotted from the enclosure and dismounted. Briar got busy fussing, hustling the animals into the stable, and marching off to fetch water. I unloaded the necessities we'd packed, found a brush, and wiped the sweat from the animals' coats, then raked hay into a mound for them.

Briar returned and accomplished the rest with vigor—too much vigor, in fact. She set down the water bucket, rearranged the hay mound, and inventoried a nearby barrel of carrots as if the horses would starve. Then her attention swung across the stable, her pragmatic mind searching for another task.

This restlessness happened whenever we found ourselves somewhere new. For a second, I leaned against the door jamb and waited her out. With a cocked head, I watched the princess exhaust her efforts, just as she had in her suite that first night. It might be unchivalrous of me not to help, but I'd never been the gallant type, and the exertion brought a marvelous tint to her cheeks. Thusly, I required a prime view.

"Your Highness," I said, my voice softening. "Briar."

Finally, she heard me. "Huh?" she puffed, turning my way.

"It's getting late. There's a bed waiting for us."

Her pupils inflated. The flush that doused her complexion made those freckles stand out like pieces of candy. "Oh, yes." She gestured toward the cabin. "It's this way."

So I gathered. Briar realized it as well, because as she passed me, her profile cringed in embarrassment.

Those creases did me in. Before she made it another two steps, my hand shot out and caught her wrist. The princess gasped and stalled in place.

Holding her gaze, I threaded our fingers together. "Now show me."

Her throat bobbed. Mutely, she allowed me to guide her across the lawn.

Logistically, I should round up our bags from where I'd left them in the stable. But fuck it. That could wait.

A walkway led to the quaint front door speckled in moonlight. Briar fumbled for a ring of keys from under her cloak, but when she fitted it into the lock's hole, her wrist shivered. I stepped up from behind, my chest aligning with her back. My hand covered hers, fingers overlapping. Like this, I nipped the princess's ear and helped her twist the key.

Together, we unlocked the door.

24

Briar

The latch squeaked. The partition swung open. And I charged into the cabin.

The scents of antique wood and nutmeg greeted me. Despite the darkness, familiar sights came into view. Rough-textured plaster walls and two load-bearing pillars. A heavy iron chandelier tipped with candles. Patterned rugs covering the floor and copper cookware hanging from a rack in the kitchen.

Two floors. Two bedrooms.

But only one bed.

The second sleeping chamber was under renovation. We hadn't had time to finish drawing up the plans since before leaving for Spring.

I plowed through the dark space. My legs carried me to the tall fireplace, its flue and stoop constructed of the same brick as the exterior walls, and the hearth inset beneath a chunky oak mantel. Quickly, I took stock of the logs piled in a brass casement and the tinderbox on the mantel.

I scrutinized the bookcases flanking the fireplace. One by one, I checked the storage bins that were packed on the lower shelves and flipped the compartments open. Damnation, the cabin had been depleted of precious Winter timber and wax candles. Fabricated by the Season's inventors, those supplies kept fires going and light fixtures illuminated for days at a time. Usually, we retained a bounty here.

Fine, then. Snatching the tinderbox from the mantel, I tossed logs and kindling onto the grate and set about lighting a blaze. My fingers jerked, swiping the flint against the fire striker over and over. Sparks darted into the air but failed to ignite.

"Blast," I swore.

"Briar," came Poet's voice from behind, the sound caressing my spine.

I shook my head. "I cannot get the kindling started."

"Briar, sweeting—"

I struck the tools once more, to no avail. "I have never had trouble before. It should be lit already. I know how to do this."

"Briar. Stop."

"No, I will not. We must warm this house." Swerving away, I discarded the tinder and flint, rubbed my hands, and marched toward a desk huddled in a corner. "Also, the kindling seems damp. Perhaps we should use paper." I rifled through the drawers, then flung up my hands. "You must be jesting!"

"Not yet," Poet murmured from several feet away. "But I'll let you know."

"Why don't we have any extra parchment?"

Giving up for now, I tracked through the first floor. From the living room, to the kitchen pantry, to the dining nook, to the study, to the bathroom, to the cellar, I audited our provisions. I threw open cupboards, inspected trunks, and surveyed closets and cabinets.

Poet braced his fingers on the back of a sofa as I quested from one end of the cabin to the other. "Not that I don't appreciate your industrious nature, but just in case you haven't noticed, we're not exiled in a snowstorm, love."

"We require necessities," I stated.

"For three days," he reminded me. "Not for three months."

"You're the one who overpacked."

"I like wardrobe options when going on a mole mission. That's not the same thing."

"You're quite right."

I left him to interpret that and continued my search. The cellar housed grains, root vegetables, frozen and salted meat, water and wine and cider and nectar. There were plenty of linens and towels and soap. We had medicine and bandages.

But we didn't have an advanced way to get a fire started. Yet even with the basics, I've never had trouble doing it before.

Returning to the fireplace, I caught sight of Poet in my periphery. He stood in the shadows, watching me. His unearthly eyes glinted through the murk like green scopes.

I tried contending with the tinder again. My knuckles strained, and my digits jerked the tinder harshly—until a hand shot out and snatched my wrists.

Poet hovered beside me. Orange radiance from the pumpkins outside trickled into the home, spotlighting the chiseled planes of his face. "Allow me," he intoned.

The gravity of the situation struck me like a mallet. I went still, thinking of how I must look, stressing and raging through the cabin like a compulsive woman. Shuffling backward, my eyes clung to Poet. Without looking away, he fastened his gaze to mine and struck the match with a single flick.

A tiny ball of flame popped from the wick. The globe of light flared between us.

Poet squatted and did the rest. A whoosh of air resounded as the logs caught fire, the wood sizzling and toasting the room.

As the jester straightened to regard me, my throat bobbed. "I do not know what came over me."

"Aye, you do," he said quietly, cupping my cheek and running his thumb across my flesh. "You don't need me to analyze it."

I flattened my palm over his knuckles. "They betrayed Autumn."

He nodded but didn't speak, spurring me to release everything pent-up inside, every source of strain that had been coiled in my gut. "They seek to harm my kingdom. They would harm Nicu and Mother. They would harm you." My eyes stung, even as they burned with anger. "They helped to build Autumn, as their forbearers did. I trusted them with this nation. Mother and I placed our faith in them. If they, of all people, can forsake us and pledge themselves to Rhys, what chance do we have to change anything?"

Poet stared at me for the longest time. "Then show them it's not that easy."

"But if we do this, we can't undo it."

"Sweeting, I knew in Spring, as I know here, as you know too. Some enemies will become our tribe. Other enemies will stay enemies. We won't be able to reach everyone."

"I never expected this would happen," I whispered. "Any of it."

"But it has. And it will keep happening."

I lifted my chin, despite how my voice cracked. "I do not regret it."

His lips tilted. "Good princess."

"Ruined princess," I corrected. "But I do not care."

"Mmm. I do have a fetish for subversive heiresses."

Yet he didn't chuckle. Neither did I.

"Father used to say our greatest achievements sprang from our harshest lessons. I'm not afraid for myself." I leaned in, soaking up the masculine whiffs of amber and vetiver. "I'm afraid for you."

The jester's gaze stroked mine. He slid one arm around my middle. "Nothing will happen to me. Most importantly, nothing will happen to you. I'll make sure of it. They'll lose their vitals before they have a chance to touch you."

"We're doing this," I realized aloud, the reality hitting me.

"We've done many things already," Poet murmured. "We've survived thus far. You and me, princess? Your wisdom and my words? Together, we're a brilliant fucking force. We can reign supreme and bring an army to its knees. I'm all in, Sweet Thorn."

"As am I," I replied. "All in. With you."

"And I do have a bit of faith in our ability to fool the fools. You should too."

A gust of oxygen raced from my lungs. "I do now."

Finally, my spine relaxed. The heat of his touch eased my muscles and reinforced my hope. Let no one sunder this thing between us. Whether it took ten years and a thousand enemies, we would triumph.

The flames swayed. Their molten temperature brushed my skirt and the carved edges of Poet's face. That's when I remembered where we were.

In this isolated cabin. In this dark forest brimming with luminous pumpkins.

Away from everyone. As we rarely could be.

We had never been secluded like this. Not without company.

Silence filled the dwelling, breached only by my thick respirations and the crackling blaze. Firelight spilled across the walls, hot colors swimming within the shadows. Although the windows were frosted on the outside, the panes were clear from inside, offering a view of the glowing orbs.

I became hyperaware of every flat surface in the vicinity. Every floor, every countertop, every wall. Every stick of furniture, from the dining table to the sunken chairs, to the bathroom shower, to the four-poster bed upstairs.

Earlier, I'd felt sheepish, still affected by what happened in the throne room. Happy but awkward. Each time I assumed we'd consummated in every way possible, this erotic jester introduced me to a new enticement, another source of stimulation.

My timidness faded. It always did the moment his words wrapped around me like ribbons.

Awareness hooded Poet's gaze. "Princess," he husked. "If you keep thinking what you're thinking, we'll never make it out of this hideout."

My folds contracted. My heart skipped anxiously—impatiently.

"I won't complain," I replied. "Or weren't you planning to fuck me tonight?"

"Oh, I was," he assured me. "Up until the second you got into a wrestling match with the tinderbox. Don't get me wrong. Now that I have you to myself, and you can't escape—"

My eyebrows shot together. "I would never escape. I ... Oh, that was ... You were teasing me."

He smirked, a sensuous light glossing his irises. "Sweeting, I haven't begun to start teasing you."

Anticipation fluttered low in my belly. My walls clenched, and my clitoris thrummed. Reflexively, I pressed against him, my breasts rubbing through the bodice and pitting into his coat. "Then what delays you?"

His sultry mouth rode across my own. "I know my thorn. Sex is what you want. But it's not what you need."

"I'm not hungry."

"That's not what I meant."

"I'm not thirsty either."

"Splendid. Because I plan to fuck you senseless on every surface that has been tiptoeing through your mind." His molten timbre oozed down my limbs and swirled between my legs. "I have every intention of making your precious little pussy come around my cock, several times in succession, once you're ready for it. For when I start, I won't stop until you've shouted for so long, it rings through this house and into the wild."

"That might get us discovered."

"Frankly, I'll be so deep inside you, neither of us will give a shit." Poet's lips scorched against mine. "But first thing's first."

I grunted. "I'm your sovereign. I can bend you to my will."

"Ambitiously insatiable princess. Be careful what you ask of a jester. You need sustenance first, if you wish to keep up with me."

"You are a bragger."

"That's hardly news. First, this." His teeth nipped my lower lip, the points sinking deviously into my skin until I whimpered. "Then, this." Out of nowhere, he fished inside my cloak pocket and held aloft the letter from Eliot, the missive poised between his fingers. "And then food. After that, I hope you're not attached to those clothes because they won't be fit to wear once—"

"—once you're done with me?" I guessed, taking the letter from him.

"Nay, love." This time, Poet bit my upper lip, sending tingles down my vertebrae. "Once we're done with each other." And when my mouth slanted in aroused amusement, he straightened. "There's the smile."

Winking, he twisted away and sauntered to the kitchen. "Sit. Read. I'll take care of our foreplay dinner."

"You don't know where—"

"I think I can find my way around a kitchen. I'm the one who made you soup at Jinny's, remember?"

"But—"

"Hush, my beautifully neurotic temptress. Open the minstrel's letter. Make yourself at home."

My insides tightened with need. "This *is* my home," I reminded him.

To which, Poet dismissively twirled his fingers in the air. The gesture wrought a short laugh from me. He truly did not know the meaning of humbleness. Also, he would pay dearly for leaving me in lustful tatters.

Sighing with laughter, I fanned myself. Nonetheless, the effort failed to cool my body.

The echoes of crockery and cutlery filled the cabin. The ambience settled in my bones like a warm bath—comforting, reassuring. Being here with him felt different from the castle or even Jinny's cottage. Whatever happened tomorrow, this interlude belonged only to us.

Eliot's letter rested in my fingers. I brought the envelope to the sofa, sank into the cushions, and draped a blanket over my limbs. Breaking open the lute seal brought his wide, loopy handwriting into stark relief.

Longing flowed through me. Wistful. Cathartic. Poet had been right. He could fuck me sweetly, make love to me hard. He could sweep away everything on my shoulders, make it all disappear. But no matter how intense the pleasure, the aftermath couldn't last unless I tended to myself first.

I needed this. And so, I nestled deeper into the couch and began to read.

Master. Monarch.

A quiet chuckle leaped from my mouth. My best friend and I always greeted each other this way.

My Spirit. My Briar.

Wetness pooled in my eyes. I felt a grin stringing across my face.

Although you've been gone only a few weeks, time has stalled. Life has been moving on, yet it hasn't without you, if you understand me, which I know you do, since you've always understood me better than I've ever understood myself.

Tell me you're okay. I agonize over this, but then I remember how strong you are, how brave and steadfast. I suppose I never told you this, not since we were twelve, but you're my idol. You might think Poet was my hero, but you would be wrong, my friend. Well, that is to say, he was my fantasy. But you were my idol, my inspiration, my first love. I mean, not in that way, but you get my drift.

I could fill this letter with all the basic bullshit—how I am, what I'm doing. I'm good despite missing you, and I'm sure our favorite ladies will fill you in on the rest. But the thing is, this letter isn't about me. Hell, it's not for me.

It's for you.

If I know my faithful princess, she's steeling herself against whatever's getting in her way. She's upright, standing tall like the towering trees and fields of her land. But she's also fretting, worrying, reorganizing every item in the room, to keep control, to keep herself together, to keep from doubting her every move.

I'm writing to say don't do that. Don't ever second guess yourself, Briar. The things I'm trying to do in Spring? The stuff I'm doing for this world to change? That's what I meant by you inspiring me. Don't discredit the effect you have.

Sometimes you need to embrace disorder, because it just might give you an edge. Sometimes the best plans are the ones that were never plans to begin with. Sometimes the unknown is the right way.

You discovered me at a midnight festival when we were scrawny fledglings, and that day shaped my future. You became the Court Jester's target, then you became his equal. You rescued a child from the claws of a Seasonal tyrant and gave the boy a reason to believe he would always be safe. You changed our lives because that's who you are.

You're a wish granter, a heroine for the ages, and you're in every song I write. You're the reason legends are created. You were a leader long before you wore a crown, and really, who needs a crown anyhow? You may look aloof to people, but you care about them, so let others say you're prissy, and then prove those fuckwits wrong.

In other words, be yourself. Poet knows who that is. I do too. You're not alone, and you never were. And now you're one of two—the princess and the jester, a match for the ages. I reckon that warrants a ballad, or two, or three. But even if you were on your own, you would survive better than any of us.

By the way, Basil and Fatima recently asked if I'd compose a raunchy song about rabbits. The shit people think of, right? We'd have a good fucking laugh about that.

I love you more than anyone.

Yours, Eliot

The note floated to my lap. Tears pushed against the backs of my eyes, and a lump inflated in my throat. Ahead of me, the fire blurred to an orange puddle.

I replayed Eliot's words, letting them fill in the gaps his absence had left behind.

Then something occurred to me. My brows furrowed as a passage cycled in my mind.

Sometimes you need to embrace disorder, because it just might give you an edge. Sometimes the best plans are the ones that were never plans to begin with. Sometimes the unknown is the right way.

I leaped to my feet. Hastening to the kitchen, I found Poet standing with his back to me, a blade in his hand as he chopped a carrot. I rushed toward him, gripped his forearms, and yanked him around.

The knife hit the ground. The carrot followed in the blade's wake.

Poet grunted. "What the fuck—"

"We have to go," I urged. "Now."

This couldn't wait. We would return here afterward, but we had to meet with the Masters tonight.

Ten minutes after I rushed through an explanation, Poet and I were mounted on our horses and galloping into the wild. Gourds pulsated, shadows laced the bracken, and starlight etched the trees as we passed from one territory to the next. The pumpkins shrunk behind us, replaced by the eastern aspens of The Fox Dell and the western brambles of The Forbidden Burrow. The serrated web of nettles, prickly shrubs, and thorns appeared like a blockade.

Except it was no barrier. Not to anyone who looked closer.

From a remote corner, an owl hooted, and a fox shrieked. Dismounting and tethering our horses, Poet and I picked our way past the snare. "It is not far," I told him, guiding us through the arteries.

Poet's agility worked in his favor. Memory worked in mine.

We navigated our way through the jagged channels, the brambles prodding our clothes. "Is this a bloody joke?" Poet demanded. "I'm all for exclusivity, but this is extreme even for my standards."

I could hardly disagree. The distance was not great, so much as it was precarious.

After a handful of twists and turns, we ducked under a thorny overhang and emerged into a compact clearing where a door embedded itself into a thick tree trunk.

The eventide chill seeped through my merino wool top. I felt the weight of numerous thorn quills camouflaged in my headband. Squaring my shoulders, I moved forward.

But Poet jerked me backward, snatched my profile, and wretched my head toward his. His mouth swooped down and caught mine. Those lips crushed against my own, tugging on me swiftly, fiercely, hotly. I barely had time to kiss him back when he ripped his mouth away and swung his arm toward the entrance. "Princesses first."

A black diamond slashed through his left eye, the way it had when I'd met him. Under that expensive cabernet-dyed coat and raven cravat, I imagined how many daggers he'd stashed into various harnesses.

Our gazes fused, welding together like iron. Unbendable. Unyielding. Time to do what we did well, to be the match they didn't see coming.

We strode to the door, where I knocked in a particular rhythm. The sound would echo down the tree trunk's hollow throat, deeply into the earth. Something twitched overhead, shaking the leaves free, so they rained down.

A moment passed before the door opened. A small face poked through the darkness.

From beside me, I heard Poet's barely restrained hiss. Much like him, I struggled to conceal my reaction.

Although I hadn't come here with Mother often, I had met with the guild enough times to know the members were adults. However, the female who greeted us lacked a mature age. This stranger couldn't be a Master, because she wasn't old enough to be. And yet, hanging at her side, dangling in her grip was a curved blade attached to a short handle.

The figure carried an axe. The figure was a child.

25

Poet

Holy wicked fucking shit. It went without saying, but I'd say it anyway. We had expected weathered features, replete with filaments of silver tinsel in the female's hair, or at least a face ranging from eighteen and older. No one in our predicament—no one in their logical mind—would expect our hostess to have barely achieved puberty.

Behold. There were indeed times when the jester was rendered speechless. We loomed over the girl, who peered at us with eyebrows that slanted downward like ramps.

A child. A motherfucking child.

Because of the hooded cloak she wore, I could only guess the wee one's age, which couldn't be more than ten years old. In the dull light blooming from inside the tree trunk, I made out a few distinct traits. Long wavy hair hung to her hips, a beauty mark notched above her upper lip, and hazel irises rimmed around her pupils.

Briar stiffened in shock. "Oh," she exclaimed. "Hello, there. We're—"

"I know who the hell you are," the girl replied, her voice as smoky as a chimney. "You're early."

"Unfashionably so," I agreed, kneeling before the moppet. "Alas, time is of the essence. And who might you be?"

"Someone," she answered with so much moxie that I repressed a dark smirk. Were this not a horrific turn of events for more reasons than I could count, I would have applauded the tyke's gumption. So much for charming her. Usually children gravitated to me, but I had the feeling it would take more than jokes and verse to entertain this one.

I shrugged. "Well, Someone. It's past your bedtime. Shouldn't you be asleep, dreaming of trees to chop down with that axe?"

The girl harrumphed. "Do I look like a toddler to you?"

"You look like you're blocking the doorway to me."

"Whatever. I don't need a fucking nursemaid."

Oh, ho, ho. The sprite had a tongue to match her crispy voice. "Evidently," I remarked. "Then let's jump to it, shall we?" I knocked my head toward Briar. "This woman favors discretion, whereas I prefer pomp and circumstance. At the risk of redundancy, I never pass up an opportunity for a grand introduction. You understand, of course. So allow me: This is Princess Briar, and I'm the infamous Court Jester who presumably corrupted her in his own fucked up way. We know being late is the stylish thing to do, but let's pretend we're starting a new trend. The earlier, the swankier. Care to bid us entrance now? It's getting cold, and the condensation is messing with my hair."

The girl drummed her fingers on the door jamb. "Like hearing yourself talk, do you?"

I quirked a brow. "You say that like it's a bad thing."

Her mouth twitched, as though she might grin. But promptly, she smoothed out the impulse and whirled around. "Shut the door behind you."

"Ever heard of *please*?" I drawled as we followed her inside, and I closed the partition.

The girl flipped a lock of her hair. "Manners are for nobles."

Hmm. So many comebacks at my disposal, all of them insulting.

The last thing I needed was for my filter to react viscerally. At least not until we figured out what the fuck was happening and why we'd been greeted by a sassy juvenile instead of an adult.

The crusted interior of the trunk dug into the earth, with a stairway winding below the surface. Instead of sconces, the tree's bark glinted with a natural light reminiscent of illuminated brass.

Ahead of us, the girl trotted down the steps. Briar shook her head at me, testifying that she'd never seen this moppet during former meetings. To that end, I hoped to hell this was a fluke or misunderstanding. Mayhap she was the daughter or granddaughter of one of the Masters.

The princess and I came to a silent conclusion. Regardless of the girl's enigma, she had to be the one Nicu encountered. I hated to think it, but when he quoted and imitated her voice, I'd noted the smoky inflection and youthful tone.

But what rattled us to the core was the second probability. Aire had said none of the Masters wielded axes, even though that's what hacked off Merit's head.

Repelled, Briar glanced at the weapon hanging from the girl's small fist. I did the same, my mood darkening further.

"Tell me, Someone," I drawled on the way down. "I appreciate the occasional prodigy, but aren't you a trifle young to be a Master? How did you manage to snag this membership? What's your secret?"

The fascinating creature windmilled her axe once, then let it swing back to her side. "I'm good at what I do."

"That's all we get? No embellishments to the backstory? How boring."

"I'm telling the truth. If you want a fairytale, open a book. Though if you ask me, stories aren't worth a damn."

What a disastrous thing for a child to say. "At minimum, I hadn't expected you to get straight to the point."

The girl continued hopping down the passage. "Bragging is fun."

I respected that. What I didn't respect were the cocksuckers who'd put this tyke up to ... whatever they'd put her up to.

A hollow, baritone sound flooded the trunk, like the inside of a cello. Muffled dialogue drifted up the corridor. We reached a landing, where several passages tunneled into various directions. They must lead to separate quarters where the Masters slept, if they met here for days on end.

Our hostess shuffled toward a grilled door and pushed it open. Inside, the vast room had thick, snarling roots for walls. Mounted to the facades were diverse emblems including iron, stone, steel, wood, and gold, among a host of others. Each one depicted a different trade symbol.

My canines ground together. The gold placard had been carved to resemble a crown.

In the room's center, opulently tufted chairs surrounded a long, rectangular table, and the sources of muted conversation came into view. Two dozen men and women ran the gamut from their twenties to their seventies. Each of them modeled distinct styles of braids and wore matching wood brooches—encrusted with a jeweled likeness of Autumn's coat of arms—that fastened their vests, coats, and mantles closed.

The same number of blades, swords, and hammers rested either in their sheaths or on the wall brackets.

In unison, the guild stood. Their reactions fluctuated between stunned and cordial as they bowed.

"Your Highness," they chorused.

One of them stood out from the others. The middle-aged man had hair as dry as straw, with the layers netted into multiple plaits, bound at his nape, and trailing down his lanky form. I assumed him to be the leader.

His patina irises flashed to me, then vaulted to the princess. "An unexpected pleasure," he greeted Briar, his inflection sounding as though he spent his free time chewing on glass.

"The pleasure is mine," Briar lied, then motioned to me. "You haven't met the Court Jester yet. Allow me to introduce Poet."

"Yes, well." The man clipped his head my way and spoke to the princess while scrutinizing my very existence. "Did we get the date wrong? How careless of us."

"Not at all. I do hope you'll excuse our intrusion," the princess said. "My schedule changed at the last moment, which made it impossible for us to conference with you tomorrow. This was the only available time. With Mother's permission, I'm eager to discuss the ongoing conflict regarding admission to the guild."

"Most appreciated that Her Highness has made this unfortunate squabble a priority. Nonetheless, we weren't prepared for you and your—" he regarded me with snooty apprehension, "—guest."

"I prefer the term *fanatic*," I drawled.

"Is that a fact?"

"One of many facts, matter of fact."

The words skipped off my tongue, which caused the man's brows to flatten. So they knew to be on the offensive with a jester. Splendid and predictable. Our original plan to show up when expected had changed. Being punctual would have relaxed these players so they wouldn't anticipate an ambush, which would have made them careless around us. By contrast, we'd reasoned that making an unannounced appearance would put them on edge, making them less susceptible.

Initially, that had been our tactic. But Eliot's letter had inspired the princess to rethink that logic. On the contrary, disorder would deny the Masters time to brace for contingencies or fabricate excuses. This would also disarm them, but even more so than the former option.

Briar had determined catching them off guard outweighed any other choice. The more apprehensive they felt, the more vulnerable they felt. The more vulnerable they felt, the easier to tell when a nerve had been struck. That made it increasingly possible, and all the more rewarding, to locate the crawl spaces in their veneers. As such, the princess and her jester could weed out the shit they tried to hide.

The girl who called herself Someone tarried at the threshold. The leader noticed her and cleared his throat, then jutted his head toward a three-legged stool in the corner. No cushion. No cup of water. Yet plenty of chalices, decanters, and flagons crammed the dining table.

The girl's feisty nature deflated like a balloon. She skulked toward the stool and perched there, her mouth sealing shut. 'Twas the very picture of an obedient little mercenary.

One of my fists curled. Whether to smash it into the leader's skull or to restrain my fury, I couldn't say. But one crucial fact relieved me of having to blame the child. She could have hurt Nicu when he caught her skulking through the orchard camp, but she didn't. And though the moppet might have chopped off Merit's head—Seasons al-fucking-mighty—this girl hadn't done it willingly.

Recruiting children to commit murder was a dealbreaker among a thousand dealbreakers. One more reason I would shave Rhys's flesh from his hide when I had the chance. The Masters took their orders from him, and I doubted he objected to them using a stripling as one more pawn in this game. Summer already took advantage of enslaving born souls when they were only fledglings; he'd almost gotten his talons into my son, and now this.

In the end, I'd make him scream until his lungs collapsed. But first, I fantasized about practicing on his cult.

I stalked toward the table, my intentions clear. But Briar had the same idea and reached the furnishing first. The members parted as she claimed a chalice and filled it with water from one of the flagons. Striding to the girl's side, the princess wordlessly handed over the cup.

The mini mercenary hesitated, then accepted the cup before tossing down the contents in one gulp. She burped and wiped her mouth with her sleeve. "Thanks, I guess."

Briar inclined her head and refilled the chalice. This time, more of the girl shone briefly in the light. The instant the princess blinked at the moppet's appearance, a glower pursed the child's face as she realized her flesh was on display. Quickly, she jerked back, causing the stool to wobble.

My brows slammed together. I'd seen it too—something uncanny about the girl's skin. It was hard to decipher since the stripling kept to the shadows, tucking the cloak and hood tighter around her. Veiny lines ran up her throat and threaded across her chin, oddly akin to wood grain. In the half-light, that was the most I could confirm.

As the mini mercenary drank, the princess recovered. She cast me a perceptive glance before scowling at the faction. "What is a child doing here?"

"That mutation?" the man with the dehydrated braids said, jerking his arm toward the girl. "She's filling in."

Mutation. Freak. Simpleton. Half-wit.

I'd heard them all. Over the centuries, every word had congealed into a noxious poison I'd love to shove down their throats, right before my dagger deprived the men of their cocks and the women of their tongues.

Except this girl didn't seem to have the conditions I'd witnessed in born souls, nor in my son. From what I saw—which, admittedly wasn't much—the most she exhibited was a skin condition under that oversized cloak. So what?

Briar scowled, and I spoke for the two of us. "That's not very mannerly of Autumn."

At last, the pack acknowledged me. They swerved my way, dubious but proud.

The leader cleared his throat. "We see your sidekick has become a permanent fixture."

"That's also a rather disappointing description," I pouted. "Guest. Sidekick. Fixture. So politely industrious."

"And inaccurate on both accounts," Briar clipped. "This child and the Court Jester deserve more. As is customary, I expect better from the Masters."

"Of course." The man bowed, along with his flock. "Forgive me, Highness."

"To them. Not to me."

Reluctantly, the leader grumbled his apologies and gestured to the table. "Please. It's not every evening we have Royal company."

Considering the place reeked of Summer's aura, I would bet

against that. Rhys tended to leave a putrid, oceanic stench behind, like sulfur marinated in bullshit. 'Twas a unique stink that lasted months and made my eyes water.

I might be hyperbolizing. Could one blame me?

We took our seats, chair legs skidding across the floor. After Briar requested the leader make introductions, he presented me to the rest of his brood—the arrowsmith, blacksmith, metalsmith, glassblower, bricklayer, stonemason, thatcher, welder, builder, lumberjack, tanner, and a drove of other occupants.

Upon closer inspection, the Masters' clothing demonstrated their wealthy professions. Their suede garments were dyed in rich, earthy colors and garnished with fine stitching. Though, each vestment lacked jeweled ornamentation apart from the fancy brooches.

They may work with their hands, but these were not the same laborers who dwelled throughout the rest of this nation. Poised at the top, they led the pecking order and benefited extensively from it, unlike the peasants and villagers I'd grown up with. Groomed despite the calluses and scars, they could have been mistaken for nobility or gentry. They certainly dressed and drank like them.

The leader set a hand on his chest, scabs encrusting his knuckles and a chunky, twenty-four karat ring encircling his thumb. "My name is Vex. I'm the Master Goldsmith."

Fuck. Him. Hard.

I thought of the anguished fury stored behind Briar's eyes, in addition to the broken crown pieces littering Merit's torso. With supreme effort, I bit my tongue. Instead of silver spilling from lips, the pressure of my teeth caused blood to wet my palate.

Apples centered the table, the orbs propped in a large, fluted bowl like a shrine. The princess spent an unordinary amount of time staring at them, her gaze tracing every facet. Her features didn't change, yet they didn't need to.

She emitted an appreciative noise that could have glamoured a rock wall. "They're beautiful," she uttered, motioning for the men and women to pass a specific one down to her. She twisted the pome in the brass light glinting from the tree trunk's interior. "Ripe. Smooth. I've rarely seen such a perfect batch."

"Picked them myself, Highness," the arrowsmith boasted.

"Is that so?" Briar replied. At which point, her pupils darted to mine, and her finger ran back and forth across the apple's flesh.

Do not touch them.

I read the unspoken message and remembered what she'd once told me about these fruits. Pick the wrong ones, and they sucked a person's greatest skill from their bones. The result could be minor or fatal, depending on what the victims considered their best assets. As such, a Royal could lose her masterful ability to reason, negotiate, or lead a kingdom.

Had these crafters expected us tonight, after all? They couldn't have.

Had any of them consumed an apple yet? Evidently not.

All the same, it seemed the height of idiocy to go near something that could potentially rob the eater of their strongest skill. So why else would the Masters fill this bowl with poison delicacies?

My fingers itched for the daggers stored under my coat. But from the look in Briar's eyes, this wasn't premeditated. So the reason was either something incomprehensible, or these figures were ignorant about Autumn's crops, or they were just plain stupid.

Briar handed back the apple and kept her posture upright. "Wherever did you find this assortment? Which orchard or farm? I'd love to procure some for Reaper's Fest."

Ah. Silence engulfed the room.

The arrowsmith's eyes flitted to the goldsmith—the one absurdly named Vex—before responding with a fabricated grin. "Got them from The Shadow Orchard. It's yielding a fine crop right now."

Casually, I flicked lint from my sleeve and made a show of wrinkling my nose like a pampered dandy. *Humor them, my thorn.*

Briar caught the signal, pretended to be unfazed, and worded her reply carefully. "Well. It's a comfort to hear some good is coming from there."

"I meant no offense, Highness," the man insisted, feigning guilt and concern. "The orchard is a traumatic subject, to be sure. If we'd known to expect you, we wouldn't have set out the bowl."

Rookie mistake. Such a rookie mistake, I almost felt let down.

Merit's death had been announced after Rhys's departure. Though as planned, we had omitted several important details about the murder.

Wisely, Vex hissed to the man. Agitated, the others stirred.

The princess waved off the apology. "I beg you. Our kingdom's most recent loss wasn't the fault of an apple." She perched her elbows on the table, folded her hands, and tilted her head. "Except I never said anything traumatic happened in the orchard."

Bull's-eye. The location of Merit's death hadn't been made public. The people only knew he was slaughtered during our voyage to Autumn.

I slouched in the chair like a lazy bastard, my mouth tipping along with the rest of me. "Tsk, tsk."

Vex's head shot my way. "What is that supposed to mean?"

Casually, Briar poured herself cranberry nectar from a flagon. Setting her chalice on the tabletop, she twisted the vessel's stem, initiating one of the many hand signals we'd invented. *What do you think?*

I snatched my own chalice and a wine decanter, filled it partway, and tossed back the liquid. *Be blunt.*

Briar's attention traveled across the table. "We know you've sided with Rhys."

26

Poet

She might as well have sucked the air from the room. The men and women didn't move, didn't look at each other. Their fingers froze, and their breathing stalled. But their eyes flared with indignation—and uncertainty.

Briar read their minds, her expression as flat as the ground. "Yes, the Queen knows too." After another round of silence, she said, "End it. Stand down against us."

That … wasn't supposed to come out so quickly. Sure, we'd planned to wrap up this discussion with an ultimatum, only not from the get-go. But the heiress's flinty exterior demonstrated just how pissed off she'd grown. Plus, she wasn't one to dance around the point.

The jester liked to play with his targets. The princess aimed for the heart and struck fast.

The girl called Someone blinked, her eyes wide and glistening with fear. I gave her a covert shake of my head and mouthed, *Not you.*

Briar and Avalea wouldn't blame a stripling for being forced into this. Thus, the girl hesitated, then her shoulders finally relaxed as she tugged the hood closer around her head.

In that time, the Masters recovered and burst into a tirade. Voices grumbled an eclectic mixture of sanctimonious denials and subsequent accusations, but Vex subdued them with his raised palm. After a tense moment, the pack relented, their faces either going slack with guilt or tightening with hostility.

The goldsmith leaned in, bracketing one forearm on the table. His movements caused the gold ring to choke his thumb. "Stand down or what? You'll have our heads on pikes?"

"That would be easy," Briar said primly, her drink forgotten. "I have more dire penalties in mind. End your allegiance with Rhys, step away from your plans, or be removed from the guild. All of you."

Again, the upheaval resumed. The men and women gripped the table, protesting over one another until the goldsmith shut them up again and spoke on their behalf. "So the reports about you are true. You would cast us aside for the sake of abominations," he barked, appalled. "They can't function. They can't think in a straight line. They're violent and incapable of fending for themselves. They can't build houses or erect monuments. They can't even sow the soil."

The Masters nodded and mumbled their assent. Their alpha continued, "Born fools make no contributions to this world, but normal people do." He stabbed his finger onto the table. "*We* do. As for our high and mighty sovereigns, you may create laws, but we created this Season. We built the foundation you're standing on—the foundation you're trying to uproot. The people will understand our actions."

"Murdering a soldier," Briar contested, her voice icy. "Threatening to massacre the public and make a scapegoat of innocent prisoners."

"Sacrifices," the stonemason defended. "Noble sacrifices of the people. Expendable sacrifices of the born. All in the name of preservation—of our culture, of this continent, which you aim to demolish with detestable notions about equality for those plagues of nature!"

"The people will condone our exploits," Vex added. "But if you condemn us—that, they won't tolerate. It will only give them fuel to hate you." He flung up his arm. "We knew the risks. Kill us if you want or ban us if you prefer. Either way, you'll suffer more while alive and free than we will dead or demoted."

The Masters jeered and squawked like a bunch of radical supremacists.

One by one, Briar trained her gaze on each member. "I wasn't finished. Not only will you be dismissed from the guild, but you'll be stripped of your ranks as elite crafters."

If I thought the silence was suffocating before, it was nothing compared to now. The tiny axe wielder in the corner mumbled an impressed "Shit" under her breath. Every other face blanched, their outrage reaching critical mass.

No matter the Season, legacy was everything. Losing one's place in the guild was already a significant blow. But the distinction of Master was supposed to be permanent, granted to a person for their lifetime, even after retirement. According to Briar, guild members carried that privilege with them to the grave, so cutting off that legacy was another matter entirely. And because these positions were inherited, this would impact their offspring as well.

"Our history. Our heritage," the glassblower stammered, his irises as pearlescent as oysters. "Your Highness would decimate tradition? Ruin us on a whim?"

I ran a digit across my lower lip. *Don't spoil them by answering that.*

"What do you expect will happen?" Vex charged. "This kingdom will splinter into riots if you denounce us. You have the public's lawful obedience, but we have their support. We have influence."

"Mother has their support," Briar lobbied. "I shall earn it too."

"You will earn nothing, Highness," he snarled. "For what you're hoping to achieve, I reckon it will be strenuous, if not unattainable, without the paragons of trade on your side. Not that any of us would assist you willingly, but making a mockery of the guild won't improve matters. You need us."

Briar's eyes tapered into thorns. "I rebelled against Spring's Crown and deceived a room full of Royals into signing a binding contract. I know this land as I know my breath. I know its roots, its seeds, and its soil. I've tilled and worked these acres, I've nurtured its fauna, and studied every paragraph of its history. I'm educated, resourceful, and steadfast. I have the continent's most alluring, silver-tongued, and dangerous scoundrel in my corner—"

"That's me," I remarked. Like a nuisance, I crossed my legs sideways, balanced one finger on my temple, and swung my head to Briar. "You forgot, hottest."

"I have a mother who has been ruling on her own," the princess went on. "At this juncture, I have the support I need. Also, I'm obstinate. Isn't that what the people say about me? Strict and stubborn." She honed the next sentence like the tip of a prong. "I think I'm capable of wearing a crown without you."

I committed the sight of this princess to memory, particularly for the next time my cock pounded into her. Until then, I thumped my chalice subtly on the table.

You've hit a nerve.

Not that she needed to be told this. I merely felt like congratulating her.

Vex glowered with umbrage. "You are nothing like your Mother."

In the past, Briar would have flinched. She didn't this time. The insult bounced off her like a pebble.

But to keep myself from ramming a belated fist through the man's cranium, I muttered, "History has, well, a history of reinventing itself. It takes decades or centuries sometimes, but it happens eventually. I'm sure in your tidy, dogmatic little brain, you're a maven at what you do. But I'm fairly certain replacing you won't be as difficult as you think. You're not the only gifted ones in this kingdom." I cocked my head. "You're just the ones more people know about."

"You belittle our craft," the welder accused from her end of the table.

"Nay, I'm expanding it," I replied. "The more, the merrier. Apart from my lovely sovereigns, hierarchy bores me. Just like your pride."

"Then are we free to assume anyone can replace the Court Jester?"

"Let's not get ahead of ourselves."

"Vanity," Vex spewed, a husk of braids flapping around his shoulders. "Vanity, profanity, lechery, and debauchery." He peered at Briar. "How low you've come."

Oh, joy. I'd been wondering how long it would take for one of them to bring up how many ways I'd fucked their princess wide open.

Instead of lamenting like Spring or raging like Summer, this exclusive pack berated, scolded, and censured. Case in point, their leader grimaced as if merely uttering the next comment violated his modesty. "Blasphemous," he listed to me. "Vulgar. Obscene. Sordid. Shameful—"

"Lewd. Crude," I rhymed, then swerved my head toward Briar and inquired, "When will he be done?" But on second thought, I redirected my gaze to the man. "Better yet, when are you actually going to insult me?"

"So little respect for Autumn ways," he carped.

"So little knowledge of Spring society," I parried.

"Your origin is immaterial. If you can't take our judgment in earnest, we must conclude you're proud of these traits."

"And if you can't appreciate those traits, I'm afraid your opinion is about as useful to me as a gilded bauble—something cheap that only looks valuable on the outside. If you paid a bit more attention to civilization beyond this cubbyhole, you might have learned that in the eyes of The Dark Seasons, I'm something of an icon. You may be a master." I rested my hands on my chest. "But I'm a masterpiece. Historically speaking, one of those tends to live longer than the other."

"Bah! The people will never bow to a traitorous, disgraceful, sympathizing whore—"

My retinas exploded. From under my coat, a dagger sped across the room and stabbed the table's surface, right between the man's splayed fingers. The next one struck a millimeter beside the opposite hand. The third ... well, the third waited in my grip, poised prettily just in case the miserable bastard hadn't gotten my point.

The girl called Someone yelped. Chairs creaked as the members skidded backward in shock. Half of them grasped the hilts of their weapons; the other half snatched their armory from the wall mounts.

Vex jerked his hand from the blade. His complexion reddened, but he stuck up his chin and regarded me like Rhys—like I was a demon set loose on the world.

"Let me guess," he muttered. "You could have aimed higher."

My mouth crooked. "I could have aimed lower."

The hooded girl in the corner snorted.

The leader grimaced. Evidently, Rhys hadn't made public how closed he'd come to being castrated by my dagger.

Briar continued to stare at him whilst smoothing out a wrinkle in her sleeve.

You've impressed them.

Despite the princess's unruffled exterior, her pupils dilated briefly at me. Seasons, I knew that look. She liked when I fondled my weapons for her benefit, did she?

Oh, but this woman didn't know the half of it. This cult might be wielding defenses, but they were fixated on me, not her. Otherwise, piles of severed body parts would already be littering the floor.

Briar glanced at the members and sobered. "Everyone is essential to Autumn. Every soul helps to build, nourish, and empower this land, including the ones you dismiss as human beings. Yes, there is a hierarchy, but it is never permanent, and it must not exclude anyone. It must give each person a democratic chance to thrive and excel. Therefore, I would have no qualms about downgrading you."

"Of all the sacrilege and hypocrisy," Vex answered. "The monarchy itself is an institution conceived through bloodlines. It's passed on, not campaigned for. That is our way and has been through The Dark Seasons for countless generations."

"It is *mostly* inherited," Briar reminded them. "Royals may appoint whomever they see fit to succeed them, either if their children don't suit the role, the monarchy hasn't produced an heir, or if someone comes forth to declare themselves. The Royals, as well as the council and the court's most faithful military leaders, determine the final selection. That structure is in place to give a chance to others who might seek it. *That* is our way."

"We know what you did in Spring," the blacksmith blurted out. "We could publicize it."

Except that during our chat with Rhys, we'd established how circulating this information wouldn't ruin Briar more than recent events already had. And while it was plausible the Masters would embellish, painting a grittier picture of the incident, I had opinions about this threat.

I tapped my chin. *They're full of shit.*

Briar considered my signal and declared, "You have no proof."

"Summer—," Vex began.

"Will not admit to scheming with you," I interjected, balancing my dagger's tip on the table and spinning it with one finger. "Do you honestly think he'll announce to the world that he has spies throughout the continent? Being pitchforked by Autumn may not be an issue, but having the monarchies of Spring and Winter discover that a Royal peer has their asses under surveillance?" I juggled the blade between my fingers, flipped it into the air, and caught the handle with the opposite hand. "That is a different matter. One, kings and queens don't like to be monitored, much less betrayed. Two, spies can be recruited in lots of places, from barnyards to brothels, whereas sovereigns are few and far between. Rhys may want you, but it's a one-night-stand at best." I lifted a brow. "He needs Spring and Winter's allegiance more. He needs the Royals eternally."

"You have no evidence we cooperated with him."

"Not yet," Briar conceded. "But once we do, it shall be easy. The public may spurn born souls, but they will not care to hear you've been arranging to take down their monarchy. Their ruined princess, perhaps. But not their beloved queen. In which case, dismissing you will be widely accepted."

"If what you say is true and Rhys denies everything, that doesn't change one important fact. Merely alleging we've conspired with the Summer King would lead him to declare war on Autumn."

"Yes, it would." She stared at them placidly. "So who said we'd involve him at all?"

Also not yet. Not until we had a plan to avoid bloodshed. Or at least lessen the chances.

Still, the princess needed the guild members to believe she'd focus solely on them. In their minds, they alone would be blamed for spying and plotting against the monarchy.

We waited to see if these cocksuckers would call that bluff. Yet no one made a reply.

After a long measure of silence, Briar inquired, "Shall I go on?"

"Allow me," I volunteered. "Just in case we need extra leverage, I did overhear one of the servants whispering in the halls at court. 'Twas something about the guild taking more than its share of rations from the previous harvest. Yes, jesters are nosy that way. And what would the public say? That offense could bring down every member here in a heartbeat."

Slandered, the men and women gnashed their teeth. Vex sputtered as if I'd accused him of fucking his way to the top of the food chain. "We would never—"

"True," I sang. "I made that one up. I just wanted to see what it did to each of your faces. Since Rhys isn't here, my funny bone needed compensation."

"Even if you tried, no one would swallow that farce."

"I'm a storyteller from the land of seduction and artistry. And I'm Poet. I've gotten people to swallow many things."

He glared at me. "You have perverted our princess with your foul Spring ways."

Nonchalantly, Briar rubbed her scarlet bracelet between her thumb and forefinger. *He's telling the truth.*

Quickly, I gave her a dry look. Hilarious, Princess.

The arrowsmith cut in and sneered at me. "You don't belong here. With a face like that, you may have fooled some, but there's no hiding the reality. You are disgusting."

A tempest stormed across Briar's features. "You will not offend the Court Jester," she said between her teeth. "Your duty is to us."

"Our duty is to Autumn," Vex protested, taking over the argument once more. "Our duty is to the future of this kingdom!"

"She appreciates that," I responded.

"You highfalutin spawn of hell!"

My blade dug into the table. Call my princess anything but the best, and the speaker would suffer. Hence, I spoke with fatal calm. "I wouldn't, if I were you."

But he didn't stop. "This is your fault."

The chair shuddered as Briar rose to her feet and plastered her palms atop the table. "I am doing my job to progress and defend this nation."

"I wasn't talking to you," the man spat.

My sweet thorn straightened. "Oh, by all means," she invited whilst gesturing to me. "Keep talking to him, then." Her voice flattened. "I dare you."

Every head pivoted my way. Their leader wavered as I stared back with an expectant look, my tongue ready to strike like a viper.

Smart chap. He turned away, composed himself, and studied Briar. "So that's it? Not only will you make us pay, but our children too. They've done nothing to you."

The princess kept a straight face. "You might have considered that before committing treason."

"Don't blame her." I pressed my hands to my chest. "I'm a morally gray influence."

My thorn repressed the evident urge to roll her eyes. Aye, I hadn't been able to resist.

Vex swapped glances with the Masters. After a moment of wordless deliberation, they disarmed, and he grunted, "If we concede?"

"No harm, no foul," I said. "Your skeletons stay down here."

From behind me, I heard the girl called Someone emit a low huff.

"The promise of a scandalous princess and her notorious jester means nothing," the leader stated. "The King of Summer won't take kindly to this. We want the protection of Autumn's military, plus a guarantee from Her Majesty in writing."

Briar nodded. "You shall have it."

In truth, Rhys would likely come after us rather than squander his energy on them. Ironically, he wouldn't see the Masters as worthy of retribution. Whereas Briar would have traded her life to safeguard these players.

Three minutes later, the meeting ended. We emerged from the tree trunk and into the forest, where Briar pressed her hand over her navel, and her steely expression collapsed. Great gusts shot from her mouth, and red flooded her cheeks.

On the threshold, we stalled, the rush of what just happened catching up with us. The girl idled behind, hovering in the entrance and about to close the door.

I swerved toward the moppet and stooped to the grass. This time, I gave her a deadpan look. "Are you here by choice? And don't lie, or this jester shall know."

"Pff. I'm no liar," the girl defended, although that feisty confidence didn't reach her eyes. "Every act is a choice. And it's my business."

Beside me, Briar lowered herself to the girl's height. "Is the axe your hobby or your vocation? You can tell us and trust that we'll know the difference."

In other words, we'd hear what she wasn't saying. Nor did she have to worry about confessing something that would imprison her. Whatever she was doing here, it wasn't for adventure or some perverse indoctrination. Based on her attitude, she wasn't being coerced or held captive either.

The girl wrenched her head sideways, peered at the ground, and clammed up.

I crossed my forearms over my upturned knee. "What's your name, Someone?"

"Names are dangerous," she muttered to the grass.

"Aye. It means we can track you down and find you. I know about keeping true names a secret." I leaned in and whispered, "I have the same problem."

Her head shot up. "Your real name is a secret?"

I nodded. "Shall we trade?"

Briar's gaze veered to mine. Only she, Nicu, and Jinny knew my real name. Whilst revealing it wasn't a risk any longer, the name had only ever been for trusted ears, and that habit proved difficult to break. Yet if this was what it took, I'd make an exception.

The girl considered, then shook her head. "I don't accept handouts. I won't take your name from you."

"Suit yourself. In that case, tell us what they promised you. A miracle? A packet of coins?" But when she rolled her glistening eyes, I took a gander. "Are you here to save yourself? Or to protect someone else?"

"Please," Briar insisted, her breath puffing out like tiny clouds. "How can we help you?"

"I don't need help," she mumbled.

"Then who does?" I wondered. "Who are you playing this game for?"

The girl's chest rose and fell. She pinched the hood tighter around her head, making it difficult for us to see her skin. "My mother." Her smoky voice cracked like a split log. "She's a Master."

"Which one?" Briar asked. "Can you tell us?"

The girl shook her head and peeked at us. "She's sick."

Ah. So that's what Vex meant about her filling in. The mother was a Master, too ill to do her job. And since this girl must be training to follow in the woman's footsteps, the elite guild had taken her daughter as a replacement and somehow compelled the tyke to do their dirty work. That must mean she had exceptional skill, if these crafters valued her.

Considering the axe, I thought of asking about the mother's trade. The lumberjack was accounted for, so some other manner of woodwork?

Unfortunately, we couldn't overstay our welcome. One more prying question, and the girl would withdraw.

Empathy flooded Briar's eyes. "We know what it's like to worry about our loved ones' suffering."

The girl blinked, her pupils watery. A second later, she sucked up the hint of tears and crossed her arms. "I'm not leaving with you, if that's what you're thinking."

"But you can," I told her. "You'd be safe. And we could send a court physician to take care of your mother—"

"No!" she yelped in panic, then leveled her voice. "No."

I squinted at her. If I didn't know better, I'd say this moppet didn't want her mother anywhere near the castle.

Agonized, Briar implored, "Come with us anyway. We won't ask questions."

"Or I could throw you over my shoulder," I suggested.

The girl stepped back and slapped the axe handle into her opposite palm. "Try it, asshole."

I would. And I'd succeed. Her aim wouldn't match my speed.

But if I did that, it might endanger her and her mother in a way we couldn't fathom. The Masters weren't abusing her physically, but emotional manipulation was another matter. Without the details, hauling this girl out of here could make her situation worse.

"Every act is a choice," Briar quoted the child reluctantly, then gave her a sad smile. "You are brave."

"And you're the liars." We balked, but she explained, "You're not punishing their sons and daughters for this. But you're not fixing to keep those two-timers as Masters either, no matter what they've chosen."

Astute, indeed. And impressive.

Briar would never spurn someone's kid for their parents' mistakes. The Masters' children would get a chance to earn their positions in the guild, as would every trade worker in this land once the rules became democratic. Be that as it may, Briar had needed the advantage, and the mere implication held weight.

As for the rest of it, this moppet was also right. Briar said she'd preserve the Masters' status. She just hadn't said for how long. We may not have physical evidence of their involvement with Rhys yet, but time would solve that problem, as well as how to expose our enemies without it amounting to a civil uproar, much less a battle between kingdoms.

We'd wait it out, then arrest the traitors. After that, the guild would be wide open to new crafters who earned those ranks fairly. And by then, hopefully the girl would have received whatever compensation she was seeking from these fuckers.

"Your boy," the girl said.

I stiffened. "You mean the fae lookalike who caught you tiptoeing through camp? That was quite a bothersome quote you regurgitated to him, by the way. With so many narrative options in existence, *'For the inheritance of the Seasons'* is my least favorite. If you live by that adage, we might have a problem."

Under the hood, patches of her face burned a penitent shade of red, making those curious grains stand out. "I was in a crappy mood and being sarcastic. That trashy saying isn't my style, but the Masters keep using it. I shouldn't have passed it on."

"Good. And sarcasm happens from time to time. Myself, I'm a frequent patron."

"And I didn't want to hurt the soldier." Her voice narrowed to a sliver. "I didn't want to hurt anyone."

"We know," Briar said quietly.

"They told me to take his head, but I didn't draw those symbols on him. The markings weren't me. Vex tailed me into camp right after I was done, and he …"

"We believe you. The broken crown pieces make sense now."

"Is he okay? Your boy?"

She directed the question to both of us. Briar nodded, her throat bobbing. "He is."

Simply by asking, this stripling made a fan of me for life. "Until we meet again, perhaps this will help." I fluttered my fingers along the back of her ear, then pulled away to reveal a silver coin worth several necklaces. The girl huffed with conceit, but a gleam broke through anyway. She snatched the coin and pocketed it. "Bet it took you no time to learn that trick."

Aye. This girl would survive without our intervention. More than trauma from killing a soldier, she embodied resilience to a confident degree. And laced within her bravado was a hint of brashness. Someday, she would grow into a plucky force of nature.

As much as we wanted to stop her, the girl called Someone strode into the tree trunk. But she kept her head aloft and her grip tight on the axe whilst shutting the door behind her. She also walked with more bounce than before.

Nonetheless my molars gnashed, my daggers weighed heavily in my coat, and my primal instincts wanted to disembowel the Masters slowly and thoroughly. But it was her life and her right to do whatever she needed. The little mercenary would be fine, even if I wasn't fine seeing her go.

I can't say if Briar tugged me, or if I tugged Briar away. Our hands molded together, and we stalked from that place, then leaped onto our mounts.

"We did it," Briar croaked, taking the reins.

"Aye," I said, cupping her jaw and pinning my gaze to her damp pupils. "We did."

This had hurt her. This had fueled her.

It was over. It couldn't be undone.

But we were alive tonight. My thorn was still breathing, and I had tamped down the urge to draw blood. Our weapons had remained attached to our clothes, apart from the daggers I'd toyed with for the guild's viewing pleasure.

How Rhys would take this news was another matter to deal with tomorrow.

We galloped from The Forbidden Burrow whilst checking periodically to make sure none of the Masters were following us. The princess and I rode in silence, our emotions fighting to settle. The further we went, the more I calmed down and Briar's shoulders relaxed. After that, we flew.

The horses accelerated, their muzzles punching out great clouds of air. While passing aspen trees in The Fox Dell, the distance kindled another impulse, akin to the one that had fired me up in Spring, when the Autumn heiress and I raced from the sunset carnival on Lark's Night.

The need to escape. The craving for release.

Celebratory relief sluiced through my veins. On the fringes of The Pumpkin Wood, the princess stalled her horse and shot her gaze to mine. Her eyes dilated, and her cheeks flushed a decadent pink, an unspoken appetite blossoming across her face. The effect made her freckles stand out like dots of paint that I longed to drag my tongue across.

We had won this first game. Now it was time to play another with her. Only this one, we'd enjoy.

This one would last all night.

27

Poet

We broke through the foliage. A breeze swept into The Pumpkin Wood, making the canopy of hickory leaves shiver. The setting glittered with molten orange hues, the gourds pumping light from inside their husks like globes. Together, they created a twinkling pattern, like a room outfitted with a thousand candles.

The whiff of apples and parchment hit me like an intoxicant. My thoughts disintegrated, and liquid heat swirled through my bloodstream. In less than a second, Briar's essence took effect. My cock vaulted upward, the stem thickening.

Grinding my canines, I dropped from the horse, my boots smacking the ground. At the same time, the princess halted beside me. In a hurry, she scrambled off her own ride and rounded the mare.

Whilst fixing my gaze to hers, I patted both creatures, sending them off to a remote patch of grass where they grazed. And good for them, for I didn't have the patience to tether the horses. For mercy's sake, I barely had the patience to fucking inhale.

The princess dashed toward me. My legs ate up the distance, and

I snatched her hips.

She uttered a needy, pleading sound as I hauled her into me. With a growl, my mouth came down hard, stamping to hers.

My sweet thorn cried out, the noise cracking from her lungs. She opened for me, those lips parting and emitting such warmth that I groaned. One my palms catapulted to the back of her skull, fastening her in place I pried her apart. My jaw worked into her, my mouth slanting and fusing with her own. She keened as my tongue flicked between those willful lips, lapping in a dizzying tempo.

My other hand veered to her ass, gripping it and steering her backward to the nearest … nearest whatever the fuck we landed against. Be it a rock boulder or a fallen trunk, I hardly gave a shit.

We hit a tree stump capped in moss, the perfect height for shackling her. Uttering a fiendish noise, I hoisted Briar off the ground. In unison, she bracketed her hands atop the trunk and hopped on.

My fingers grabbed her knees and split them apart. Slinging my arm around her middle, I yanked her to me, the motion scissoring her legs wide. Her thighs pitched around my waist as my ferocious lips seized hers.

I went deeply, harshly. And the princess took it.

Oh, how exquisitely she loved to take it.

I tasted her, feasted on her like a banquet. Briar's mouth rode mine whilst the temperature between her legs rose, prompting thoughts of how wet she must be, her body ready to clamp around my cock like a vise.

Seasons. Fuck.

This woman.

My mouth plunged. The flat of my tongue rowed inside her, swabbing in a hectic, sensuous rhythm. Briar drove her fingers through my roots and shoved her lips against mine. She rocked herself into me, her motions spreading the cloak, her nipples so tough they poked through the wool top.

My cock shot high, and my sac ached. Desire vaulted from the hilt to the pome of my erection.

Insatiably, I peeled my lips away with a grunt and sank my teeth into the delicate cove of her neck. Briar's moan pitched through the forest. She arched, extending her throat for me, which forced her thighs to flex and cling around my waist.

Like a glutton, I sucked her skin into my mouth. I pared my incisors over her flesh, used the pressure she liked, and drew on her with force. This manipulation had a glorious impact on her moans. Staggered whines fell from Briar's mouth, the noises soaring into the treetops and breaking apart.

Ah, my loud one.

But I could make her louder. And for longer.

The possibilities whirled in my head, all the locations I would have her, all the ways I would make her come. Releasing the sensitive skin, I swirled my tongue into the crook of her neck until she was delirious and her pussy emanated heat against my cock.

At length, I pulled away to relish the sight of her panting. Those lips were swollen, her cheeks mottled, and her pupils grew hazy.

I dragged my finger across her lower lip, my black nails flashing. I could fuck her right here, cover her eager screams whilst my cock pistoned into her, the impact of my hips shaking her atop the stump. Perhaps I would do so later, after we'd christened the cabin.

My voice came out husky, dangerous, intentional. "Get inside."

Whereas her voice came out sharp. "No." Then she cut off my growl by ordering, "Stay out here."

Commands from her often did it for me. Pent-up but intrigued, I watched as she detached herself from me, slipped off the trunk, and headed for the cabin.

That her legs wobbled caused my lips to tilt. She was soaked. Seasons help me, I wanted to lick every drop purging from her.

Briar glanced over her shoulder, ducked her head at me like a coy creature, and disappeared into the house. Several minutes passed in which I struggled to regulate my intakes and console my raging cock. Walking wasn't an option, so I maneuvered to a tree and leaned one shoulder against it.

Except idleness wouldn't do. Restless, I swiped a dagger from under my coat and flipped it like a short baton, then juggled it between my fingers, and then—

"Jester," she said.

I glanced up. And I saw her.

Wicked. Fucking. Hell.

I froze, nearly impaling my hand in the process. Only two parts of my body reacted to the sight that greeted me. My mouth dropped like a stone, and my fingers loosened, the dagger falling to the ground.

Briar stood several feet away wearing a sheer robe, the diaphanous material patterned in a whorls of moody Autumn colors. The garment draped off her shoulders like fluid, the material pooling down her sides and exposing her naked body.

Her tits puckered at the centers, nipples perking like beads. Freckles trailed down her stomach, where a patch of hair nestled between her thighs, the curls shielding her cunt. All the same, a pert little kernel of flesh peeked from the thatch.

More freckles sprinkled across Briar's skin, from the planks of her collarbones to her straight hips. A set of darling toes poked through the grass. Her chin was smooth and as flushed as the rest of her.

But that wasn't the most glorious part. Nay, it was the paint adorning her face.

A bronze diamond slashed through her left eye, the shape formed by a series of leaves. Feline streaks of the same bronze etched her right lids, which connected at the outer corners and looped toward her temple like a cat's eye. At the tip, a maple leaf bloomed.

The princess wore my face paint and nothing else.

Those fiery tresses cascaded down her figure like lava. With hair that ignited this brightly, she didn't need a crown. The color penetrated this murk like an inferno, whilst her eyes pierced like gray blades. This Autumn goddess radiated before me, a figment of my imagination.

Mine. All fucking mine.

My addiction. My fantasy. My obsession.

My equal. My sweet and savory thorn.

Correction. One other part of me responded with aplomb. For fuck's sake, my cock grew so broad, 'twas a miracle the monster didn't tear through my leather pants.

My lungs were depleted of oxygen. If I didn't close my mouth soon, I'd start to drool.

That I couldn't speak weighed on Briar's expression. Her feet shuffled, then stalled. She waited for me to articulate a coherent word—or at least grunt.

Slowly, I crooked my finger, beckoning her. Her skin baked with a rosy hue. Pleasure gleamed in her irises, melting them like mercury.

This woman knew I liked what I saw. She also knew I was about to take what I saw.

As she stepped into my shadow, I found my voice. "I see you've been nosing through my things."

"You brought a considerable amount of makeup with you," Briar said. "I thought it should not go to waste. I've watched how you apply the pigment, and I may have had additional instruction."

I took a guess. That instruction had come from three ladies who'd recently been inducted into Briar's coterie.

"Indeed," I murmured. "Dare I say, you wear it better than me."

"You would never utter that to anyone," she whispered.

"My dear sweeting." I towered over her and traced the painted leaves with a single digit. "You forget. What I would never utter to anyone, I'll always utter to you."

"So ..." She cleared her throat. "So you like it?"

"Oh, I'm about to do more than just like what you've done. Except there's one problem."

Her eyes kindled with uncertainty. I withheld a smirk, which proved easy considering how my tongue had lost its knack for kinetics. At least, with my sanity in this state.

Sweeping past her, I stalked into the cabin and returned seconds later with a face brush. I prowled her way like a panther whilst juggling the object across my fingers. "The problem is you missed a spot."

Holding her gaze, I banded my arm around her midriff and swung her toward the mossy tree stump, urging her to sit once more. The sheer robe fell wider apart, baring her to my famished gaze. Once her lovely ass rested atop the stub, I stepped into the vent of her thighs.

Then I pressed the plume against the tip of her breast. Briar's respiration caught. Slowly, I dragged the brush across her skin, which pebbled and caused her nipple to darken.

The princess's eyelids fluttered. She dipped her head and watched me decorate her. In advance, I had coated the tool in paint. Attentively, I drew another maple leaf beside her nipple, sketching its shape over her skin.

Then like a villain, I circled the brush's peek around that same nipple, urging it to pinch tightly. A small gasp leaped from her mouth as I dabbed at the point. Her thighs spilled farther, as if in reflex.

As though she knew what was coming.

Because the pigment was made of natural fruits, it was harmless. Nonetheless, I pulled back and tasted the fibers, my lips consuming the color.

This allowed me to do my worst. Nonchalantly, I returned the brush to her beautiful tits. From there, I drew over her navel and dipped the object between her thighs. Briar whimpered and clutched my shoulders. She kept her eyes on me whilst I reeled the tip up and down her drenched crease, moping her arousal into the bristles, collecting it. The faint brushing coaxed more wetness from her body, her pussy glistening and laminating the brush.

Her mouth fell open. An afflicted expression creased her features, which shifted the leafy diamond framing her eye. I wanted badly to look, to see the brush swabbing the flanks of her cunt. But even more, I wanted to see what it did to her face.

Lightly—viciously—I sketched her slit. Then I skimmed the tip to her studded clit and circled the ridge, smearing the wet proof of her desire there.

Briar whimpered. She scooted closer, parting her limbs more.

Aye. That's it, my thorn.

Let me mark you, as you've marked me.

Her whimpers narrowed into moans as I skated the plumed nib around the distended flesh and began sweeping it over the apex. Back and forth. Back and forth. Briar chanted and gripped my muscles harder. Daintily, she rolled her ass, rubbing her folds against the bristles.

She continued swiveling her lower half, her cunt abrading the tip. At last, she made a pained noise, her forehead collapsed against mine, and her eyes squinted shut. I watched, the muscles in my face tensing to the point where I might give myself a migraine. Not that I gave one fabulous fuck.

I feasted on my princess's visage as it crumpled in despair, like she might shatter into a million pieces. Yet she needn't worry. If she chipped into fragments, I would collect the broken particles and put her back together. Until then, I dabbed her pussy and felt her walls contract against the soft fibers.

Briar bumped her waist forward, bracing her clit over the peak. Her moans tapered and accelerated, heavy breaths chuffing between us. I made a ravenous sound and anchored her with my free hand, slowly towing her my way, helping her ride the brush. Her brows furrowed in pleasure as she smeared herself onto the plume, her clit jutting into it.

Finally, I spoiled myself with a glimpse. Almighty Seasons, she looked stunning. Her folds slickened, and the top of her clit projected, the bead of skin inflating.

The thought of washing this brush later pissed me off. But the thought of using it again—to make her shiver, to line my eyes in kohl—enticed me. To that end, a heady vibration rumbled from my chest.

"I'm going to come," Briar confessed brokenly, her words fracturing. "Oh Seasons, I'm going to come."

My head lifted to savor her. "I know, sweeting."

I saw it in the tight flush of her pussy and the quiver of her clit. I heard it in the octave of her voice, the rapid speed of her outtakes. I felt it in the way she trembled, the way her fingers burrowed into me, and the way my cock broadened to an unmanageable size.

Briar stalled. Her body strained, and her eyes compressed. Another second later, she burst into shards.

Wheezing cries shot from her mouth—grievous, triumphant. I watched her combust, relished the view, and suffered through it. Her body erupted, limbs spasming and cunt leaking from pleasure.

Fucking hell. My pulse rioted. That same all-encompassing feeling filled me to the brim.

Her. It had always been her.

She had ruined me for life.

As Briar's orgasm ebbed, she sagged against me like a fallen temptress. I held her and groaned. Could this woman ever be hotter or more divine?

Aye, she could. For the princess wiggled from me suddenly, her eyes reams of sterling. She'd let her lover have his fun.

Now she would have hers.

Straightening, the princess shook out her red hair. Her tits lifted from the open robe, the erect nipples pointing and stimulating my tastebuds.

She panted, "Back off, jester."

I withdrew the sodden brush and slipped the bristles into my mouth, then sucked on it like candy and watched her pupils bloat. Finished, I licked my lips, enjoying her musky flavor. "Who? Me?"

"You," she rasped, stealing the brush from my hand. "I came out here like this for a reason, and you will not distract me."

"Seems I've already done that."

"Do as I say."

Oh, but she had my attention. Sauntering backward, I leaned against the column of a hickory tree. That seemed to satisfy Briar because she held the brush to the side and purposely let it fall to the ground.

And then she followed.

The princess scooted off the trunk and stepped in my direction until those enticing breasts scraped my coat. Then she stooped to her knees and craned her head to look up at me, her irises as polished as nickel. And I knew.

"Shit," I muttered, but that was all I could manage.

My useless tongue flopped in my mouth. I had done many things to her, in many places, and in many positions. But she had never done this to me.

She had asked about it a few times, how it felt with other women and men. Even when I'd answered her, she revealed not a shred of jealousy. Rather, my thorn had been curious, absorbing every graphic detail like text in a book.

Beyond that, I never asked, never pushed. I had expected it would take some pacing. I'd been waiting until she wanted it. But I always fantasized, particularly whilst groping myself.

Now she balanced on her knees. An inexperienced blush flared along her cheeks, and a hungry light brimmed in her pupils. I could help her, but two obstacles stopped me.

One, her stern expression instructed me not to open my mouth.

Two, even if she had let me, this jester couldn't have babbled a fucking comprehensible word to save my wretched soul.

The force of Briar's gaze tacked me to the tree and had my cock standing so high, it threatened to punch through the waistband. My mouth dried, and my lungs emptied as she captured me in her stare and unclasped the front of my pants. Sensory perception drained from my being, every ounce of awareness narrowing to each fastening she broke open. I swear to almighty Seasons, I'd never cared about a set of buckles more in my life.

The fabric rustled. The flaps sprang apart, and blessed relief gave way to a new form of torture. My cock sprouted from the opening, the head dark, ruddy, and expansive. Veins threaded up the stem. From my aching sac to the slit in my crown, the circumference of my erection had grown as solid as cement.

Briar focused her attention there, appreciative and concentrated. The moment she licked her lips, several prayers and confessions flitted through my head, like my life depended on it. If she didn't do something soon, this woman would have me begging.

"Exquisite," she whispered.

"Yours," I husked.

My fingers itched to comb through her hair, but not yet. This princess didn't want or need encouragement, much less assistance. She could do any fucking thing she wanted on her own. By all means, she could do it to me.

The instant her fingers feathered across my heavy sac, all reason vacated my mind. She sketched the pouch of skin, her touch causing my rationale to shrivel. Her digits traveled to the base of my erection, ascended the twitching stem, and circled the apex.

A droplet pushed through the faint line of my cock. Briar mopped it with her thumb, then draped it on her tongue. And every possible sound that existed, every possible noise I could make, clogged in my throat.

Once more, Briar followed the path her fingers had made. Only this time, her tongue flexed from her lips and did the honors. The point of her tongue pressed against my balls, patiently glided up the column, and skated over the head, where she swabbed another bead from the crease.

I proceeded to lose my mind. Every reverberation that had been packed in my throat unleashed, hoarse and as jagged as rocks. "Briar."

The gritty echo of her name spurred the princess onward. Encouraged, she sighed as if sampling a delicacy—and licked my crown again.

Oh. Merciless. Shit.

I struggled to keep my head aloft, to watch what she did to me. The prim, proper, princess of Autumn genuflected, had sunk to the ground, and now lapped at the round peak of my cock. The tip of her tongue swatted gently over the incision, drawing opaque droplets to the surface, which she consumed like honey.

This heiress serviced her jester. This future queen lowered herself before him.

I'd never felt more dominated. Incidentally, I was the one being claimed, taken captive, and conquered.

Bewitched, I could do nothing but let her work me into a stupor. And work me, she did.

Briar swirled her tongue around the radius of my crown, then up and down its length. Puffs of air blew from her lips and warmed my sensitive flesh. I cursed, fighting to restrain myself, to shove my cock between her lips.

Erotism was an enjoyable pastime. Yet with the effect she had on me, I barely managed to pace my hips.

Sparks flew up my legs. Heat rushed from my sac to the crux of my erection, the onslaught of her damp tongue downright brutal. She draped it over my engorged flesh, rolling up and down, wetting me.

But when Briar reached the feverish head again, she stalled for a beat. Then with a needy sound, she parted her lips and sealed them around the crown. At the taste of me, the princess moaned, the noise vibrating over my swollen cock.

My vocal cords snapped like severed ties. I growled—and growled more, a short sequence of noises grating from my lungs, each one in tandem to her mouth as it puckered and descended around me.

Briar's head dipped. She took me in … and in … and in.

Soaked heat clamped onto my flesh. The flat of her tongue braced along my stem.

For a second, I thought I might be dying. Then she began to pump, and I was done for.

With a gentle, experimental tempo, the princess strapped her lips around my cock and bobbed. She reeled up slowly, sucking her way to the roof, where she stroked the incision with her tongue, then engulfed me again.

My knees threatened to buckle. I'd been digging my fingernails into the tree bark, but now I reached for the closest overhead branches and shackled myself to them, lest I should grab Briar's hair and pull on it. I might as well be chained, my body at her behest as she fed on my cock.

Groaning in confidence and desire, Briar increased her pace and pressure. She pulled on my cock with famished tugs, and I groaned in rhythm to her mouth.

Her fingers climbed up my thighs and slid to my ass, welding me in place whilst her lips hauled on my erection. The back of my scalp thumped against the trunk, my haggard moans escalating.

My cock grew firmer, thicker. My arms burned with the effort to hold myself up, to stay upright despite the ground evaporating under me.

At this rate, I would detonate.

Because my hips couldn't resist, they rocked into her. The impact nudged my cock further, which Briar caught in her mouth. She keened and suctioned onto my shaft, exerting more force as if rewarding me.

I flexed my ass and bucked against her lips. With shallow juts, I matched her cadence, her tongue and my cock surging together. Her hair scorched through the eventide, light from the pumpkins illuminating gold strands hidden in all that red. My waist rolled toward her face, and my head fell forward, and my eyes blazed at the vision below me. I held onto the branches, casted my body forward, and saw my erection disappear between her lips.

Fuck.

Fuck.

Like a vixen, Briar swallowed me whole. Like a reigning heiress, she commanded my body.

I should last longer. Much longer.

But not like this.

The visual of her sent my blood into a frenzy, each vessel bursting and searing through my veins. My cock twitched, and my balls tightened, bolts of release shooting up my length to the bulbous head. My groans quickened. I increased the momentum of my hips, snapping harder, faster.

Briar recognized the sounds and doubled her efforts, devouring my cock to the hilt. Magnificent. Incomparable. I thrust every inch into her, my growls expanding into something turbulent, something feral.

She gripped my cock in her mouth and sucked me into a trance. My heart rammed into my chest, both about to fracture in half. The avalanche hit me, the ecstasy so intense stars flared before my eyes and liquid heat blasted up my stem.

I paused. Then I came with a roar, the drastic clamor smashing through the woods. My crown spurted its release, twitching and gushing across her tongue.

Briar made an elated sound as she gulped my orgasm to the last drop. She continued sweeping her tongue over my cock, as if searching for remnants of my climax. The thought ripped me from my position, my body still levitating but unable to keep still.

Fucking princess. I'd had enough.

Uttering a harsh noise, I let go of the branch and snatched Briar an instant after her lips released my cock. She yelped as I heaved her off the ground and into the air. On instinct, her legs latched around my waist and held fast.

My mouth seized hers. Like this, I stalked us across the grass, my boots incinerating a path to the cabin. With a single blow, I kicked the door open. It whipped backward, smacked the wall, then crashed back into its frame when my heel knocked the partition closed behind us.

Briar had lit a fire before emerging with the makeup on her face. Presently, logs split on the grate, their flames writhing and torching the walls.

I charged across the rug. Rushing Briar to the nearest pillar, I braced her scalp and thumped her high against the surface. A gasp lunged from her mouth, her lips still attached to mine, so that I tasted her surprise and excitement.

We broke apart, breathing labored. Frantic, we panted and tore at my clothes. She clawed my coat and shirt open, yanked them from my arms, and flung both items to the ground. I toed off my boots, which took some balance and self-control, neither of which I possessed.

"Motherfuck," I groused, which made Briar chuckle.

That throaty sound could have lit a match. She found this comical, did she?

With a lopsided, devilish smirk, I shred my pants. I had toppled over the edge once already. But if I waited a second longer, I'd crash.

We thrashed, ripping the rest of my garments. Naked, I surged my waist between her thighs, opening them wider for me.

Briar's translucent robe trickled on either side of her. The leafy diamond spearing through her eye had a smudge, but the maples were otherwise intact.

Her tits pitted into my chest. Warmth radiated from her pretty cunt and saturated the crest of my cock.

I secured her right wrist overhead, our scarlet ribbons meshing. Then I hooked her left leg over my hip and notched my crown at the drenched slot. The friction wiped the mirth from her face.

After securing her limb to me, I let go and reached up to pinch her chin with my thumb and forefinger. "Now you shall pay, Highness. I'm going to make you come until you fucking pass out."

With that, I lurched my ass upward. And my cock pitched between the flanks of her pussy.

Briar gave a stunned, enthusiastic cry. "Oh!"

She jolted upward, her breasts straining as she arched into the pillar. On a hum, my head fell forward, bowing between the swells of her chest. Yet I didn't wait, couldn't wait for us to recover.

I rolled my waist, skidded out of her, then lunged my hips into her wet pleat again. Wasting no time, I locked our hips and threw my weight into it, pivoting in and out. With each rush of my cock, Briar's arousal coated both of us. Her folds spread wider, the hot clamp agonizing.

My muscles clenched as I ground my ass between her thighs. My sweet thorn joined in, gyrating her hips against mine. We heaved ourselves into one another, the urge instinctive, the momentum primal.

Briar unleashed, devastated whines tumbling from her lips and inundating the cabin. Her body straddled my own, my frame buoying her in place, bolting her to the facade. The better to hit every dark, deep, delicious spot inside her.

The princess's mouth hung ajar, and her gaze crashed into mine.

Staring at each other, we flailed into one another, crashing together repeatedly. For the bloody life of me, I couldn't tell if I was pounding up into her, or if she was pounding down onto me.

I dedicated myself to the sounds she made, determined to wring each possible noise to the surface. Kinetic training worked to my advantage. For I used every nimble, sinuous, jester move in my arsenal.

My hips wheeled in an illicit rhythm, circling into the gap of her thighs. The impact split her farther around me, so that I had her pinned like a butterfly. Whilst fixating on her slack face, I lunged my cock from base to crown, the engorged head striking those tight, tapered places that made the princess wail.

Her soft cunt sucked me in, the walls strapping around the rigid length of my erection, all the way to my crest, which grew broader with each pump. The narrow clutch of her folds squeezed me, meeting the force of my waist as I fucked deeply into her.

"Such a tenacious one," I crooned. "Are you enjoying yourself like a good princess?"

"More," she demanded, swiping her cunt onto my erection. "I need more."

The cinched heat of her walls nearly destroyed me. "Careful, Your Highness," I gritted out. "The more you flay my cock, the longer I'll make your pussy wait."

"That's a challenge I will win," she moaned. "My will is stronger than yours."

A carnal chuckle rolled across my tongue. We would see about that.

Overhead, our hands bolted together. My free fingers snatched her steepled thigh, whereas her own palm spanned my flexing ass, urging me higher, harder. Thusly, I elevated that thigh further, which altered the axis of my thrusts.

My cock vaulted so far, it struck a place that had Briar sobbing. The sound played like an aphrodisiac, like a lustful melody in my ears, like every erogenous page I've ever read. Only a hundred times more potent, a million times more effective. The echoes of her pleasure reached bone deep, tracked down my spine, and fused into my blood.

My sac hung heavy, throbbing with need. I shuddered and hoisted my cock into Briar, my energy running purely on her moans. Her slit parted, the crease spreading around the length of my erection. She encased me up to the round peak and pooled onto my flesh.

Damnation, she was so wet, so perfect. The princess poured herself on me as I worked into her, sweat surfacing across our skin. Her freckles shifted as she moved, and the firelight trickled through her hair, and I wanted to consume every ounce of her.

My head bowed as I nipped the top of one breast. Briar cried out, ecstatic. She pushed her tits toward my mouth, encouraging another bite.

Indeed. She belonged to me.

And I belonged to her.

I lowered my mouth and grazed my incisors over that jostling breast, then pinched her nipple between my teeth. Briar moaned and nodded. Each abrasion sent her into a tailspin, pleasure and pain coalescing in her ragged voice.

My lips nicked and marked that nipple, then licked a path over her bare throat. In the basin of her collarbones, I drew her flesh into my mouth and sucked, all the whilst pistoning my hips.

Briar's thighs shook astride me, her limbs riding my waist as it slung into her. The tiny kernel of flesh at the crux of her pussy rubbed against the seat of my cock. When it did, a hysterical cry soared from Briar's lungs, and my fucking head dissolved.

With renewed vigor, I angled my cock and attacked that place with swift, shallow juts. Her inflated clit brushed my base repeatedly. The increasing friction pulled cry after cry from Briar as I deliberately went after the dainty spot.

Piercing tingles spread across my skin. My muscles contorted, sizzling with exertion of the most enjoyable kind.

Releasing the skin of Briar's clavicles, I tilted my head to watch her melt into euphoria. With open-mouthed groans, I committed the sight to memory. The princess's features twisted, the maple leaves adorning her face slanting.

Her eyes fanned shut, but that simply wouldn't suffice.

"Don't," I hissed. "Open your eyes and watch me fuck you."

The command caused her eyelids to flare. Obediently, she stared down as I hefted my erection between her soaked folds. Despite our speed, I used agility to make sure she felt every solid inch, every fluid pass of my cock.

Her brows crinkled. Short wheezes of air escaped her. Both told me how good it made her feel, how much it satisfied and tormented her.

Excellent. Misery loved company. Fickle bastard that I was, I hated and adored this, wanted it to end and never end.

The princess's arousal seeped from her, flooding my cock. Together, we felt each liquified pump, each urgent jut of our waists.

Briar flattened her heel on the pillar and used it to push herself onto me. We slammed into each other, her pleat stretching, bringing my cock deeper.

The blaze from the living room seared up my back. The smoldering hues glowed across the princess's naked body—all but the robe rustling on either side of us.

Brittle noises filled the cabin. I inhaled the fragrances of sweat and the woman bounding atop my pelvis.

My growls amplified, fraying at the edges. Her sobs multiplied, splintering at the seams.

Both noises tangled.

The inside of Briar's pussy contorted, the slot gripping me tighter. Her clit twitched, and her orgasm mounted as my cock lurched through her.

I fell into her, my torso flush with hers. Those tipped nipples abraded my pectorals, and my abdomen clenched with each pitch of my hips. Our open mouths mashed together, her shouts and my bellows colliding like the rest of us.

Deeper, harder, faster. We rode each other into fucking oblivion.

Heat swam from my sac to the stem of my cock as we stiffened, then unraveled into a frenzy of hollers. Briar's walls pulsated, her pussy coming so long, so wetly around me.

Yet I didn't stop. With renewed urgency, I quickened my pace to another breaking point. My waist jetted between her thighs, my erection pitching into Briar until she bowed, and another wave crested across her tongue.

"Take it from me," I husked. "Take as much as you can."

"Oh, gods," she yelled. "Oh, my gods!"

She came again, her joints rattling and the inside of her pussy clasping me. My cock twitched, the taut head spilled into her slit, and I howled my release three seconds after her.

We convulsed against the pillar and screamed ourselves hoarse. The shrill noises cut through the cabin like battle cries.

28

Briar

I slumped against him. Boneless. Weightless. Mindless.

My body perspired and heaved for oxygen. Joyous. Precious.

Poet's strong arms encased me, buttressing me to the pillar. The muscles in his physique flexed, equally spent and damp with sweat. My breasts inflated into his pectorals as we sucked in air, our breathing ragged.

The fireplace popped with embers and bathed the cabin in simmering light. All was still and quiet in a way it hadn't been since our caravan trundled into Autumn. Warmth flowed through me, mingling with remnant streaks of pleasure, from my soles to my scalp.

Everything tingled. Everything brimmed.

The jester's head rested in the crook of my neck. I threaded my fingers through his disheveled hair.

After a few moments, he craned his head to gaze at me. Those verdant eyes swallowed me whole, the irises enameled with such a vibrant color, they hurt to look at. Like my own makeup, a diamond slashed through his left eye, only his was as black as his fingernails.

Possessiveness, pride, and pity converged within me. Fate was cruel, as it should be outlawed to look that perfect and for there to be only one of him in existence. I felt sorry for the admirers—the countless number of men and women—who desired him but would never know his touch.

However, a greater part of my conscience lacked remorse. He belonged to me.

The jester's cock remained tucked inside my soaked folds, the width of him still hot and hard, to the point where I felt the crown cradled in a spot that made me dizzy. Seasons forgive me. I should have had my fill, yet I wanted to bite him. To claim him again.

His eyes gleamed, as if reading my mind. He nipped my chin and murmured, "Patience, minx. Otherwise, you'll destroy me."

I grinned, sheepish. He peeled the robe from my shoulders, letting it flutter to the ground, then pulled us from the column and carried my limp body to the fireplace. Tugging a blanket from the sofa with his free hand, Poet unfolded the knit fabric atop the rug and sank us onto it.

Dropping to his back, he let out an exhausted grunt while nesting me against his side. We'd perfected this position, always moving in sync with each other. As he slipped his arm under my head, I cushioned my cheek on his marbled torso and extended one leg over his thighs.

His fingertips swayed along my hip as we stared at the ceiling. We were sticky and sweaty. We should bathe. I should drag a comb through the knots in my hair, because surely he'd done damage to it. Yet I refused to move, to break from this moment.

Let us be rumpled. Let us be imperfect.

The fire danced across Poet's cobbled abdomen and my unshod feet. In my periphery, sparks flew from the timbers.

The naked jester hummed, his voice husky and masculine. The sound oozed through my blood like thick syrup.

"You know," he spoke to the ceiling beams. "At some point, I plan on slowing things down."

My brows crimped in amusement. "Isn't that what we're doing

right now?"

"Merely an intermission. But what I meant was, we've been feral since we got to Autumn. The balcony, the throne room, and now this cabin. I fancy rough and ready, and believe me, I have no complaints. But I also favor slow and savory—a seductive, sensuous pace. I'm a man of variety when it comes to sex. Besides, if we don't ease up, my cock will chafe, and I'll be hobbling for days."

"I thought you were an expert lover with stamina."

He skated a digit over my hip. "That, I am. However, a sharp and relentless princess requires more effort." I yelped as he pinched my skin. "And with you, I can't help myself. You bring out the savage in me, more so when our lives are on the line."

Rising on one elbow, I thwacked his shoulder and gave him a mock glare. "So you're blaming me?"

Another yelp jumped from my lips as he snatched my bicep and jerked me atop his chest. "I'm complimenting you," he murmured against my mouth. "High maintenance meets high maintenance. We're a match made in heaven. Be that as it may, it's a missed opportunity if we don't continue to indulge in a range of spicy pursuits, including speed."

I inched my lips from his and stared down at his unearthly body. My head ducked, and I addressed the grid of his chest. "If I'm not mistaken, we've been covering that range quite extensively. Defiant sex, angry sex, makeup sex—"

"Makeup sex?" Poet lifted an intrigued eyebrow. "That sort of vocabulary is out of character, Princess. Does this have anything to do with three certain ladies-in-waiting?"

"Victory sex," I finished, then looped a piece of hair behind my ear, formality edging into my voice. "And yes, if you must know."

"Oh, I must know everything where you're concerned," he flirted, the words dangerously soft. "Including how rapid you breathe, how high your temperature gets, how wet you grow, and how loud you cry out."

An electric current sprinted up my thighs and into the cleft between my legs.

I cleared my throat. "In terms of having an expansive range, you're discounting what we did in The Pumpkin Wood."

"I'll never discount that." He thumbed the leafy diamond etched on my face. "You in this kinky jester paint and my brush on your glorious cunt. Not least of all, you have ample skills with that tongue of yours."

Now heat spread though my being. I peeked at him beneath my lashes. "You enjoyed it?"

Poet tugged me firmer against him, then flopped me onto my back, so that half his body hovered over mine. My limbs spread for his waist, cradling every sculpted and erect part. "I worshiped it," he hummed, skimming his finger down the side of my neck. "I'd like to capture the moment and frame it among my pleasure toys in the closet—my favorite secrets. I'd like to declare a pagan holiday in honor of that moment."

I wrapped my arms around his shoulders. "Bring it to my attention the next time I hold court, and I'll consider it."

"Most of all, I'd like to relive that moment."

"You will," I promised, then nibbled on my lower lip. "By chance, where in your new closet do you keep your pleasure trinkets?"

"In case you'd like to get sneaky?" he taunted. "Why, they're in the same place your little drawers are stored."

Seasons, this man. I doubted he would return the intimate item he'd stolen after our dalliance in the throne room. Though the prospect of my undergarments stashed among his hoard sent a flutter through me.

The jester's pupils darkened, and I felt his cock jolt against my crease. "And you?" he intoned. "Did you have fun coming against the brush and sucking me to within an inch of my life?"

By now, I must look feverish, my complexion as crimson as a pomegranate. "Yes," I demurred. "Both. One, more than another." The confession came out easily. "Your cock tastes of sugar and sin."

Poet crooned and seized my lips with his. His mouth clamped

to mine, urging me into a swift, scorching kiss. Like a tease, it had scarcely begun when he pried himself away and chuckled at my protesting whine.

He rolled us toward the flames and reclined behind me, his larger frame bracing my shorter one like a shield. My back aligned with his chest, both siphoning air, in tune with each other. I ran my fingers across his forearms, his heat seeped into me, and we watched the blaze dance.

A bleak thought crawled into my mind. It wasn't a revelation but rather a conclusion we'd already drawn.

"They will never side with us now," I rehashed in a whisper. "After this, they won't forget."

Poet grunted, a honed edge to his words. "If they're willing to enact treason for Rhys, slaughter citizens and blame innocent people for it, and bribe a stripling to commit murder, they're never going to be on our side."

I scooted deeper into him and studied the fire. "But I need to believe anyone can change."

After a beat of silence, he said, "You're right."

"And the girl will be okay. Won't she?"

"If she isn't, I'll tear their hearts out with my bare hands. I'll take their fingers, throats, and dicks too."

"The only guild member absent from the meeting was the carpenter, so that must be the child's mother. I've not interacted with the woman much, but I wasn't aware she had a daughter. Mother and I make a point of knowing about our subjects' families." Briar shook her head. "I suppose carpentry could possibly train a child to excel with an axe, enough for her to wield it violently. But what could make it worth that child committing heinous acts against her will? What would motivate her to work for the Masters? And how is the mother's illness involved?"

Poet traced the top of one breast. "It's something the girl doesn't want people to find out about. To that, I can empathize."

"Still, the Masters must know whatever plight she's dealing with,"

I concluded. "If they're using her like this."

"Not necessarily. Not if she went to them first. She might want to keep the guild away from her home. They may know bits and pieces, but not the whole thing." Poet thought about it. "The moppet has a look of secrecy about her, to the point of desperation. That's why she didn't want our help. In any case, she must have impressive skills with that axe, mayhap in addition to other advantages. For a start, she was small enough to get past your troop and young enough that they wouldn't have suspected a thing, had they caught her."

To soothe my worries, the jester kissed my temple. "But she's a survivor. Like you." Then as if to distract me, he reached around to tap the painted leaves on my face. "So what brought these on?"

I smiled and shrugged. "I just wanted to try it. Or perhaps since we're nearing the eve of Reaper's Fest, I was feeling adventurous. Although that could also be your influence."

"Ah. Reaper's Fest." His tone lightened. "How long do I have to commission an outfit for this bonfire ball?"

I kept a straight face. "A fortnight."

Poet launched partway off the blanket and gawked. "Excuse me?" he complained as I twisted in his arms and tried not to laugh. "You do realize my taste will need more time if I'm to dazzle the court."

"You can do that with a smirk and a flick of your wrist."

His brows shot together. "Flatterer."

"Flaunter," I criticized with mirth.

A devious grin broke through his face, all sensuality and vanity. That snaggletooth poked out like a morsel.

"Be warned," I said. "Citizens take the masquerade costumes seriously, and they aim to outdo each other."

Poet rolled his eyes and wiggled his fingers. "No one outdoes the Court Jester."

In fact, he felt so confident about this, that he swooped down. With a greedy snarl, he burrowed into my neck and grazed his mouth over my flesh, as though debating which area to sample first.

A rather undignified sound uncurled from my tongue, even as I chortled. "They might disagree with you." I arched my throat for his mouth. "In fact, rumors and conspiracies have spread. The court has denounced you as a fashion victim."

Once more, Poet lunged off the ground. Insulted, he sat upright. "They said I'm a *what*?" he demanded.

But I merely kept laughing until the jester glowered at me with predatory humor. Flattening his palm beside my face and hovering like a specter, he insisted, "Think that's uproarious, do you?"

I raised my bare thigh over his hip. "Are you denying it?"

"Hardly. I'm not offended by the label. I'm offended that they think it's offensive. 'Tis another cardinal rule this Season has yet to learn. Fashion victims aren't victims. Why? Because they know when to take a risk. That, in itself, is a weapon."

"Noted," I teased.

Poet crinkled his brows. "Mmm. I detect a hint of sarcasm. It's a good thing I'm hungry, otherwise I'd start plotting my ensemble for the revels, all with the intention of proving my point."

It was true, we had worked up an appetite. I doubted we were done with each other, which meant sustenance was required. "Should we see what we have in the pantry?"

Poet cocked his head, mischievous. "Who said I wanted food?"

"You said—"

I gasped as he grabbed my ankles, jostled me toward him, and split my legs apart. "I said I was hungry, sweeting. I didn't say what for." He slithered over my body, hips nudging my limbs farther apart. Then he proceeded to nuzzle my breasts and nipples.

Aroused chuckles skipped up my throat. Hearing the sound, Poet bracketed himself above me. The firelight sketched his features, throwing shadows across them.

Something profound brimmed in his eyes, stoking them. "Aye," he rasped. "We've been quite prolific sexually. But indeed, that's not what I'd meant." His mouth lowered onto mine. "*This* is what I meant."

Then his lips melted with my own.

My heart rate quickened, and I sighed into his hot mouth. He was right about the intensity between us these past weeks. There had been sensuality and passion, but each bout had culminated in a riot of drastic sounds and hectic movements. As rapturous as they'd been, they had often spiraled out of control.

This time, we moved languidly. Poet coiled over me, his solid form spanning my body. Our limbs tangled as his tongue swept into me, flicking deftly until I whimpered. Lost in the grip of his mouth, I knew this would be slow and concentrated—agonizingly so.

Thick, heady sensations poured through my blood. I wanted it right here, in front of the grate, while the inferno turned to ash. The notion resurrected a memory of when he first brought me to orgasm in his chambers, after we traipsed through the Spring labyrinth, after the most sumptuous dance of my life. Before a fire, the jester had spread me out on his floor and reduced my inhibitions to cinders.

His cock had slid in and out of the gap in my drawers. The head of his erection had rowed back and forth against the furrow in my core, until I unraveled like a ribbon. I wanted that again, only time with his cock buried inside me.

Yet instead of spreading my pussy and probing it gently, Poet crooned with a different sort of intent. One powerful arm slung around my middle and hauled me upright with him. That's when he severed the kiss to gaze at me, mesmerized.

Overcome, I stared back. His fingers traced my cheekbones and chin, and my digits etched the ledge of his jaw, both of us entranced in the movements. He ran the backs of his knuckles over my leaf-painted breast, while I sketched the lattice of his abdomen.

Then more. Naked, he hefted me close while his free arm snuck under my thighs. Affixing his mouth to my own, the jester gained his feet.

Like this, he carried me from the living room and up the narrow staircase to the bedroom. Moonlight leaked through the windowpanes, and although there was another hearth in this chamber, we didn't use it. Instead, we sank into the darkness, shrouded and hidden.

Unspooling me across the four-poster bed, Poet stood at the edge, his eyes fuming and his cock upright. The broad head was smooth like a finial, the skin ruddy, and the length of him jutted firm and weighty. I glimpsed the line across his crown, and my respirations hitched.

With attentive motions, he massaged my ankles, heels, and soles. Every fiber and nerve ending relaxing under his skilled hands. After that, he tugged me to the rim and splayed me wide.

His eyes seared over me, the force of his attention sending a pulse of need to my clitoris. The peg throbbed. My walls ached. But Poet forced me to wait, tamed me with his ministrations, his fingers skimming my calves, behind my knees, and over my navel.

Every place he made contact with flickered to life. Simultaneously, my bones liquified like wax. I dissolved into his touch, giving myself over fully.

He rubbed the cove of my waist, thumbed my nipples, and charted my throat. He coasted over my open lips. He readied me for a long, arduous bout.

When the jester had me sufficiently thawed, he fastened my heels to the footboard and then nudged his cock at the slot of my thighs. "Hands over your head. Now."

My heart pounded like a hammer. I did as he instructed and fisted the quilt.

Poet stared, reveling in the sight. Holding my gaze fast, he swiveled his hips.

His long, feverish cock glided between my open walls. Deep … deeper … deeper still. I cried out softly but kept my eyes on him, on his anguished expression. With his mouth parted on a silent groan, Poet reeled his waist backward, exiting me completely—then slipping in once more. The girth of his erection filled me to the rim, rooting the solid flesh high.

I had thought I'd known the meaning of slow. Yet the jester proved me wrong.

He began a torturous rhythm. His sinuous cock pitched in and out with patient lashes of his hips. The peak bumped into a tight space that wrenched moans from me, my pussy clinging to his length and wetting him to the hilt.

Looming over the mattress, Poet did more than fuck me. He made love to my body, to my mind, to the very edge of my consciousness.

So I made love to him in kind. I gripped the sheets overhead and lifted my waist to meet his cock, swaying my folds over him. Rolling my waist and expanding my thighs, I caught each flex of his length.

My walls expanded and clamped onto him. His cock whipped through them at a gradual pace.

Heated sensations eddied across my skin, the stimulation calamitous. It felt inebriating, enlivening. My cries hardened into moans, the noise rushing through the bedroom.

Poet grunted and whisked his hips sluggishly. Deeply. Intensely. The impact caused my spine to bow off the mattress.

At length, he hunched forward. Grabbing my overhead wrists, he shackled me to the bed, suspended himself over my body, and continued the onslaught. My joints shook like scaffolding about to shatter, and plaintive whines gushed from my lips.

I couldn't take this. I could not.

No one could possibly withstand this bliss. Surely, I would crumple.

Yet I did take it. We kept going, and I committed myself to making Poet feel the same afflictions, the same euphoric effects.

My hips linked with his, rocked with his. My pussy rode his cock delicately, and my sobs cracked, and every gash in my heart sealed.

Not once did we increase our speed. Not once did we hurry this. Not once did we yield.

Not once, because we would fight for this. Seasons, we would earn this. The groans and cries escalated. With our damp bodies bolted together, we emitted shallow gusts of oxygen—heavy, frayed, and quivering at the ends.

This was all. This was everything.

Blood swirled in my clit, which swelled. Arousal coated my pussy, which contracted.

My mouth split wider. Poet saw the climax cresting—and he slowed down even more. Irises flaring, he flexed his cock lazily between the flesh of my pussy.

Over and over.

And over. And over.

"Poet," I implored. "Please."

"Please, what?" he panted, his backside pumping. "Say it."

"Make love to me," I begged. "Make me come."

"How badly, sweeting? Like this?"

The jester tilted his hips. He snapped them patiently into a condensed place that wrung more cries from me.

Yes, that badly. Yes, like that.

Poet pinned my wrists harder above us and pressed his forehead against mine. We watched each other, his grunts tangling with my sobs.

Those whipcord muscles clenched with every pass. His naked form sprawled me wide, his buttocks ground leisurely, and his erection plied me to the brink. My moans heightened, my bones quaked, and the muscles of my pussy seized him to the crown.

There. Right there.

All at once, I combusted. The climax sprang from my core to each point of my body, my folds constricting around his rowing cock. I released a guttural noise, this one contained, kept between us.

Poet came at the same time. He let out a jagged growl as the prominent flesh of his cock spasmed inside me.

Shocks of pleasure wracked me off the bed. The mattress quaked under us as we rode out the last streaks of sensation. For as long as we could, the jester and I made it last, just as we had vowed to from the beginning.

And when he lugged the quilt over us later, I fell into his arms. Safe. Sure. He murmured until my thoughts faded, and then we slept.

29

Briar

Hours later, he took me again. And over the next several days, our bodies consumed one another. We indulged, savoring it like a honeymoon, unable to keep our hands to ourselves.

Poet and I fluctuated between sleeping in an assortment of positions. His arms cocooning me. My back tucked into his chest. His head between my breasts. My body splayed atop his torso.

Me, watching him rest. Him, watching me dream.

We alternated between fucking and lovemaking. In bed, with him behind me. On the floor by the fire, his erection grinding me into the rug. On the dining room chair, with me straddling him. In the shower, up against the tiled wall while steam swirled around us, our wet bodies plastered, water racing down his muscles, and the rhythmic brunt of his cock jolting me upward.

Later, Poet towel dried me and bit my lower lip. I combed my damp hair and stared at his naked buttocks, admiring the smooth, taut shapes as he sauntered into the bedroom for fresh clothes.

We snacked, drank, and feasted. I watched him putter around the cupboards in low slung pants that failed to stifle my craving. My arms entwined around his abdomen from behind. Like this, I felt him grin as he knotted our fingers together.

With the meal baking, he observed me shuffling through the kitchen in nothing but his shirt. Feigning nonchalance, I moved about while deliberately skating my hands over his forearms, or draping my palms across his tailbone, or bending in front of him, all on the pretense of gathering table settings.

"Excuse me," I said coyly, the shirt lifting as I bowed forward, my backside popping into view.

Poet stamped a flagon onto the counter, the hard thump matching my pulse. He uttered a gruff noise and murmured, "Think I don't know what you're doing?"

"Hmm?" I pretended. "I have no idea—"

Then I gasped in delight as he hauled me upright, spun me toward him, and flung me onto the counter, plates and cups shattering to the ground. Seconds later, he arched me into the cabinets, which rattled from the impact of his hips snapping between my thighs. I cried out and linked my feet across his waist. My heels shoved the waistband down enough to free his cock, allowing me to take its length so deeply that my scalp tingled.

We worked ourselves into such a stupor that our food nearly burned to a crisp.

Afterward, we shared a plate. Poet propped me astride his lap and fed me helpings with his fingers. When the juice of an overripe pear leaked down my throat, he licked up the remnants, then folded his mouth over mine to taste the flavors.

We managed to drag ourselves from bed—or whatever surface we ended up on—and came up for air by curling on the couch. The jester and I talked until we lost our voices, though Poet constantly found mindless ways to touch me, as I did him. We caressed, bantered, debated, whispered, and laughed until my sides ached.

Outdoors, we rode our horses through the wild and trained on the front lawn. Because we'd brought our weapons, he and I challenged each other to a second match. Except Poet complicated things by divesting himself of his shirt, so that his endowments rippled into view. Though to be fair, I repaid him in kind by wearing only a thin camisole and leggings. Barefooted, we paced around each other, teasing and tempting and tracking.

An hour later, we called a draw. Sweat lathered his pectorals and drizzled between my breasts.

Like this, Poet offered tips on how to throw my quills while in motion, and while using a few unexpected postures. He also demonstrated hand-to-hand combat moves. Those were more difficult to learn than I'd hoped, but I proved an apt pupil. At least until he loomed behind me.

Poet molded my fingers into a fist and clicked our bodies together as he pantomimed a series of quick jabs. His frame rotated with mine, the heat of him launching sparks across my skin.

Noticing my reaction, his deceptive mouth scraped along my neck. "Like this," his voice ruptured into my ear.

My eyes rolled back. My hands shook.

The next thing I knew, my back hit the nearest tree. Only the lower half of our clothes made it off before we attacked each other. After which, Poet knelt before me, and his head vanished between my thighs.

The days melted into one another. It felt like being drunk and lucid, all at once. I'd never grinned, moaned, begged, conversed, or chuckled so much in my life.

At dawn, the jester and I bathed in the mill pond, where he prowled after me like a serpent, making me shriek with laughter. We splashed each other, though it became impossible to concentrate with Poet dripping like a sea god and shaking droplets from his hair. Rivulets licked his torso, trickled down his narrow waist, and vanished under the surface.

My desire became apparent. In seconds, Poet responded.

He crushed our mouths together while my legs clung to his hips. Then my voracious jester fastened me to the mill wheel, where he surged his cock between my spread pussy, and I hollered to the treetops.

By afternoon, he surprised me with a gift as we hunkered nude and sated in front of the fireplace. "Searching for this?" he asked, lifting a book to my stunned gaze.

I gasped, recognizing the cover and title, even though the tome had been missing from my collection. Grabbing the book, I traced the embossing and then pressed it to my chest. "Where did you find it?"

"Where I knew to look," Poet said, eyes glinting with satisfaction. "Your favorite place."

"A library? Which one?"

"All of them."

My head snapped up from the cover. "All the libraries in Autumn? But I checked. Over the years, I've sent inquiries."

The jester spoke quietly. "Not just in Autumn."

Spring. Summer. Autumn. Winter.

That would have taken ages. Longer than we'd been here.

Poet tucked a lock of hair behind my ear. "It required a lot of messengers, chiefly owls, hawks, and ravens. They travel quicker. Turns out, their services are also rather pricey, but what can I say?" He tapped my nose. "I have expensive taste, and I'm not accustomed to the word *No*."

He'd remembered our conversation that first night in my suite. He recalled how hard I'd been searching for this volume. According to Poet, the book had been shelved in one of Winter's universities.

Tears stung my eyes. I flung myself at him and rode my jester until he was roaring.

Afterward, I read him the first chapter while he nibbled on my shoulder, then the following five chapters as we became engrossed in the story and made predictions of what would happen next to the characters.

At dusk, I awoke to find him gone. Unable to locate Poet, I shuffled through the shadows, the cabin silent and still. Hyperawareness assured me all was okay, my senses attuning to some type of game.

As I stepped around a corner, a creak alerted me. A nervous thrill shimmied up my limbs. Then a shadow swept out of nowhere. Like a specter, the jester's outline materialized and snatched me into the corridor.

I barely had time to utter a noise. Poet hoisted me off the floor, pinned me to the wall, and spread my legs around his upright cock. He fucked me where he caught me, with my feet planted on the opposite facade for balance, my shouts colliding with his.

We wore ourselves out, then started all over again. We teased and mocked. We faced each other on the pillows and confided. We made each other burn.

We stole this time. We claimed it as ours.

We loved to the point of wildness.

All the while, I tamped down the strange premonition that this perfect intermission was too easy, too good to be true.

Just like that meeting with the Masters.

30

Poet

Eventide fell across the house, slathering the walls in indigo. The fire crackled, its hues burnishing Briar's profile whilst she slept. Her features were relaxed, eyelashes fanning across her face.

We'd piled a nest of blankets in front of the hearth, shortly before I made her come for a second time that evening. Presently, I leaned on one elbow and studied her with a smirk. Dare I say, she was having a splendid dream. With any luck, I played a key role in that fantasy.

Elation rippled through every vital organ I possessed. I fetishized all that I'd done to her in the span of seventy-two hours, plus everything I'd yet to do to her before we returned to court. As much as I had an itch to wake her, I let the heiress sleep, the better to restore her energy. Feeding and fucking Briar in solitude had been sheer magnificence.

Happiness. Hope.

That's what this was.

Those pivotal emotions kept me from reclining next to Briar and passing out. I snuck from the mountainous bedding and shrugged into the loose pants I'd tossed to the floor earlier. After stepping into boots and shrugging on a thin, open coat, I harnessed a dagger to my calf, grabbed the steel staff I'd been training with—including during my practice session with Briar—and sauntered through the front door.

Undergrowth cushioned my steps, the soil damp and fog settling over the wild. Mist snaked through the trees. Pumpkins glinted throughout the property, but I'd learned how daylight snuffed them out until they resumed glowing at dusk.

I crossed the grass, paused, and sucked in a current of air. Exercising a few choice moves would staunch the restlessness. Lazily, I spun the weapon between my fingers like a propellor, then scissored it along the backs of my shoulders to the opposite hand while contemplating the landscape.

I thought about Briar growing up here, retreating to this hideaway as a girl with her parents. The notion wheedled a grin from me. It seemed I hadn't been the only one who'd spent part of his life tucked away, however short that time had been.

As I tumbled the pole around my waist—merely a warm-up—and flipped it between my digits again, my eyebrows furrowed. My smirk flattened, and an ominous premonition stunted my movements. I stalled the weapon overhead, my arm cranking and freezing that way.

Usually, crows flitted through here, their caws scratching the air. Typically, a wandering critter rustled the leaves and rained hickory nuts to the ground. Routinely, this place made noise.

My eyes scanned the layers of forest, from the high timbers to the burning gourds. Something else occurred to me, as it had periodically since we left The Forbidden Burrow.

The meeting with the Masters had gone well.

Too well.

Every deceiver knew two crucial rules. Traps were made to feel harmless. Tricks were made to feel unlikely. Alas, that was the thing about happiness and hope.

It made you forget.

My ears perked. My gaze skewered the environment.

Skilled jesters also learned this: Be aware of what was around you—and who.

My lips tilted without humor. "Come now. Don't be shy."

They didn't answer. So we were doing this, were we?

Fine. Briar was in the cabin, unconscious but safe. So help me, it would stay that way. My molars pressed together, and my thumb slid across the weapon.

The open coat flapped as I whipped around and spiraled the staff. Then I halted. My mercenary gaze landed on the visitor, the sight arresting me in place—one second before I also remembered a fatal lesson about decoys.

Truly, I should have seen this coming.

That realization struck me right before the hammer did.

31

Briar

The fire must have recently died. It no longer sputtered, yet I inhaled the crisp aroma of smoke, and the grate still emanated warmth. Copious blankets encapsulated me, because my jester tended to overindulge.

Images of his touch and taste stirred my consciousness. Thoughts of what we would do next, of how we'd spend tomorrow before going home, wrought a grin to my lips. With my eyes still closed, I sighed in contentment.

Perhaps we would take a walk. I could show him more from the wilds of Autumn. Once he woke up, of course.

And assuming he didn't roll me onto my back first.

My intimate center ached with soreness from how often his cock had pumped into me. The illicit memories scalded my cheeks. A thrilling vignette of skin and sinew curled through my mind, every second with him replaying.

Along with the lingering scents of the extinguished fire, the residue of amber and vetiver hung in the air. Longing to feast my eyes on Poet, I twisted in his direction. Except when my eyelashes fluttered open, only his unoccupied pillow greeted me, the space beside me vacant.

Blinking, I sat up and brought one of the blankets with me, using it to cover my breasts for absolutely no reason. With my free fingers combing through my tousled hair, I glanced around the cabin. The living room was empty.

Leaning forward, I peeked into the dining room. "Poet?"

No answer. No flirtatious quips or naughty comments drifted from the kitchen.

Rising, I threw Poet's discarded shirt over my head. The sleeves hung past my wrists as I padded through the first floor.

He might be hiding again. He might be hunting me, playing a dark game like he had yesterday. He might be stalking my every move, waiting to lurch from the shadows and fuck me in whatever spot he found me.

"Poet?" A sleepy, amused grin coaxed my lips apart. "Anyone there?"

Tiptoeing to the corner leading into the hallway, I paused for effect. Then I jumped around the bend, expecting him to leap out at the same time.

No one. The passage lay uninhabited.

Checking the bedrooms and bathrooms upstairs yielded nothing as well. My grin faltered. Baffled, I retraced my steps. Clammy sensations crawled across my skin, warning me the jester wasn't toying with his princess.

I raked my gaze across the house, which suddenly felt exceedingly quiet. A slow buzz started in my navel. The kitchen knives were too far away, as were my own small weapons, which I'd stored in the bedroom. We had spare defenses, but they required a trip to the cellar, since I hadn't retrieved them when we got here. With Poet around, why would I have needed to?

I inched toward the fireplace while scanning the living room for movement. Behind me, I reached out and fished the poker from the hearth's tool set. After several rapid heartbeats, I crept across the cabin to the front door. Instinct pushed me toward the exit, yet another reflex reminded me the wild could be less safe.

I dashed over the threshold and into the forest. My head veered this way and that.

Where are you?

My fingers gripped the poker. I dared not utter a word yet.

Crows rasped from the canopy. The pumpkins flared with orange light.

I had hoped he might be training outside. Whenever he couldn't sleep, the jester preferred exercising his weapons, if not making love to me. But he wasn't here either.

Trepidation pinched my chest. My lips sagged, and I turned about quicker, the makings of panic rippling across my flesh.

He would not disappear without leaving a note. He would not leave me at all.

And he would not go anywhere without his weapons. Belatedly, I remembered his daggers; their harnesses had been resting on the living room trunk. Perhaps all but one.

As for his staff …

My eyes scanned the woodland, then stumbled across the bloody length of steel abandoned in the grass.

32

Briar

My stomach bottomed out. Hysteria gripped my lungs. I dropped the poker and darted to the staff, my knees smacking the dirt. My shaky fingers picked Poet's weapon from the ground. Crimson coated the rod, trickled across the underbrush, and trailed west.

No.

Fear unlike anything I'd ever known seized my throat.

No.

That, and fury.

No!

Wrathful emotions burned through me. My jaw tightened, and my eyes tapered to slits. "No," I snarled.

Releasing the staff, I stalked into the cabin. In seconds, I strapped myself into a fitted black jacket dress with gold appliqués and a slit that revealed my stockings and boots. Although leggings would be ideal, such material would be easy to pare through. This thicker ensemble provided more of a barrier and enabled me to conceal defenses under the skirt, plus the numerous appliqués provided a modicum of armor.

I braided my hair, stashed thorn quills into a set of gold hair pins, and stabbed each one through the weave as if I wore head jewelry. The stocking garter hugging my upper thigh carried a few more quills, each one accessible through the skirt's gap.

Finally, I collected Poet's daggers. Grabbing their harnesses, I sprinted outside to my horse. I retrieved his staff on the way and loaded everything into the saddle's compartments.

Stupidly, the perpetrators hadn't thought to untether the equine and send her galloping. Even so, the mare and I had forged a bond. She would not have abandoned me.

Like a one-woman army, I hefted myself onto the saddle. We galloped through the wild as though a brushfire chased us. The creature must sense the storm raging within me, for she pounded across thickets and creepers, heeding my signals as I guided us through the forest.

Hot coals burned in my stomach. My teeth bared like fangs.

If they hurt him, I would destroy them.

Crashing through the shrubs and into The Forbidden Burrow, I leaped off the animal. After securing her to a dense area, I thrashed through the bramble path, down the hidden arteries, and smashed my way to the tree door. My fist rammed into the facade with such vitriol, the door shuddered on its hinges.

The partition flew open. The girl's hazel eyes glistened into view, while the rest of her face was nonetheless shrouded in that oversized mantle. Gone was her bravado, that bright and bold nature having been reduced to a memory.

Horror flashed through those adolescent pupils when she saw me. "Your Highness," she begged. "I'm sor—"

I blew past her and catapulted down the stairwell. My heart was a fist in my mouth. My blood was a boiling kettle about to shriek. At the landing, I thwacked my palms against the next door and charged into the Masters' meeting room.

And I stopped. And I saw him.

Poet slumped on the stone floor, his pose negligent, as if he were merely reclining in his element. Except his head hung forward, and irons clamped around his wrists, shackling him to a wall. One of the chains choked the scarlet ribbon clinging to his wrist.

His chest rose and fell, like he'd been taking a break from being impertinent. The men and women surrounding him proved he'd been virtually impossible to tame. The Masters clustered around the jester, looking mentally winded and visibly traumatized from the onslaught of his silver tongue.

Upon my entry, they turned in unison, appearing anything but surprised.

A gravelly noise slipped from my mouth. Hearing it, Poet's head snapped up.

That's when another sound vaulted up my throat, the impending scream threatening to cannon into the air. A brutish slice carved across his cheek, red soaked the white of his left eye, and maroon welts likely made by a hammer decorated his torso.

They hadn't merely beaten him. They'd tortured him.

But not before he'd gotten his hands on the guild. Bruises, gashes, and contusions littered their faces. A broken jaw. A hemorrhaging lip. A dislocated shoulder. Many of them winced and groaned while attempting to nurse their injuries, and others kept a wide berth from the jester.

Poet's good eye glittered. Wicked green flashed my way, testifying that he hadn't succumbed without taking verbal or physical bites out of the Masters. That accounted for the gag they'd wedged into his mouth, the solution evidently coming to them too late.

Regardless, the instant Poet fully registered my presence, that self-satisfied gleam disappeared. Violence cluttered his face. He didn't want me here. He didn't want me near them. With his hands bound, he couldn't protect me.

Three seconds after processing the sight of him, I unleashed. A bellow ripped from my lungs as I tore across the room and launched at the Masters' leader. I smashed into Vex's frame, my fingernails clawing at his face.

Blood squirted from his countenance. I lacerated his flesh with my bare hands, but before I could pull the thorn quills from my braid, bodies swarmed me like hornets. Someone yanked me back by the hair.

Poet thrashed against his restraints. He growled into the gag, the sound murderous.

The stonemason held me in his viselike grip. The members glowered, each of them armed as though they'd anticipated I would bring a squad with me.

Vex wiped the blood off his face. "You see?" he barked as I struggled to break free of his comrade's grip. "You see what this devil and his simpleton spawn have reduced you to? A wild, wanton slut instead of a sovereign."

"You will *release him*," I seethed. "Or I will kill you."

The members muttered without remorse, my comment fueling their animosity.

"You call yourselves stewards of Autumn," I spat. "We do not condone torture. We do not solve our problems with violence unless we're defending our nation."

"No, we don't," the leader replied. "But Summer does."

"So you're still taking cues from Rhys."

"And protecting this kingdom," the thatcher defended. "You're the one who's forsaken us!"

"Kill us, you say?" Vex echoed. "We have a better idea. You'll cooperate. Or—" He jerked his plaited head toward Poet, and the blacksmith squatted beside the jester, then braced a small hammer and iron nail over Poet's palm—and drove both down.

A howl barreled from Poet's chest, the sound pushing against the fabric stuffed in his mouth. The noise shredded past the wad and speared through my heart.

I flailed against the stonemason. "Poet!"

He bowed off the ground, agony contorting his face before he collapsed in a shaking fit.

That's when the Masters had the decency to look ashamed.

However, the repentance lasted for all of a moment, until their consciences reminded them about the alleged greater good.

This was Rhys's influence. This was what intolerance and indoctrination did to people.

My eyes stung. My fists curled.

Poet. My Poet.

Mine.

The goldsmith regarded me. "As I was saying, you'll cooperate or we'll take care of the other hand, and so forth," he finished. "You shouldn't need coaching about our vocations, Highness. The Master welder and blacksmith make shackles very difficult to breach."

"I'm sorry, Princess," the cloaked girl blubbered from the entrance, tears glazing her orbs. "They forced me to distract Poet! I didn't mean to—"

The welder clammed a hand over the child's mouth and shoved her into a corner. "Be still, little mutant," the member commanded.

"If you wish to receive compensation, you will hold your blasted tongue," their leader warned. "Otherwise, it shall be chopped off by the lumberjack."

"Abuse is a crime," I hissed.

"Then it's fortunate we don't answer to you or your mother anymore," another Master reproached, though I couldn't see which one.

Vex gestured. The obedient blacksmith yanked the nail from Poet's hand.

My jester groaned, his nostrils flaring and blood oozing from the crater. They could have severed an artery. Without the right treatment, they might have marred his hand permanently.

My gaze clung to Poet's. Despite the aftershocks of pain, his eyes sliced past everyone and tacked to mine. A territorial energy radiated from his being, like that of a cougar waiting to be set free. If he got loose, none of these occupants stood a chance. Already, his tongue had done its own damage.

The Masters cast him nervous looks, regardless of their weaponry. Rightly so, as Poet possessed a sharper weapon than any tool they wielded. He grunted something, a hint of mockery laced in his tone.

As if pushed to his limit, the blacksmith backhanded him across the face. I cried out, but the Master's reaction accomplished what Poet wanted. The gag popped from his lips like a cork.

He spit out a glob of blood, concealed his rancor at the stonemason who held me, and veiled his true feelings with a smug smirk. "Thanks for that," he told the blacksmith.

Jittery, the metalsmith hastened across the room and shoved the wad of cloth back into Poet's mouth. My lover groaned theatrically— then headbutted the member.

And drummed his heels into the man's bowels.

And wrung his own leg around the metalsmith's limb, hooked the crafter in place, and twisted. A sickening crunch resounded through the space. The man wailed, staggered backward, and struck the wall where he toppled over.

The girl jumped out of his way, her arms in the air. "Shit!"

My scalp burned as the stonemason hauled my hair backward. "Try that again," the member warned.

Poet ceased and hissed around the gag.

It took the goldsmith a moment to regain his composure while the others rushed to aid their bleeding, whimpering peer. Despite Vex's crusade, rampages weren't in Autumn's nature. But to my despair, Rhys's influence had pushed through that long ago.

At the leader's nod, the stonemason shoved me toward the meeting table. My hands shot out and caught the ledge, breaking my fall.

Poet was right. These players were lost to me.

They would force the hand of a child.

They would violate their sovereign.

They would dare touch my jester.

These were the consequences I had signed up for. These were the risks Poet and I would take for each other.

For Nicu. For this continent.

Instead of anger, I thought of Father and Mother, and what they had taught me. I thought of what Eliot had written to me. I thought of what Poet and Nicu had shown me.

My eyes clicked to Poet's. His stare bore into me, and he inclined his head.

Vanquish them, Sweet Thorn. I'll take care of the rest.

Cold steel reinforced my bones. I straightened, hoisted my chin high, and leveled my former subjects with a stare as sharp as needles.

Disquiet strung across the room. They absorbed my expression and shuffled, the reality of their choices coming to the forefront. My features reminded them, they had just chosen one monarch over another. And I would not accept that penalty sitting down.

Vex wavered, then remembered himself. "The deal we made," he said. "You and your perverted whore had us convinced. A harlot you might be, but you do not give your word lightly. That much, we had remaining hopes about." He gestured to the girl. "Unfortunately this morning, we caught the runt rambling to herself—"

"I wasn't talking to myself, asshole," the girl protested.

"Yes, our mistake," he belittled. "She was chattering to a wood-pecker." His derisive expression demonstrated what he thought of that. "What we overheard was disconcerting. Your vow to keep us as Masters wasn't genuine. You planned to rescind that promise and remove our titles when you had the chance. Or are we wrong?"

No, they were not. "How did you know the retreat's location?"

"Because our ancestors helped to build it. Did you not assume they'd pass down such confidential information to their successors?"

"Unlike you, I have more respect for my own judgments. I do not assume anything unless I see the evidence with my own eyes."

"In any case, it was hardly a chore to trespass on your property and wait until you and the jester exhausted your baser needs."

Fury outweighed my mortification. Since sunrise today, they had been watching us, holding out for an optimal moment to take Poet from me.

Vex approached the opposite end of the table and slapped his palm atop a leaflet of paper. "So we'll try this again. This time, with an immediate guarantee."

He shoved the paper forward, along with a quill pen. They coasted across the surface and landed on my side.

"Sign it," the man said.

My attention ticked to the parchment. One short passage. To the point. No fuss. No loopholes. I scoured the paragraph for a technicality, a semantic misstep, an escape clause I might use to my advantage.

Nothing. The language and wording were too simple for an outlet. And without Poet, there was no one to take a second pass to confirm this.

The Masters will forever be a recognized and essential branch of the Autumn Court. Henceforth, no Royal may sunder or imprison this faction, nor strip its members of their titles. For that license is hereby granted only to the guild members themselves.

These crafters would be an eternal fixture in this kingdom. Neither Mother, nor I would be able to replace them with hardworking citizens who deserved the ranks. These spies would be able to interfere in our quest for emancipation, able to influence the public against us. If any society had a chance of posing a threat to our hopes, it was them.

As a Royal, I had the authority to sign this document and set it into law. Regardless of my status as a future monarch rather than an acting queen, the signature would hold. That was the way of The Dark Seasons and its rulers.

The astute jester didn't need assistance in guessing the content. Yet I felt him waiting for a sign, an indication of a way out.

My eyes sheared toward him. My head shook covertly, moving scant inches so the men and women wouldn't catch it.

The walls shrunk, closing in like a trap, a drawbridge about to slam shut if I didn't make a choice soon. I rubbed the scarlet bracelet between my thumb and forefinger, signaling the text was truthful. It was valid and binding in every way.

Trenches dug into Poet's face. His eyes just might incinerate the manacles. Now it was his turn to shake his head.

Don't fucking do it, Briar.

The plea bulldozed through my chest. But how could I possibly obey him?

Nicu. That was how.

The choice swung before my eyes like a noose. Poet or his son.

I could execute the Masters for this treachery. If they harmed another millimeter of Poet's flesh, I would do it myself. But then we would forfeit any chance of gaining widespread approval. If I prompted a mass death sentence to these members, in addition to lacking proof of their treachery, their supporters would riot and rue the day I became queen. As a result, Nicu would lose the opportunity for a safe and equal future, as would every born soul.

The fate of this nation or Poet.

The freedom of citizens or Poet.

The little boy who loved the color orange or his father.

Briar, no! Don't!

His desperation blistered me like acid. My body shook, about to cave in on itself. I stared at him, heat stinging the backs of my eyes. But with just as much vigor, resistance seared through my veins.

Father would never oblige this group. Mother would never capitulate to their demands. The jester would never gratify them.

Not without a fight. Not without trying.

How to comply without the signature holding weight?

How to get us out of here before the Masters realized this?

A princess does not play their game.

A princess changes the rules.

A princess tricks.

This wasn't the first time I'd had to decide on a course of action within the span of seconds. Nor would it be the last. My mind foraged for an answer.

Beside the paper, a bead of ink bubbled from the tip of Vex's pen. The gold fluid sparkled like a melted nugget.

At the same time, something red and glossy split my concentration. The bowl of apples still sat untouched and unconsumed on the table. The sight broke through the clamor in my mind, flushing out the dismay.

During those blissful days with Poet in the cabin, at one point I'd reflected on these fruits. I told him not all the pomes had appeared noxious. But some had.

My attention darted between the gold-inked pen and the apples. A risky idea presented itself, tickling my scalp.

Mere seconds must have passed. No time for them, but a lifetime for me. My plan was scarcely foolproof, but what plan ever was? To that end, I had limited options.

My fingers plucked the writing instrument from the table.

Poet growled and jolted his arms forward. The magnitude of his movements shuddered the chains, dislodging the wall nails a fraction. If I pushed him too far, his strength might uproot the hardware like putty.

I fixed him with a look. *Trust me.*

Like a mechanism fastening into place, he read my expression and stopped. His chest rose and fell, thick pants surging from his nostrils.

Yet he ceased. *At your service, Highness.*

My mouth almost twitched. Instead, I schooled my features and scratched the quill across the parchment. Gold ink leaked into the surface.

As I signed, Vex scoffed. "Not a shred of hesitation. Not a moment to deliberate. But that isn't because you believe in our cause. No, it's because you wish to save your whore." Disillusionment tarnished his voice. "Tragically, the apple has fallen far from the tree."

I ignored the jab. I had never claimed or attempted to be like Mother.

Notwithstanding, we were more similar than people assumed. Like me, she wouldn't have given them what they wanted.

The parchment curled inward at the ends when I let it go. Tossing down the quill, I made sure to aim the instrument strategically, so that it landed on the leaflet. The pen's weight bore down on the flaps, closing them like doors.

I spoke quickly, trampling over the man's impulse to cross around the table and claim the document. "Speaking of apples, now you must do something for me," I stated. "Prove your worth."

The leader grunted. "We do that every day, as opposed to you."

"Prove your connection to this kingdom," I clarified. "As crafters, prove your knowledge of this nation." I smeared a temptation across my next words, a morsel these zealots would be persuaded to enter- tain. "Change my mind. Convince me to endorse you confidently. Despite our history, I have neglected to consider how well you truly know this land, down to its roots."

One thing the jester had taught me, one thing court life had prov- en no matter the Season, was that flattery accomplished a great deal. Likewise, nothing motivated extremists like the opportunity to re- cruit people to their beliefs.

I garnished my last statement with sugar. "Show me what I have to learn from you."

Reluctantly, the members motioned nearer and speculated my words.

After consulting their silent reactions, Vex squinted. "How?"

The word *game* wouldn't have the same effect on them as it would in Spring. No, they required a more dignified term.

"A challenge," I said.

They could simply release Poet, and we could walk out of here. The problem was, they would see my signature soon enough, poten tially before Poet and I made it to my horse. I needed something to distract and delay them.

Leaning forward with my body shielding the document, I contem- plated the fruit. "Beautiful apples," I repeated, admiring them as I had last night. "But which is the ripest, therefore the most flavorful?"

As I straightened, I caught Poet's gaze under my lashes. What he saw drew a mischievous glint to his countenance.

Setting one hand nonchalantly on the parchment, I offered the crafters a stately expression. "Only the most astute Autumn native would know."

Ego. Hubris.

They existed in every Season too.

Like carnivores sniffing raw meat, the Masters transformed. An eager light swept through their visages.

I made certain to exhibit both misgivings and conformity. They might view me as a fickle princess, seeing as I had changed so remarkably after returning from Spring. Yet they also knew Briar of Autumn to be a willful princess.

That balance convinced them I was being genuine.

"With these crafters as our witnesses, we shall each choose what we think is the ripest apple," I dared. "If your selection outdoes mine, you'll have my sponsorship. If not, I'm sure you'll find other ways to mobilize your princess—wait a moment," I instructed as the goldsmith moved to sit. "Release him first."

Vex nodded to the blacksmith. No matter how this went, I had signed our agreement.

Poet grimaced as the crafter twisted a key into the manacles. When the chains collapsed, so did my breath. Every fiber of my being yearned to rush to him, to snatch him, to haul him out of here. I longed to absorb him into me.

I did no such thing. That would only show the Masters how much he truly meant to me, which would make them doubt my intentions. In that regard, I needed to appear capricious.

The blacksmith had the audacity—and the barest civility—to offer Poet his hand. I withheld a vindicated sneer as Poet smacked the man's hand away with the backs of his knuckles, as though swatting a pesky fly.

Blood still dribbled from the pit in his hand. The jester winced but tore the gag from his lips, the movement causing everyone to tense, unsure of what would come out of his mouth. Instead, he made a show of wrapping the cloth around his wound to staunch the blood.

Then he considered the crimson staining his pants and swung his gaze to the goldsmith. "You'll get the bill for this, sweeting."

Unbelievable. I ducked my head, relishing the sound of his mockery, sinking into it like water.

The nails mounted into the wall sagged, exposing how close Poet had been to ripping the irons from the facade. Noticing this, the members hustled backward, and the mysterious girl gawked.

Poet was only playing docile and dandified because he knew where I was taking this. Otherwise, I doubted these crafters would still possess their vitals. I saw him straining to conceal the ferocious impulse. Though between us, he wasn't the only one.

Instead, Poet slouched lazily on the floor, feigned annoyance with me, and ridiculed, "Don't keep us in suspense."

"Very well," the leader said, lowering himself into the chair. "After you, Your Highness."

I did not thank him. Nor did I sit across from him.

One of the members slid the bowl to me. I studied the apples, reviewing their skin and plumpness, appraising their shades and stems. Rifling through the options, I weighed several in my palm and felt their coolness. Holding one to the light, I examined the leaf at the stem's tip, then rejected it with a flourish.

At last, I plucked a rotund pome and cradled it in my hands. "Now you."

The goldsmith's pupils had been stalking my every move. When the bowl was passed to him, he reconsidered the batch. Yet his concentration kept straying to the one I'd given the most attention to—the one I'd held to the light but then dismissed.

I maintained an impartial countenance. With confidence, he chose my reject.

We watched each other in an unspoken agreement. We would test our choices before switching and sampling our opponent's.

I bit into the apple. Crisp juice spilled along my tongue, tart and sweet. As the flavors danced down my throat, I felt the jester watching every pump of my neck.

Vex slurped on the flesh of his own apple and hummed in satisfaction.

We exchanged fruits, the thatcher carting them between us on opposite ends of the table. I kept one hand firmly planted on the document and sank my teeth into the second apple. Chewing, I wedged the chunk carefully into the side of my cheek.

The leader gulped his portion down and then rammed his fist on the table. "I think we have our winner."

"I agree," I murmured.

We had found a winner. But it wasn't him.

The man gloated, and his peers nodded to him in congratulations, then they bowed to me. My participation had thawed them, gave them an ounce of hope that I might see the light soon enough, might absolve myself in their eyes.

I inclined my head and strode to Poet's side. His scent hit me like a draft of fresh air, and his warmth seeped into my bones. Doing my utmost to contain myself, I squatted and looped my arm around his waist, and we hauled ourselves upright.

The Masters genuflected. I fantasized about stabbing them in their sleep.

Vex cleared his throat and regarded Poet. "Apologies for the hand."

"You should be apologizing for the clothes," the jester drawled, his voice thick with pain. "By the way, go fuck yourself."

The man blustered as we hobbled to the stairwell.

On our way out, Poet winked at the girl. At which point, I mouthed to her, *Run. Now.*

Her eyes widened. "I gotta pee!" she blurted out, then dashed from the room.

From above, we heard the tree door thump open. The Masters grumbled at her indelicate announcement, Poet rolled his eyes at their prudishness, and I nestled him close as we vacated the room and mounted the steps.

The Masters assumed I would not broadcast these meetings with Mother or the Royal Council. They believed none of this would be made public. In short, they believed many unlucky things.

Like others in this world, these crafters had branded me a deplorable princess who spent her time reading, scowling, and harvesting. They assumed I engaged in the latter purely to win civic approval.

They didn't think I invested genuine time learning about the crops, and they weren't at court, so they never witnessed me toiling in those areas. These members didn't know everything about me, because I had kept myself withdrawn and stoic.

Nor were they farmers, so they did not visit the orchards. They were too busy priding themselves on being elite citizens. With such a high status, why bother with anything other than their own practices?

The basics of survival were known everywhere. The irony about humanity was how quickly we forgot.

It took one second to discount certain perils. Do not cross the road without checking for incoming carriages. Do not walk alone at night without a weapon. Do not touch a boiling kettle. Do not turn and run from a wild animal, because that could mark you as prey. And do not trust everything that grows in the woods.

In our arrogance and haste, sometimes we overlooked how close to danger we came. Or we didn't take measures to learn, assuming ourselves to be an exception to the rules of nature. Or sometimes for all our wisdom, we were simply foolish. And sometimes, for one moment, we did stupid things.

The Masters didn't know the difference between a good apple and a bad one. They did not know how to angle the pome in the light, the better to see if the leaf was green or brown. They did not know which option was safer. They did not know the consequences of making the wrong choice and eating the wrong fruit. They did not, because they hadn't taught themselves what to look for.

Poet and I blew through the tree door. Eventide filtered through the branches, scattering shadows across the grass. Out of eyeshot, I spit out the wedge of apple that had been tucked into my cheek.

In an instant, the jester and I were on each other. He hauled me into him, and I tangled my arms around his body, my own frame shaking. With a groan, he pulled back and snatched my face.

Crying out, I flung my lips at his. He plastered me to him, his mouth on mine, kissing me over and over while gritting, "You stubborn woman."

Kiss. "You."

Kiss. "Fucking."

Kiss. "Stubborn."

Kiss. "Woman."

Sticky liquid coated my cheek. Blood from his wound streaked my skin and leaked into my clothes. Poet hissed from the pressure, but I veered back and tugged on him urgently. He nodded yet refused my assistance. Taking my hand with his good one instead, he guided me through the barbed lane and back to the horse.

"What the hell did you sign on that paper?" he asked.

"Something they deserved," I told him.

"Humor me, sweeting. My pants are ruined, and I'm upset."

The sentence flitted through my mind. The response I'd given them, comprising of words scripted in gold, penned from the bottom of my heart.

I shrugged and stated with as much virtue as possible. "The same thing you told them."

Sincerely,

Go Fuck Yourself

When I explained my actions, guffaws rumbled from Poet's mouth. He laughed through his pain, chuckle-hissing intermittently. "Sharp thorn."

Sharp, indeed. It had been a risk, but I knew Vex. If a poisonous apple stole from its victim the skill they valued most, I had theorized what the apple would take from him.

Not only would he lose the talent for crafting gold. He would hopefully lose the ability to recognize it. In which case, my signature would vanish from his sight.

Reaching my horse, I untethered Poet's staff and hurled it to him. He caught the weapon in his uninjured hand and affixed it to his hip with one of the harnesses I'd brought, then outfitted himself with the daggers I'd also packed.

As for the quill thorns in my braid and garter, I prayed we wouldn't need them. That aside, naivete had rarely ever served me well.

Poet grunted as we climbed onto the horse. The jester landed behind me, securing his arm around my middle. We fought over who got to steer the animal, but he finally gave in.

Digging in my heels, I sent us flying. As we plowed our way from The Forbidden Burrow, shouts and bellows launched from the tree trunk's open door.

Therein lay the flaw in my plan. Vex might not have been able to see my signature, but everyone else in the room could. Inevitably, they'd read the parchment aloud.

I urged the mare to go faster. Poet cursed, unsurprised. Because by challenging the goldsmith and falsely conceding defeat, I hadn't rescued us.

I'd merely given us a head start.

33

Briar

We speared through creepers and thickets. The horse's mammoth body contorted beneath us, her hooves punched the soil, and sharp blasts of air launched from her snout. I whisked the animal around shrubs and stumps, then veered her over a creek that cleaved into the forest. Fountains of water ejected from the surface as the mare's weight tramped through.

Resplendent leaves of yellow and ruby poked through the darkness, their colors impervious to the shadows. The canopy blasted us with Autumn hues as we raced from one terrain to the next.

Behind us, more hooves resounded, stamping the earth. The Masters had mounted their own fauna quickly. Not foxes, for those were worshiped and guarded by the fox mavens of the dell. Rather, the Masters straddled colossal steeds and stags, which they oftentimes leashed out of sight from The Forbidden Burrow's entrance. If we'd had time, I would have thought to free the animals, preventing the crafters from gaining on us.

The main thoroughfare would allow Poet and me to make greater headway, but it would also render us visible. I detoured, keeping to denser areas. Shrubs. Patches. It took longer, yet in an ideal world, it would prevent us from being spotted.

That, providing we discounted my hair. The locks burned red like a furnace.

Nevertheless, the ground shook. Poet and I cranked our heads over our shoulders, to where a stampede belted through the underbrush. Stags with lofty crowns, each bracket tipped in leaves or pierced with hoops. Steeds with ink markings on their limbs. Hooves ripped debris out of the way, and antlers battered through saplings, hurling trees from their roots and sending them crashing to the ground.

Atop the creatures, a gang of cloaked figures powered forward. They shot toward us like missiles, straight and sure. Hammers, blades, and swords flashed from their hilts.

Poet unleashed a gritty, aggravated noise. We whirled forward, and I spurred the horse faster over the creek, then propelled us through hedges.

We blasted into The Shadow Orchard. Apples glistened from the branches like silk globes. They detached and dropped as we flew through the rows.

The mare navigated the route with some difficulty, but I whispered to her and steered the creature true. She swerved around the trunks with the agility of a bobcat, but she would tire soon. At this velocity, the female had her limits. But so did the other fauna.

A primitive sound grated from Poet's mouth. He twisted and leaned far to the ground, as if he were about to topple over. A shout bunched in my throat, and my arm whipped backward to catch him, only for me to stall in realization. The elastic jester executed a maneuver impossible for average mortals. He arched low and sideways, as if his spine were made of string, and wielded his staff.

The weapon snagged onto a hulking tumbleweed. In my peripheral vision, I caught Poet rolling back to a sitting position while launching the mesh at our chasers.

The tangle of offshoots projected across the air like a grenade and struck one of the riders in the face. The filed prongs stabbed him through the eyes, blood spraying his countenance. With a howl, he pitched off his stag and smashed into the dirt, the tumbleweed spikes shredding his visage and throat.

He would not survive that. The punctures were too deep.

The stag belatedly registered its rider's absence, then skidded to a halt.

Vomit clogged my esophagus. I wheeled forward and drove our mount quicker.

Poet's muscles signaled tension but not remorse. Instead, he seized a dagger from his waist harness. I felt his body contort, indicating he was juggling the blade. Then he ejected the weapon with a backhanded flick.

The shriek and fall of another rider penetrated my ears, followed by another. One by one, the jester spun, flipped, and fired his daggers. I leaned over the horse, urging her to fly. Meanwhile, I listened to the impact as every weapon impaled its target and blew them off their rides.

Unsaddled, the animals either slowed or scattered through the wild. The latter creatures vanished into the trees, choosing to get out of harm's way, unaware that Poet would never hurt them. No, he concentrated on the Masters with deadly focus.

We accelerated. I forged ahead at such a momentum that the wind sliced across my cheeks, and my eyes watered.

When all five blades had been cast, Poet swiped a sixth one from under his pant leg, which he must have been hiding when the guild captured him. Armed, he gripped the weapon and hissed in my ear, "Slow the horse."

"Are you daft?" I yelled behind me. "Or are you jesting me?"

"Slow. The. Horse. Sweeting."

How dare he *Sweeting* me right now. But I knew him too well. If I didn't quell our pace, he would reach around me, steal the reins, and do it himself. Hating to but trusting him nonetheless, I eased on the straps.

The horse slowed while emitting a confused noise. Before I could predict it, the jester had sprung upright onto the creature's back, with nothing anchoring him.

Poet steadied himself as the mare galloped. "Circle that tree," he shouted.

What confounded tree?

Then he disappeared. Poet's weight lifted like smoke. I shrieked and swerved the animal around the next trunk, then directed the horse in a circuit. Overhead, a sleek body landed on a branch, hunched like a cat, and then launched off the edge.

Poet crashed into one of the Masters. Savagery constricted the jester's features as he wiped the blade's tip across the figure's mouth, which opened it wide like an oversized grin—a grotesque caricature.

Poet dove off the horse just as I rounded near him. As slick as water, he landed on the mare, and I charged forth.

The Shadow Orchard gave way to beech trees. If we continued in this direction, it would lead to The Wandering Fields, in view of the castle and its sentinels patrolling the towers.

This battle should not be witnessed. I directed the horse east, away from the boundary. Yet I spotted the remaining riders breaking apart, gaining traction, and fencing us in. On either side, the Masters galloped, as if pushing us toward the stronghold, herding us in that direction.

Why? Why would they urge us toward the one place where their actions would be seen?

I sensed Poet questioning the same thing. My rationale fought to catch up, but steering the horse hindered me from speculating.

The Masters hollered and pressed in on us. My horse panted, her limbs faltering, sweat clinging to her coat. She couldn't anymore.

I yanked on the reins. The creature skidded in place, hooves throwing brittle leaves into the air.

Poet and I jumped off the animal. I flattened my palms on her face, murmured my thanks, and planted my lips to her muzzle. She would be safe, find a spring, and rest. The loyal horse would wait, and I would retrieve her if we survived this.

The jester and I ran. Left with no other outlet, we sprinted down the main road to The Wandering Fields. In the distance, the lower town's pitched roofs clustered the vista, followed by the pasture with its gargantuan maples, and finally the castle towers rising into the foggy sky.

In the fields, titanic stalks loomed from the soil, each maize and brown silhouette fringed in corn tassels and wheat beards. A thought rippled through my consciousness. Relief pulsed through my veins.

I hustled toward the endless rows spanning before us. Poet understood and tore into a run beside me. At the fields' threshold, he seized my arm and hauled me into him.

Grasping my profile, the jester hoisted my lips to his. That breathless mouth snatched mine, prying me open. His tongue swept in, and with a desperate gasp, I wove my own tongue with his.

One brief kiss. Only one.

Poet jolted his mouth away, clamped onto my hand, and hurled us into the fields. He remembered. Based on how rapidly he bolted us into the maze, he remembered what I had told him about this place.

The tapered channels extended into a vanishing point, a black dot that seemed to lead nowhere. Stalks rose like spectral monoliths on either side, their outlines skewering into the firmament. We sprinted down the lanes, which multiplied and spread.

Air chopped through my lungs, as dry as sawdust. My side ached, but I forced my limbs to keep moving.

Muffled shouts plowed through, the Masters' clamor bringing up the rear. Boots thumped in our direction. They must have dismounted, since their fauna would not fit through these passages.

"This way," I told Poet, tugging us right, then left.

After years of harvesting, I knew this acreage blindfolded. The Masters did not.

Yet fury and spite had a provoking influence on people, especially if they believed it would be easy to follow their quarry. And most pertinently, if they wanted to exact revenge.

Still, my ears counted a reduced number of footfalls. Not all of them had elected to venture inside the enclosure.

Poet grimaced. Blood from his wounded hand seeped into the cloth and smeared across my palm.

Our fingers broke apart. Wrenching my head this way and that, I conjured the path in my mind's eye. Poet tracked my movements like his own, scarcely needing to be guided. Each corner I turned, he was there. Every time I doubled back the correct way, he aligned himself with me.

As we jetted through, the lanes seemed to bend and shift. Shadows embroidered the leaves, beards, and kernels of wheat. Their heights appeared to increase, as if distorted by a trick of ethereal light. I'd witnessed this before, while venturing here after dark with Mother and Father.

The stalks swayed, their leaves curling. A current rippled through, progressing in a single direction. This reminded me of an alternative trajectory.

I darted north. Poet followed. We carved a path I rarely used but remembered from strolling with my parents.

A shortcut.

From someplace within the fields, one of the Masters squawked in confusion. Promptly, that noise shriveled into a frightened whimper. I glanced back, taking stock of how truly vast this maze appeared when ensconced inside. People underestimated it, just as they did the perilous height of a tree until climbing its trunk and then peeking down.

Kernels bristled like needles. Gusts blew through the expanse, which distorted the rows and made it harder to navigate without proper knowledge.

Behind us, our chaser's whimper erupted into a delirious howl. Puzzled. Lost. The sound was followed by another, this one belonging to a female.

Poet and I surged across the rows and columns, then spilled into the brick road leading through the lower town. As our pursuers wailed in bafflement, we turned to stare. The acres oscillated like waves, the motions reverberating with a collective, audible hiss that engulfed the guild members' shouts.

The Masters would not find their way out.

I shuddered. "I'm sorry."

Poet snarled, "I'm not."

Foreboding clung to my ribs. I had lost count of our chasers and could no longer tell how many remained.

Poet snatched my wrist, and we blew through the alleyways while the locals slept. Candles twitched on windowsills. Pumpkins and hay bales decorated the front stoops of timber and plaster buildings. Lanterns hung over the avenues.

The denizens were preparing for Reaper's Fest.

I wheezed, my throat scalding. Only pure adrenaline kept me on my feet, whereas the jester barely broke a sweat. Finally, we barreled down the maple pasture, through the castle's barbican, and to the drawbridge.

Sentinels along the parapet walks caught sight of us. My flaming hair alerted them, and they called out, "Make way for the princess!"

The portcullis raised like fangs. Hinges groaned as the barrier opened.

I sprinted alongside Poet, and we hurled ourselves into the main courtyard. The exhalation I'd been about to release stalled on my tongue. Poet seethed, his boots freezing on the pavement beside mine.

Vex stood in the quad. He and the surviving Masters idled beneath one of the soaring maples, their hammers and blades braced.

34

Briar

nlike their comrades, the rest of the guild had wisely chosen to avoid the fields. Their presence could only mean they'd predicted the night watch would admit them. Although the Masters were not residents of court, they'd visited enough times to be recognized, particularly while wearing those signature brooches. Admired and respected by all, why wouldn't the sentinels bid them entrance?

With a growl, Poet maneuvered in front of me, his dagger in one hand and the staff primed at his hip. Momentarily shielded, I took advantage. I plucked a thorn quill from one of the jewel receptacles woven through my hair.

Except as I stepped around the jester, his muscles stiffened. Not because I was showing myself. But because of what he saw.

The goldsmith had a diminutive, cloaked form pinned to his side. He clamped onto the girl's nape, exhibiting her like a puppet. Through the oversized hood that blotted her grainy skin, those hazel eyes flashed terror at us.

Her body trembled. Her short axe rested on the ground, several feet away.

A feral noise shot from Poet's mouth. Neither of us had noticed the girl when the Masters gave chase to us. Patently, the goldsmith had been shrouding her on his mount. Even more likely, the man had kept to the rear of the stampede rather than the helm, the better to stay out of sight and range.

"You take my kin," he warned, "I'll take your own."

The jester flipped his dagger. "Tsk, tsk. Has no one cautioned you never to provoke a jester's temper? The last ones that did ended up as roadkill."

"Try it, and I'll snap her bones like kindling."

"Try it, and you won't have an arm to manage the task."

"You may have attacked us, but I have no fear of you."

Poet cocked his head and bragged, "Who said I was talking about me?"

The man balked. He and the surviving members glanced briefly at me.

Without looking, Poet knew I had armed myself. While I appreciated him talking me up, Vex shook off the possibility as though it was laughable. Apart from that training exhibition between Poet and me, the notion of Autumn's princess wielding anything more penetrating than a scowl had never been entertained in this kingdom.

I squeezed the quill in my palm and felt a gelatinous stream of blood pour between my digits. Pain bit into my flesh, but with these particular weapons, the coating would make the projectiles soar faster. I discovered this years ago, after accidentally cutting myself on one, back when Father was alive to explain it to me.

"Release her, and we'll negotiate," I told the man.

"Negotiate, and I'll release her," he countered.

"Keep being stubborn, and after my princess lops off your wrist, I'll polish off that tongue of yours," Poet murmured, a lethal grin in his voice. "I assure you, I'm quite good at aiming. Even better at juggling sharp things."

"What do you want?" I demanded.

"The guarantee you've denied us," Vex fumed. "The signature you failed to provide. The skill you've stolen from me with that apple. The penance you deserve for massacring our members and betraying this nation!'"

Confusion clashed with dread. They dared to pursue us to the castle, in perilous view of witnesses. Even as we spoke, curtains shuffled from hundreds of overhead windows. Heads poked from the draperies, while other figures threw open their sashes.

The courtiers and nobles were too many levels above to hear what was being said, much less to see clearly beyond the maple tree's canopy. Still, it proved difficult to tell whether these obstructions were insufficient to convict this cult.

Still, they had taken the chance. And their motives were obvious now. They risked arrest and execution because of their legacy. These men and women could endure death, so long as they were still titled as Masters. But they would rather die than have that privilege stripped. At least this way, they would perish before Mother or I had the chance to deprive them.

Beyond that, some other intuition fizzed along the nape of my neck—a missing puzzle piece about why else they'd be eager for such a gruesome end.

This, assuming Poet did not pierce these members in half before then. Regardless of the chase that had turned some members into carcasses, they disregarded his agility and precision.

They underrated me as well. But more importantly, they had forgotten the girl.

No more than a minute could have passed since entering the courtyard. Hence, the sound of rushing footfalls cluttered the quad, a legion of boots striking the bricks. The sentinels bellowed, the tower horn blared, and shouts rumbled from the soldiers' dormitories.

Steel rang. The onslaught grew louder.

Visibly, the girl recognized the clamor of knights storming our way. Beneath the cloak, her eyes narrowed.

That bold attitude resurfaced. When Vex propped his blade to her temple, the girl ejected a howl that could have stripped bark from an oak tree. She made a show of wailing like a frightened doe, to the point where her performance impressed the jester. I sensed his brows vaulting into his hairline and imagined a devilish smirk wreathing across his lips.

The Masters' leader grumbled. Distracted, he veered toward the girl—"Be quiet, you freakish bitch!"—and absently loosened his hold on her.

Poet and I tensed, both of us predicting the inevitable before it happened. The girl snatched the man's arm and sank her teeth into his flesh.

Vex brayed like a mule as crimson oozed down his skin. Bucking forward, he released her, and she hurled herself toward the abandoned axe.

Chaos erupted. The Masters yelled and streamed our way.

I launched forward, thorn quill in hand. But with a growl, Poet hooked onto my midriff. He pivoted us around, lashed his arm backward, and executed a backhanded throw.

The dagger spiraled. It rammed into one of the Master's throats, blood spritzing on impact.

A throng of bodies blasted into the quad. Autumn's military wielded axes, archery, halberds, hammers, sickles, saw blades, and swords. They bulldozed into the scene and joined Poet, spreading out to form a crescent around me.

As they did, I recognized the surrounding faces. The soldiers who had journeyed with us from Spring. The ones who had listened to Poet's campfire tale about me and him. The ones who had witnessed me honor Merit's death. These men and women had arrived first and formed a barricade, their expressions harsh on the Masters.

Among them stood Aire. The First Knight aligned himself with Poet.

The jester's livid voice spoke, his tongue flicking like a knife. "Touch the princess and suffer her jester's wrath."

"Harm our sovereign as you harmed our brother-in-arms," Aire gritted, "and forfeit your lives."

The legion crowded in on all sides. Some of them cast me quick glances, loyalty blooming across their faces.

Salt stung the backs of my eyes. A boulder squatted in my throat. I knew these looks from all the times they'd been directed toward Father and Mother—but never me. These weren't the countenances of fighters obligated to safeguard their ruler. Rather, they had transformed. They were now the faces of warriors who respected their princess.

One of them muttered to me, "For Merit."

Gulping, I whispered, "For Autumn."

The Masters regained their bravado. With a unified screech—"For the inheritance of the Seasons!"—they shot toward us. And with a blare to defend the Crown, the knights collided with our enemies.

Honed noises cleaved through the night, shrieks clashing with crossing blades.

Hammers whacked opponents. Halberds jabbed into stomachs.

Wheeling me the other way, the jester shoved me behind the maple tree. I stumbled against it and grunted with umbrage. He'd just finished complimenting my skills, yet at the first sign of danger, the man deposited me into a corner?

Whipping out his staff, Poet windmilled the instrument in his good hand. Then he launched into the maelstrom and vanished along with the troop.

Horror clamped onto my throat. "Poet!"

Although injured, he moved like steam, passing through attackers as if intangible. Those serpentine reflexes and panther instincts kicked in. He rotated his weapon, spinning it like an extension of his body.

The staff flipped and wheeled around Poet's form with a speed that dizzied his opponents. He blocked, ducked, sheared across the ground, and cracked through bones. The fighting traveled across the expanse, with Poet using the architecture to his advantage. He rebounded from benches and flipped backward off walls, all while dicing though anyone who got near him.

Skulls shattered. Limbs were crushed, misshapen and warped at inhuman angles as the jester shifted from a glorified rake to a deadly enemy.

Deafening cries inundated the area. The soldiers brandished their own arms. Swords clanged while other weapons speared through flesh.

Body parts scattered across the quad like detritus. Men and women hollered. Geysers of blood puddled the ground.

The girl could be in trouble. She could be hurt.

I swerved my head. My eyes stumbled across a small figure armed with an axe and dashing along the outskirts. A ripple of shock buzzed through me as she cried out in fear, dodged an incoming fist—and instinctively chopped it off.

The mangled hand popped from the assailant's body. Her victim bellowed and clutched his arm as she kept going, squirreling around everyone.

Just then, another of the Masters bounded in front of her and raised a hammer. I broke into a run while aiming my thorn quill. However, I skated to a standstill as a broadsword flashed out of nowhere. The blade looped like a wing and smashed into the Master's weapon, stalling it a hair's breadth from the girl's cloaked face.

Aire held his weapon aloft, his arm extended and the sword braced as if it weighed nothing. His eyes darkened like a midnight sky. Without looking at the girl, he maneuvered in front, blocking the assailant from her.

"Where are your Autumn manners?" he snarled to the crafter. "Try picking on someone your own size."

The Master was nowhere near Aire's size. Still, he lunged.

The soldier deflected, whirled, and produced a second sword from his hip. As if wrought from thin air, the set of blades clipped the man's own weapon again. At which point, the pair of fighters vaulted into it, their instruments flying.

The First Knight battled with the same precision as Poet. Except whereas my jester attacked like a shadow, this man advanced like a bird of prey. His movements cut to the quick, airborne and swift as a cyclone.

The girl stumbled back. She gawked at the soldier, momentarily dumbstruck. But as the men battled over her, I flapped my arm to get the female's attention.

"Hide!" I shouted.

She got wind of her senses and scrambled like a crab into the nearest bush. Once certain of her safety, I skirted around the maple in time to bear witness to another influx. More soldiers swarmed the perimeter, the rest of Autumn's army smashing into the scene.

The Masters should have been vastly outnumbered long ago. They should have, if it weren't for a significant downfall. Amid the tumult, sentinels had trickled from inside the castle, except not all the guards aligned with the troops.

Instead, they grumbled and defended the Masters. And to my distress, I realized why. It wasn't because they wanted their princess killed. It was because they wanted the Masters harmed even less.

In the confusion, they had lost sight of me and couldn't say which side they were supposed to be on. All they saw were the Masters struggling against trained warriors. Because of that, some forces shielded the elite crafters instead, switching loyalties along with a parcel of the military who arrived late—the ones who hadn't quested with Mother, the jester, and me from Spring. Thus, disorientation gave way to violence.

Poet's face materialized from the throng. A knife jolted toward him from behind, intent on carving into his spine.

Rage and panic torched a path up my fingers. *Touch him and die.*

Like a monster, I tore from my spot, squatted into position, and pitched my thorn quill into the air. It whorled and clipped the figure across his face, dislodging a chunk of his skin. Blood splattered from the wound as the jester's attacker hit the ground.

Poet whisked around, registered what just happened, and snapped his gaze to mine. Pride and protectiveness blazed across his face. But when the quagmire expanded my way, those green eyes detonated.

A team of Masters charged at me. I reacted on impulse, invoking all the moves Father had taught me, applying the new maneuvers Poet had inspired during our training session at the cabin. I veered while snatching the next quill from my braid and throwing it at my assaulters. I leaped aside and ejected two more from my thigh garter, then additional ones from my braid. I twisted and fired each projectile, knocking my attackers off balance. On impact, the men and women sprang into the air, mists of crimson squirting from their wounds.

I agonized, fighting to aim correctly. I targeted the Masters, anyone racing my way with a weapon, and no one else. Yet with the tide constantly in motion, my fingers shook, and terror iced my blood that I might harm someone on our side.

With the main doors splayed open, part of the battle spilled into the castle.

From within, screams echoed. Glass blew outward from some of the windows, and a silhouette went tumbling from a sill. Rivulets of blood slithered across the ground.

I staggered in place as the combat extended inside the palace walls. "Stop!" I entreated. "Please, stop!"

But no one heard me. Pandemonium catapulted from my lungs, but the havoc swallowed my cries in its maw. Paralyzed, I beheld the slaughter as citizens, guards, and warriors ripped one another apart. I watched blood flow through the courtyard, the massacre hellbent on turning this castle to ruins.

A familiar weight wrapped around me. I glanced sideways to where Poet stood, having just felled another perpetrator. Welts branded his face, blood stained his open coat and torso, and his injured hand quaked from exertion.

Yet he was still alive, still breathing, still mine. Relief slackened his features when he spotted me. Tears pricked my eyes as we locked gazes across the anarchy.

One of the Masters blared while hustling into the castle, "The dungeon! Get the born!"

Hysteria seized my chest. Putridness sloshed up my throat.

They would raid the cells containing born souls. They would un-shackle the mad from Summer. They would send those innocent beings to their own slaughter.

And Nicu! Mother!

Some sort of blur shifted in my periphery. Poet's eyes darted to something closing in on me like a wraith. Instantly, a frenzied emotion distorted the jester's features, and his pupils erupted with fear.

A primal noise shredded from his lungs. He broke from his stance, plowed through the crowd toward me, and roared, "Briar!"

Time slowed. The faces of born souls, Mother, Father, and Nicu swarmed my vision.

"Briar!"

I had exhausted my supply of thorn quills. Still, my will broke through the paralysis. Recovering from my stupor, I clenched my teeth and whirled toward the castle.

"Briar!"

And as I turned, my body pivoted into the path of an outstretched object.

Smooth edge. Sharp tip. Expertly forged.

The blade pared through me like a spike through pudding.

35

Poet

The howl stripped my lungs to tatters, the force of it rupturing across my tongue. It reverberated in my ears like a thousand alarm bells. From across the quad, Briar blinked as if puzzled by the noise that catapulted from me.

There was my princess, standing amid the bricks of her home. There was my thorn, surrounded by a fortress stained in crimson, her frame standing upright among the desolation of bodies.

She swayed, then glanced at her stomach. The hollow dug into her gut, blood spewing down her frame like strands of scarlet.

Like severed ribbons.

The world faded to black. The screams from both sides evaporated.

My pulse seized, my heart stopped beating, and my voice lost all meaning.

'Tis the lovely cruel you are.

With another bellow, I tore across the courtyard. My boots ripped from their foundation like chains splitting from iron. I hacked and lashed my way through the mutiny, my staff cracking scalps, my free fingers swiping knives from warrior's hands. While eating up the distance, I ducked fists, pivoted around weaponry, and flung blades at every figure that blocked my route.

I no longer felt my injured hand. I no longer gave a solitary shit.

A vignette cycled through my head. Briar, glowering at me from her seat in the great hall, back when I denied her a lit candle. Briar in that Spring hall, when I interrupted her paltry attempt to dance. Briar, braving a leenix attack in the wildflower forest. Briar, meeting my son. Briar, tossing pebbles into a stream and repressing the first true smile I'd ever seen from her. Briar, caked in mud and fucking kissing me in a meadow. Briar in the kitchen at midnight, unaware how close I'd come to shredding the nightgown from her body and hoisting her onto the counter. Briar, dancing in a moonlit labyrinth. Briar, breaking Nicu from a dungeon with me. Briar, holding her chin aloft under the judgment of the Royals.

Briar, splayed and panting on my chamber floor, then on her bed when my head sank between her legs, then in the woods during a sunset carnival, then in a traveling carriage, then on a balcony overlooking Autumn, then on her throne with a lopsided crown on her head, then in the cabin, then during every heated moment in between.

Her crinkling chin. Her sterling irises.

Her sharp features. Her stubborn voice.

Her face painted in jester makeup. Her body arching beneath me, arousal and pleasure staining her lips pink as she came.

Her mouth on mine. Her shaky exhales. Her heart beating.

Briar twisted to see who'd stabbed her. Vex stared back, flabbergasted as though just registering what he'd done. His blade stuck out of her womb like a lever.

Repentance clashed with defiance. Vex yanked the hilt from her body. Before he could recover and overpower her, Briar used the last vestiges of strength to crank her right arm backward—and punch him in the face.

His nose spewed like a red fountain. On a shriek, the man spun like a disk and toppled to the ground. And like a moth freed from its pins, Briar followed him.

She buckled and fluttered to the floor, her knees striking the ground. And my limbs exploded with movement.

While the fight raged on, I diced and cleaved a ferocious path to that flaming hair and those steely eyes. Verily, I smashed through the combat whilst serrated noises grated from my throat.

So help me, I would raze this castle if she lost another drop of blood. I would burn this land to cinders if those eyes closed.

My knees crashed into the stones as I landed beside her. An instant before her head would have cracked against the foundation, I caught her limp form and hauled her upright against me. "Briar!"

Fluid bloomed through her jacket and seeped into my clothes. I rushed to peel off my coat and ball the fabric against the wound, pressing firmly to staunch the flow. The nail gash in my own hand poured over her injury, so that it became impossible to tell where her blood ended and mine began.

My free hand cupped her face, smearing crimson onto her freckled cheeks. The fractured word scraped from my mouth, "Briar."

Her eyelashes fanned open. As she registered my face, a grin trickled across her lips, and those gray irises softened.

A garbled sound clotted her mouth, then leaked into the air. "Fashion victim."

The phrase stalled my touch. My brows slammed together. Briar … wouldn't say that if she were fatally wounded.

Pained eyes gazed back at me, accompanied by lucidity. My head snapped from her face to the gash. Dumbfounded, I lifted my quaking hand and took a second look at the red pit in her stomach. The puncture was deep, but not deep enough to impale an organ.

Over the place where she'd been stabbed, one of the gold appliqués lining her jacket had cracked. The accessory had blocked the weapon's depth like a shield. It had provided a barrier, the way leather sometimes did against blades, especially effective if crafted by someone with indisputable skill.

Someone like a Master goldsmith. Someone who, at the moment, hadn't been able to register the gold decorating her jacket. Someone who'd bit into a poisonous apple and lost that most valuable ability.

Had I not been about to uproot the ground everyone stood upon, I would have noticed this. Had I not been ready to decimate this world for her, I would have been sane enough to inspect the wound more thoroughly.

My muscles deflated. This time, it was my turn to unleash a clotted noise.

"Wicked hell," I hissed, gathering Briar to me. "Wicked fucking hell."

"You once ... told me ... fashion victims aren't victims, because they know when to ... take a risk." Briar licked her lips. "Wanted to wear leggings ... but I took a chance ... and the dress became a weapon, like you also said."

I thumbed her cheeks. "Finally, someone who's smart enough to quote me."

"Hurts," she muttered, her respirations choppy. "But I still ... look better ... than you."

Broken chuckles tripped from my tongue. I wanted to clamp my mouth to hers. I wanted to kiss life back into this glorious woman. Except the long-suffering groans coming from the goldsmith snagged my attention.

My humor tapered into a low, menacing noise. My relief sharpened into something deadly. My knuckles curled like talons.

Gently, I positioned Briar upright, making sure she was able to sit fully. I urged her to maintain pressure on the wound, to keep my coat wedged there.

Then slowly, I turned my head.

Vex rolled around the floor like a capsized cockroach. He cradled his nose, streams of red oozing between his fingers.

"Poet?" Briar drew out.

Not enough. Oh, but he hadn't endured nearly enough.

"Poet, don't," the princess implored.

The backs of my eyes burned like coals, red hot fury clouding my vision. My blood boiled, the rampage gushing from my head to my fingers. A primitive hiss scrolled up my throat as I lifted myself onto my haunches.

"Poet, no! Don't—"

I was on him before she could finish. One second, I'd been coaxing her into a sitting position. Then next, I flew across the quad and slammed into the man like a cannonball.

Savage noises ruptured from my lungs. My fist rose and lowered, rose and lowered, rose and lowered. Vex groveled under my weight and shielded his arms over his face, but I would have none of that.

My knuckles rammed his cranium into the ground. With each blow, crimson splattered my chest. Swiftly, the man's face shape-shifted to a mass of pulp, bones crunching and trenches distorting his flesh.

Briar's shouts slipped through my mind like water. My canines bared, and I blasted my arm downward like a battering ram until that failed to satisfy me. Catching sight of the weapon he'd used to stab my princess, I snatched the blade off the ground. Three seconds later, the man's shirt was gaping open, and he was yowling.

Recalling the symbols carved into a dead soldier's chest, I repaid him that courtesy. With deft flicks, I sketched the knife's tip across his flesh. Lines of red pooled and formed the shape of a knotted ribbon.

I would do this and more. I would flay the skin from his bones. I would snap every ligament.

Briar's weight thrust against my side. She screamed for me to stop, to please stop. Her fingernails burrowed into my biceps, and concern stalled my movements. If she didn't release me, she would aggravate her wound.

Another pair of hands grabbed my shoulders. Aire materialized in my periphery, that cloud of ashy hair complimenting the man's astringent expression. He tried to haul me backward, but though he possessed the strength of a warrior, I remained cemented on top of Vex.

It took another pair of hands. Then another. Then another. With four soldiers clamping on, they finally pried me from the goldsmith and hauled my weight off the ground.

I staggered backward into Briar's waiting arms. Having managed to stand, she clutched my side, her free hand racing over me until I blinked and swerved her way. Pain, fear, and love gripped her features.

Alive. She was alive.

With a haggard growl, I grabbed her. With a dry sob, she flung herself at me.

Banding my arms around her, I encased the princess into my frame and angled her from the goldsmith, who no longer resembled himself. Briar's digits balled against my torso. Her muscles shook as violently as my own.

At some point, the fighting had stopped. Blood splashed across the quad and stained the maple tree's bark. The carnage of bodies, limbs, and mangled flesh lay across the castle grounds like fractured chess pieces, along with shards of glass from broken windows. The rancidness of sweat and blood crowded my nostrils. Cries resounded from overhead as the courtiers stared down into the destruction, trauma stringing across their features—the ones I could make out, at least.

The survivors stumbled nearer, including the soldiers who'd arrived late. But every Master lay unmoving, and each knight who journeyed with us from Spring had fallen.

All except the First Knight. Aire wavered in place with his swords hanging at his sides and contusions littering his face. Grief creased his features, and his irises dulled as he absorbed the aftermath. Some of his unit muttered Autumn prayers, and others knelt beside their kin.

Several knights bolstered what was left of Vex. The man teetered on his knees, his features a husk of his former self.

"Get him out of here," I gritted between my teeth. "Get him out of Briar's sight before I fucking kill him."

The shriveled goldsmith managed to lift his head and sputter, "Too late."

Then he took advantage of the knights' momentary indecision. In

391

one final act of stupidity, Vex hurled himself to the ground, retrieved his blade, and slit his wrist.

More blood. More gasps. More cries.

Briar keeled forward. Her mouth fell open as the bastard crumpled in a dead heap. I held onto the princess, carefully wrapping my arms around her, in case she lost her footing once more.

Commotion blasted from inside the castle. More silhouettes raced outdoors, many of them carrying torches and lanterns.

Gasping with horror, the Royal Council stumbled in place.

Cadence, Posy, and Vale dashed through the crowds. "Briar!" one of them called out whilst all three females rushed to the princess's side.

Because I wouldn't let her go, and she wouldn't release me, the ladies settled for wiping Briar's brow, replacing my coat with a proper cloth for her wound, and clasping her dazed face to kiss it.

Afterward, shock cluttered the women's features. Cadence paled, her complexion going as sallow as porridge. Posy clamped a hand over her mouth, and Vale's jaw hung open.

"Briar!" came a terrified shout from the doorway. Avalea fisted the skirt of her gown and sprinted to her daughter's side. "Oh, my girl!"

Still numb, Briar peeled herself from me as the queen threw her arms around the princess. Unshed tears rimmed the queen's lashes, and chilled tendrils of air burst from her mouth as she muttered unintelligible things to Briar.

"Nicu—," Briar and I began.

"He's safe," Avalea said, winded and shaken. "The skirmish never made it to our level; however, the lower floors are in shambles."

The princess hugged her in kind, then sagged against me once more. Anguish glittered in her pupils as her head swiveled to and fro over the expanse. Bereavement twisted her expression, along with remorse.

From behind, I lowered my mouth to her ear. "Don't you dare."

This was not her fault. She didn't cause this upheaval.

Yet she braced the cloth against her wound and glanced around as though the opposite was true. Her eyes quivered over each fallen soul, from knights to sentinels to crafters. "Forgive me," she whispered in a shattered tone, like she might choke on her guilt. "I'm so sorry."

I read her thoughts. The Masters had been traitors, but they had still cared about this nation. They'd had families and children, as had the soldiers who fought to protect her.

I felt Briar's pain and wanted nothing more than to absorb it, to free her from it. Helpless, I pulled her close, as though it might be possible to leach the emotions from her.

From the sidelines, a small form scurried out of the bushes and tried to make a break for it. Mid-run, the girl named Someone grunted as a mighty hand shot out and seized the back of her cloak. Aire shackled her in place. She thrashed and snarled, all the whilst keeping her face tucked inside the hood.

The exchange unfolded on the fringes, unnoticed by everyone but Briar and me. With nods from us both, the First Knight released the girl.

She scurried backward and craned her head to glare at him, but the moment her attention landed on the knight, those hazel irises flared wide. I couldn't see the girl's expression, but there was no mistaking the blush racing up her throat.

The knight frowned at the girl's shrouded features. "Are you all right?"

That blush faded into what I imagined was a glower. "Fuck off," she snapped.

To which Aire's eyelashes flapped in umbrage. The sight of this bulky soldier being taken down a peg by a female ten years his junior should be amusing. And it would be, if it were any other night but this one.

Another knight snatched the tyke's arm, about to demand she apologize. But without taking his eyes from the girl, Aire thrust the flat of his sword against his comrade's chest.

"Hands. Off," he ordered.

The girl hopped backward, then glanced my way. From across

the distance, Briar and I detected what the soldiers hadn't. Under the hood, the female's mouth trembled. She feared what she'd seen. More than that, she was frightened of being discovered.

Whatever her motivation had been for working with the Masters, whatever she'd aimed to gain, she had just lost it. The Masters were dead, taking her hopes with them.

Briar's profile softened, and she pointed to a narrow, inconspicuous exit from the quad. Likewise, I inclined my head and winked.

A grateful expression loosened something in the moppet's eyes. She exchanged one more hostile look with Aire, then skulked the way Briar had pointed. Someday, that feisty force would grow into an even greater contender. But if we ever saw the little slayer again, that would depend on her.

No more than several minutes had passed. The moment was short-lived as the reek of dead bodies festered around us.

Avalea watched her daughter not merely with relief. Nor did she digest the casualties merely with sorrow.

To the contrary, another emotion drained the color from the queen's complexion. "I didn't know."

I flattened my hand over Briar's, right where she clutched her wound. We waited for more, but all Avalea did was shake her head and repeat, "I didn't know."

"Know what?" Briar murmured.

The queen's pupils quavered. Her next words came out in a low rush of sound. "I didn't know he would be here."

Somehow, the princess and I comprehended. We fucking knew to glance at the castle's threshold, which loomed wide open at the top of a flight of steps.

There, Rhys stepped into the firelight.

36

Poet

A brutal noise grated through the courtyard. Yet it hadn't come from me. For I was still processing the macabre sight of this cocksucker.

Nay, the grisly sound had erupted from someone else. It came from the heiress at my side.

Briar's eyes turned into blisters. With another shrill cry, she launched into motion and raged across the courtyard, baring her fingernails like claws toward the Summer King.

Aire's arm shot out, looped around her middle, and yanked her backward. Unaware of her injury, the First Knight restrained her too tightly. Her furious shriek dwindled to a whimper.

Stunned, Aire released the princess. The echo of her pain spurred me to action, my limbs blowing past everyone. With a growl, I caught Briar, shackling her upper frame as she flailed against me with renewed ferocity.

Heedless of her wound, the princess thrashed like a hooked fish. Her limbs scratched the air, scrambling to get loose and reach the king's smug leer.

"Let me go!" she shrieked. "Let me fucking go!"

"Nay, sweeting," I muttered, struggling to tamp down my panic. "I'm afraid that would make things a tad dramatic."

No matter that I understood her. No matter that I wanted to steal the nearest weapon and use it to disembowel Rhys, slowly and methodically. No matter that I wanted to pare out his spleen, tie him to a tree in the forest, and watch as the wild's rabid fauna polished him off. No matter that I wanted all of this and more.

For we had an audience. And as one familiar with audiences, I knew some performances won admirers. Alas, others did irreparable damage. I had spent my days and nights in Spring learning to repress the urge to slit throats and speak out of turn, the better to fool my targets and prospects. I had taught myself when to unleash and when to keep my enemies close.

Briar showed no sign of caring. From one minute to the next, the reputedly aloof and prudent Royal broke. Ballistic, she ignored the gash in her side and wrestled against me.

Around us, courtiers crept from the interconnected quads and various castle doors located throughout the grounds. The Royal Council gaped at Briar. The queen rushed to her daughter's side, attempting in vain to quell the princess. The ladies hustled behind Avalea and tried to help, to no avail.

The surviving knights grimaced at the scene in distaste. Aire was the exception, the First Knight's face crimping with worry. That, and trepidation. He knew just as I did, just as the queen did, just as Briar's ladies did, just as the advisors did.

A set of grim facts remained. Apart from the First Knight, every other soldier who traveled with us from Spring had fallen. Every warrior who could testify that Briar had paid Merit the utmost tribute in The Shadow Orchard—setting a leaf on his forehead and covering his throat with her torn skirt—was gone. Except for Aire, each knight who could vouch for Briar's honor lay dead and maimed.

Nobles and servants had viewed the battle from windows, but they couldn't say whether the soldiers had protected Briar out of a vow of servitude and duty, or if they protected her out of loyalty. The First Knight though he might be, Aire would be incapable of helping us prove the truth. Without the backing of his crew, the man's testimonial wouldn't hold water. The court knew he had developed a friendship with me and Briar. They would consider him biased, regardless of his pristine reputation.

Rhys's wife emerged into the scene. Queen Giselle's eyes broadened around the courtyard, which had morphed into a graveyard.

Ah. So he'd come here on the pretense of another social visit.

I didn't know he would be here.

Avalea's confession prickled my flesh. So soon after his last conjugal visit, Rhys must have heard we invited Spring to Reaper's Fest and decided to include himself.

Either that, or he'd never left. In fact, he might have been here the whole time, stashing himself somewhere private in Autumn. Someplace where he could meet with the Masters on a regular basis, as well as keep tabs on me and Briar.

Rhys couldn't have known any of this would happen. He wouldn't have known to show up at this exact moment. But I wouldn't put it past him to stick around for a while, should anything go amiss and we refused to succumb to blackmail.

He would have known not to underestimate us.

A snarl pushed against my teeth as Rhys and I locked gazes. He stood there, patently aware he didn't have to do a fucking thing, hardly needed to lift a pinky, much less utter a word for this shitshow to work in his advantage.

Like a coup or an unexpected boon, Briar was accomplishing plenty for him.

"Monster!" she trilled.

"Murderer!" she damned.

Anxiety squeezed my chest. Whilst keeping my vehement gaze on Rhys's miserable sneer, I whispered "Hush" in Briar's ear. "Hush, sweeting."

At last, the princess slouched against me. She panted, her breaths slamming into the air. She struggled to calm down, but her voice came out raw as she hissed at the king, "You did this. You're responsible. And for that, I'll fucking butcher you."

Audible gasps rung through the crowd. To threaten a monarch was treason, even if it came from the mouth of a fellow Royal.

In response to Briar's accusations and threats, Summer shook his head. The menace stood there, as he had the first night he darkened Autumn's doorstep—like a praying mantis from the pit of hell.

If it were up to me, I would relish Briar tearing into the fucker. By Seasons, I would join in on that delight.

Instead, I held her fast. My tongue lost its leverage, artifice abandoning me, my skills withering. I clasped my thorn, protecting her yet helpless to stop the domino effect.

Rhys extended his arm. "You see now what I witnessed long ago in Spring? A princess who has lost a grip on her faculties. An heiress spiraling into a crazed state of hysterics, all because of her infatuation with a notorious, whorish, bastard jester who kept his simpleton son a secret from the Crown. Seduction has claimed her sanity."

I bared my teeth and snarled, "Stop. Right. There."

But like an idiot, Rhys ignored my warning. "My queen and I have come here with the hopes of sustaining our peaceful alliance. We came to show goodwill and take part in your Reaper's Fest celebrations. Yet it seems our grand gesture can no longer be fulfilled," he bullshitted, practically foaming at the mouth. "We mustn't align ourselves with this nation when its future sovereign is on the verge of collapse. Pray, don't blame your queen. But from simpletons to the mad, Briar of Autumn supports the born and seeks to liberate them. Mark my words, this woman and her jester lover intend to lawfully emancipate a scourge. The princess will set free a pestilence of nature and infest your Season with abominations. I daresay, she isn't fit to reign."

"How dare you!" Avalea seethed. "You will not speak thusly of my daughter!"

My arms secured Briar closer and felt her stiffen. Verily, I sensed the moment logic returned to her, the instant when my prudent princess recognized the gravity of her behavior.

Rhys barely cast the deceased Masters a glance. I couldn't say the degree to which he'd plotted with them, nor did it make sense that he would have foreseen this outcome. One more puzzle piece was missing.

Nonetheless, the Prick to End All Pricks seized this opportunity like a bonbon. Tickled fucking pink, he increased the volume of his speech, his propaganda going airborne like a virus. "Because of her sympathizing choices, and because of her sordid passions, soldiers forced to stay loyal and commoners—" now he gestured to the dead Masters, "—forced to rebel are dead."

Cadence, Posy, and Vale stationed themselves on our side and scowled at the king. Aire hardened his jaw and stepped in our direction as well, positioning himself beside us.

The solidarity did nothing to impress the spectators. Like tar, Rhys's expression slid across the crowd, covering them in a thick, black heap of slander.

"How many more of you will she sacrifice for her vulgar desires?" he questioned. "Tonight, she drove a once-benevolent court to violence. But how long before she incites a civil war?"

"No!" Briar yelled. "I won't ... I will not ..."

But her denial faded. The king had planted his words strategically like landmines, and Briar knew better than to step on them. Still, she understood as well as I did that any defense was too late. The more she protested, the worse it looked.

Bravo, for the court listened to Rhys and watched Briar, their stunned features warping into something more dangerous than doubt. Their faces reflected suspicion and finally contempt.

They stared as if she'd gone mad.

As if she'd ... gone ... mad.

37

Briar

There existed different types of darkness. The total absence of light, like plunging into the depth of a well or falling into slumber. The foiled sheen of a forest at dusk. Murky paths or chambers inked in moonlight.

The depths of a jester's pupils. The black of a diamond painted down his face. The ebony enamel of his fingernails. The shadows that draped across his features.

But there also existed a morbid sort of darkness. The type that could not be measured in pigmentation but in feeling. It dwelled in even the most altruistic of kingdoms, as impossible to avoid as nightmares.

Hours after the battle ended, I stood on the dungeon's threshold and felt that same darkness crawl over my flesh like a phantom. The guards lurched to their feet when I entered. To their credit, they did their utmost to avoid staring at my tattered gown and the crimson splotch where my wound had leaked through. I gathered they'd already heard of my demise and Rhys's misrepresentation of my sanity.

To that end, it was hardly prudent or wise to show my face here.

The timing could not be worse. Yet it could not be more important.

This wasn't my first visit here. And who knew if I would have another chance.

I cranked my chin as high as it would go. "I require a moment."

The men exchanged wary glances. "Did the queen—"

"She approves," I lied, forcing my eyes not to narrow and thus illustrate how the question offended me.

Without further inquisition, they stepped aside. My boot heels thumped onto the stones as I turned a corner, and my eyes strayed down the hollow of cubicles.

Rushes lined the floors. High, shallow windows permitted air to flow through and leach the odor of feces from the area. Torches provided a semblance of light, and each cell contained a latrine and a wash basin.

Nonetheless, I knew better. None of these pitiful attempts at Autumn charity absolved Mother or me.

This was no life for anyone. It was deplorable and unforgivable at best.

However quickly we hoped to change things, it would never happen fast enough. If it weren't for Poet, I wouldn't have a prayer of sleeping at night. In fact, I marveled how Mother managed while knowing what born souls suffered, in addition to any citizens living in squalor and poverty outside the citadel.

One by one, I passed by the cages where the group from Summer languished My pulse knocked against my breastbone, and perspiration bridged across my clammy palms. With my arms hanging at my sides, I peeked through the grilles.

A young man rocked in a corner and mumbled to the wall, as if expecting the facade to reply. He turned to me and croaked, "Did you hear that? Did you hear what they said to me?"

My throat bobbed. I nodded. "Indeed, I did."

A woman with a cascade of blonde hair repeatedly counted her mud-caked fingers. But when she glanced my way, I stared back and counted my digits too. The gesture relaxed her shoulders and tipped her lips into a grin.

One lanky figure tried to grab the hem of my jacket dress and yank me forward, but I stopped the guards from intervening. "It's all right," I told them, aware they wouldn't approve of this response. Not that I cared what they thought.

Further down, a man hissed. He was the same one Poet had blocked from me during our first visit.

Another person slapped the floor.

All the same, my trepidation ebbed like a tendril of smoke. I did my best to communicate with them, to see them fully, to absorb their presence.

In one cell, I halted to watch a young woman hunching over the floor. She had gathered a mound of dirt and was sketching what appeared to be sentences mashed together. The grainy font proved remarkable, the attention to detail so meticulous and intricate that it resembled a clam. Or if one peered harder, perhaps some type of land mass?

"Be careful with that one, Highness," one of the guards grumbled, his meaty hand resting on a halberd.

He said this every time. One would think I hadn't interacted with this female on prior occasions.

Dismissing the nonsense warning, I squatted beside the bars. "That is lovely."

At the compliment, the female's head sprang up. Her bronze skin shone in the torchlight, and her sooty, matted hair desperately needed a brush. Most of all, her irises robbed me of speech; two reams of gold flared my way, the metallic color stunning in their clarity.

A gasp tripped across my tongue, but I swallowed it. Although I'd spent time with her before—offering biscuits and milk without the wardens noticing—I had never discerned the girl's eyes. She usually kept to the murk, shielding those irises like buried treasure, accessible only to the ones who earned it, who struggled for it, and who cared to look deeply enough.

Still, I had the feeling that staring too long would upset the female. Instead, I glimpsed her depiction in the dirt. The sentences were squished together, making it difficult to discern much. But from what I made out, the passage had something to do with an island.

"Does this hold a special meaning for you?" I coaxed.

But she merely glowered and continued drawing. Her movements were swift, almost erratic but passionate—dedicated. This amount of skill rivaled the artists of Spring, the design captivating me.

Poet would know what to say. I searched for some other way to connect with her, but the longer I tarried, the more aggravated her gestures became. Finally, I forced a smile and murmured, "I hope you find what you're looking for."

Her fingers ceased, then trembled. Those eyes kindled like fire, then glistened like the surface of the ocean. She closed her eyes, absorbed my words, and resumed drawing with the hint of a smile in her profile.

It was the most I could do. Another moment down here, and I would overstay my welcome.

I pried myself off the ground and retraced my steps to the exit. Before leaving, I stalled and angled my head at the guards. "Give them clean blankets, fresh water, and hot food. Nothing cold or on the brink of spoiling." But when the astonished men failed to bow or reply, I pruned my lips. "Is there a problem?"

"No, Your Highness."

I nodded once, gripped my skirt, and commanded while mounting the steps, "And see that it's done on a regular basis."

Brazen. Imprudent. Unhinged.

That's what they would think. Poet and I had planned to take these risks later, in small chunks and when the timing was perfect. Yet these people did not have the luxury or freedom of waiting for perfect. After tonight, I could not fathom what tomorrow held.

And at this point, what more did I have to lose?

Truthfully, I knew how to answer that. It's why I found myself sneaking into the castle vault minutes later, grabbing what I needed from there, and ascending one of the towers.

I stood at the parapet. Pebbles collected under my bare feet, which pressed into the stones. Fresh gales thrashed the torn skirt of my dress, the garment's hem fraying, its threads unraveling. The higher one climbed in this palace, the more violent the wind became.

The same could be said about power. Certainly, the same could be said about a Royal.

That irony sat on my shoulders like rocks.

Hectic currents whiplashed my hair. Red strands flew around my face, most of my braid having loosened long ago. Though it wasn't the only part of me that had come undone.

My mind. My soul.

My fear. My love.

Everything unspooled. It came apart like the tattered fibers of my jacket dress.

Blood crusted my knuckles. My flesh stung from the goldsmith's blade.

So this was what a ruined princess truly looked like.

Crenelations encircled the castle's highest peak like teeth, the fortress barricading me in—for a little while longer, at least. With one hand, I seized the ledge and leaned forward. At these heights, only the maple trees clustered amid the palace's courtyards were visible. Despite the midnight sky tarred in black, lush branches glittered with shades of red and orange.

Autumn leaves. Many of them rattled against the tempest like cymbals.

From up here, the tumult felt stronger—sharper. The summit was vast, the drop long, and the wind eager to snatch anything tossed into its flux.

The fall wouldn't take much.

My free hand choked the crown I had stolen from the vault. I'd worn this relic while making love with the jester on my throne.

The crown's tips projected like golden spikes, flawless but for a crack running down one side. That had required several hard smashes. However, the rift would make it effortless to finish the task now.

As I stroked the crown with my thumb, my grip trembled. I extended my arm over the precipice, and my throat stung.

A princess does not break.

But a crown can.

My fingers opened—and released. The weight of a nation vanished as if no heavier than a plume, the gale swallowing the object whole. I brushed the hair from my eyes and watched the descent, those serrated tips reducing to metallic specks.

The crown smacked a lower tower. It shattered, the piercing sound audible. Thousands of pieces splintered, reminiscent of mirrored glass or flecks of brilliant dust. They plummeted into the maples, the shards disappearing into the broad leaves.

I had been right. The higher one stood, the harsher the wind, the harder the fall.

Yet it had to be done. I'd had to let go. Come what may, this crown had been forged by an ancient goldsmith who'd believed in principles and laws I could not support. That centuries-old crown had represented an old way of thinking, an intolerant canon of morals. It had not been made for me, nor what I stood for.

A princess must forge her own crown.

In the dark, the scarlet bracelet around my wrist flashed. Blood stained the fabric, but the band was still there, its knot secure. I had made my choice long ago, and it was a true one, even if it meant risking all else I held dearly. Because when a ruler didn't behave, the consequences could be fatal. Though I couldn't yet say what to expect from here, one certainty existed. If not careful, tactful, and heedful, even a princess could lose everything.

Including this kingdom.

Including the crown.

Including him.

38

Briar

I had barely turned the knob to my suite when Poet yanked open the door. At the sight of me, his haggard features slackened. He snatched my elbow, hauled me inside, slammed the door shut behind us, and heaved me against his chest.

My muffled sigh rushed against his torso. A magnetic force adhered me to him, and I wrung my arms around his frame, inhaling the fragrances of amber and vetiver.

The aromas of safety and ardor. The essences of home.

Fiercely, the jester clasped me to him and buried his face in my neck. "Wicked fuck, Briar," he hissed. "You gave me a heart attack. I searched the library wing, prowled to the stables, and had a conniption in the pear orchard. After stalking every one of your refuges, it felt like you'd vanished. Goddammit, I've been pacing this room like a beast."

"I'm sorry," I said, my voice splintering. "I went to your suite first, but you weren't there."

"It seems we had the same thought, for I came to yours the instant I finished checking on Nicu. But when I found your suite empty, I looked everywhere before finally retracing my steps here." I opened my mouth to ask after Nicu, but Poet jolted back and seized my cheeks, his thumbs racing over my skin. "Where were you?"

"I went to the dungeon."

His expression transformed, that shrewd mind deciphering my own. "We must have missed each other."

I blinked. "You were there too?"

"Aye. No matter what your mother said about the fight and the Masters not reaching other parts of the castle, I knew you'd want to make sure the people were unharmed. Not least of all, I had a feeling you would be pulled there by other princessy impulses. I must have arrived shortly after you left."

Once the crowd dispersed, Poet and I had been ushered to the infirmary. Mother had accompanied us, refusing to leave my side until we urged her to watch over Nicu and tend to the troops.

After she left, physicians tended to the jester and me in a private chamber. The healers cleaned us of grime, stitched us up, and treated our injuries. We'd stared at one another with our hands clasping, our fingers bridging across the empty space between our cots. But because my side injury wasn't as intricate as the nail cavity in Poet's hand, I stayed until a sleeping draught took effect on him. He'd needed it to combat the pain.

While he rested, I looked on Nicu as well, then entered that subterranean hell, then climbed to the tower and sent my crown flying. I must have been up there a while, seeing as Poet had awakened during that time and descended into the dungeon after me. Certainly, he'd expected to find me there.

At Poet's wince, I ducked my head to examine the bandage strapped around his hand. Blood speckled the white dressing, not unlike the cloth affixed to my own wound.

I caressed the gauze, "Does it still hurt?"

"Not with you touching it like that," that silken voice assured me. "Winter medicine has its perks. If only they didn't use shitty methods to study it, I wouldn't have a problem with this."

Truer words could not be uttered. As the most scientifically advanced Season, Winter possessed the continent's leading physicians, as well as the most competent treatments and cures. Such remedies enabled the skin to mend itself infinitely quicker, all while preventing infection. As a result, our injuries would close fully within several days.

Nevertheless, the price was steep. It costed the lives of many born souls, the people whom Winter tested in order to derive those restoratives. That Autumn possessed its own limited supply—a former donation from Winter—was more a curse than a blessing.

I consoled myself by knowing the soldiers and sentinels would recover swifter. Privately, I vowed to visit them soon, to check on Aire and his brethren.

Poet emitted a gruff noise. "I know that head of yours, Briar. I hear the wheels turning. Permit the trained fool to guess."

I rested my palms on the plate of his chest. "Summer and the Masters turned born souls into pawns because of me. It was my duty to visit the prisoners, to offer some measure of comfort, whether or not they registered it. I had to make sure they were looked after, and I requested better treatment before whatever happens to me—"

"Nothing will happen to you," the jester rasped, clutching my face once more. "Nothing."

"I failed them." My words cracked, shattering like my crown had on its way down. "I failed all of them."

"Forgive this jester for objecting, but the fuck you did."

"Instigating a massacre is a felony. Inciting one on castle grounds and endangering the court is treason. It's punishable by ..."

Poet's eyes sharpened like green glass. "They would have to kill me first."

Nonetheless, I could barely stand still. Nerves fizzled up my limbs, and restlessness tracked up my vertebrae. I tugged myself away, ducked under his arms, and strode across the room while thrusting my fingers through my hair.

Behind me, Poet stressed, "Sweeting, your mother would condemn herself before letting anyone come near you. More critically, I would rip out the executioners' hearts with my bare hands."

"I know, but what consequence will I face instead? What if it's worse?" I whirled on him and flung one arm out to the side. "I know what they're saying. I know what Rhys implied about my sanity—"

"Fuck him," the jester snarled. "And fuck treason."

I started to shake my head, but he came forward and framed my jaw. "Heed your jester. If they try to touch you, they'll be corpses before their fingers make contact."

I clasped the nape of his neck and braced my forehead against his. "Poet," I whispered. "I'm scared."

"I'm here," he husked, his warm breath gusting across my mouth. "I will always be here." He ghosted his lips over mine. "I'll be here to bicker, banter, and beguile you for eternity."

We swayed as he walked me backward, maneuvering us from the antechamber, through my bedroom, and into the bathroom. A copper tub stood before a crackling hearth, with acorns carved into the mantel. Candles dyed the color of rum glowed from inside wall recesses, and a window overlooked one of the towering maples. Soapstone covered the walls, and penny tiles dotted the floor.

Steam rose from the water, which smelled of eucalyptus and lavender. Towels had been stacked on a wooden stool. Besides that, stoppered bottles filled with liquids stood on a brass tray, which nestled on the pocket windowsill overlooking the tub.

My eyes brimmed with unshed tears. The jester had prepared for my arrival.

At the foot of the tub, Poet unclasped the gold appliqués of my jacket dress. "I'll be here to entice and entertain you."

Then he spread the dress open. "I'll be here to enrage and encourage you."

After that, his fingers peeled off my bloody garment. "I'll be here to flirt with and flatter you."

Next, the jester nudged my chemise to the floor and pulled my embroidered drawers down my legs. "I'll be here to taste and fuck you."

Lastly, he rolled the garter and stockings from my thighs. "Most of all, I'll be here to keep you safe—and accept your compliments, of which there will be an abundance."

A laugh escaped my lungs, which bubbled into a sob. Poet gathered me close, burying my face in his torso. He did not try to quell or wipe the tears. Not yet.

Instead he merely held on while the dam burst. Salted liquid streamed down my face, and my body convulsed against the jester, his frame catching every movement. My cries pushed against his bare chest under the coat, his flesh absorbing every droplet.

Naked but for the scarlet bracelet and the cloth protecting my gash, I curled into him. I dug my fingernails into his back, wishing I could infuse myself into this man, if only for a moment. Rather, I emptied myself. Loss wracked me to the core, but the jester soaked it up like a sponge and kept me upright. At least until I could hold myself aloft once again.

He brushed through my hair, unspooling what little remained of my braid. Thick locks of hair tumbled down my back. All the while, his mouth traced my forehead, grazed the top of my scalp, and skimmed my temple.

The tears subsided. That menacing weight from seconds ago dissipated, replaced by a flux of warmth. A strange sort of peace settled in my bones, so that my mind and body felt like putty.

The release was instantaneous. A sigh floated from my lips. However, the skin around my eyelashes stung, the flesh raw and swollen.

Poet spoke at last. "Now hush, sweeting."

Now. Hush. Because a princess did not wilt forever.

She recovered. And she endured.

He'd waited until I was ready to hear and remember it. Lifting my head, I clamped onto his gaze, aware of the mess I'd made of us both. "I must be a sight."

"Aye." He scrolled his mouth over each set of eyelashes, swabbed the tip of his tongue over remaining tears, and riveted his gaze on me. "Aye, you are a sight."

The gruffness in Poet's voice coiled low in my belly, unfurling in my core like a vine. He stared in that devastating way I'd come to know. His expression told me everything he'd also said aloud many times. My jester beheld me as though I were faultless, yet he never made me feel as if I needed to be. With him, I was perfectly imperfect. I had power, but I was not weapon-proof. In his arms, I could shed my Royal skin and reveal a flesh-and-blood woman.

Even if I wore rags and was covered in sludge, he would find me dazzling. To this man, I could wail until my eyes turned red, and I would still rob him of breath.

I knew this sentiment well. No feelings could be more requited.

I latched onto his features and gripped his coat collar. My fingers urged the fabric from his shoulders, the garment torn, stained in filth, and mottled in crimson. Careful not to trouble his wounds, I divested him of the tattered material.

Flames sketched his torso, laminating every groove and contour. The broad pectorals, flushed nipples, and carved abdomen. That sculpted body, which could twist one moment, flip the next instant, and wield a dagger with deadly precision in the end. Those powerful forearms and juggler's hands. The smattering of faint scars where he'd been injured during years of training. Among these facets, a fine line of hair trailed to the waistband of his pants.

Poet's inhalations quickened. The shadow of a bulge inflated between his narrow hips.

Anguish, comfort, and desire swirled through me. The emotions tangled as my fingers undid the closures of his pants. While tugging on the clasps, I marveled how such contrary sensations could inundate me effortlessly.

I mourned, and I yearned, and I anticipated.

I ached, and I needed, and I relished.

Holding his gaze, I stripped the pants down his body. His cock rose from the material, the length and width of him springing into view. Dark and inflated at the head, with a slim line bisecting the crest.

Firm along the stem and pointing high. The vision rarely failed to thrill me—evidence of the pivotal effect I had on him.

The folds in my center tightened. A deluge of liquid pooled there.

I must have been admiring his size for too long, because a rough sound echoed from his lips. It might be an obscenity. Knowing this man, it most certainly was.

Our bandages did not require removal. Unlike common dressings, these were impervious to water. With Autumn being a conservative nation, we had managed to save such provisions for times like these.

Poet helped me into the tub, then sank in next. Fluid sloshed against the rim, and curtains of moisture lifted into the air. Heat melted into my flesh, seeping to the marrow of my bones.

Yet a source of greater temperature penetrated me deeper. I could have slid into the cocoon of Poet's arms, but I twisted to face him instead. Our movements magnetized one another, instinctual and primal.

As I turned, Poet wound his strong arms around my middle and hefted me onto his lap. I straddled him, my hands hooking over his shoulders. Water lapped against us, wet warmth licking my skin.

In the half-light, rivulets dragged down his solid chest like beads of sweat. Droplets scraped over his muscles and sank under the surface. My nipples tightened, the damp peaks skimming his pecs.

The hard length of his cock skated lightly over my clitoris. The barest trace of friction threw embers across my pelvis.

Poet emitted a gritty noise. Those molten eyes consumed me, and that black satin voice intoned, "Remember what you said in Spring? When you knelt before me?"

Lark's Night. The sunset carnival.

After he took my virginity, Poet almost ended it. He'd attempt to sever ties for my sake, to spare me from public ridicule, to prevent my suffering for having chosen him. Yet I had refused to give him up, refused to stop what could no longer be stopped.

I opened my mouth, but Poet chose that moment to dip his head. His lips rushed across my collarbones. Fleetingly, the quote died a lovely death on my tongue. In its place, a trembling gasp toppled from my lungs.

My eyes fanned shut. My fingers wove into his hair. My head lulled backward, the tips of my hair floating in the water.

Poet flattened his palms on the small of my back, urging me farther. As I arched from him, he bowed into me. His mouth latched onto the flesh between my clavicles, then dragged up to the crook of my neck. "Tell me what you said."

Then he snatched my skin into his mouth and sucked.

Another gasp flew out of me. The weightless water combined with the humidity added a new sensitivity to my flesh. With every erotic crevice his lips reached, those sensations magnified.

In a daze, I consulted my memory. "If I make a vow, I do not break it. My will is as strong as my promise." As I spoke, that former pledge resurfaced. "I'm not ashamed to love you, and I will fight for that with everything I am, and I won't hide it. I have pretended long enough. I'm not afraid of Autumn's judgment or retaliation."

The jester hummed into my throat. His mouth pulled on my skin, and his tongue flicked lazily, repeatedly over a spot that wrung a moan from me.

"Someday we'll make a difference together ...," I quoted, my voice quivering as I bowed at a harsher angle, "... be a finer nation for it, and show them that no other match could have existed for me than with you."

He made another haggard sound of approval and cupped my backside, towing me closer. The possessive gesture splayed my thighs wider around him. A gentle splash struck the tub, and the surrounding fluid reduced my bones to jelly. That, and his fervid mouth, which glided lower and seized one pert nipple.

I cried out. "We'll rule and love like warriors."

Poet crooned against the apex of my breast, his tongue fluttering over the dainty peg. A riot of pleasure swarmed my blood. The stud of my nipple toughened under his licks, every stroke blasting me with need.

Then he rolled his mouth to the opposite nipple. He etched the point until it ruched, then clamped onto me, kissing my breast like it was my lips.

I became inarticulate. My mouth fell open on a soundless moan.

My pussy clenched. Slickness dripped to the slit of my opening. Of their own volition, my hips furled against his in a single, sweeping gesture.

With a groan, Poet released the nipple and rocking me upright. His hooded eyes charted my features, as though committing every freckle to memory. My lips tingled as those pupils landed on them.

A second later, the jester grabbed my face and held it steady. My respirations stalled. As he captured me in his gaze, an anticipatory sensation washed through me, familiar yet new.

Like that moment shortly before the first kiss. Like experiencing it all over again.

With his feverish gaze clinging to mine, Poet swooped in. His mouth tilted and crushed to my own. With a steep slant of our lips, his tongue licked the crease, and I parted for him. Like this, I relived that scene in the meadow, when I discovered his taste and touch.

Except he achieved a feat I hadn't imagined possible. This time, he probed me deeper, longer, lusher.

The jester's head pushed forward. His mouth folded over mine, rowing us into each other. The heat of his tongue slipped between my lips and flexed against me. With agile strokes, he looped that tongue with mine, pitching the flat in and out.

The strength of his jaw worked me to new heights. I shuddered, the vibration tracking up my throat as he kissed me fully, thoroughly, endlessly. Plaintive, I scrambled closer to him, plastering my drenched body against his.

When my tongue curled around Poet's, he hissed and vaulted backward. On a breathless whine, I forced my eyes open. Those pupils dilated, consuming the green irises.

Poet watched me, then shook his head. He muttered what sounded like a profanity and mashed his mouth to mine again. I keened and launched myself into it, my lips fastening to the jester's, his tongue licking into me.

Clutching my buttocks, Poet shoved me against him. I rose on my knees and came down hard on his lips. This forced his head to crane backward, my mouth overtaking him.

My waist gyrated. My pussy skidded over the distended crown of his cock, bolts of stimulation probing the slot of my thighs.

The agitation splintered us apart. Panting, we drifted back, the better to watch one another's reaction.

Poet gripped my backside and leaned into my ear. *"I will be vicious, if her pain is deep."*

That obsidian voice drizzled into me like a sin and a benediction. With his hands spanning my rear, he used the leverage to reel me into him. The forward motion pried me farther apart. My jaw hung ajar, and I settled my hands atop his shoulders as he swung me softly astride his lap.

He hissed while wheeling me against his erection. Thick gales of oxygen blew from my throat. I couldn't tell if the texture of his voice, the lilting words, or his hold on me caused this vivid response. Perhaps it was everything.

All of him. All of me.

"I will be darkness—" he positioned my pussy over his cock, *"—that she may sleep."*

And then he drew me down. We groaned as the pome of his upright cock pitched between my walls, its girth stretching me. Inch by inch, he lowered me around his erection, my soaked crease spreading and sealing around the rigid length of him.

On a cry, I landed astride his waist. Poet's mouth parted on a silent *Ah*.

With my core encapsulating him, we admired each other. I savored every twitch of his face, and he relished every crimp of mine. The jester filled me to the brink, and I melted over him, my folds quavering and dripping down his solid flesh.

In unison, we swayed into another. Poet framed my buttocks and bobbed me up and down, the tempo patient to the point of luxurious. With every rise and fall, my slot expanded for his cock, and my cries hardened.

Poet husked against my whimpering mouth, *"I will be damned, lest she should weep."*

While his voice spilled wickedness into my head, he pumped me onto his cock. I sobbed at the pleasure, at the words pouring from his tongue. Both sensations burned a path up my thighs, which hooked and trembled over his hips.

Poet propped his thumb on my lower lip, then dragged the finger downward. The gesture pulled my flesh with it, baring my teeth. Emboldened, I caught his digit with my mouth and sucked on it.

The jester's face tightened. His erection broadened inside me, and his muscles clenched, on the brink of losing control.

Being with him like this—claimed, shared—imbued me with vitality. Although he directed the motions, the jester teetered on the edge with me. More than him taking charge, Poet grappled for me, like he needed to satisfy a hunger. At the same time, he serviced me, held himself steady while I rode him.

His embrace turned me into a siren, a temptress, a woman, a queen. His possessive touch shaped me into a rare and coveted thing he couldn't get enough of.

Always, consummation with the jester did this to me. I felt equal parts dominated and dominant, unanimously reckless and enduring. But when he combined this mayhem with that velveteen voice, I went up in flames, sweltering like an inferno.

My head tipped back. My lips released his finger, allowing him to focus.

"I will be shameless, for the pleasure she'll reap," Poet purred against my upturned chin.

My joints liquified. Our sodden bodies aligned, rubbing and clasping. After several laps, my forehead dropped to watch our hips shove together.

Beneath the water, Poet swiveled me into his waist, the rhythm lethargic. I caught sight of his cock, primed and ruddy in hue. My walls flared over the rounded head every time I fell on him. Seasons, I puddled all over the jester, my arousal coating him to the sac.

Enveloped in mist, I urged Poet against the rim. He reclined, so that I hunched over his body, able to view the soaked expanse of his form. Suds leaked down his abdomen, and the tips of his hair grew as dark as raven wings.

While I hovered above, he thrust into me from below. The new position altered the slope of his hips and the incline of his cock. Like this, Poet increased the momentum by a fraction, and I seized the tub's rim for balance, my pussy widening for him.

"I will submit, if power she seeks," he intoned.

When his erection hit a tapered spot, a short cry leaped from my being. Taking that as a sign, Poet's crown repeatedly tapped that place, so deeply ensconced within me. Gradually, I rotated my lower half, bucking tenderly.

Humming, the jester arched his agile body, swooping his cock higher and deeper. Despite the angle, he kept his eyes tethered to me. He licked those naughty lips, and the next stanza came out stuttered. *"And I have been hollowed ..."*

The jester whisked into me, and I bobbed onto him. His long cock flexed in and out, each fluid lash burrowing farther. In tune to the movements, I keened aloud, my broken moans tangling with his gravelly pants.

We dissolved into each other. Our hips linked and thrashed gently, the cadence steady, as if time did not exist here. Over and over and over.

The cleft of my thighs contracted around Poet's cock. Yet we kept going, drawing it out for a century. My thoughts evaporated like the condensation surrounding us, to the point where our wounds disappeared.

My core leaked onto him. My muscles sizzled like firecrackers—hot and combustible.

Poet moved faster. The slap of water flooded my ears, manifesting the sounds of our lovemaking. He whisked between my thighs, prying my folds apart, fucking into me. In kind, I bounded on him, taking and giving.

His fingers faltered on my waist, and a jagged noise escaped his mouth. *"And I have been hollowed …,"* he repeated but couldn't finish.

I whined. Strands of red hair fell around my face and swam in the water. The peaks of my breasts stiffened into pebbles, and splashes resounded through the room.

Even as Poet began to unravel, he never lost his hold on me. The jester didn't let me go. And how I wanted to stay like this, to freeze this moment.

Every memory collided, the visions spiraling into a montage. Enemies. Lovers. Rivalry. Friendship. Tension. Passion. Humor. Lust. By Seasons, we had felt and done it all.

Yet there would be more. Please let there be more.

The familiar and the unknown. The darkness and lightness.

I longed for every bit of it, every scrap of it, every second of it. My body pleaded for it as my hips galloped onto his, both of us moving faster now. But not rougher, nor harsher. Tonight, we'd weathered enough aggression to last a lifetime.

In this place illuminated by flames and starlight, I had no more room for ugliness. Only affection. Only fortitude. I chased after that feeling, the stimulation he never failed to wring from me.

Balmy warmth filled the space. Sweltering water bathed my flesh. Awash in these sensations, I splayed myself for Poet and undulated with abandon.

His engorged head whipped up into me, that feverish cock pistoning through my open walls. He fucked me sinuously, deeply, hotly. I returned the pleasure, swiveling my waist with his, my pussy clutching his length and siphoning over him.

We maintained that sweet tension. Regardless of how my folds convulsed or how firm Poet's cock grew, we did not give in, nor allow our restraint to crack.

Only our voices succumbed. My moans frayed. His growls fractured. Both sounds scattered into the air, echoing as though we were in a cavern.

The water made everything supple and sleek. Liquid dashed over the ledge and smacked the penny tiles.

My clit throbbed, the bud skating over his groin. The flanks of my core constricted, wetness gushing freely.

The precipice drew nearer, yet it seemed leagues away. Beneath me, Poet's green eyes squinted, concentrating on me. His jaw loosened, on the fringes of collapse.

I knew the signs and could never decide whether to torment, enrapture, or sever that control. All choices appealed to me, each one profound.

While hurling into one another, labored puffs of oxygen vacated my lungs. Meanwhile, Poet chuffed air, the masculine rumble coaxing more arousal from me.

On his next moan, I whimpered in kind.

Poet jabbed his hips upward into me. "Do it, sweeting," he hissed. "Let it out."

The whimper swelled into a cry.

"That's it," he droned. "Just like that, Princess."

Water lapped my skin. The jester's hips flew into mine, spreading me, working into me. His cock plied my slit with quick thrusts, shallow juts that had me wheezing in tandem.

Unable to stand it, Poet thrashed us upright, then hunched forward. He switched our positions, so that my scalp rested on the tub's ledge. My knees steepled high, and my limbs fell apart, then draped across the rim.

Poet looped one arm around my middle and tucked the other under my nape. Nestled in the vent of my legs, he revolved his hips in a nimble way that had me chanting. Inconsolable noises erupted from some dormant place inside me.

The acoustics from the bathroom's coffered ceiling reverberated those illicit sounds. I wailed for this, for more, for all of it. Poet gave himself over, exercising his whole frame into the effort.

His cock stiffened beyond measure. It pitched into my pussy, every long stroke provoking another bout of cries. The crest of his erection struck a new crevice, a cinched place that had me in tatters. I vaulted my hips to catch the movements, which launched a heady groan from Poet.

We turned the floor into a river. We hauled ourselves against each other.

The scream built in my lungs, writhing to break free. "Fuck," I hollered. "Oh, fuck."

"Tell me how it feels," Poet heaved. "Tell me how it feels when I fuck you."

I nodded aimlessly. "It feels like everything. It's all I've ever wanted." Grabbing the sides of his face, I savored the vision of him crumbling, those pupils swallowing his irises. "It's you, I think about every moment. It's you, I imagine when I touch myself. It's you, who has my heart. It's you, I live for. It's you, I would die for."

Finally, Poet detonated with me. He snapped his waist into my body, lovingly, fiercely, and growled against my mouth, "'Tis you I would kill for."

Blood rushed from my toes to my navel. My pussy clenched his cock, then sprang apart. I tensed and unspooled on a single howl, my wet walls rippling around him.

Every part ignited. Waves of pleasure wracked my body into spasms, a hot black haze eclipsing my vision.

Poet roared. He flung his cock, pounding into me once, twice, three more times. Then his hips stalled. An instant later, the jester's muscles quaked, his choked bellow engulfing the room.

That wondrous face collapsed into rapture. His eyes darkened. His mouth hung open, letting out a slew of untamed noise. And this, I would never get over—the sight of him when he came.

I cried out, my pussy fluttering over and over to his image. In the throes of release, my consciousness condensed to one thing. One thought. One truth. It spilled through my blood, visceral and innate.

I love this.

I love you.

I love us.

Together, we slumped in the tub. Poet's mouth rested against my throat, where he panted, *"And I have been hollowed, for she has struck deep."*

The verse caressed my ears. I wrapped my limbs tighter around his muscled form and strayed my fingers through his damp hair. Rather than spent, my body coasted like a raft. And within time, I knew that same body would reinforce itself like a tree after a storm, abiding and unshakable.

Perhaps that's what love did. Perhaps that's what happened when two people bonded.

Or perhaps this was different. Like every pairing, perhaps this was uniquely our own story. A rebellious, seductive, passionate tale for campfires.

"Yours," I implored.

Poet lifted his head and gritted, "Mine."

Now I understood. Both of those words meant the same thing, because each one was intertwined.

Like ribbons.

39

Poet

On and off, I awoke to watch the princess rest, lest nightmares should bleed into her dreams and she needed me. Or mayhap 'twas I who needed her to ward off the demons. My coping mechanism often included expensively tailored clothes, a chalice of quality wine, a splendid performance replete with an ovation, any second I spent in my son's company, a heady combination of Briar's laughter and her orgasms, and …

Well, my list was long.

Tonight, the source of my sanity narrowed to one detail. The vision of Briar nestled into the down—with her face relaxed, her breasts exposed over the blanket, and her freckles in disarray across her body—temporarily slayed the black thoughts plaguing my mind.

Tendrils of air slipped from the princess's mouth and stirred the fibers of her hair. Sometimes, those tresses darkened like the rust of her mother's locks. Other times, it shone in gradients, from scarlet to a burnished gold-red. Lounging naked beside her, I strung a few threads around my digit.

Were it a simple morning, I would contemplate waking Briar up with my head between her thighs. Instead, I drifted in and out of consciousness whilst making sure the woman slept through the night.

Mission accomplished. We dozed into the next day and until dusk. The prospect from her balcony gave way to a thicket of clouds floating like shredded cotton in the gray sky. It might drizzle later, which would help wash the blood from the courtyard.

The notion brought other fucked-up memories to the surface. From the bodies strewn throughout the quad, to the sight of that blade jammed into Briar's stomach, to the bone-deep savagery I'd felt seeing her hurt, to Rhys's miserable fucking sneer, to Briar's debilitating scream of rage, to the way everyone had stared.

What they'd concluded. What they assumed.

The court had given my son the same reception when they first saw him. And so I knew what the bigots thought whilst observing the princess's breakdown. I knew what it meant, because I'd lived that horror from the day Nicu was born.

The toxic conclusions they'd drawn about Briar had been etched across their faces. But although a jester was often a dozen steps ahead of the game, my addled brain deflated. I couldn't predict where this chaos would lead.

Either way, I wouldn't let it happen. I would raise this palace from its foundation before then.

Last night, calming Briar had been my priority. I'd made her come twice in the bathtub, then we rinsed each other off before sinking into her bed. But this morning, my agenda changed.

They thought they knew the extent of a jester's rage? The limits of his power and cunning? Oh, but they hadn't begun to learn how badly I could sting. Aye, if they came after her, this kingdom would find out.

A downy sigh drifted from Briar's lips as her eyelashes fanned open. "Mmmfff."

My lips ticked sideways, a thousand emotions playing inside my chest. "Afternoon, sweeting. Or rather, good evening."

With our limbs entwined, she glanced from my naked body to my rather excellent face. For a second, a blissful pink puddled in her cheeks. But then reality crept across her features, bleakness furrowing her brows.

Despite that, her chin refused to crinkle. Instead, she lifted it.

Ah. Behold my resilient thorn.

She nuzzled into me and whispered, "I want to go somewhere."

"Anywhere," I answered.

But from that soft tone, I knew her destination. 'Twas the same place I longed for—the only person who mattered outside of this room.

We dressed and padded across the hall to Nicu's chambers. Aire waited at the entrance and straightened when we appeared. Loss weighed down his features like wet cement, and his irises had dulled to something resembling blue metal. Yet the grief vanished as he registered our presence.

Ignoring all semblance of protocol, Briar genuflected to the soldier. She ducked her head and curtsied as if greeting a fellow Royal. "Sir Aire."

This man had been guarding Nicu. He protected my princess and our secrets. He sided with us last night, regardless of what happened to his comrades.

I followed suit and bowed to him. And as much as I enjoyed hearing myself talk, I didn't need to utter a thing. Briar's tone conveyed plenty—sympathy, remorse, gratitude.

Rising, we met the shocked knight's eyes. A tinge of color returned to his sallow features, and finally he inclined his head. Nothing else needed to be said, for the world had made enough noise since last night. We left the knight alone, giving him the space he deserved.

No surprise, my son was awake. That he hadn't dragged Aire to my bedside or to Briar's suite before dawn was a rare occurrence.

As we stepped into this sanctuary, Nicu looked up from where he sat cross-legged on the floor. He wore a robe the color of chestnuts, his scarlet ribbon peeked from under the cuffed sleeve, and his toes were bare.

When he saw us, those wide-set eyes gleamed like clovers. He shouted, "Papa! Briar Patch!" Then he pointed at us rather than the window. "The sky is tired, so we need to wake it up."

That meant he wanted us to play with him, so the evening could officially begin.

An unconditional response pinched my chest and reflected in Briar's profile. But between us, she did better to shield those emotions. "I trust your judgment on these manners," she conspired with a bright smile. "If you say so, we must do our best to rouse the sky."

Only sixteen hours had passed, yet Winter's remedy had begun working its magic. The ointments, stitches, and bandages had mended our wounds to the point where pain had become less of an issue. Briar's stomach looked much better, the gash in my cheek wouldn't scar—thank fuck—and the white of my left eye was losing its red film. As for the welts across my torso, those hadn't begun to fade yet, but most of the stiffness in my joints had.

Briar strolled forward, sank to the floor beside Nicu, and fluffed out her skirt without wincing. Tucking her legs sideways beneath the fabric, she asked, "What shall we play?"

"Tumble decides," Nicu instructed, then whistled.

That silvery voice chimed through the chambers, demonstrating a hint of his singing talent. At the sound, Tumble poked his beady eyes from under the bed. The creature squeaked and galloped like a log across the carpet, where he circled Briar and my son twice.

Nicu set three options on the floor. They included a set of potions, a card game with pieces shaped like stars, and marbles carved into acorns.

"Watch," he ordered the princess, then snapped his finger. "Choose, please."

The ferret trotted to each item and sniffed, then nudged his nose against the stars. Nicu squealed with glee and snatched the card game. "I'll go first," he chirped. "Then you. Then Papa."

I hadn't moved. With my shoulder slumped against the doorway, I watched Briar and Nicu set up the pieces whilst mumbling to one another like accomplices. Tumble pawed at several stars, then contented himself with the marbles, which he swatted across the floor.

"Papa." Nicu patted the rug. "We're playing now. You have to juggle the cards."

"Bossy little fae," I teased and sauntered over to them.

Lowering myself across from the pair gave me ample opportunities to shuffle the cards and watch as Nicu explained the rules to Briar. Any games involving distances and locations confused him. But this game had to do with memorization and solving a legend about the celestials, which required the player to have a keen sense of riddles and word play. I suspected the game had been inspired by Winter, since lore existed there about certain uncharted stars.

The cards jumped across my fingers with a whiz and snap. For my son, I juggled them, as he liked to call it. Then I propped the stack between us.

"Whoever wins is the hero," Nicu finished to Briar, then patted her hand. "But don't worry. You have a crown."

In other words, Briar had an advantage. As a leader, she was an established hero in Nicu's eyes.

For a long moment, Briar stared at him. Her eyes dampened, as luminescent as silver coins.

Twisting her hand upside down, she clasped Nicu's small fingers. "It takes more than a crown. It takes something even more special." Her wobbly grin reflected pride, plus a thousand other sentiments. "That means someday you might become the hero," she insisted. "You might grow to be the one who saves us all."

My son studied her with those broad, inquisitive eyes. I saw him committing what she said to memory. At length, that winsome, faeish face beamed. "Okay," he chirped. "For you, I'll try."

I swallowed the pit that had been stuck in my throat. Briar's eyes clicked over to me. We exchanged sober grins, then bowed over the game.

As Briar helped Nicu deal the cards, a furious sort of tenderness prickled across my knuckles.

Two hours hence, I left Briar with Nicu and Tumble, the three of them curled in a chair and reading aloud the first book in that series

Briar loved. With everything that happened since I gifted her the final installment, we hadn't had time to fetch it from The Royal Retreat. At some point, I'd ride there and snatch the book for her.

For now, I made the excuse that I needed something from my suite. Nicu made me promise to come back. And that, I would.

But first, I had residual energy to burn off.

My boots torched a path from Nicu's chambers to my own, where I collected a token of my affection for certain, recent visitors. After that, I strode to a classified passage leading to another portion of the Royal wing. At this hour, our esteemed guests would be dining on quail eggs in the great hall, if not choking on their lack of humanity.

I stalked from the concealed entrance and slipped into a mezzanine. It wasn't hard to guess which space Rhys festered in. I needed only to follow the stench of bigotry and bullshit.

Moving undetected had become child's play. Sidestepping the sentinels, tossing out an object to distract them, and gliding behind their backs charged my blood. High on the nostalgia kick, I slithered into an apartment embellished in metallic shades. Mostly gold.

It was the same here as in Spring's palace. Every Royal from each Season had an appointed dwelling.

Summer's lair included adjoining bedrooms. According to rumors, Queen Giselle had requested this because she couldn't stand the thought of fucking her repugnant husband on a routine basis. If that was true, I applauded the woman's taste.

I turned into a shadow, my boots ghosting across the antechamber and stalking to the owner's desk. Papers covered the surface, numerous sheets crumpled or torn. Had the man actually jotted down anything or just thrown the leaflets about during one of his many tantrums?

I did my part snooping, flicking through correspondence and ledgers. My eyes scanned the contents for anything I could use to incriminate the king, if not stuff in his mouth and suffocate him. Unfortunately, Rhys wasn't that stupid.

Grinding my teeth, I nudged every slice of parchment back into place. Fine, then. If I couldn't toy with some type of damning evidence, we would play in a different way.

Who knew when or how, but he would know my retribution. To be sure, I'd take my time planning every meticulous detail of the monarch's suffering.

Targets like these were worth the patience.

With that in mind, I fished into my coat pocket and withdrew a scarlet ribbon. It slumped over my index finger like a dead worm. Overturning my digit, I let the band of fabric drop onto the fucker's desk.

If he paid any attention to gossip, he would know what it meant. But just in case he didn't, I let the words echo and seep into the walls.

"You're mine, bitch," I hissed.

It had been more than a trap. It had been a trick.

The gist became clear as I retraced my steps to Nicu's chambers. Rhys couldn't have plotted that infamous chase from The Forbidden Burrow to the castle, because he couldn't have foreseen what would happen there. The man couldn't have known Briar would outwit the crafters and incite their ire. But with some foresight, Summer had orchestrated its outcome, nonetheless.

My mind replayed our meeting with Rhys in the library, the breadcrumbs he'd dropped without realizing it. Namely, this brilliant puzzle piece.

Always best to have spares on hand and alternative stratagems in place.

As a precaution, Rhys had prompted the Masters in case Briar and I became difficult—resistant to his blackmail. He knew we might unearth the identities of his spies. If that happened, he was aware we'd act.

During the chase, Briar and I hadn't understood why the guild would continue stampeding after us once we reached the castle borders. Soon enough though, it made sense.

The king had manipulated those men and women to forsake themselves. As a backup, Rhys must have instructed the Masters to give chase to the castle if all hell broke loose. The agenda had required at least one of two outcomes. Briar's compliance—hence, Vex taking that hooded moppet hostage—or bloodshed.

The latter would scapegoat Briar. Pursuing us to the stronghold would ensure the knights' interference, plus an audience who'd witness the Masters get mutilated.

Both the crafters and Rhys had known the kingdom would see this slaughter as a betrayal. Once abreast of certain details—doubtless circulated by Rhys—the citizens would deem the Masters innocent of any wrongdoing. From the public's point-of-view, the guild had uncovered Briar's intentions for emancipation and sought to prevent it.

Of course, the citizenry wouldn't find out the particulars, such as Briar and I being spied on during the Spring carnival, because that morsel would expose Rhys's own duplicity. The Seasons would learn he had moles stationed in every court, a fact he wouldn't be eager to advertise.

Unfortunately, Briar and I had no proof of that. And at this juncture, no one would believe the accusation.

Thus, those bits would be withheld. Not that fully formed facts mattered when propaganda burned throughout any nation.

All the public would know was the Masters objected to Briar and her jester's campaign for equality. And because the nation's most elite crafters had protested it, those men and women ended up dead. In this way, the princess would be denounced for supporting born souls over loyalists.

So Rhys convinced his cult it was their duty to forfeit their lives, to preserve the future of this Season. Their deaths also guaranteed Briar wouldn't have the clout to strip them of Master status, neither before nor after they took their final breaths. The guild must have concluded that last part after Briar duped them with the apple.

I stormed through the corridors. I would target Rhys for this. I'd do it carefully, slowly, effectively. I would—

A hollowed noise resounded into the halls. My boots halted several feet from where Aire guarded Nicu's door. The giant, baritone call of a horn blew through the complex, the spacious echo traveling from its perch and carrying across the grounds. The noise expanded to the lower town and perhaps farther, so that I guessed its intent.

In Spring, announcements and alarms rang from a bell. In Autumn, it came from that massive horn suspended from the castle's highest tower.

Foreboding crawled up my spine. I whipped toward Aire, who frowned at the commotion, his eyes darting to the nearest window, as if decoding a message in the clouds. "Something's wrong," he said. "There's a punitive charge in the air, like a reckoning." Creases dug into his features. "Her Majesty is calling for an assembly."

The fuck? Briar and I had planned to meet with Avalea in an hour. Why would she request the court's presence before meeting with us first?

I whirled to my son's door, about to blast inside. Except the partition barged open too soon, and Briar spilled into the hall looking nonplussed.

We stared at each other. Over a rust skirt and bodice, she wore a fitted black corset that clutched her ribs and capped her shoulders. Rust-dyed puffed sleeves inflated from there, then cinched into tight, quilted sleeves down her arms. Tonal suede gloves of the same shade encased her fingers, and she'd swept her hair into a loosely braided updo.

Briar never made a single absentminded decision. Everything was considered, so this style felt intentional. Each piece strapped her in like a girdle, as if she depended on the extra support to hold herself up.

I drew out the words. "Since when does your Mother call for a conference before talking to you in advance?"

The princess's throat pumped. "She doesn't."

"Papa?" Nicu's head popped into view, his little face bunching in confusion. Holding Tumble in his arms, my son's head darted between me, the princess, and the knight. With that fucking horn funneling through the air, Nicu searched for clues about how to react. If any of us looked panicked, he would sense it.

I knelt and ruffled his hair. "'Tis nothing. Merely a ghastly instrument that cannot hold a candle to your voice."

Briar lowered herself beside me. "Go back to reading the story," she encouraged. "Find out how it ends."

Because my son wasn't a fool, he hesitated. Yet something in Briar's features made him straighten. "I'll go learn to be a hero, Briar Patch. You go and be a ruler."

She gave him a fixed smile, then grabbed his face and kissed his forehead. I playfully tickled his side, which made him giggle as he cantered into the room with Tumble draped over his shoulders.

The instant the door shut, we took off. Briar and I strode down the passages whilst Aire muttered to another soldier, "Watch the Royal Son."

The Royal Son. I admit, I fancied the sound of that.

Fastening his fingers around one of his sword hilts, the First Knight patrolled behind us. Whatever he sensed, the same uneasiness chipped across my skin. I snatched Briar's hand and stalked in front of her, blocking her from anything we didn't see coming.

"They sacrificed themselves," I murmured to Briar whilst prowling ahead.

The princess's breath hitched. "The guild?"

I nodded and whispered my theories as we navigated the path. Briar listened but didn't respond, signaling she agreed with me. Half of this had been plotted, the other half a happy accident for Rhys.

One question remained. What would we do about it?

A lethal kick of adrenaline cut through me as I thought of the scarlet ribbon waiting on the king's desk. I would tell Briar about it later.

After an eternity of hallways and stairways, we emerged at the landing of the castle's main entrance. From the top of the steps overlooking where the battle had taken place, we stalled.

A sea of heads materialized. Under the maple tree, courtiers packed the expansive quad to capacity. The Royal Council formed a crescent to one side of the landing. Cadence, Posy, and Vale idled nearby, apprehension stringing across their features. They knew as little as we did.

Aire moved around us and descended several steps, where he stationed himself like a bodyguard. Except none of the other troop members joined him.

Rhys and his wife hovered like smog—noxious, poisonous—behind Avalea, who stood with ramrod posture. But the moment she laid her eyes on Briar, the veneer faltered. She stared at her daughter with the sort of tortured agony reserved for parents who had run out of options.

A hiss rolled up my throat. I maneuvered in front of the princess.

Briar's eyes skated across the crowd, then swerved to the queen. "Mother?"

Avalea's lips trembled. She opened her mouth, but a new racket cut through.

One of the sentinels hollered from the parapet walks. A tinkling noise rang through the air, bright and flashy like wind chimes. Recognition bolted through me like a shock to the system.

Bells. With all the pandemonium going on, Briar and I had forgotten about Spring's arrival for Reaper's Fest. The invitation we'd sent had apparently been accepted, all whilst neglecting to inform Autumn of this decision. Typical of my homeland.

Everyone turned, whispers rushing through the court. A caravan of horses and carriages trundled down the road, traveling past The Wandering Fields, the lower town, and finally the maple tree pasture. The portcullis rose, admitting a line of vehicles, their horses clomping over the bricks.

Knights shouted, "Make way!"

Like ants, the crowd parted for the queue of carriages, which rolled into the quad. Riders in dark green military cloaks appeared, one of them leaping from his steed and pulling open a door. Basil and Fatima poured from the vessel in a spectacle of silk and gemstones.

The court gasped and fell into a wave of bows and curtsies.

"Such a reception," Basil cheered, thwacking his palms together with glee.

"Your Majesties," Fatima boasted, surprised to see Summer. "I do hope we're not late."

No, they weren't fucking late. If anything, they were really fucking early.

On that score, the king and queen must have traveled via the confidential river reserved for their use. That was how Briar's ladies had gotten here so quickly.

Though, Avalea's astonishment made it clear. Whatever this assembly had amassed for, evidently it had nothing to do with welcoming Spring.

Hardly eager to have the proceedings interrupted, Rhys shouldered his way to the front. "Quite the theatrical timing, Spring," he grumbled. "However, quite tragic as well. Most unfortunate that you must bear witness to this transition."

The Spring monarchs blinked, perplexed.

Indeed. "What fucking transition?" I snarled.

At the rear of the procession, another carriage door creaked open, though only several people noticed. A head of blond waves exited the vehicle, followed by a pair of expectant blue eyes. The markings of a lute tattooed the traveler's neck, and his gaze veered across the crown, searching and finding Briar's.

By Seasons. Seeing him, the princess released a gale of oxygen.

"Eliot," she breathed.

I wanted to share in her happiness, but that joy was fleeting. Likewise, the minstrel's elated grin faded into bafflement. Gobsmacked, Eliot's features twisted with concern as he took in our expressions.

What's wrong? he mouthed to us.

All other eyes swung from me, to Briar, to Avalea.

The queen gulped, so overcome she neglected to greet Spring. Her gaze pinned to Briar's. "Come forward, Daughter."

Formality. Shit, this was going from bad to fucked. In that instant,

I remembered something vital. Princesses and jesters weren't the only figures who had to perform. More than anyone, so did queens.

It took Briar ages to pry her eyes from Eliot's worried face. In a daze, she met her mother's gaze but didn't budge. Instead, she reached for me.

Uttering a predatory noise, I seized Briar's fingers and stepped deeper in front of her. Our hands wove together, tight and unbreakable.

Avalea nodded in understanding. The words manifested as if they had to be shoved out. "Daughter of Autumn," she announced. "Blood has been spilled at our doorstep. As sovereign, the people seek retribution and look to me. Therefore, hear your punishment now."

The growl leaped from my throat. No private conference? No legitimate trial? This court had to be fucking kidding.

Briar's features collapsed. Sweat pooled in her palms and seeped into my flesh.

My thorn's fingers shook. More than that, her chin crinkled. In that instant, she seemed to understand something that took me an extra second to register.

And then I knew.

We figured it out, even before Rhys decided to exercise his miserable gullet. "You were banished from Spring," he blared for everyone to hear, then glowered in triumph at the princess. "But why stop there?"

My chest caved in. An invisible mask toppled from my face, because I couldn't hide it. No way could I hide what this did to me.

Autumn was calling for Briar's punishment. They deemed her a disloyal heiress on the brink of madness.

But they weren't interested in imprisoning her. Nay, in front of her subjects, friends, and witnesses—the Royal Council, the Spring Crown, Aire, Cadence, Posy, Vale, and Eliot—they aimed to do worse.

They would claim everything she worshiped. They would strip her of what she valued most. They would separate her from each one.

From her homeland.

From her crown.

From me.

40

Briar

The ground tilted. Blood drained from my body, the flux leaching from my system. For a moment, every fragment of noise and every silhouette blurred, as though someone had dunked me underwater.

You were banished from Spring. But why stop there?

Heckles and demands seemed to ring through the courtyard. Yet I could not tell who was speaking or how many of them.

Mercifully, a strong hand squeezed my fingers. Because my own digits had turned to ice, the person holding me attempted to infuse warmth into my system.

Poet. His hand encased mine like a protective sheath.

At last, my vision cleared. Sound flooded my ears, as sharp as a knife.

Mother came into focus, her distraught features on the verge of crumbling. Poet loomed in front of me. His fingers tightened on mine, lest I should keel over.

Mother's expression and the proximity of Poet's body wrung the shock from me. I could not have heard correctly. There must be a mistake.

Yet as the numbness wore off, blessed heat returned. It rushed through my veins and enabled me to think lucidly. Rationale cracked my mind open like an eggshell. Because of this, worse sensations assaulted me.

Pain. Loss. Bereavement.

I knew what to expect. I knew from Mother's face, from Poet's unyielding grip, and from years of breeding. I knew without needing anyone to speak another word.

Life had instructed me. My upbringing had taught me. Tradition, history, and experience had supplied me with sufficient knowledge.

Like Poet, I'd been aware that Mother would never sanction my execution, nor stomach throwing me into a prison cell. Yet I hadn't been able to predict an alternative—until now.

Yesterday, Mother had left the infirmary to check on Nicu and the troops, then to speak with Rhys. She'd done so at his request. This moment was what they'd talked about.

The purple crescents under my mother's eyes testified that she hadn't slept, that this decision had strangled her all night. Moreover, the council's weary features signaled they'd concurred with my fate. Surely, they had advised it, seeing no other recourse.

Therefore, hear your punishment now.

I forced myself to step around Poet, ignoring his string of curses. On wooden limbs, I approached Mother, my eyes clinging to hers.

"Mother," I beseeched in a low tone. "Mother, please."

She twisted so the masses would not see. With our bodies blocking their view, she snatched my hands and curled our fingers together. Her eyes glistened like puddles, but she spoke fiercely. "They will hurt you," she whispered shrilly. "If you stay, they will *hurt* you."

Yes, that's what I had predicted. Her plea ate through my flesh. If I served out my punishment here, in any capacity near this insulted court, someone would retaliate. And no matter how much Mother and Poet vowed to protect me, they could not ensure this promise.

They would die for me, as I would for them. But there would never be a guarantee. One glance in the wrong direction, one moment with me out of their sights, and it could happen.

A blade to my throat. A pillow mashed against my face, depriving me of air.

Or if not a physical attack, the assassin would attempt the unexpected. Poison, for instance.

Any time. Any place.

Like the Masters, the attacker would see it as their duty. They would view themself as a charitable savior of Autumn. To that end, I would be in greater peril if I remained.

In turn, I would put the ones who mattered in jeopardy. That, I would never allow.

"You know what I must do," Mother implored, anguish creasing her visage. "But I cannot."

Right then, she looked like Father used to when facing an unspoken choice, when trapped between being a leader and being a human being—a friend, a relative, a parent. Or perhaps for my mother, this was no choice at all.

So I took the choice from her.

I gave her one more long look, committing her features to memory. The rust hair, swept above her head in a corona of braids. The beauty mark on her earlobe. The voluptuous figure I had always envied. The bravery I'd aspired to. My unsung heroine.

A princess did what she must to keep herself safe.

A princess did everything to keep her family safe.

Releasing her, I shuffled backward until my spine bumped into Poet's solid chest. Heat brimmed from his clothes, and his muscles radiated like a volcanic thing. I closed my eyes, absorbing the feel of him while I still could.

My attention clicked over to Cadence, Posy, and Vale. My friends gazed back in distress, their expressions crinkling like paper.

Nearby, Aire glowered as if he foresaw my fate. His hands braced the swords at his hips, the knight's broad form creating a barrier between the crowd and me.

And then my eyes found him. Those tormented blue irises. The face I had grown up with, which reflected disbelief and fury. Eliot's helpless gaze clung to mine.

I blinked away and lifted my head. Then I curtsied, folded my hands in front of me, and waited.

Mother strained her features back into place. "Inciting a battle between commoners and knights is grounds for treason, a crime independent of title and rank. For these penalties—" her voice faltered like a rickety bridge, "—for these penalties, I hereby strip Briar of Autumn—"

"Nay!" Poet ground out.

"—of her title as heiress to the throne."

The world capsized. Momentarily, I fell against Poet.

The remainder of my sentence leaked into the air like fumes, suffocating me. I had lost my right to the crown. I was banished from Autumn, forbidden to return.

"Upon pain of death," Rhys finished when Mother could not.

Shouts tore through the quad, many in support of the words that echoed across the castle.

Basil and Fatima gawked. Giselle of Summer snapped her astounded—and discriminating—gaze to her disreputable husband.

Cadence, Posy, and Vale shrieked in protest. "You can't do this!" one of them yelled.

Aire barked, "This is not justice!"

Eliot bellowed and surged forward, shoving his way through the throng.

But no one made as much noise as my jester. Poet whipped me behind him and roared.

No trial. No defense.

I swayed once more before straightening. If anyone possessed greater power than the queen, it was the people. The quad consisted of courtiers who stared with disenchanted indignation. In their eyes, I was guilty. Betrayal by one's sovereign did much to stoke a person's anger, even if that person was of Autumn.

My people took disloyalty, dishonesty, and disobedience far more seriously than any other nation. They wanted me to pay without haste or the benefit of a hearing. Anything less, and the crowd would rage before the sun went down. If that happened, who knew how many more innocents would be harmed.

Ultimately, it would give everyone another excuse to blame their princess. Public scrutiny had pushed Mother into a corner.

The Summer King put up a front. He observed me behind a veneer of disappointed pity. Despite the pretense, victory inflated his pupils.

From the way Poet seethed at the spectators, I sensed him grasping the situation, the cause for persecuting me swiftly, and the reason they excluded him from all this. The people believed their princess deserved to be denied the one thing that had influenced her to begin with. Perhaps they hoped to purge those feelings from me, not comprehending that would be futile.

The time it would take to stop loving my jester? That amount of time was impossible.

"Poet," I murmured, my heart in my throat.

Regardless of the clamor, he heard my whisper and spun on his heels. I saw his intention—his plan to fling me over his shoulder and haul me as far from this nightmare as possible. I saw the protective malice lurking across his features. But I also saw the moment he read my mind.

Poet's expression crimped. Flames writhed in his irises as he seized my face. "Nay."

"Poet." I tore off the suede gloves, jammed them into my pocket, and planted my palms on his jaw, anguish shredding my voice to ribbons. "I must."

"The fuck you do," he hissed. "You're not going anywhere—"

My mouth slammed against his. The shaky press of my lips muffled the rest, because if I heard more, I would never stop hearing it. And if that happened, I would never move from this spot—never leave.

The jester's nostril flared, but he grabbed me just the same. His mouth smothered mine, clutching desperately, as though to cement us together. Tears pricked the backs of my eyelids as my kiss fused with his.

Too soon, I pried myself away and mumbled against his mouth, "You have to let me go."

He sucked in a fractured breath. "Never."

Because that was what we'd sworn. Because that was the one thing we promised not to do.

I brushed our lips together. "Always."

Tension strung his muscles into knots. I felt his need to capture me, to safeguard me against my will, to love me ferociously.

The memories surged through my veins. Each touch. Each word. Not a single one would I forget.

With a cry, I flung myself from his arms and knocked my way past the jester. Every step crushed my chest. Every inch buried the knife deeper. Without a backward glance, I dashed down the stairs before he could catch me, my skirt rippling in my wake.

Aire swooped the tip of his sword at anyone who attempted to get closer. On my way down, I muttered to him, "My horse. Now."

He nodded and called out an order. Thankfully, the mare had been retrieved from the forest while I'd been resting.

Poet's scream ripped across the courtyard. Over and over, my name peeled from his lungs.

My eyes clenched shut, barricading the tears. As one of the knights rushed my horse from the stable, I charged across the bricks, my heels burning a path to the animal.

Keep moving. Just keep moving.

Don't look back. Do *not* look back at him.

I could delay. I could pack my bags and say proper goodbyes. I could prolong the torment, aware that taking such liberties would place the ones I cared about in positions of newfound danger.

Or I could spare them.

The mare nickered when she saw me. I retrieved the suede gloves from my pocket, stabbed my fingers into the material, and hoisted myself onto the female's back. Grasping the reins, I twisted us in the maple pasture's direction.

But one more desperate bellow, and my soul could no longer endure. I wheeled and looked back, my gaze colliding with those green eyes.

Poet was slashing his way through six guards. He ducked weapons, blocked fists, and swiped his blade across every knight who attempted to restrain him. Blood spritzed from their mouths as the jester erupted into movement, ripping and slicing a path to me. He blew past them like a mallet plowing through paper.

Yes. No.

Come to me. Stay away.

Don't let me go. Don't come any closer.

Out of nowhere, Aire's arm swooped in like a raptor's wing and caught Poet by his torso. The First Knight's armor might as well be made of straw. He fought to maintain a grip on the jester, who exploded and thrashed to the point where he would snap the knight's bones.

"Briar!" Poet roared. "Don't do this! Please! Briar!"

I swallowed a mouthful of sobs and raised my trembling fist to show him the ribbon. The scarlet band entwined my wrist like an unspoken pledge. Poet's eyes landed on the fabric, and he stopped.

His slack countenance watched me as if I'd just plunged a blade into his gut. But when he focused on the bracelet, understanding skewered through his features. Of all our hand signals, this one did not need further interpretation. It pointed to the one reason he could not stop me, nor join me.

Covertly, I shook my head. Poet would uproot hell itself to get to his princess. My jester would walk through fire to stay with me.

He would, if not for one thing.

Nicu.

Poet could not leave his son. He would never do that.

I was safer away from the castle. And with me gone, Nicu was now safer inside of it. Even so, that boy needed his father to protect him while among the lions and cobras of this court, because no Season was without its limits.

Our friends would be there to help him. The ladies and the First Knight would always be there, even if I couldn't be.

I allowed myself one moment to luxuriate in the memory of Nicu's laugh as we played a game of stars, and he swore that he'd try and be a hero someday. Then I shut that memory in a private compartment, locking it inside my chest.

Another set of hooves clomped to my side and halted. My head swung toward a head of blond hair and a pair of eyes like a morning sky. The sight of him pulled a cry from my lips. "Minstrel."

Eliot grinned sadly and reached out. "Monarch."

Our old greeting.

My fingers shot toward his. We clasped hands, the sensation wrapping around me like an old quilt.

Soft. Familiar.

The monarchs of Spring must have insisted on bringing him, perhaps to show off their new celebrity for Reaper's Fest. Yet I'd thought it would be years before I saw him again. If I blinked, would he disappear?

Belatedly, I registered his steed and frowned. "Where did you get the horse?"

"Stole it from the carriage," Eliot answered, knocking his head toward the vehicle that brought him here. "Did you really think I'd let you go without me?"

I should not allow it. I should refuse him.

Instead, my mouth lifted into a watery smile. "Thank you for the letter."

"I meant every word," he answered. "You were a leader long before you wore a crown."

As we gazed at each other, one more set of hooves trotted into our huddle.

On my other side, Cadence straddled her own mare and quirked a brow at us. "What?" she scoffed, nudging her chin at Eliot. "Did you really think I'd let you two have all the fun?"

But behind the flippant veneer, I caught a flash of something unprecedented in the lady's expression. Something selfless and dedicated. Something like friendship. And so, I gulped and nodded, welcoming her to accompany us.

Eliot's lute rested in a saddlebag, along with what appeared to be some type of garrote. A knife sat in the belt of Cadence's sweater dress. Thorn quills were hidden in the jewels strewn through my loosely plaited updo, like a new type of crown.

None of us were veteran fighters, but we had weapons. My earrings alone were worth a fortune, enough for us to live off. As for the rest, I knew where to go.

But my heart could not help itself. I swiveled in my saddle.

Just one more look. Just one more.

My gaze slammed into Poet's. He stood apart from the crowd now, his features haggard, that powerful chest rising and falling like a pump about to detonate. Fear and fury churned in his pupils, the questions mounting.

Who would protect me? Who would defend me? Who would make sure I ate well, slept through the night, and kept warm?

Silently, I communicated. A princess was resilient, tenacious, and willful. Even if she wasn't a princess anymore.

Poet's irises glittered. Slowly, a smirk twitched across his lips—wickedly heartbroken. And slowly, tearfully, I grinned back.

Every word. Every kiss. Every touch.

Every secret, confession, and regret we shared. Every plan we'd ever made. Every hope we had.

Every time his tongue shocked me. Every time he made me laugh. Every time he held me while I dreamed. Every time his hot mouth claimed mine. Every time he tasted me, stripped me bare, pitched his body inside me.

Every time I cried out and came around his naked hips. Every time I breathed.

In that look from across too many yards, I remembered. From his end of the castle grounds, so did he.

At length, the jester's smile faded. His features darkened with intent, resembling a feral panther about to go on a hunt.

Then Poet mouthed, *I love you.*

That was all. That was everything.

And at the last moment, he finished with, *And I will find you.*

My heart lifted. Yes, he would.

I branded those parting words into my mind. Like a beacon, I let his promise guide me forth as I whirled my horse around.

My jester danced in the shadows, fooled his enemies with stealth and a silver tongue, and knew me better than anyone. No matter where I went, he would find me. And being his stubbornly resourceful princess, I would find him.

This was not the end. If I had to guess, Poet had already deposited a scarlet ribbon in Summer's room on behalf of us both. The jester's targets were my targets, just as his passions had become my passions.

Soon, we would fight our way to each other.

Until then, I steered my horse. My features sharpened into thorns as I galloped with my companions from the castle. The further I went, the faster I accelerated. The wind sliced through my hair and stung my eyes, or perhaps my livid tears were the culprits.

Even as I wept, I ground my teeth and raged across the landscape. All the while, I made a new promise.

I would come back to him. He would come back to me.

And together, we would burn our enemies to ashes.

Poet and Briar's spicy story continues in book 3

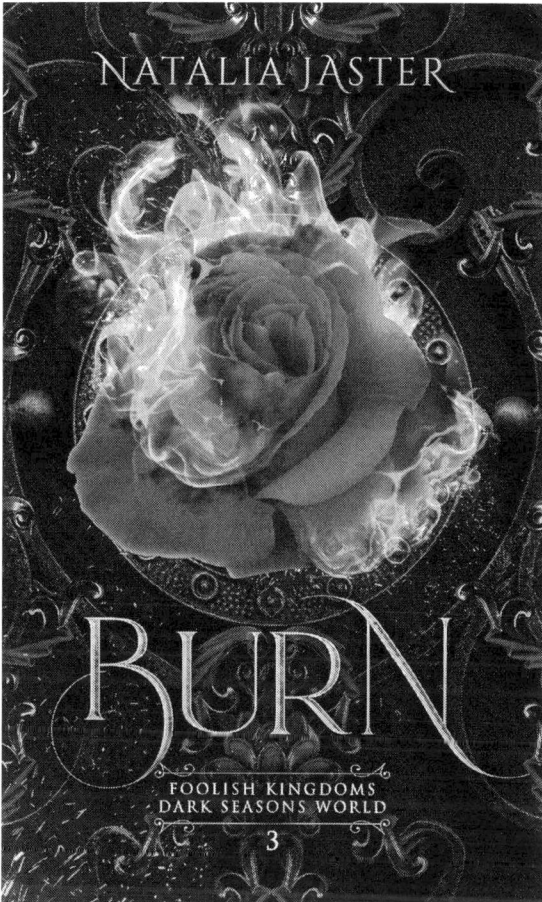

Want steamy NSFW character art of Poet and Briar?
Sign up for my newsletter to unlock an exclusive
digital download for subscribers' eyes only:
nataliajaster.com/newsletter

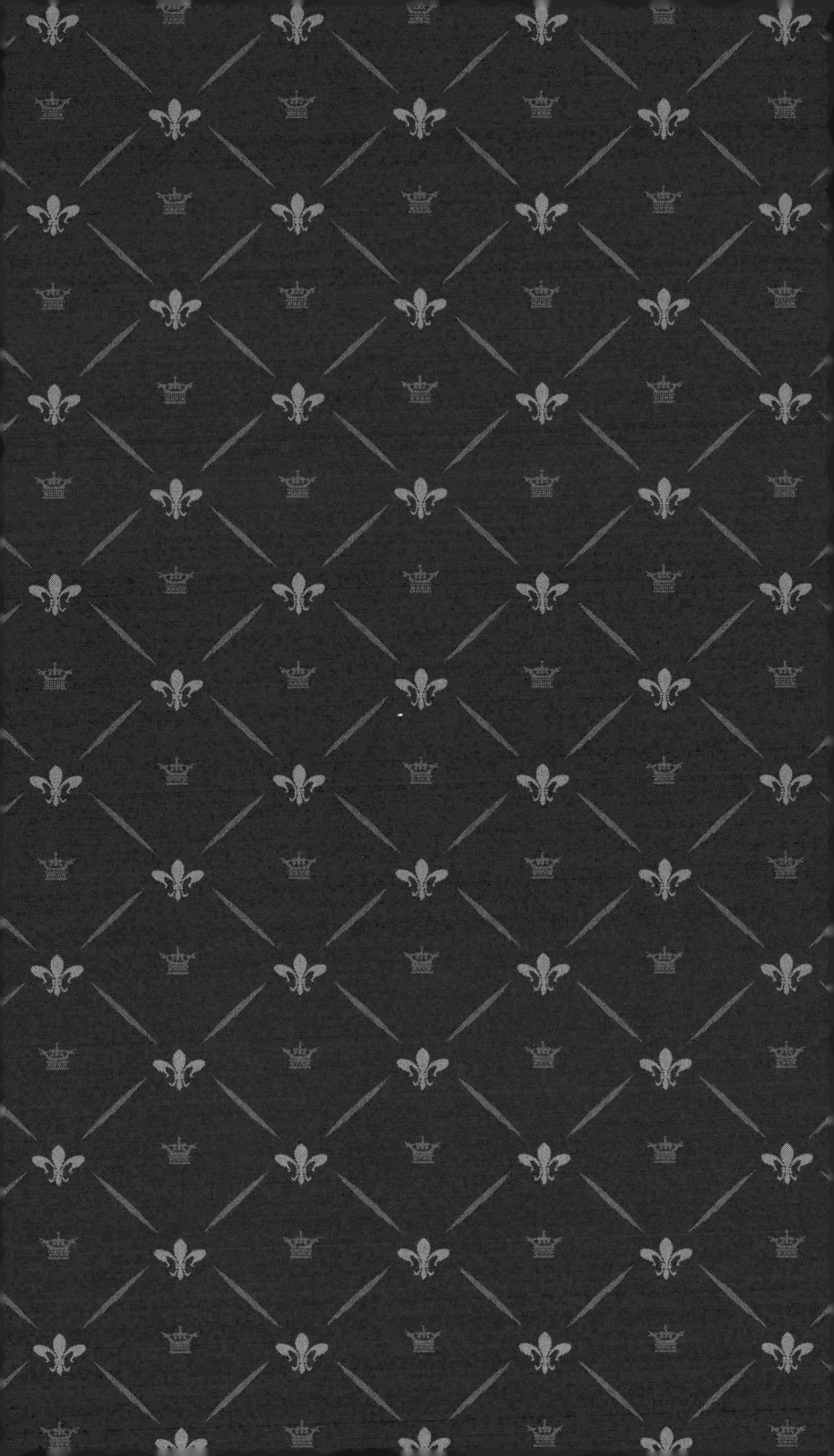

AUTHOR'S NOTE

Sooooo have you recovered yet? Trust me, I'm still clutching my heart.

Wicked hell, this book. It drew so many unexpected emotions to the surface, ripped me out of my comfort zone, and brought me to tears more than once.

I love returning to Poet and Briar. I love their banter, devotion, and passionate tension. I love how their journey has gotten more dire, tested their limits, and made them stronger. I love how they make mistakes and piss each other off, but then emerge from the upheaval closer than before. I love that they can't keep their eyes (and hands) off each other. I love how amidst everything thrown at them, their bond just gets more intense—enduring and everlasting.

How I love this power couple, so damn much.

This magnum opus is slowly becoming a saga, and I hope you're excited to see where my jester and princess go from here. Don't worry. That cruel cliffy only means we get to relish in one hell of an anticipated, breathtaking, and steamy reunion.

Hugs to the court of beta and sensitivity readers, who generously read and offered feedback for this story. I'm eternally grateful to you.

My heartfelt thanks to Michelle, Candace, and Amber for your beta prowess and friendship. I heart each of you.

To my family, always.

To Roman, my muse, soul mate, and silver-tongued troublemaker.

To my ARC team, the Myths & Tricksters and Vicious Faeries FB groups, and every reader who opens my books and turns the page. You are Royals.

There's more Poet & Briar ahead, so be ready for it…

Their spicy story continues in *Burn* (Dark Seasons: Foolish Kingdoms #3).

About Natalia

Natalia Jaster is a fantasy romance author who routinely swoons for the villain.

She lives in a dark forest, where she writes steamy New Adult tales about rakish jesters, immortal deities, and vicious fae. Wicked heroes are her weakness, and rebellious heroines are her best friends.

When she's not writing, you'll probably find her perched atop a castle tower, guzzling caramel apple tea, and counting the stars.

Come Say Hi!

Bookbub: www.bookbub.com/authors/natalia-jaster

Facebook: www.facebook.com/NataliaJasterAuthor

Instagram: www.instagram.com/nataliajaster

TikTok: www.tiktok.com/@nataliajasterauthor

Website: www.nataliajaster.com

See the boards for Natalia's novels on Pinterest: www.pinterest.com/andshewaits

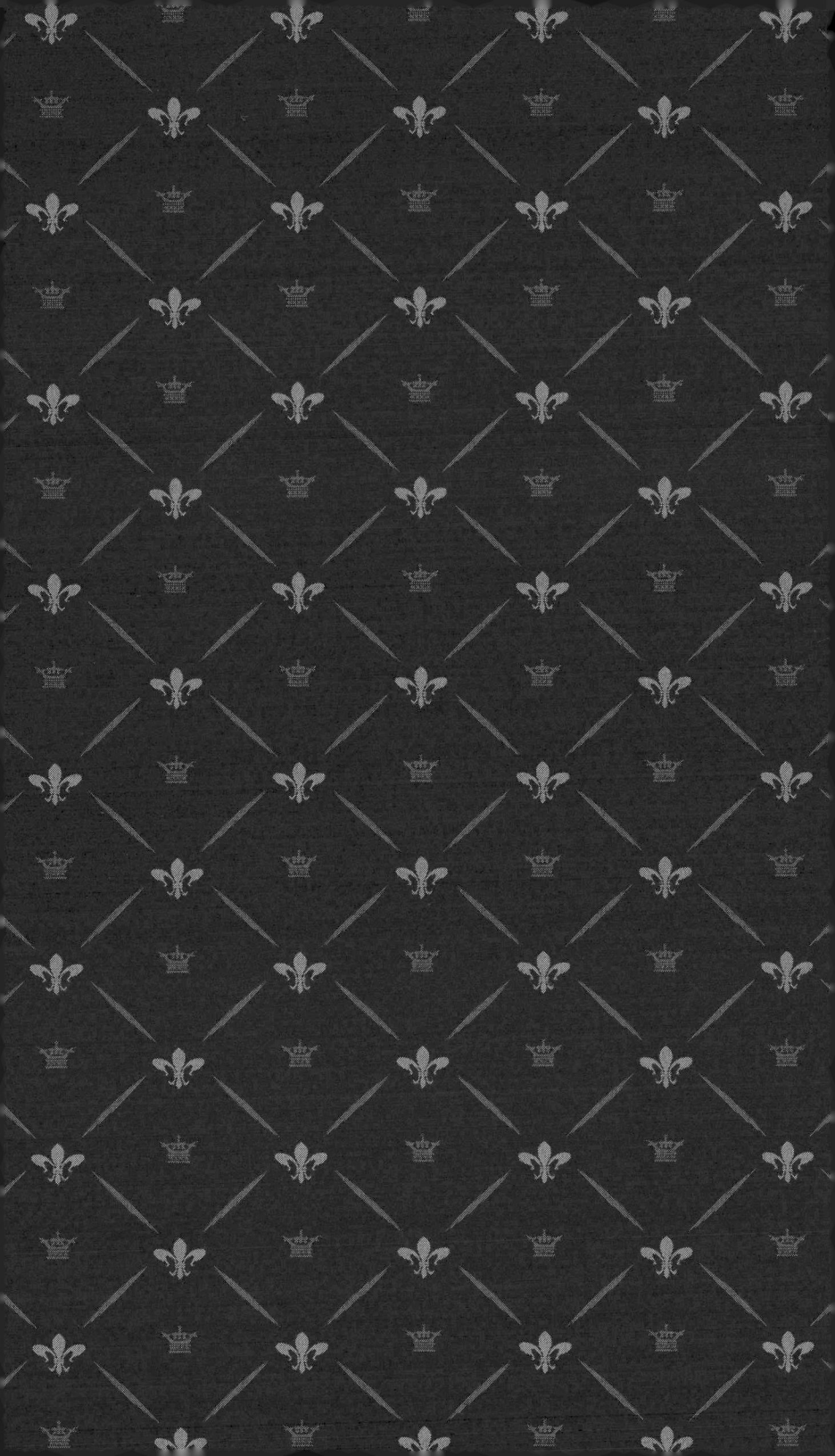

Printed in Great Britain
by Amazon